"STORIES THAT STRETCH OUR
IMAGINATION AND PREPARE US FOR THE
ENDLESS POSSIBILITIES OF THE FUTURE."
—*VOYA*

"Very good reading . . . confirms that SF in the
short form is alive and well."
—*Science Fiction Book Review*

"An essential collection . . . the science fiction
short story has really taken off again."
—*The Washington Post Bookworld*

Over the years, the short story has been a
means for new authors to test their skill, and for
established writers to hone their talent. And, year
after year, Donald A. Wollheim's *Annual World's
Best SF* has continued to showcase the finest
stories of the year, whether by long-time masters
or talented newcomers.

So welcome to the 22nd volume in the series
that has consistently charted the evolution and
new trends in the science fiction field, brought to
you by that dean of science fiction, Donald A.
Wollheim.

THE 1987 ANNUAL
WORLD'S BEST SF

THE 1987 ANNUAL WORLD'S BEST SF

EDITED BY
DONALD A. WOLLHEIM
with Arthur W. Saha

DAW BOOKS, INC.
DONALD A. WOLLHEIM, PUBLISHER

1633 Broadway, New York, NY 10019

First Printing, June 1987

1 2 3 4 5 6 7 8 9

PRINTED IN THE U.S.A.

CONTENTS

INTRODUCTION

The year past saw two events which should give thoughtful pause to anyone who reads science fiction and is thereby interested in the future of humanity on Earth. These two events were the disaster of the space shuttle *Challenger* and the melt-down of the nuclear reactor at Chernobyl. There were other events, less publicized, but of basically similar natures, but it was these two that caught the world's attention.

The disaster at Cape Canaveral was a serious setback for the United States space program. It was also an inevitable product (inevitable as many engineers and astronauts testified after the event) of workmanship undertaken first to produce dividends for wealthy corporate executives and only secondarily to produce efficient space technology. There were also the elements of hypocritical public relations involved with a sacrifice crew composed like the cast of a cheap Grade B movie: one person from each standard category of American ethnic citizenry, plus the hastening of the launch time to permit personal PR before a nationally televised session of Congress.

It also turned out that the United States, which had been the leader in space, had placed all its eggs in one basket, that of the space shuttle. The lesson of this was underlined by the marvelous success of the Uranus fly-by and the information gained by astronomy from this. The vehicle that performed that feat was nine years old and the product of a virtually abandoned system—and it worked perfectly.

The Chernobyl affair was more serious in the way it affected humanity. It demonstrated once and for all the insanity of nuclear warfare. Any accident of nuclear dimension would affect all the world. Any nuclear bomb dropped—even one—would have much the same result—contamination of the air and the soil for hundreds of miles around and across national boundaries without regard to flag or social systems. The Earth is one planetary unity. That was the lesson to be learned. Has it been learned? The radioactive gases released by that one accident traveled around the entire globe. The results . . . they will show up in the course of years. But they *will* show up. The news, however, may be kept secret for years after, if possible. That is how things function politically today.

There are, as usual, the secret wars, the lies about the victims of those wars, the sponsoring of an enormous public and private arms trade—stuff designed for the sole purpose of killing people, preferably fast and efficiently.

What sort of a world do we find ourselves in during the last fourteen years of the Twentieth Century? Does it make sense? Is all this a form of species suicide? It is said that nature tends to cut back species that over-extend themselves. Let there be too many rabbits or deer and the excess starve. Let there be too many wolves and the same thing occurs. There are undoubtedly too many human beings—but thus far human ingenuity and the pace of medicine have kept disaster from coming in the natural way—starvation and plague. But perhaps the madness of war will prove to be nature's remedy. We hope not. We hope that some will get out into space in time to keep the spark of our species glowing.

It is not surprising that science fiction is booming. It deals with the future and this is the secret concern of anyone alive since 1945. As a genre it is not the mere escapism that publishers assume it to be. It supplies answers—sometimes grim, sometimes hopeful, but answers they are to the ineradicable worries of intelligent people. Fantasy, too, appears to be escapism, with its tales of magic and wizards and curses and quests for Holy Grails. Not as clear-cut as science fiction, fantasy nevertheless represents a vision of a world more glamorous than the mess we are currently in—and the quest, which is so much a part of so much fantasy, is the quest for salvation and life.

In the year past both SF and fantasy have been strong on the readers' market. Publishers of books have increased their lists and more and more good writers are turning up thereon. The magazines have been sustained and anthologies of original stories have grown in number. All this in spite of inflation, of rising costs and rising prices.

So we proceed to 1987 with determination and the will to keep on dreaming great dreams. We dare not predict what will happen to resolve the world's crises, but we still believe that they will be solved. And that is why we read science fiction.

—DONALD A. WOLLHEIM

PERMAFROST
by Roger Zelazny

*Many elements mingle to make this remarkable
story. Some of these elements belong to the
structures of fantasy, some to those of science
fiction. The talent of Roger Zelazny combines
then all in a colorful yarn through which runs
the steady thread of the sense of wonder.*

High upon the western slope of Mount Kilimanjaro is the
dried and frozen carcass of a leopard. An author is always
necessary to explain what it was doing there because stiff
leopards don't talk much.

THE MAN. The music seems to come and go with a
will of its own. At least turning the knob on the bedside
unit has no effect on its presence or absence. A half-
familiar, alien tune, troubling in a way. The phone rings,
and he answers it. There is no one there. Again.

Four times during the past half hour, while grooming
himself, dressing and rehearsing his arguments, he has
received non-calls. When he checked with the desk he was
told there were no calls. But that damned clerk-thing had
to be malfunctioning—like everything else in this place.

The wind, already heavy, rises, hurling particles of ice
against the building with a sound like multitudes of tiny
claws scratching. The whining of steel shutters sliding into
place startles him. But worst of all, in his reflex glance at
the nearest window, it seems he has seen a face.

Impossible of course. This is the third floor. A trick of light upon hard-driven flakes: Nerves.

Yes. He has been nervous since their arrival this morning. Before then, even . . .

He pushes past Dorothy's stuff upon the countertop, locates a small package among his own articles. He unwraps a flat red rectangle about the size of his thumbnail. He rolls up his sleeve and slaps the patch against the inside of his left elbow.

The tranquilizer discharges immediately into his bloodstream. He takes several deep breaths, then peels off the patch and drops it into the disposal unit. He rolls his sleeve down, reaches for his jacket.

The music rises in volume, as if competing with the blast of the wind, the rattle of the icy flakes. Across the room the videoscreen comes on of its own accord.

The face. The same face. Just for an instant. He is certain. And then channelless static, wavy lines. Snow. He chuckles.

All right, play it that way, nerves, he thinks. *You've every reason. But the trank's coming to get you now. Better have your fun quick. You're about to be shut down.*

The videoscreen cuts into a porn show.

Smiling, the woman mounts the man. . . .

The picture switches to a voiceless commentator on something or other.

He will survive. He is a survivor. He, Paul Plaige, has done risky things before and has always made it through. It is just that having Dorothy along creates a kind of déjà vu that he finds unsettling. No matter.

She is waiting for him in the bar. Let her wait. A few drinks will make her easier to persuade—unless they make her bitchy. That sometimes happens, too. Either way, he has to talk her out of the thing.

Silence. The wind stops. The scratching ceases. The music is gone.

The whirring. The window screens dilate upon the empty city.

Silence, under totally overcast skies. Mountains of ice ringing the place. Nothing moving. Even the video has gone dead.

He recoils at the sudden flash from a peripheral unit far to his left across the city. The laser beam hits a key point on the glacier, and its face falls away.

Moments later he hears the hollow, booming sound of the crashing ice. A powdery storm has risen like surf at the ice mount's foot. He smiles at the power, the timing, the display. Andrew Aldon . . . always on the job, dueling with the elements, stalemating nature herself, immortal guardian of Playpoint. At least Aldon never malfunctions.

The silence comes again. As he watches the risen snows settle he feels the tranquilizer beginning to work. It will be good not to have to worry about money again. The past two years have taken a lot out of him. Seeing all of his investments fail in the Big Washout—that was when his nerves had first begun to act up. He has grown softer than he was a century ago—a young, rawboned soldier of fortune then, out to make his bundle and enjoy it. And he had. Now he has to do it again, though this time will be easier—except for Dorothy.

He thinks of her. A century younger than himself, still in her twenties, sometimes reckless, used to all of the good things in life. There is something vulnerable about Dorothy, times when she lapses into such a strong dependence that he feels oddly moved. Other times, it just irritates the hell out of him. Perhaps this is the closest he can come to love now, an occasional ambivalent response to being needed. But of course she is loaded. That breeds a certain measure of necessary courtesy. Until he can make his own bundle again, anyway. But none of these things are the reason he has to keep her from accompanying him on his journey. It goes beyond love or money. It is survival.

The laser flashes again, this time to the right. He waits for the crash.

THE STATUE. It is not a pretty pose. She lies frosted in an ice cave, looking like one of Rodin's less comfortable figures, partly propped on her left side, right elbow raised above her head, hand hanging near her face, shoulders against the wall, left leg completely buried.

She has on a gray parka, the hood slipped back to reveal twisted strands of dark blond hair; and she wears blue trousers; there is a black boot on the one foot that is visible.

She is coated with ice, and within the much-refracted light of the cave what can be seen of her features is not unpleasant but not strikingly attractive either. She looks to be in her twenties.

There are a number of fracture lines within the cave's walls and floor. Overhead, countless icicles hang like stalactites, sparkling jewellike in the much-bounced light. The grotto has a stepped slope to it with the statue at its higher end, giving to the place a vaguely shrinelike appearance.

On those occasions when the cloud cover is broken at sundown a reddish light is cast about her figure.

She has actually moved in the course of a century—a few inches, from a general shifting of the ice. Tricks of the light make her seem to move more frequently, however.

The entire tableau might give the impression that this is merely a pathetic woman who had been trapped and frozen to death here, rather than the statue of the living goddess in the place where it all began.

THE WOMAN. She sits in the bar beside a window. The patio outside is gray and angular and drifted with snow; the flowerbeds are filled with dead plants—stiff, flattened, and frozen. She does not mind the view. Far from it. Winter is a season of death and cold, and she likes being reminded of it. She enjoys the prospect of pitting herself against its frigid and very visible fangs. A faint flash of light passes over the patio, followed by a distant roaring sound. She sips her drink and licks her lips and listens to the soft music that fills the air.

She is alone. The bartender and all of the other help here are of the mechanical variety. If anyone other than Paul were to walk in, she would probably scream. They are the only people in the hotel during this long off-season. Except for the sleepers, they are the only people in all of Playpoint.

And Paul . . . He will be along soon to take her to the dining room. There they can summon holo-ghosts to people the other tables, if they wish. She does not wish. She likes being alone with Paul at a time like this, on the eve of a great adventure.

He will tell her his plans over coffee, and perhaps even this afternoon they might obtain the necessary equipment to begin the exploration for that which would put him on his feet again financially, return to him his self-respect. It will of course be dangerous and very rewarding. She finishes her drink, rises, and crosses to the bar for another.

And Paul . . . She had really caught a falling star, a swashbuckler on the way down, a man with a glamorous past just balanced on the brink of ruin. The teetering had already begun when they had met two years before, which had made it even more exciting. Of course, he needed a woman like her to lean upon at such a time. It wasn't just her money. She could never believe the things her late parents had said about him. No, he does care for her. He is strangely vulnerable and dependent.

She wants to turn him back into the man he once must have been, and then of course that man will need her, too. The thing he had been—that is what she needs most of all—a man who can reach up and bat the moon away. He must have been like that long ago.

She tastes her second drink.

The son of a bitch had better hurry, though. She is getting hungry.

THE CITY. Playpoint is located on the world known as Balfrost, atop a high peninsula that slopes down to a now-frozen sea. Playpoint contains all of the facilities for an adult playground, and it is one of the more popular resorts in this sector of the galaxy from late spring through early autumn—approximately fifty Earth years. Then winter comes on like a period of glaciation, and everybody goes away for half a century—or half a year, depending on how one regards such matters. During this time Playpoint is given into the care of its automated defense and maintenance routine. This is a self-repairing system, directed toward cleaning, plowing, thawing, melting, warming everything in need of such care, as well as directly combating their encroaching ice and snow. And all of these functions are one under the supervision of a well-protected central computer that also studies the weather and climate patterns, anticipating as well as reacting.

This system had worked successfully for many centuries, delivering Playpoint over to spring and pleasure in reasonably good condition at the end of each long winter.

There are mountains behind Playpoint, water (or ice, depending on the season) on three sides, weather and navigation satellites high above. In a bunker beneath the administration building is a pair of sleepers—generally a man and a woman—who awaken once every year or so to physically inspect the maintenance system's operations and to deal with any special situations that might have arisen. An alarm may arouse them for emergencies at any time. They are well paid, and over the years they have proven worth the investment. The central computer has at its disposal explosives and lasers as well as a great variety of robots. Usually it keeps a little ahead of the game, and it seldom falls behind for long.

At the moment, things are about even because the weather has been particularly nasty recently.

Zzzzt! Another block of ice has become a puddle.

Zzzzt! The puddle has been evaporated. The molecules climb toward a place where they can get together and return as snow.

The glaciers shuffle their feet, edge forward. Zzzzt! Their gain has become a loss.

Andrew Aldon knows exactly what he is doing.

CONVERSATIONS. The waiter, needing lubrication, rolls off after having served them, passing through a pair of swinging doors.

She giggles. "Wobbly," she says.

"Old World charm," he agrees, trying and failing to catch her eye as he smiles.

"You have everything worked out?" she asks after they have begun eating.

"Sort of," he says, smiling again.

"Is that a yes or a no?"

"Both. I need more information. I want to go and check things over first. Then I can figure the best course of action."

"I note your use of the singular pronoun," she says steadily, meeting his gaze at last.

His smile freezes and fades.

"I was referring to only a little preliminary scouting," he says softly.

"No," she says. "We. Even for a little preliminary scouting."

He sighs and sets down his fork.

"This will have very little to do with anything to come later," he begins. "Things have changed a lot. I'll have to locate a new route. This will just be dull work and no fun."

"I didn't come along for fun," she replies. "We were going to share everything, remember? That includes boredom, danger, and anything else. That was the understanding when I agreed to pay our way."

"I'd a feeling it would come to that," he says, after a moment.

"Come to it? It's always been there. That was our agreement."

He raises his goblet and sips the wine.

"Of course. I'm not trying to rewrite history. It's just that things would go faster if I could do some of the initial looking around myself. I can move more quickly alone."

"What's the hurry?" she says. "A few days this way or that. I'm in pretty good shape. I won't slow you down all that much."

"I'd the impression you didn't particularly like it here. I just wanted to hurry things up so we could get the hell out."

"That's very considerate," she says, beginning to eat again. "But that's my problem, isn't it?" She looks up at him. "Unless there's some other reason you don't want me along?"

He drops his gaze quickly, picks up his fork. "Don't be silly."

She smiles. "Then that's settled. I'll go with you this afternoon to look for the trail."

The music stops, to be succeeded by a sound as of the clearing of a throat. Then, "Excuse me for what may seem like eavesdropping," comes a deep, masculine voice. "It

is actually only a part of a simple monitoring function I
keep in effect— "

"Aldon!" Paul exclaims.

"At your service, Mr. Plaige, more or less. I choose to
make my presence known only because I did indeed over-
hear you, and the matter of your safety overrides the good
manners that would otherwise dictate reticence. I've been
receiving reports that indicate we could be hit by some
extremely bad weather this afternoon. So if you were
planning an extended sojourn outside I would recommend
you postpone it."

"Oh," Dorothy says.

"Thanks," Paul says.

"I shall now absent myself. Enjoy your meal and your
stay."

The music returns.

"Aldon?" Paul asks.

There is no reply.

"Looks as if we do it tomorrow or later."

"Yes," Paul agrees, and he is smiling his first relaxed
smile of the day. And thinking fast.

THE WORLD. Life on Balfrost proceeds in peculiar
cycles. There are great migrations of animal life and quasi-
animal life to the equatorial regions during the long winter.
Life in the depths of the seas goes on. And the permafrost
vibrates with its own style of life.

The permafrost. Throughout the winter and on through
the spring the permafrost lives at its peak. It is laced with
mycelia—twining, probing, touching, knotting themselves
into ganglia, reaching out to infiltrate other systems. It
girds the globe, vibrating like a collective unconscious
throughout the winter. In the spring it sends up stalks that
develop gray, flowerlike appendages for a few days. These
blooms then collapse to reveal dark pods that subsequently
burst with small, popping sounds, releasing clouds of sparkling spores that the winds bear just about everywhere.
These are extremely hardy, like the mycelia they will one
day become.

The heat of summer finally works its way down into the
permafrost, and the strands doze their way into a long
period of quiescence. When the cold returns they are

roused, spores send forth new filaments that repair old damages, create new synapses. A current begins to flow. The life of summer is like a fading dream. For eons this had been the way of things upon Balfrost, within Balfrost. Then the goddess decreed otherwise. Winter's queen spread her hands, and there came a change.

THE SLEEPERS. Paul makes his way through swirling flakes to the administration building. It has been a simpler matter than he had anticipated, persuading Dorothy to use the sleep-induction unit to be well rested for the morrow. He had pretended to use the other unit himself, resisting its blandishments until he was certain she was sleep and he could slip off undetected.

He lets himself into the vaultlike building, takes all of the old familiar turns, makes his way down a low ramp. The room is unlocked and a bit chilly, but he begins to perspire when he enters. The two cold lockers are in operation. He checks their monitoring systems and sees that everything is in order.

All right, go! Borrow the equipment now. They won't be using it.

He hesitates.

He draws nearer and looks down through the view plates at the faces of the sleepers. No resemblance, thank God. He realizes then that he is trembling. He backs away, turns, and flees toward the storage area.

Later, in a yellow snowslider, carrying special equipment, he heads inland.

As he drives, the snow ceases falling and the winds die down. He smiles. The snows sparkle before him, and landmarks do not seem all that unfamiliar. Good omens, at last.

Then something crosses his path, turns, halts, and faces him.

ANDREW ALDON. Andrew Aldon, once a man of considerable integrity and resource, had on his deathbed opted for continued existence as a computer program, the enchanted loom of his mind shuttling and weaving thereafter as central processing's judgmental program in the great guardian computerplex at Playpoint. And there he functions as a program of considerable integrity and resource.

He maintains the city, and he fights the elements. He does not merely respond to pressures, but he anticipates structural and functional needs; he generally outguesses the weather. Like the professional soldier he once had been, he keeps himself in a state of constant alert—not really difficult considering the resources available to him. He is seldom wrong, always competent, and sometimes brilliant. Occasionally he resents his fleshless state. Occasionally he feels lonely.

This afternoon he is puzzled by the sudden veering off of the storm he had anticipated and by the spell of clement weather that has followed this meteorological quirk. His mathematics were elegant, but the weather was not. It seems peculiar that this should come at a time of so many other little irregularities, such as unusual ice adjustments, equipment glitches, and the peculiar behavior of machinery in the one occupied room of the hotel—a room troublesomely tenanted by a non grata ghost from the past.

So he watches for a time. He is ready to intervene when Paul enters the administration building and goes to the bunkers. But Paul does nothing that might bring harm to the sleepers. His curiosity is dominant when Paul draws equipment. He continues to watch. This is because in his judgment, Paul bears watching.

Aldon decides to act only when he detects a development that runs counter to anything in his experience. He sends one of his mobile units to intercept Paul as the man heads out of town. It catches up with him at a bending of the way and slides into his path with one appendage upraised.

"Stop!" Aldon calls through the speaker.

Paul brakes his vehicle and sits for a moment regarding the machine.

Then he smiles faintly. "I assume you have good reason for interfering with a guest's freedom of movement."

"Your safety takes precedence."

"I am perfectly safe."

"At the moment."

"What do you mean?"

"This weather pattern has suddenly become more than a little unusual. You seem to occupy a drifting island of calm while a storm rages about you."

"So I'll take advantage of it now and face the consequences later, if need be."

"It is your choice. I wanted it to be an informed one, however."

"All right. You've informed me. Now get out of my way."

"In a moment. You departed under rather unusual circumstances the last time you were here—in breach of your contract."

"Check your legal bank if you've got one. That statute's run for prosecuting me on that."

"There are some things on which there is no statute of limitations."

"What do you mean by that? I turned in a report on what happened that day."

"One which—conveniently—could not be verified. You were arguing that day. . . ."

"We always argued. That's just the way we were. If you have something to say about it, say it."

"No, I have nothing more to say about it. My only intention is to caution you—"

"Okay, I'm cautioned."

"To caution you in more ways than the obvious."

"I don't understand."

"I am not certain that things are the same here now as when you left last winter."

"Everything changes."

"Yes, but that is not what I mean. There is something peculiar about this place now. The past is no longer a good guide for the present. More and more anomalies keep cropping up. Sometimes it feels as if the world is testing me or playing games with me."

"You're getting paranoid, Aldon. You've been in that box too long. Maybe it's time to terminate."

"You son of a bitch, I'm trying to tell you something. I've run a lot of figures on this, and all this shit started shortly after you left. The human part of me still has hunches, and I've a feeling there's a connection. If you know all about this and can cope with it, fine. If you don't, I think you should watch out. Better yet, turn around and go home."

"I can't."

"Even if there is something out there, something that is making it easy for you—for the moment?"

"What are you, trying to say?"

"I am reminded of the old Gaia hypothesis—Lovelock, twentieth century. . . ."

"Planetary intelligence. I've heard of it. Never met one, though."

"Are you certain? I sometimes feel I'm confronting one."

"What if something is out there and it wants you—is leading you on like a will-o'-the-wisp?"

"It would be my problem, not yours."

"I can protect you against it. Go back to Playpoint."

"No thanks. I will survive."

"What of Dorothy?"

"What of her?"

"You would leave her alone when she might need you?"

"Let me worry about that."

"Your last woman didn't fare too well."

"Damn it! Get out of my way, or I'll run you down!"

The robot withdraws from the trail. Through its sensors Aldon watches Paul drive away.

Very well, he decides. *We know where we stand, Paul. And you haven't changed. That makes it easier.*

Aldon further focuses his divided attention. To Dorothy now. Clad in heated garments. Walking. Approaching the building from which she had seen Paul emerge on his vehicle. She had hailed and cursed him, but the winds had carried her words away. She, too, had only feigned sleep. After a suitable time, then, she sought to follow. Aldon watches her stumble once and wants to reach out to assist her, but there is no mobile unit handy. He routes one toward the area against future accidents.

"Damn him!" she mutters as she passes along the street, ribbons of snow rising and twisting away before her.

"Where are you going, Dorothy?" Aldon asks over a nearby PA speaker.

She halts and turns. "Who—?"

"Andrew Aldon," he replies. "I have been observing your progress."

"Why?" she asks.

"Your safety concerns me."

"That storm you mentioned earlier?"

"Partly."

"I'm a big girl. I can take care of myself. What do you mean *partly*?"

"You move in dangerous company."

"Paul? How so?"

"He once took a woman into that same wild area he is heading for now. She did not come back."

"He told me all about that. There was an accident."

"And no witnesses."

"What are you trying to say?"

"It is suspicious. That is all."

She begins moving again, toward the administrative building. Aldon switches to another speaker, within its entrance.

"I accuse him of nothing. If you choose to trust him, fine. But don't trust the weather. It would be best for you to return to the hotel."

"Thanks but no thanks," she says, entering the building.

He follows her as she explores, is aware of her quickening pulse when she halts beside the cold bunkers.

"These are the sleepers?"

"Yes. Paul held such a position once, as did the unfortunate woman."

"I know. Look, I'm going to follow him whether you approve or not. So why not just tell me where those sleds are kept?"

"Very well. I will do even more than that. I will guide you."

"What do you mean?"

"I request a favor—one that will actually benefit you."

"Name it."

"In the equipment locker behind you, you will find a remote-sensor bracelet. It is also a two-way communication link. Wear it. I can be with you then. To assist you. Perhaps even to protect you."

"You can help me to follow him?"

"Yes."

"All right. I can buy that."

She moves to the locker, opens it.

"Here's something that looks like a bracelet, with doodads."

"Yes. Depress the red stud."

She does. His voice now emerges clearly from the unit.

"Put it on, and I'll show you the way."

"Right."

SNOWSCAPE. Sheets and hills of white, tufts of evergreen shrubbery, protruding joints of rock, snowdevils twirled like tops beneath wind's lash . . . light and shade. Cracking sky. Tracks in sheltered areas, smoothness beyond.

She follows, masked and bundled.

"I've lost him," she mutters, hunched behind the curved windscreen of her yellow, bullet-shaped vehicle.

"Straight ahead, past those two rocks. Stay in the lee of the ridge. I'll tell you when to turn. I've a satellite overhead. If the clouds stay parted—strangely parted . . ."

"What do you mean?"

"He seems to be enjoying light from the only break in the cloud cover over the entire area."

"Coincidence."

"I wonder."

"What else could it be?"

"It is almost as if something had opened a door for him."

"Mysticism from a computer?"

"I am not a computer."

"I'm sorry, Mr. Aldon. I know that you were once a man. . . ."

"I am still a man."

"Sorry."

"There are many things I would like to know. Your arrival comes at an unusual time of year. Paul took some prospecting equipment with him. . . ."

"Yes. It's not against the law. In fact, it is one of the vacation features here, isn't it?"

"Yes. There are many interesting minerals about, some of them precious."

"Well, Paul wants some more, and he didn't want a crowd around while he was looking."

"More?"

"Yes, he made a strike here years ago. Yndella crystals."

"I see. Interesting."

"What's in this for you, anyway?"

"Protecting visitors is a part of my job. In your case, I feel particularly protective."

"How so?"

"In my earlier life I was attracted to women of your—specifications. Physical, as well as what I can tell of the rest."

"Two-beat pause, then, "You are blushing."

"Compliments do that to me," she says, "and that's a hell of a monitoring system you have. What's it like?"

"Oh, I can tell your body temperature, your pulse rate—"

"No, I mean, what's it like being—what you are?"

Three-beat pause. "Godlike in some ways. Very human in others—almost exaggeratedly so. I feel something of an amplification of everything I was earlier. Perhaps it's a compensation or a clinging to things past. You make me feel nostalgic—among other things. Don't fret. I'm enjoying it."

"I'd like to have met you then."

"Mutual."

"What were you like?"

"Imagine me as you would. I'll come off looking better that way."

She laughs. She adjusts her filters. She thinks about Paul.

"What was he like in his earlier days—Paul?" she asks.

"Probably pretty much the way he is now, only less polished."

"In other words, you don't care to say."

The trail turns upward more steeply, curves to the right. She hears winds but does not feel them. Cloud-shadow grayness lies all about, but her trail/*his* trail is lighted.

"I don't really know," Aldon says, after a time, "and I will not guess, in the case of someone you care about."

"Gallant," she observes.

"No, just fair," he replies. "I might be wrong."

They continue to the top of the rise, where Dorothy draws a sharp breath and further darkens her goggles against the sudden blaze where a range of ice fractures rainbows and strews their shards like confetti in all directions.

"God!" she says.

"Or goddess," Aldon replies.

"A goddess, sleeping in a circle of flame?"

"Not sleeping."

"That would be a lady for you, Aldon—if she existed. God and goddess."

"I do not want a goddess."

"I can see his tracks, heading into that."

"Not swerving a bit, as if he knows where he's going."

She follows, tracing slopes like the curves of a pale torso. The world is stillness and light and whiteness. Aldon on her wrist hums softly now, an old tune, whether of love or martial matters she isn't certain. Distances are distorted, perspectives skewed. She finds herself humming softly along with him, heading for the place where Paul's tracks find their vanishing point and enter infinity.

THE LIMP WATCH HUNG UPON THE TREE LIMB. My lucky day. The weather . . . trail clean. Things changed but not so out of shape I can't tell where it is. The lights! God, yes! Iceshine, mounds of prisms. . . . If only the opening is still there. . . . Should have brought explosives. There has been shifting, maybe a collapse. Must get in. Return later with Dorothy. But first—clean up, get rid of . . . it. If she's still there. . . . Swallowed up maybe. That would be good, best. Things seldom are, though. I—When it happened. Wasn't as if. Wasn't what. Was. . . . Was shaking the ground. Cracking, splitting. Icicles ringing, rattling, banging about. Thought we'd go under. Both of us. She was going in. So was the bag of the stuff. Grabbed the stuff. Only because it was nearer. Would have helped her if—Couldn't. Could I? Ceiling was slipping. Get out. No sense both of us getting it. Got out. She'd've done the same. Wouldn't she? Her eyes. . . . Glenda! Maybe . . . No! Couldn't have. Just couldn't. Could I? Silly. After all these years. There was a moment. Just a moment, though. A lull. If I'd known it was coming I might have. No. Ran. Your face at the window, on the screen, in a sometime dream. Glenda. It wasn't that I didn't. Blaze of hills. Fire and eyes. Ice. Ice. Fire and snow. Blazing hearthful. Ice. Ice. Straight through the ice the long road lies. The fire hangs high above. The screaming. The crash. And the silence. Get out. Yet. Different? No. It could never have. That was the way. Not my fault. . . . Damn it. Everything I could. Glenda. Up ahead. Yes. Long curve. Then down. Winding back in there. The crystals will. . . . I'll never come back to this place.

THE LIMP TREE LIMB HUNG UPON THE WATCH. Gotcha! Think I can't see through the fog? Can't sneak up on me on little cat feet. Same for your partner across the way. I'll melt off a little more near your bases, too. A lot of housecleaning backed up here. . . . Might as well take advantage of the break. Get those streets perfect. . . . How long? Long. . . . Long legs parting. . . . Long time since. Is it not strange that desire should so many years outlive performance? Unnatural. This weather. A sort of spiritual spring. . . . Extend those beams. Burn. Melt in my hot, red-fingered hands. Back off, I say. I rule here. Clear that courtyard. Unplug that drain. Come opportunity, let me clasp thee. Melt. Burn. I rule here, goddess. Draw back. I've a bomb for every tower of ice, a light for any darkness. Tread carefully here. I feel I begin to know thee. I see thy signature in cloud and fog bank, trace thy icy tresses upon the blowing wind. Thy form lies contoured all about me, white as shining death. We're due an encounter. Let the clouds spiral, ice ring, Earth heave. I rush to meet thee, death or maiden, in halls of crystal upon the heights. Not here. Long, slow fall, ice facade, crashing. Melt. Another. . . . Gotcha!

FROZEN WATCH EMBEDDED IN PERMAFROST. Bristle and thrum. Coming now. Perchance. Perchance. Perchance. I say. Throstle. Crack. Sunder. Split. Open. Coming. Beyond the ice in worlds I have known. Returning. He. Throstle. The mind the mover. To open the way. Come now. Let not to the meeting impediments. Admit. Open. Cloud stand thou still, and wind be leashed. None dare oppose thy passage returning, my killer love. It was but yesterday. A handful of stones. . . . Come singing fresh-armed from the warm places. I have looked upon thy unchanged countenance. I open the way. Come to me. Let not to the mating. I—Girding the globe. I have awakened in all of my places to receive thee. But here, here this special spot, I focus, mind the mover, in place where it all began, my bloody handed, Paul my love, calling, back, for the last good-bye, ice kiss, fire touch, heart stop, blood still, soul freeze, embrace of world and my hate with thy fugitive body, elusive the long year now. Come into the place it has waited. I move there again, up sciatic to spine, behnd the frozen eyeballs, waiting and warming. To me. To me now. Throstle and click, bristle and thrum. And runners scratching the snow, my heart slashing parallel. Cut.

PILGRIMAGE. He swerves, turns, slows amid the ragged prominences—ice fallen, ice heaved—in the fields where mountain and glacier wrestle in slow motion, to the accompaniment of occasional cracking and pinging sounds, crashes, growls, and the rattle of blown ice crystals. Here the ground is fissured as well as greatly uneven, and Paul abandons his snowslider. He secures some tools to his belt and his pack, anchors the sled, and commences the trek.

At first, he moves slowly and carefully, but old reflexes return, and soon he is hurrying. Moving from dazzle to shade, he passes among ice forms like grotesque statues of glass. The slope is changed from the old one he remembers, but it feels right. And deep, below, to the right. . . .

Yes. That darker place. The canyon or blocked pass, whichever it was. That seems right, too. He alters his course slightly. He is sweating now within his protective clothing, and his breath comes faster as he increases his pace. His vision blurs, and for a moment, somewhere between glare and shadow, he seems to see. . . .

He halts, sways a moment, then shakes his head, snorts, and continues.

Another hundred meters and he is certain. Those rocky ribs to the northeast, snow rivulets diamond hard between them. . . . He has been here before.

The stillness is almost oppressive. In the distance he sees spumes of windblown snow jetting off and eddying down from a high, white peak. If he stops and listens carefully he can even hear the far winds.

There is a hole in the middle of the clouds, directly

overhead. It is as if he were looking downward upon a lake in a crater.

More than unusual. He is tempted to turn back. His trank has worn off, and his stomach feels unsettled. He half-wishes to discover that this is not the place. But he knows that feelings are not very important. He continues until he stands before the opening.

There has been some shifting, some narrowing of the way. He approaches slowly. He regards the passage for a full minute before he moves to enter.

He pushes back his goggles as he comes into the lessened light. He extends a gloved hand, places it upon the facing wall, pushes. Firm. He tests the one behind him. The same.

Three paces forward and the way narrows severely. He turns and sidles. The light grows dimmer, the surface beneath his feet, more slick. He slows. He slides a hand along either wall as he advances. He passes through a tiny spot of light beneath an open ice chimney. Overhead, the wind is howling a high note now, almost whistling it.

The passage begins to widen. As his right hand falls away from the more sharply angling wall his balance is tipped in that direction. He draws back to compensate, but his left foot slides backward and falls. He attempts to rise, slips, and falls again.

Cursing, he begins to crawl forward. This area had not been slick before. . . . He chuckles. Before? A century ago. Things do change in a span like that. They—

The wind begins to howl beyond the cave mouth as he sees the rise of the floor, looks upward along the slope. She is there.

He makes a small noise at the back of his throat and stops, his right hand partly raised. She wears the shadows like veils, but they do not mask her identity. He stares. It's even worse than he had thought. Trapped, she must have lived for some time after. . . .

He shakes his head.

No use. She must be cut loose and buried now—disposed of.

He crawls forward. The icy slope does not grow level until he is quite near her. His gaze never leaves her form as he advances. The shadows slide over her. He can almost hear her again.

He thinks of the shadows. She couldn't have moved just then. . . . He stops and studies her face. It is not frozen. It is puckered and sagging as if waterlogged. A caricature of the face he had so often touched. He grimaces and looks away. The leg must be freed. He reaches for his axe.

Before he can take hold of the tool he sees movement of the hand, slow and shaking. It is accompanied by a throaty sigh.

"No . . .," he whispers, drawing back.

"Yes," comes the reply.

"Glenda."

"I am here." Her head turns slowly. Reddened, watery eyes focus upon his own. "I have been waiting."

"This is insane."

The movement of the face is horrible. It takes him some time to realize that it is a smile.

"I knew that one day you would return."

"How?" he says. "How have you lasted?"

"The body is nothing," she replies. "I had all but forgotten it. I live within the permafrost of this world. My buried foot was in contact with its filaments. It was alive, but it possessed no consciousness until we met. I live everywhere now."

"I am—happy—that you—survived."

She laughs slowly, dryly.

"Really, Paul? How could that be when you left me to die?"

"I had no choice, Glenda. I couldn't save you."

"There was an opportunity. You preferred the stones to my life."

"That's not true!"

"You didn't even try." The arms are moving again, less jerkily now. "You didn't even come back to recover my body."

"What would have been the use? You were dead—or I thought you were."

"Exactly. You didn't know, but you ran out anyway. I loved you, Paul. I would have done anything for you."

"I cared about you, too, Glenda. I would have helped you if I could have. If—"

"*If?* Don't if me *ifs*. I know what you are."

"I loved you," Paul says. "I'm sorry."

"You loved me? You never said it."

"It's not the sort of thing I talk about easily. Or think about, even."

"Show me," she says. "Come here."

He looks away. "I can't."

She laughs. "You said you loved me."

"You—you don't know how you look. I'm sorry."

"You fool!" Her voice grows hard, imperious. "Had you done it I would have spared your life. It would have shown me that some tiny drop of affection might truly have existed. But you lied. You only used me. You didn't care."

"You're being unfair!"

"Am I? Am I really?" she says. There comes a sound like running water from somewhere nearby. "*You* would speak to me of fairness? I have hated you, Paul, for nearly a century. Whenever I took a moment from regulating the life of this planet to think about it, I would curse you. In the spring as I shifted my consciousness toward the poles and allowed a part of myself to dream, my nightmares were of you. They actually upset the ecology somewhat, here and there. I have waited, and now you are here. I see nothing to redeem you. I shall use you as you used me—to your destruction. Come to me!"

He feels a force enter into his body. His muscles twitch. He is drawn up to his knees. Held in that position for long moments, then he beholds her as she also rises, drawing a soaking leg from out of the crevice where it had been held. He had heard the running water. She had somehow melted the ice. . . .

She smiles and raises her pasty hands. Multitudes of dark filaments extend from her freed leg down into the crevice.

"Come!" she repeats.

"Please . . ." he says.

She shakes her head. "Once you were so ardent. I cannot understand you."

"If you're going to kill me then kill me, damn it! But don't—"

Her features begin to flow. Her hands darken and grow firm. In moments she stands before him looking as she did a century ago.

"Glenda!" He rises to his feet.

"Yes. Come now."

He takes a step forward. Another.

Shortly, he holds her in his arms, leans to kiss her smiling face.

"You forgive me . . ." he says.

Her face collapses as he kisses her. Corpselike, flaccid, and pale once more, it is pressed against his own.

"No!"

He attempts to draw back, but her embrace is inhumanly strong.

"Now is not the time to stop," she says.

"Bitch! Let me go! I hate you!"

"I know that, Paul. Hate is the only thing we have in common."

". . . Always hated you," he continues, still struggling. "You always were a bitch!"

Then he feels the cold lines of control enter his body again.

"The greater my pleasure then," she replies, as his hands drift forward to open her parka.

ALL OF THE ABOVE. Dorothy struggles down the icy slope, her sled parked beside Paul's. The winds lash at her, driving crystals of ice like microbullets against her struggling form. Overhead, the clouds have closed again. A curtain of white is drifting slowly in her direction.

"It waited for him," comes Aldon's voice, above the screech of the wind.

"Yes. Is this going to be a bad one?"

"A lot depends on the winds. You should get to shelter soon, though."

"I see a cave. I wonder whether that's the one Paul was looking for?"

"If I had to guess I'd say yes. But right now it doesn't matter. Get there."

When she finally reaches the entrance she is trembling.

Several paces within she leans her back against the icy wall, panting. Then the wind changes direction and reaches her. She retreats farther into the cave.

She hears a voice: "Please . . . don't."

"Paul?" she calls.

There is no reply. She hurries.

She puts out a hand and saves herself from falling as she comes into the chamber. There she beholds Paul in necrophiliac embrace with his captor.

"Paul! What is it?" she cries.

"Get out!" he says. "Hurry!"

Glenda's lips form the words. "What devotion. Rather, let her stay, if you would live."

Paul feels her clasp loosen slightly.

"What do you mean?" he asks.

"You may have your life if you will take me away—in her body. Be with me as before."

It is Aldon's voice that answers "No!" in reply. "You can't have her, Gaia!"

"Call me Glenda. I know you, Andrew Aldon. Many times have I listened to your broadcasts. Occasionally have I struggled against you when our projects were at odds. What is this woman to you?"

"She is under my protection."

"That means nothing. I am stronger here. Do you love her?"

"Perhaps I do. Or could."

"Fascinating. My nemesis of all these years, with the analog of a human heart within your circuits. But the decision is Paul's. Give her to me if you would live."

The cold rushes into his limbs. His life seems to contract to the center of his being. His consciousness begins to fade.

"Take her," he whispers.

"I forbid it!" rings Aldon's voice.

"You have shown me again what kind of man you are," Glenda hisses, "my enemy. Scorn and undying hatred are all I will ever have for you. Yet you shall live."

"I will destroy you," Aldon calls out, "if you do this thing!"

"What a battle that would be!" Glenda replies. "But

I've no quarrel with you here. Nor will I grant you one with me. Receive my judgment.''

Paul begins to scream. Abruptly this ceases. Glenda releases him, and he turns to stare at Dorothy. He steps in her direction.

"Don't—don't do it, Paul. Please.''

"I am—not Paul,'' he replies, his voice deeper, "and I would never hurt you. . . .''

"Go now,'' says Glenda. "The weather will turn again, in your favor.''

"I don't understand,'' Dorothy says, staring at the man before her.

"It is not necessary that you do,'' says Glenda. "Leave this planet quickly.''

Paul's screaming commences once again, this time emerging from Dorothy's bracelet.

"I will trouble you for that bauble you wear, however. Something about it appeals to me.''

FROZEN LEOPARD. He has tried on numerous occasions to relocate the cave, with his eyes in the sky and his robots and flyers, but the topography of the place was radically altered by a severe icequake, and he has met with no success. Periodically he bombards the general area. He also sends thermite cubes melting their ways down through the ice and the permafrost, but this has had no discernible effect.

This is the worst winter in the history of Balfrost. The winds howl constantly and waves of snow come on like surf. The glaciers have set speed records in their advance upon Playpoint. But he has held his own against them, with electricity, lasers, and chemicals. His supplies are virtually inexhaustible now, drawn from the planet itself, produced in his underground factories. He has also designed and is manufacturing more sophisticated weapons. Occasionally he hears her laughter over the missing communicator. "Bitch!'' he broadcasts then. "Bastard!'' comes the reply. He sends another missile into the mountains. A sheet of ice falls upon his city. It will be a long winter.

Andrew Aldon and Dorothy are gone. He has taken up painting, and she writes poetry now. They live in a warm place.

Sometimes Paul laughs over the broadcast band when he scores a victory. "Bastard!" comes the immediate response. "Bitch!" he answers, chuckling. He is never bored, however, or nervous. In fact, let it be.

When spring comes the goddess will dream of this conflict while Paul turns his attention to his more immediate duties. But he will be planning and remembering, also. His life has a purpose to it now. And if anything, he is more efficient than Aldon. But the pods will bloom and burst despite his herbicides and fungicides. They will mutate just sufficiently to render the poisons innocuous.

"Bastard," she will mutter sleepily.

"Bitch," he will answer softly.

The night may have a thousand eyes and the day but one. The heart, often, is better blind to its own workings, and I would sing of arms and the man and the wrath of the goddess, not the torment of love unsatisfied, or satisfied, in the frozen garden of our frozen world. And that, leopard, is all.

TIMERIDER
by Doris Egan

*Traveling back and forth through time is some-
thing never yet experienced, but when and if
chrononautics comes into existence, it will not
be as simple as taking a train or an airplane.
It presents problems of paradox and historical
distortions. For the person who becomes such
a timerider, the problems could be acute
indeed—especially if they take their natural
human emotions along with them.*

Mark had me on a manic-depressive cycle because of what
happened in Byzantium. It was everything you might think,
humiliating, frightening, self-disgusting; but the worst thing
about it was the energy drain. As I climbed up the hill to
manic it poured out of me, rushed out of me in torrents,
while I ran down corridors half-dressed, calling out to my
colleagues in filthy language. I danced, I screamed, I hung
over railings and yelled at the passersby. No one, of
course, stopped me.

Four or five days of this; then, when my body could
stand no more, the downward slide. A few days of rest,
time to breathe, even the ability to think clearly. Then the
tumble into the depression pit.

That phase I will not talk about. But it was in the days
between, the almost-peace, that I decided to keep the
journal I write this from. I would write as long as I could,

until I lost interest as I climbed the peak, or realized there was no point in writing at all, as I slipped into the gray fog of defeat. The amazing thing was that the cycle cost me no status among my friends. Status is everything to a rider. But being singled out for punishment by Mark and still to be alive was a mark of attainment, like being cursed by the gods. If anything, they regarded me with awe. It does not appear in my journal, but I remember—I think—one or two of my crew coming to clean me. Things like washing or finding a public toilet sometimes seemed too trivial when I was on the peak. And once I found myself finishing up a striptease on the steps of the D'drendt Liaison Hall, to no apparent audience reaction, when I heard lone applause and a whistle behind me. I turned and bowed to a young man in gray jeweled shorts. His companion, an older woman, hustled him away. "You idiot," she said, embarrassed. "That's Ceece, the Timerider. Don't gawk at her." So even the citizens were ignoring me, with an eerie politeness that wrote me out of their existence.

Three months went by; Mark kept me on full pay, considerate as always. And one day Banny came to see me, where I sat in the main Spoke. "Mark wants to see you," she said, handing me a handkerchief. I had a cold, and the medico was off-limits to me during the punishment. Banny was my Second, a sweet-natured, chunky, black-haired girl. She was only nineteen, the youngest Rider I knew of. I picked her straight out of School, and if she hadn't made Probationary Citizenship I don't know what I would have done.

"What's the news?" I asked.

"You think he tells me?" She helped me up. I was midpoint in the cycle—Mark had timed it well. "Want me to call you a chair?"

"I can *walk*, you know."

"Sorry, Ceece. I didn't mean anything."

Of course she didn't. I was irritated by a vague memory that was tickling the back of my head, of yelling at Banny—actually hitting her? Hell, I probably dreamed it. My dreams had been varied, of late.

I dug up a smile for her. "I know. Just don't worry about me. I'll let you know how it turns out."

I watched the people I passed on the way to Mark's, saw them politely not watching me. Maybe today I'd be taken off the cycle. Maybe I'd be back at work in a few hours.

I killed that thought with the ease of long practice. I never anticipate what Mark's plans are.

In Arizona, a long way away from me, Brian Cornwall was experiencing his first vision. It was a hot night in June, 1957. His room was on the top floor of the boarding house, a small, dark room with lilies on the wallpaper, a cracked window, and one forty-watt bulb on the ceiling. The window was open.

He turned over again, wondering if he should go downstairs to the porch. No one would mind if he did, but the other boarders would rise early and he hated to have strangers watch him when he slept.

He fell into a troubled sleep at last. One dream led to another in a succession of shadowy figures and places, until suddenly a light broke through his mind, a fierce and compelling light that cleaned away all lesser images. He dreamed that he was sitting up in bed, and the light had become softer. It suffused the room, covering the bed, the bureau, the trunk and bookshelves in a glow like a night-time snowfall back home in Vermont.

In the center of the glow now he could see a figure. A woman in a long white robe with a white crown on her head, her arms held out. Her face was still unclear.

When he saw her, he knew she would be beautiful.

Before Mark there comes Narses, the lion at the gate. More of a bad-tempered cat, actually, but with claws and ready to use them. Narses is never a welcome sight, but even less so then; he reminded me of Byzantium.

"You'll have to wait, Ceece. He's conferring." Narses claims he used to sing with the boys' choir in the church of Saint Sophia; his voice is still soprano, but in my opinion, not a very fine soprano. If they made him a eunuch it was for political rather than artistic reasons. Before Narses, I had pictured all eunuchs as fat and middle-aged, with knobbly hands and too many rings, and probably not all that bright, either. Narses was just on the full side of plump, by about ten or fifteen pounds, quite tall for his locus-of-origin, and rather good-looking in a blondish way. (Another stereotype fallen, as I had thought all Greeks and all Turks were dark.) He was sharp enough when it came to petty details . . . sharp enough to cut yourself on. And he reported everything to Mark.

He barely finished speaking before the door split open. Mark looked a careless twenty-five, with curly brown hair and dark eyes and not a worry in his head. He had looked just that way when I met him, ten years ago. "Carol, please come in. Narses, you can empty the tubes."

Environment tubes? Had he really been conferring with D'drendt, as rumors had it? I followed him in and saw the tubes retracting into the floor. Too late, whatever had been in them was gone.

"Carol, I trust you've been well. Take a seat; the one by the pandidor is the best." He's the only one who calls me Carol. Carol Celia Cordray, that's me; but it's been Ceece since I was two, back in the sunny mornings of southern California. The only other person who called me Carol . . . never mind, it was a long time ago, in all senses of the word. And we don't have to talk about what it was like before we were recruited.

Mark smiled politely. "I hope my point has been made about following procedure in your step-throughs. Convenience for one's crew is all well and good, but we can't let it conflict with D'drendt policy. May I assume I need not bring up Byzantium again?"

I said evenly, "I guess you can assume that."

"Excellent. Please report to the medico after our chat and have him take you off the cycle." He handed me a folder. "I have something rather unusual coming up, that I think you can handle. Keep it low-key; I don't want anyone outside you and your crew hearing about it."

I was looking through the folder. There were stat sheets and a picture of a young man, dressed circa 1955. Close enough to my own starting point to recognize. There were other pictures, at various ages, and a medical profile; none of the pictures showed him any older than the first. "Brian

Cornwall," said Mark. "Twenty-eight years old, locus 1957; born in Montpelier, Vermont, in July of 1929."

"The name seems familiar."

"He was an artist of some reputation. Mostly posthumous, I gather, but you might have heard of him; it was near your timeframe, wasn't it?"

Actually, I had been—I did some mental arithmetic—about five years old at that particular locus; and if anyone else had asked that question, he would have been livid. Riders do not ask these things. But after all, he was my recruiter; I could hardly pretend he didn't know.

"Close enough. I suppose I could have heard of him in college. My memory is pretty hazy about that time."

"Not important. Nor is Brian Cornwall, actually; have you checked the sheets? High intelligence, introverted, low self-esteem . . . a personality pattern that would have been labeled in the picturesque parlance of the age as a potential schizophrenic."

"We could cure that now."

"So we could. We're not interested in curing it, though, but of aggravating it. Notice how his lifeline comes to an abrupt dead-end. He was killed in a fire at the place where he worked."

"So we're recruiting Brian Cornwall?" It fit well enough. A high potential and a self-perceived failure, a life easy to pick up without disturbing the pattern—like me and everyone else.

"We have no interest in Brian Cornwall. We are interested in *this*."

Not a sheet-photo this time, but a real three-dimensional repro; a sculpture of some mellow, shiny stone. I took it for an abstract at first, but as I followed the flowing lines I realized there was a neck, and an eye . . . "It's a bird," I said, delighted.

"Mmm. A seagull, carved in chalcedony. Created sometime in the late 1870s, by an unknown Japanese artist. It made its way through a succession of small museums and shows for a century or more. Finally it started to be noticed. Its value has been growing, little by little, ever since . . . it's been priceless for quite a while now."

"We're salvaging it? Doesn't sound difficult. Who was the 'unknown artist'?"

"Literally unknown. I tried to track it, to establish its provenance, but it was created at a bad window. The time weather around Kyoto was awful; there's a storm going on there for a six-year span. It showed up in San Francisco twelve years later, though, and its history is well-documented from that point on." He took back the repro. "You'll have to take my word that the best locus for salvage is 1957. I've been waiting for a good weather report for years; the watchers notified me this morning that a perfect window will be opening any time now. The wave is close enough to us, in fact, that you should be able to observe—as soon as you're through with the medico, take Banny to the lab and start getting the feel of it."

"O.K. And Brian Cornwall?"

"We may be able to use him as a sort of extended agent. He's practically on top of the locus, for one thing; the seagull is in the museum where he works. He's perceived by his neighbors as being out of touch enough with reality that we can contact him without worrying about what he might say. And his past suggests that he might be amenable to persuasion. Read the stats."

He said it in a you-may-go-now type of voice, so I stood up. "By the way," he added, "I've already begun contact. Don't be surprised."

Surprised by what? Why should I care if he'd already begun contact?

We walked out of the office to where Narses sat, looking sour. Mark said to him, "Why don't you give Carol an O.K. for the medico?"

Narses reached slowly into a drawer for the stamp. As he pressed it into my hand, I said, "Cheer up, honey. Next time it could be you."

Mark smiled; he liked it when people were rude to Narses. I would have been rude to him anyway, just as a personal inclination. I saw as he put the stamp away that his bracelet was silver-and-sapphire, a twin to the one Mark was wearing. It had been gold-and-rubies when I'd last been in a condition to notice. The punishment cycle had kept me away for longer than I had thought. I hoped all the changes were so minor.

I told Banny to wait for me at the lab while I saw the medico. Angelo Poguno had been a rider for almost as long as I had, though he worked the medical end and never actually rode the waves. I should say just "Angelo," as Mark confined us to one name apiece, a policy he felt made us more like the citizens—and possibly more like the D'drendt. So far as I know, I am the only one to this day who knows Angelo's full name. I once got a long look at some personnel records . . . there's a story behind that, and no one's ever going to hear it. But sometimes the gaps between the records and the stories riders tell about their pasts are amusing.

"Ceece, love, it's about time you came off punishment. I've been holding this for you for weeks." He picked up a stoppered tube with "Ceece" written on the front, and began fiddling with his needles.

"I'm back riding, too, starting today."

"Huh! That screws up your system worse than drugs. Face it, honey, you're a genetic misfit. You should be in the service corps, like me. Say the word, my sweet, and I'll find you a place in medical . . ." As he spoke, he let the first needleful into my vein.

"You've said this before, paisan. But you don't get Merit points in the service corps—I'd have to live another five hundred years to buy my citizenship."

"What's being a citizen mean? I like my life as it is. I've got my friends, my status, living quarters I never dreamed of back in Napoli. And the citizens fall all over us, like we were movie stars."

"Only because they're too ignorant to know better." It must have been the effects of coming off the emotional cycle, but I found myself talking more than I would have, even to Angelo. "Ang, when I first came to the Spokes, I thought the citizens were Olympian. You know what I think now? They're the dregs. They're the scum that got left behind when the real humans left."

"Oh? Where did they go?" He went on working with

quiet efficiency as he spoke. A second needleful found its
way painlessly into my arm.

"Where do the riders go who buy their citizenship? Out
there, to see the universe. That's what I'll do someday, if I
live through this. I want to see where we've gone. I want
to see if D'drendt are everywhere. I want to find our
descendants and ask them if the D'drendt really won the
war."

Angelo looked a trifle alarmed. We were probably being
recorded. But speculation is no crime; or at least, everybody does it—rather like marijuana-smoking in my locus-
of-origin. "Love, you of all people must know who won
the war. You've got access—look in the timewaves."

I shook my head. "They keep those years sealed up.
Bad weather, they say. All over the planet? And another
thing—"

Now he looked really alarmed. I knew I shouldn't tease
him, so I laughed and said, "Angelo, unknit those unkind
brows. There are perfectly good, orthodox, government-
approved reasons for keeping those years sealed. And it's
just as well, or I might try following my second ambition."

"What might that be?" he asked, on cue—one of the
reasons I like Angelo. In him curiosity and discreet self-
preservation mingle in equal, massive doses.

"I want to kick over the traces—stick my fingers in the
pie—see if time can be altered."

"It can't be."

"Hell, sugar, don't just spout back what we both heard
in school. Who says it can't be, but a lot of people who
have a vested interest in seeing that it isn't? I'm tired of
maintaining the status quo. I'm tired of lugging holocams
through the timewall and bringing back documentary evidence of whatever the government wants to prove this
week."

"I never heard that Mark's assignments were all that
boring."

I ignored him. "I want to either get out, or make my
own assignments. I want—"

"You want a lot of dangerous things," he said firmly.

"Don't worry, my friend. I'm a coward at heart. What I
want has nothing to do with what I'll actually do, given

the chance. I just came off punishment, remember? I'm going to be a good girl."

I meant it, too. Which meant I wasn't going to mention to Angelo some of the things I'd been thinking about between the emotional hills and valleys I'd just been riding. Like: Why were some of my assignments more than just off-site recording? I could understand the removals—salvage was an accepted part of our function—but a couple of times I'd been ordered to leave things behind. And once to destroy some machinery. Was it all part of a fixed pattern laid down at the Big Bang? Or was I changing history, making it somehow easier for a D'drendt victory? Was this what they'd meant in training school about the "retroactive rights of the victor?"

The trouble, you see, wasn't so much that I wanted to *do* dangerous things—it was that I wanted to *know* dangerous things.

Angelo was shaking his head. "I stay away from policy entirely, darling. We Neapolitans much prefer the emotional and artistic life."

Neapolitan, hell. Angelo was Jersey City, 1964. I said, "And have you made any progress in that area?"

"It's not my progress I'm worried about. It's yours. I don't think you've slept with anybody since you've been here."

"What can I say? I'm naturally reserved."

"Naturally reserved! Tell me about it! Do you realize we were in the same class in training school, and then you had to come in here for treatment practically every day when you started riding—and it was still two years before you said anything to me outside of 'Should I roll up my sleeve for this one?' "

I had to smile sheepishly. "I was a little preoccupied in those days. Honestly, Angelo, it was nothing personal. Psych put me through a rough program when I first came; I still don't remember a lot about my past, I mean, before recruitment. But I've opened up a lot, haven't I?"

He rolled his eyes. "When was the last time you went to a citizen's party?"

"Oh, Ang, they're the most incredibly boring things."

'There's one at North Spoke tonight. One of my ex-lovers will be there. You can come with me, and I'll impress her with how I've gotten Ceece the star timerider, cold fish who goes with nobody, to come to a party with me.''

"Is that how everybody thinks of me?"

"Don't worry, love, it only adds to your status. But risk it a little, as a favor to me, all right?''

"I suppose it won't kill me. All right. It should be interesting to see what bizarre fads the citizens are following now.''

He kissed me on the cheek, chastely for a supposed Neapolitan. It was a pity there was no real attraction between us; I admired Angelo a great deal. Certainly he did very well for himself in the society we had found ourselves in. Which reminded me . . .

"Ang, have you heard anything about this assignment I've got from Mark?''

His face went expressionless. "What should I have heard?''

It was so annoying, and so like Angelo. He felt about information the way some people feel about the old junk in their attic. It may look useless now, but why give it away when someday someone might want to buy it?

I sighed. "I'll see you tonight, then.''

Banny and the crew already had the locus under observation, which jarred me; I wasn't used to coming into something midway. I drew her aside. "What goes, Ban? Have you heard anything about this? Or should I go over the stats before I ask?''

She looked troubled. "I don't know. We've just been going ahead with Mark's instructions. Nobody's even given us a script.''

"Mark's been instructing you himself?''

"Sometimes he sends Narses. But, yes.''

So Mark was doing his own timework under the table. I knew something was up when he told me how he had tried to establish the seagull's provenance; he would never have concerned himself with such details unless he planned on selling the piece himself. There were signs that Mark had clandestine dealings with D'drendt; certainly he had far more money and power at his disposal than could be explained by his rank. After all, he was only a section chief, one of four, and a human at that.

I didn't know just what his plans were, but Banny was my Second. She would have to know more. "Sit down with me for a few minutes before we start. We'll go over the stats."

She smiled with relief. We spread out the hard copy and began learning about Brian Cornwall's life.

He had been a withdrawn child, with few playmates. He grew up on his father's farm in Vermont, with his father and two older sisters—his father was a gentleman farmer apparently, a successful artist himself. The stats enclosed a copy of an ink drawing Brian had made at the age of nine; it was remarkable. An Arthurian knight, riding in a forest, with a bowman hidden behind a tree. Utterly professional, engrossing, somehow . . . *ruthlessly* beautiful. It was difficult to believe that any nine-year-old could have done it. "Good lord, Ban." I handed the picture to her.

She looked up after a few minutes. "It says he was *nine*— "

"I know, I know." I read on. He and his sisters spent a great deal of time going through their father's library, which leaned heavily toward Sir Walter Scott, Tennyson, the Morte D'Arthur, and the like. He had been remarkably old for a twentieth-century child when he learned that fairies aren't real. But where had the failure complex come from? Anyone who could draw like that . . . ah, here we were. His father, a wise and supportive man who educated Brian at home and then paid his way through Yale, had never spoken to him about his art. Out of jealousy? Out of some misguided wish not to interfere with his son's talents? We were never going to know. But Brian had interpreted it as shame at his lack of ability.

"Psych spent a lot of time watching here. Must have run Mark quite a bill," I said.

"He'll just charge it to the D'drendt," said Banny, puzzled.

Not if he's running something on his own that he doesn't want to make official, I thought. Sometimes I wonder about my co-workers—are they being discreet, or just dense?

Even Banny, sharp as they come . . . well, they probably were being discreet. Probably they were all perfectly aware of Mark's little tricks, and were simply too interested in self-preservation to comment on them.

I put the stats aside. "What's the hook? How are we getting him to cooperate?"

Banny looked embarrassed. "We were just following orders, you know, blindly. We didn't know what it meant."

I looked at her. "Well?"

"We ran a holo on him. I guess Psych set it up. It was one of those archetypal things—we started it while he was asleep and let him wake up while it ran—"

"Let me see it." It wasn't like her to wander around the point like this.

She played it for me. There was a soft radiance, and then Brian's name just at the threshold of awareness. An archetypal figure appeared in the center of the light, a goddess/madonna, shining and beautiful. I could imagine the associations with his childhood worlds—Mary, Guinevere, the Queen of the Fairies; there was an aura of gentleness and innocence about the whole thing that made you ache to believe it. As the holo faded I found that I was clutching my chair in sheer anger.

Mark had given her my face.

I helped the crew set up for my watch without saying anything, and they avoided speaking to me. They seemed embarrassed to have gone ahead with this without me, but as Banny said, they were only following orders. Riders didn't get choices. "What are the waves like?" I finally asked Banny.

"We're almost parallel," she said. "Right now they're .7 faster than we are. We're in synch enough to watch, but not to take or send any objects through."

"Except for holos," I said, regretting it immediately. I forced a smile. "I forgot to say, you've kept things going nicely while I was away. Thank you."

"You're welcome." She strapped me into my chair. Then she said, "We missed you, you know." She went over to the console to establish the link, pausing only long enough to swallow her pills. I wished I could take some too, but I'm allergic to them. It's ironic, in a way. I'm one of the best riders around, but my body is defenseless against the waves.

"Go ahead when you're ready," I told her, and almost before I finished speaking the ocean swirled up around me and pulled me along.

It was a fast current. There were shapes here and there in the mists, but I shot past them. I felt the exhilaration of speed and freedom from the body rush through me, making me drunk. It had been too long. Far too soon the current slowed almost to a stop; I was at the time window. I could see people and shapes coming into sharper view and I knew if I stayed at the window it would become clearer still. But I didn't want to stay; I wanted to ride the current some more. I pulled away, trying to reach the stronger waves that ran just outside the current I had taken. But Banny's voice was beside me, linking me to the lab. "The console says that you're at the window," she said. Banny, my reminder of duty and the possibilities of punishment. I forced myself back to the window.

The center of the window was at the museum. Things were in sharpest focus there. But I couldn't see Brian Cornwall there, although it was daytime and his job would presumably require him to be present. I found a cross-current and rode it outside, to a small park with a fountain that didn't run. Brian was there. I hoped he was sketching something that I could have the console take a picture of; it was too out-of-focus for me to steal a look right now. As I came closer I saw that he was only feeding some pigeons. I was disappointed, but took the moment to look at him in "real life." I suppose someone who wasn't a rider might have wanted to laugh at him; his time was flowing by at .7 of mine, and to me it was as though I were watching a speeded-up tape. He jerked his arms out suddenly, scattering seed on the pavement. I knew enough to discount the effect and merely watch his face. It was a fine, thoughtful face; but with an uncomfortable look in the eyes, as though he went through life with shoes that pinched. Poor Brian. Perhaps he would be relieved if he knew how little time he had left.

*   *   *

Back in the lab after my reconnaissance, I took advantage of my two minutes of grace to talk to Banny about our strategy.

"Do they have any projections as to when we'll reach synchrony? If it's not till after his death, we're wasting our time with him."

"They're not sure. They're never sure, you know weather forecasters. But he's not due to die for another three months, his time. It looks good."

"For us it does," I agreed. "It's too bad. That drawing was incredible."

"He's not bad-looking, either," said Banny, and I saw she was holding his picture in her left hand.

I hadn't thought he was anything special physically. He was blond, first of all, which made him not my type, and other than that he just seemed rather ordinary. A thoughtful face, though, as I said earlier. "To each her own taste, I guess; I prefer Dervan's people, myself."

"Dervan's people are like a dream. For a human, this man is good enough."

I shrugged, because no one can argue this sort of thing. "Ban, have you heard anything about a party at North Spoke—" I stopped, and motioned wildly. My two minutes were up. Banny withdrew, and left me alone to be sick into the bucket we kept by the chair. The next half hour would be a long one for me. God, I wished I wasn't allergic to the pills.

I decided to take a walk through the Riders' Spoke before going back to my quarters. For one thing, it had been a long time since I really paid attention to the scenery. For another, I had had a look at the next holo they were going to run on Brian Cornwall, and I wanted to get the taste out of my mouth.

I passed a lot of people I knew, and they smiled and sometimes saluted me. I was glad that my status was still good. I picked up some Chinese food at "Chan & Chin's" —the place was crowded with riders, as usual. Chan and Chin are the only two riders I ever heard of who bought their citizenships and stayed in the Spokes. They had gone off Basic Allowance years ago, and were making a bundle

of money. I saw a couple of teachers I remembered from
training school, and at the table with them some retired
riders. I could tell they were retired because they were all
fat. It's hard to get out of the habit of gorging after a
timeride, even if you skip the ride. They were still high-
status, still valued, still helpful in training the new recruits—
but they weren't citizens, and they weren't on antigy.
Their faces were getting wrinkled with age. Don't let that
happen to you, Ceece, I told myself; get your citizenship
and get out of here.

That's an easy order to give, but tough to carry out. If
my status got high enough, I might be offered antigy; and
with the added years of antigy I could accumulate enough
Merit to get my citizenship. One twenty- or thirty-year
span couldn't do it. But status is a hard thing to control,
and I would have to be careful never to let it slip—I might
get it back, but I couldn't afford the time it would cost me.
Look at those riders there, I thought; they're off the rolls,
they'll never make full citizen now, whatever their status.

I was depressing myself, and I had had enough of that in
the last few months. So I left and went out along the
Spoke past the training school. There was a concentration
exercise going on in the yard, led by a teacher I remembered from my own student days. She didn't look any
older (Antigy? or just biology? The only rule about antigy
was never to ask or tell—) and she wore a heavy gold
Cretan necklace around her olive neck. "Let yourself go,"
she was telling them in her soft voice. The conditioned
memories I had were such that I almost went under myself. The students, twenty or so, were sitting with their
faces toward the console in the middle of the yard. Most of
them were blank-faced, with their eyes closed, breathing
in a rhythm that matched the console screen. About a third
of the students appeared restless, bewildered, unsure as to
what was expected of them. They would have to get the
point rather quickly, I thought. I had never asked what
happened to failed students, but the answer seemed clear.

I took a short-cut tunnel out past the school into Main
Spoke—and almost ran smack into Dervan. Dervan had
been in my dreams (oh yes, *those* sorts of dreams) since I
was recruited. His back was to me now, but I knew

without having to look the fine, delicate face, the arched brows and cobalt eyes, the aquamarine feather-hair that swept back past perfect ears and touched the back of his neck. I tensed myself—as always around Dervan, I would have to be very, very alert.

It took me a moment to realize that there was someone else in the tunnel. A student of about nineteen or twenty years, still in uniform, and Dervan was talking to him. The student was oblivious to me, wrapped up in Dervan's eyes and voice and the way all Dervan's people have of creating intimacy with whomever they choose.

Damn Dervan, anyway. Taking his victims from training-school was like picking ripe apples. After all, what sort of students do we get? They don't just want people who are "spoken for"—marked to die or disappear. They don't just want people with intelligence and adaptability, and the impossible-to-pick-for talent of riding the waves. They want people who have screwed up their lives so badly they will docilely follow anyone who promises to make things make sense. New recruits are a pitifully cooperative lot. I know I was.

"Excuse me," I said loudly. The student looked angrily at me, no doubt annoyed at having Dervan's music interrupted. "Why, Dervan! How nice to see you. I don't know if you're heard, but I was out of things for a while, on a punishment cycle . . ."

"I'd heard." He said it calmly, without the added something in his voice that he been using on the student. Even so, it was a pleasure to hear him speak.

I tried to think of something to say that would separate him from the student. I don't know why the Good Samaritan compulsion came over me, but there it was. "Will you be going to the North Spoke party tonight? I'm on my way there now."

"I may. I haven't decided yet. Perhaps Paul here would like to come with me." Paul looked eager, like a puppy being promised a walk.

"He'd need a pass from the teachers, though, and you know how they hate to give those out." Don't glare at me, you idiot, I thought at the student. You'll be lucky if they lock you up until training is over. How did I ever make it through to graduation alive? That must have been mostly luck, too.

"Oh, we might just go to the party and apologize later. I have some influence with the teachers, Ceece, if you'll remember."

I looked at him. "I don't think that would be a good idea, Dervan. I really don't."

He watched me speculatively . . . Lord, that incredible face. "I suppose not. Someone might tell the teachers before I had a chance to get my words in. Never mind, Paul," he said, turning back to the student. "We can do it another time."

The idiot was practically ready to cry. I said to Dervan, "Go on ahead and I'll see you at the party. I'd like to talk to Paul for a minute."

Dervan smiled. "If you like wasting your time, go ahead." And he walked off down the tunnel and disappeared, as Paul and I watched in silence for a moment, leaving us only an impression of grace.

Paul turned to me fiercely. "What do you think you're doing? I don't even *know* you—"

"Shut up!" I said it like a Timerider Crew Captain, which I am. He shut up, surprised. "Now why don't you think about it for a minute, and tell me what I've done?"

"You—we were going to go to this party, you know—"

"What party? Where?"

He tried to remember. The party, of course, had made no impression on him; it was not what he was angry about. He just had the feeling that something terribly important and beautiful had been happening, and I had stopped it.

Luckily for him. I tried to tell him some of the facts of life, starting with the idea that it was not all rainbows here in the Far, Far Future.

"I know things aren't easy," he said with contempt. "The teachers told us that we'd have to earn our livings, and it would be hard."

"Bully for them. But they don't have time to warn you about every lion you're going to meet in the jungle. They deal in percentages. They let you rookies wander around unprotected, and if half of you make it to graduation they pass around champagne and have a party.''

"You're twentieth century, aren't you?" said Paul suddenly. "So am I."

"Good for you," I said, and I wasn't being ironic that time. "You've got a high probability of being picked up by a top team when you do graduate. A good section chief will weight his force heavily toward twenty/twenty-first century recruits."

Paul frowned. "Isn't that illegal?"

"Never mind. The point here is that you make it to graduation. Dervan is someone you want to avoid, and anyone who looks like Dervan. They're not human, and they're not D'drendt, and they're not good for humans to mix with. Some of them, anyway, and you're not sophisticated enough to tell the good from the bad."

He looked stubborn. I didn't take it personally, I understood Dervan's effect.

"All right. Let's have a little xenobiology lesson. First of all, you're only going to meet the males of Dervan's race, never the females. The females aren't really as intelligent . . . well, that's not quite true. But the females are off doing the shitwork of the moment for whatever males they're attracted to. You see, the males are the pampered peacocks, and the real scholars, and the travelers, and the people who have all the fun. Dervan's wives, if he has any, are back on his home planet living for his memory, see?"

"No."

I sighed. "It's like imprinting ducklings, all right? Have you ever read Konrad Lorenz?"

He was getting annoyed again. I said hastily, "The way Dervan's species bonds, for mating, is by having the male imprint the female. It usually happens in adolescence. Then the female is emotionally tied to that male for life. She thinks only of him, wants to bear his children and raise them, and loses all interest in life outside of him. I guess from her point of view she's having fun too, since she gets to see her personal god every day . . . but I don't think you had that in mind for your life, Paul, did you?"

"Huh?" I'd gotten his attention.

"This imprinting power only works on the females of their own species, not on fellow males. Imagine how shocked they were when they found out it worked on humans of either sex. Some of Dervan's people were so thrilled at the ability to do it to males—people of equal status, from their habit of thinking—they became perverts. In the eyes of their race, at least. That's why Dervan lives in the Spokes. His own people would ostracize him if he lived at home."

He looked a little like I'd hit him. I said gently, "Dervan is a crew-captain, just like me. Only his crew would die for him, literally. Sometimes they do, when step-throughs don't go the way they're planned. If you don't want to be cannon-fodder, stay away from Dervan."

I left him there to think about it.

Timewave under surveillance, 7.3 concurrence (someday I'll tell you how I know these things):

Brian had been waiting for her to speak. That he would dream again, he knew already. He did not doubt his sanity, or at least he discounted the question as trivial. His painful and beautiful childhood had left him enormously vulnerable, but also enormously adaptable.

This time she came to him in his little room at the museum, where he sat after hours cataloging and updating the files. It was routine, dusty work, but he didn't mind; it left his mind free to remember.

Her coming followed on his thoughts so well, he thought at first it was only a memory. His visual memory was so sharp that it often led him astray.

"Forgive me, Brian." She knew his name! Her voice had undertones of music—no, that was too crude. Of *remembered* music. "Forgive me, but I need your help."

Second Holo, Brian Cornwall, June 28, 1957.

Sonic attachments. Refer Psych, 96/4RC.

. . . Forgive me, but I need your help. I've come a long way to find you. [2 sec. pause] No, don't speak to me now; I can't hear you, we're still too far away from each other. [Up sonics .4] I can't tell you now what I need, except your understanding. I only wish that you were here with me and we could speak to each other the way I want us to. Maybe someday it can happen. But for now, all I can say is that I am in great danger. . . .

I was more happy to try to forget about the holos and Brian Cornwall by going to the party with Angelo. I had my bathroom paint me and powder me and oil my skin. North Spoke Park was in summer mode, so we would probably be wearing the usual dress for citizens in summer— not much beyond a loincloth, a bra for those women who felt they needed one, and lots of jewelry. But when the house announced Angelo, I was disappointed to find he was in top hat and tails.

"Oh, Angelo, don't tell me they're *still* on the historical kick."

He shrugged a good-humored "don't blame me" sort of shrug. "Lady Mary's giving the party, and she's a little slow on picking up hints."

For the better part of a year now all the citizens' gatherings had had historical themes. It was part of their general tendency to watch and emulate timeriders, but we found the whole process tedious—not to mention annoying, when the historical inaccuracies crept in, as they always did.

"Is there a time range for this one?" I was half-tempted not to go. But that would mean sitting at home, thinking about things . . .

"Nineteenth-century Britain."

"You're a little off, I think. That looks more 1920s, 1930s."

"Only some of the riders will be able to tell. Now get dressed, darling—I'm starving, they're bound to have tons of food, and I'm not going to give you a chance to change your mind."

I made a face at him and went off to be fitted up. The house wardrobe found me a gown it claimed was in the London style of 1898; I took it, but left off the corset. Torturous things women allowed to be done to them—but I guess the things people will do to appear attractive to potential lovers cannot be taken lightly.

North Spoke Park was full of people that night. There were lanterns and torches and a soft breeze was blowing. It rustled through the gowns of the ladies and made the damask tablecloths sway. Lady Mary was holding court in the center of the park; she had had a fountain put up, with a cluster of statues in the middle and a score of fishes spouting what looked too dark to be water. I tasted it; it was Coca-Cola. (One of the things I hold against the D'drendt is that they have a grudge against alcoholic beverages. They don't prohibit it, but nobody has the bad taste to serve alcohol in public.)

"Ceece! I'm so glad you came!" Lady Mary made a point of knowing the name of every rider of reputation. "You haven't been to a party in ages." She stopped for a second, feeling she might have trodden too close to the subject of my recent punishment. Then she brightened. "But here you are at mine. Have you tried the fountain?"

"Yes. Very nice." It's hard for me to match the citizens' enthusiasm for Coca-Cola.

"And Angelo, it's been far too long." She took his hand and smiled up at him slyly. Another of my Angelo's past lovers, no doubt. Lady Mary looked about nineteen and lovely, but so did practically every female citizen I'd ever met, except for the eccentrics. I tried not to be contemptuous of them, I really did, but why they were here in Earth orbit when an entire universe was open to them . . . Damn them, and not to me. Not yet.

"Should we go mix?" I asked her, trying to be polite.

"By all means. Now don't just stick to other riders, you two. Get around, talk to people; you'll have a better time. There'll be a surprise later."

And she batted her eyes, so help me, and patted Angelo's hand as she dismissed us.

"I can't wait," I told Angelo.

"Patience, Ceece. We only just got here." He steered us straight to the food tables, pausing only long enough to wave or smile at about ten ex-lovers, male and female.

There was a slight stir near the fountain. "Oh, lord," I said, "Dervan's shown up after all."

"Are you still interested in him?" Angelo's attention was almost wholly on the food, and a half-eaten sandwich made his words hard to catch.

"I am *not* interested in him. I mean, no more than any

other warm-blooded human being would be. It's a simple
biological fact—"

"Ummm." I couldn't tell if he were referring to the
sandwich or to what I just said.

We wandered around the tables, found Banny sitting on
a statue, and talked shop talk and gossip with a few riders
we passed. I congratulated myself on not having thought
about Brian Cornwall in over an hour.

Then Lady Mary called us together for her surprise. It
was to be an old English fox hunt, with hunting horns and
red coats for everybody. They brought the fox in in a cage.

"It's going to be difficult to ride horses around the park,
isn't it?" I asked her. "Especially in these clothes."

"Horses?" she repeated blankly.

"I'm not running after the damn thing," said a rider
standing nearby.

"How are we going to know where it is in the dark?
And where are the dogs?" There was some general nega-
tive murmuring. Lady Mary looked upset.

Then there was a laugh I would have recognized anywhere, and Dervan stepped to the front of the crowd. He
released the catch on the cage and pulled the door up. The
fox was gone in one frightened blur. Dervan lifted some
torches from their poles and passed them to his hangers-on.
Then he pulled off the long black jacket he was wearing,
followed by the ruffled shirt. He kicked off his boots and
threw them into the bushes. "Don't fall too far behind,"
he called to his hangers-on, and laughed again. And he ran
into the darkness after the fox.

Sometimes it is not hard at all to remember that Dervan's
people are descended from birds of prey.

People still milled around the fountain, talking rather
uncertainly. Lady Mary started to cry; I wondered how old
she really was. Angelo apologized to me and sat down
beside her on the fountain edge and told her that everyone
had had a grand time, him included, and that you couldn't
expect everything to work out all of the time.

No wonder he had so many lovers. It was all superficial,
though; the truth of the matter was that he couldn't stand
to live with any one person for more than six weeks.

I passed the time with Banny. We rather rudely threw

stones into the Coca-Cola fountain. Banny told me that she
had spoken with Dervan earlier in the evening, and he hd
seemed angry with me. As angry as Dervan ever gets,
anyhow; what happened?

"Just a misunderstanding. It all depends on your point of
view. Maybe he was right, and I should have minded my
own business."

There was no need to go into detail, and anyway, the
hunting party was coming back. From what I could see of
their faces in the darkness, the torch-bearers looked tired;
but one of them carried the dead fox across his shoulders.
The man's shirt was bloody around the collar and down
the back. Dervan entered the clearing last, his face flushed
with victory. He had left the corpse-carrying to one of his
crew, but he raised the palms of his hands, showing the
bloodstains. There was general applause, particularly from
the citizens. The light in his eyes and the look on his face
made him seem more than ever like some god; Dionysus,
perhaps, or some hunters' god I didn't know about.

He saw me watching and walked through the crowd to
where I stood.

"I won't forget your interference earlier today."

The torchlight flickered across his face, making it a
gorgeous light-and-shadow mask. I shrugged and controlled
an impulse to throw myself in the dust at his feet.

He motioned to one of the torchbearers. "Not that it did
you any good." The man came nearer and I saw that it
was Paul, the student from the tunnel.

Well, it was none of my concern. I had crew of my own
to worry about, and my own skin.

Banny had sidled nearer to hear what was going on.
Dervan said, "When Paul graduates, I'm going to bid for
him. Do you think my chances are good?"

"Very good, I'd say." Paul looked pleased at my words,
which were the truth. Who else would want him, now that
he was imprinted?

Banny looked concerned at the tone of conversation.
But as a rider, I was technically safe from Dervan's tricks.
Had I ever shown signs of imprinting (and like love, it's
impossible to hide), Mark would have had him stretched
on the rack, and rolled on carpet tacks. Perhaps literally;

Mark had once or twice taken people on private step-throughs into the timewaves, and they had returned much chastened.

True, Dervan was a citizen who chose to be rider, not a refugee like me; but we both worked for Mark, and we both knew who could make us sorry if we got out of hand.

Dervan measured me for a while, perhaps hoping I would be more argumentative. Then he took Paul away and went to celebrate his kill.

Banny said to me, "Isn't it dangerous to annoy him? I mean, he *could*, you know, do that thing to you." Dear Banny, she actually blushed. Banny is one person I have never dug up background on, but I strongly suspect a Victorian childhood.

"It's not that likely." I explained to her that Mark wouldn't stand for it. "But just in case," I added slowly, thinking about it, "you shouldn't talk to him much. Especially not if you're feeling any kind of emotion. The imprinting needs interaction from the victim, you know, answering his questions, talking back to him. That speeds up the process. If you ever suspect it may be happening, just close your mouth and walk away."

Banny shook her head, clearly planning to avoid the entire situation.

We broke apart for the night soon after, Banny allowing herself to be picked up by a male citizen who, physically at least, looked the same age as she. I looked around for Angelo, but could find neither him nor Lady Mary. Poor woman—she had had an awful night. And much as I respected Angelo, I hoped that she didn't come to depend on him for any emotional support. It wasn't in him to give. Maybe that was why my mind turned stubbornly away from finding him the least bit attractive, although he was popular enough with the citizens. He was too easy to lean on, and you forgot it was temporary. I could grow to hate him if he let me down, and I wouldn't like that at all. I had never been able to tolerate ambiguity in a relationship. There was a lot in my past that was fuzzy, but that fact seemed to stand out in my mind. No . . . that wasn't quite accurate. It was just that I couldn't tolerate it in anyone close to me. Luckily, no one was really close to me, so it wasn't a problem.

I spent the next few weeks hard at work on the Brian Cornwall project—or, as Mark referred to it, the seagull project. As you can see, we both had it tagged in our minds according to what each of us felt was the major factor involved. I badgered Psych into giving me a copy of the shots they'd taken of Brian's personal journal. There were sketches in it, essays, observations, descriptions of people he'd met. It reminded me rather of the pillow books I liberated from Heian Japan and kept on a shelf in my bedroom. I read from the journal every night; it was like taking a nice, cool bath after a hot day. Meanwhile, we played three more holos for Brian. By the last one, Psych had stopped pussyfooting around and let the poor guy know that his goddess was interested in the chalcedony seagull in his museum. This sudden descent into materialism was accepted by Brian in good part; mythical people were always looking for some sort of talisman, and if he could help to provide it, he was more than willing.

I threw my souvenir silver fountain pen across the room after that session. He was being so nice about everything! He was clearly intelligent, educated, imaginative—how could he be so *nice* about everything?

"Idiot!" I fumed to the crew. "Psych has him down to a T."

Banny shrugged, knowing I wasn't really mad at Brian. She changed the subject. "Henry's done a new design for us," she said, pointing to one of the banners that hung on the lab wall. It was a red circle on dark blue, with two black triangle-shapes in it, suggestive of wings. Every crew had a nickname, usually some kind of bird or flying thing; this symbolized our nickname, Darkwings. It wasn't a name I would have chosen, tending as it did to remind me of shrieking things whirring up out of cave mouths, but I'd inherited the name along with the crew. It wasn't as bad as some names I'd heard.

"Henry!" I called to him, where he was screwing jacks into the console. "You did a beautiful job." He smiled and went on working. Henry used to be a famous writer in his locus-of-origin, and I happened to know he was working on a novel now. I had read all his books myself, in my own locus; it would be interesting to see what he came up with.

We shared labquarters with two other crews, and Henry's Darkwings design was far better than the designs on the banners that hung beside it. Anything that added to our status was welcome.

I began to feel guilty about throwing the pen against the wall. I didn't want to sound depressed when I was with my crew, for they would interpret it as our being in some sort of trouble. And I didn't want them to think I was unhappy with their work. On the contrary, I was far too proud of them; they were all talented, quick-witted riders, with enough power to send me as deep into the timewaves as any rider has ever gone, and indeed, enough power to maintain *five* of us during an actual step-through—as in the most recent step-through when I directed the looting of the palace in Byzantium. If I hadn't been so concerned about the energy drain on them, I wouldn't have taken the short-cuts I did and ended up in trouble with Mark . . . but the past is the past, except when it isn't, and there's no use crying over spilt milk when someone's paying you to clean it up.

"I'll grant you one thing, though," I said to Banny. "He's not bad-looking, after all."

Mark called me out of the lab one day soon after. I walked down Riders' Spoke to his office, my mind full of the project. Brian's timewave—the one we had been observing all this time—had finally reached full concurrence with ours. It was 1/1, and had been for two hours. Weather watchers estimated it would probably stay concurrent for several days; of course, they added (as they always did), "you never know." Several days or not, the time had come to retrieve the seagull. There would be a fire at the museum twenty-two hours further down the line, and Brian would be dead.

"You'll have to wait," said Narses, as usual, where he sat at his desk outside Mark's door. He began filing his nails ostentatiously, and I saw that each nail was inset with a small sapphire in the center. "Do you like them?" he asked, seeing my glance. "They were a present from Mark for my birthday."

"Lovely," I said.

Narses was in a mood to gossip. "Did you hear about the two riders they caught making private step-throughs? They were picking things up and selling them on the black market."

"No!" I said in surprise, gratifying him immensely. "Anyone I know?"

"I shouldn't think so. Hideo's section. Not any of *our* people."

"So what happened to them? Are they dead?"

"Not yet. They're being outcast, though, so it's only a matter of time."

It *would* only be a matter of time for a noncitizen without the weight of the timeriders behind him. Anyone could do anything they liked to an outcast. Citizens could use him for their next foxhunt, instead of a fox. And there were aliens I had seen, whose inclinations didn't bear thinking of. Dervan was a saint beside them.

"In my time," went on Narses, "we would have dealt with people like that much more severely. Why, they were barely questioned as to who their black market contacts were! One thing of which I have never approved in this society is its lack of understanding in regard to torture. I think that its absence simply means that the government no longer *cares* what its people do and think. In my time, we cared. We questioned. We followed every postulate to its logical end. We had the rack, the fire, the iron bands—"

"Uh, yes, those were the days. Look, Narses, I think maybe Mark is waiting for me. Have you told him I'm here?"

He sniffed. "He's quite aware of your coming, Ceece. He has important guests in his office. When he's ready—" A light lit on Narses's board; apparently Mark was ready. Narses sniffed again and coded open the door.

Yes, Mark had important guests. The two environment tubes were occupied, and by two D'drendt. It was the closest I had ever been to our conquerors. I tried not to show how scared I felt.

Each D'drendt was more than half again the size of a man. They did not stand or sit, but *clung* to one side of the tubes with little pink hands covered with suckers. The rest of their bodies were black, and wet-looking, and there were big, folded up parts that looked like wings. They may even have been wings, but I had never seen them unfolded, even in pictures. I stood in the middle of the office, wide-eyed.

"Please have a seat, Carol," said Mark gently. He motioned to a chair. I walked to it slowly, not wanting to take it because it would put one of the D'drendt partly out of my line of vision. The thought made me nervous, though I knew it couldn't leave the tube. I had a sudden visualization of where these two D'drendt would go when the tubes retracted into the floor; I saw them crawling out, along the D'drendt pathways that ran through every important building and under the streets, into the D'drendt-environment rooms everywhere. I suddenly wondered if these pathways were more extensive than I had ever guessed; I imagined D'drendt crawling behind the wall of the lab, or under our floor; I shivered involuntarily and quite noticeably. Perhaps they were too unfamiliar with human reactions to catch it. Certainly Mark was not. However, he simply said, "Carol, these visitors are interested in the project you are currently working on. Would you tell us the status of it, please?"

I opened my mouth. Before I could say anything, the speaker box on the tube nearest me sputtered and said, "This is the human you told us of."

Mark nodded. "Carol-Celia-Cordray," he said, giving it as if it were one word.

"You will tell us more of her history." It was a fine, round voice, with a citizen's accent.

"In a little while," said Mark. I wondered that he could speak to them like that. "Please bring us up to date first, Carol."

I nodded. "The timewave we've been observing is in full concurrence, so theoretically we could send or receive solid objects any time now. The best focus we've gotten is on the floor above the place where the seagull is kept.

Rather than take any chances on losing the wave, we're going to use that as the transfer point.''

The D'drendt interrupted. "How will you move the art-object from its present location to the transfer point? Will you make a step-through yourself to do so? Is this not expensive? Will it not have to go in the record? I do not perhaps feel—''

Mark could also interrupt. "It's taken care of,'' he said briskly. "Explain it to him, Carol.''

I turned to the D'drendt and forced myself to look at him. Experience is good for you, I told myself. And if there really were D'drendt everywhere, I would have to learn to deal with them. "This is not a step-through assignment,'' I said to him patiently. "We are using an on-the-scene person, native to the timeframe, to move the seagull to the point of focus.''

"And will he not talk? There are laws about interference—''

I decided to interrupt someone myself; everyone else was doing it. "He's not going to talk. He's due to be dead within the next twenty-two hours, his time.''

The D'drendt shut up, apparently to chew that one over.

Mark looked quite pleased with himself, in a quiet sort of way. "You're doing a fine job, Carol. Only keep it up.''

That was true actually, but he may have just been saying it to reassure the D'drendt that their project was in good hands.

I said, "Thank you.''

The other D'drendt's speaker box came to life. "You were going to tell us of this one's history.'' It was a warm, female voice, that would have been appropriate to a woman of about fifty. I had not been expecting that, and wondered if it meant anything.

Mark said, "Carol's locus at the time of recruitment was 1974. That's very near the point we're watching now, so you can see that she is an appropriate choice for the project. She's naturally discreet, and won't cause anything to happen that would attract attention in 1957.'' Naturally discreet, indeed. What a lot of fertilizer he was laying out for the guests. I almost missed what he said next. "I recruited Carol myself, in California State Prison, where she was awaiting trial for murder." I looked at him, unbelievingly.

"This does not sound like a stable recruit," said the (possibly) woman D'drendt.

Mark shrugged. "She was on trial for killing her father, who was a very disagreeable human, one that any sane society would have dispensed with for her. Believe me, I've had the chance to observe many disreputable humans in my time here, and even pass on some for training, and this man was not worth anyone's time. Certainly not worth Carol's time, so I offered her a job instead of a prison term."

"Surely she was missed—"

"We paid for her lawyer and saw that she was sent to a mental institution, where she was due to commit suicide soon after. We fudged that a little." He smiled. "No one paid a lot of attention. Someone else's body—a drowned face isn't that recognizable, anyway. Psych had to work with her heavily when she first arrived, but I must say she's been worth every penny."

"We will have to rely on your evaluation," said the D'drendt. "And surely Psych must have passed her, or she would not have been allowed in school."

"Oh, yes. They had to remove rather more memory than they'd anticipated. And she probably doesn't believe what I'm saying now—another safeguard they put in. But they really brought her back to peak efficiency. I defy you to find a better rider, in anyone's section."

"This is well." The box stopped speaking, and began instead to chirp and squeal. The other D'drendt squealed back. I was in no shape to pay any attention. How could he *say* things like that? I looked at my feet, feeling a little dizzy.

It was true, my first memory of Mark was connected with some sort of institution; but I had thought it was a school or a hospital.

The D'drendt with the male voice said, "We would speak to you now alone."

Mark gestured me to the door and I found my way out. I paid no attention to Narses as I walked away.

Probably it *was* a school or a hospital. The horrible thing about Mark was that he was quite capable of inventing all that for reasons of his own that concerned his guests, or even just to keep me off-balance.

I was, I decided, just not going to pay any attention to it. Mark was no person to go to for the truth, after all. I postponed going back to the lab for a while, and decided to see if Angelo had anything in his medicine chest to calm me down.

"I've just had a session with Mark," I said to him, without preamble. "Do you have any suitable drugs for that?"

He laughed. I hadn't seen him since the night of the party, but I gathered that he and Lady Mary had cut a swath through the North Spoke before they gave out the following morning. He even moved in with her for a week, which wasn't bad compared to his usual timing, and there were no recriminations. Gossip travels fast in the Spokes.

He pulled out a bottle of wine and looked at me with a question.

I shook my head. "Work to do."

He then pulled out a little glass container of crystal powder and handed it to me. But I didn't take it. A thought had come to me.

"Angelo," I said, "the two riders being outcast—the government must be taking them off all time drugs, so they can't escape. Are you the one administering the counteragent?"

"I might be," he replied (typically). "Why do you ask?"

If he wasn't the one, he could arrange to be. I said, "I'd like you to do some modification work on one of them."

He looked at me.

"They're going to die anyway," I said logically.

He sat back and folded his arms. "Talk to me, Ceece."

I felt wonderful. And it wasn't the crystal powder, because I didn't take any. If Mark had spun that tale to keep me off-balance (and all right, I would never know for sure), then the most obvious fact he would not want me to notice was that the two D'drendt visitors were his black-market contacts. There was a thriving market for genuine Earth art objects (the key word being genuine, and not a perfect copy—though a perfect copy seemed good enough to me, so I guess I don't have the collector's mind). I doubted that our seagull was ever going to see the inside of the government museum, or be sold to a rich tourist to help the Treasury.

For all the propaganda, I myself had rarely done an assignment that had anything to do with recording history. What I had done was a lot of looting. Riders are discouraged from talking about their assignments, so I had to wonder. Were we all engaged in looting on a grand scale, cleaning out mother Earth of her treasures? Or were the Darkwings just Mark's private circle of thieves? Oh, there are thing I would love to know.

I met Banny back at the lab. She said, "Mark says to go ahead with the retrieval as soon as possible. He just sent down a message."

Maybe the D'drendt were getting itchy. I said, "It's night, Brian's time, right? And the museum's closed."

She nodded. "He's inside, just like we asked him to be."

"Okay, play through the last holo. The one that asks him to move the seagull to our focus."

There was no point in my watching it again as it went through, so I concentrated instead on our crewwork. They were quietly efficient, as always, and there was the quick understanding between them that marks people who have been together for a while. I give myself some credit for that; on the couple of occasions when Mark sent us lemons instead of recruits I had bid for, I had carefully given the lemons a chance. I gave each of them several chances, in fact, because I didn't want the rest of the crew to think I was being arbitrary. When I saw them getting nervous, though, I would send the incompetent in question into a situation I knew he couldn't handle but he knew he could; thus getting him out of the way before he could be a danger to everybody. There had been a marked lessening of tension after these incidents. I don't know if Mark knew

I had killed them purposely; they could so obviously have done it to themselves.

But the result of it was the best crew around, in my opinion. I was proud when I heard people say "Ceece's crew," the way I had heard "Fielding's crew" or "Balthasaar's crew" when I was in school. Not counting the lemons, we had the lowest fatality rate in the section.

"Ready to go," said Banny, interrupting my thoughts. I walked down to my chair in the pit and she strapped me in. Then she went back to the console, and everyone but me swallowed their pills.

"Let's take it," I said. The ocean pulled me in.

It was a fine, heady current; I flew along, the spearpoint of the effort being made by Banny and the crew. But as always, I was only tenuously aware of them. The seduction of riding is that you feel that it's all under your own power.

The ride was over too soon, and I was at the window. It was easy to see the focus—it was literally the clearest point I could see in the waves. The third floor of the museum, a dull wooden floor with showcases of Indian artifacts, starlight shining through the windows. Brian was waiting. He was holding the seagull in both hands, as though he were afraid to drop it. He couldn't see me, of course. Damn it all, Brian . . . I looked down at my own right hand, where I carried a perfect copy of the seagull. I put it down on that dull wooden floor, stepped back, and said, "Now!" to Banny. My crew pushed against the timewall for all they were worth. The seagull began to lose its look of reality and take on the dead-looking, artificial light that seemed to me to surround the waves. At the same time, Brian's eyes widened. Then he snapped to awareness, knelt down and picked up my seagull, and replaced it with his own. The crew was on it in a second, like a pack of wolves. It became more and more real, and I picked it up.

"Done," I said—to myself, because my crew already knew it. I let the waves take me back, dragging my feet a little. My image of Brian standing alone in the museum got smaller and less real, as though I were looking at him through the bottom of a glass.

Banny came to me first, as she always did. "I don't want to talk now," I said tiredly. "Wait until after I'm sick."

When I was ready I said, "Let me see the recorder." Banny moved away from the console. I played back the retrieval as the recorder would have seen it (and as Brian saw it); the materialization of the false sculpture and the vanishing of the true. I followed Brian as he picked up the false one and carried it out of focus, into the fuzzier areas of the museum. He brought it downstairs and propped open the case he had taken the first seagull from; he was placing the substitute inside when another figure appeared on the screen. A man in uniform, who reached out a hand to Brian's sleeve, clearly interrogating him. I felt sick, although I knew it couldn't matter. His coming death made lesser matters trivial. Still, what could he possibly say? Surely he didn't make a habit of removing museum property in the middle of the night.

He was saying something, though, and quite calmly and naturally. The museum guard nodded. He helped Brian close the case on the seagull. They spoke for a minute, the guard offered a cigarette, Brian shook his head, and they separated. I realized I had been holding my breath. I turned to Banny, watching over my shoulder. "That's my boy," I said, a little shakily. "He was pretty good, don't you think?"

"Damned good," said Banny, and from the way she said it I heard Victorian echoes, as of a gentleman with great red mustaches congratulating his chums over cards.

I switched off the console. "Where's the bird?"

"On its way to Mark. I sent it up, via Narses, as soon as you brought it through."

"Good. This one seemed important to him; maybe he'll give us all Merit points."

Banny made a noise through her nose that suggested she wasn't going to hold her breath. Then she said, more thoughtfully, "I wonder how many Merit points Mark has."

To my mind there was no point in speculating, even as to Mark's citizenship. The only thing you could be sure

about with him was that he was on antigy, and that only
because the facts spoke for themselves. If he wasn't on
antigy, then he wasn't human; and Mark's sicknesses were
human sicknesses.

Banny went on, "He lives in the outer ring, I hear he's
got *citizens* for servants. Do all the section chiefs live like
that? It must cost ten times the Allowance—I don't know
how he does it."

I looked at her, but kept quiet. My fellow riders were
always *saying* things like that. What was wrong with
them?

It had always been perfectly clear to me how he did it.

The crew was ravenous after the salvage, and if I kept
them too long, it would be a toss-up whether they would
eat first or fall asleep. I let them go ahead to Chan &
Chin's, all but Banny; I told her there were a few odds and
ends we needed to clean up. When we were alone, I told
her what Angelo and I wanted to do.

"You don't have to get involved, Ban. There's always a
chance it won't work out."

"Don't be silly. Is there anything I should do, or do I
just 'hold myself in readiness'?"

I smiled in relief. "The first thing we do," I said, "is
make a holo."

It was several hours later before I finally got to sleep; I
had never held myself conscious so long after a timeride
before. All this activity, I thought, was to partially assuage
my guilt. I kept thinking of what Brian was going through
on his parallel timewave . . . he had been led to expect that
something earthshaking would happen when he brought us
the seagull; he had asked his vision if he could join her in
the other world when he did so, and certainly nobody had
told him "no." What an anticlimax for him. No, use the
exact work, I said to myself; what an *abandonment*. His
suffering couldn't possibly last more than a handful of
hours, but that thought did nothing to improve my state of
mind. At last I let sleep suck me down into darkness, like
a timewave pulling me under.

I usually sleep about twelve hours after a timeride,

longer if it's a salvage job or step-through. This time I had postponed the sleep and it was deeper and harder to wake up from because of that. Finally I became aware that my bedroom was trying to tell me I had a visitor wanting entry. "Who?" I said blearily.

I let Angelo in, and he brought water from the bathroom and wet my face. "Wake up, Ceece. I can't afford to give you a stimulant right now."

"What time is it?"

"Six."

"So, I still have some time. Give me another half-hour . . ." I tried to slip down into the bed.

"You don't have any time at all. The weather watchers say we're losing concurrence with Brian's timewave. If you're going through with this, you'll have to do it now."

I stared at him. I shook my head roughly, trying to become alert. "Angelo, hit me."

"I'm not good at hitting people, Ceece."

"Do something. Wake me up."

He stood up, rolled me off the bed onto the floor and, with devastating simplicity, began to tickle me.

"No! Stop! Stop! Please . . . I—can't—*stand*—it!"

"Are you awake?"

"I'm awake. I'm awake!"

"We medical men are so put upon. Always on call to our friends, ready with the latest achievements of science . . . should I get you some food?"

'Yes. Something I can eat while I'm walking. I'll be dressed in a minute."

Two minutes later I was dressed and out the door, munching an apple.

"Better go ahead and have Banny send the holo," I told him.

"Change in plan," he said to me. "There's another crew using your lab."

I stopped walking. "What?"

"You'll have to get permission to clear them out. I know you were going to go ahead with this and try to talk your way out of it later. You'll just have to talk your way out of it in advance, that's all."

"Ang . . . it might not work. Before, I thought at least

if I was successful first . . . but this way . . . I couldn't stand going through punishment again and know it was for nothing.''

''You want to call it off?''

''No.''

''Then what do you want me to do?''

I took a breath. ''All right. Tell Banny to send the holo. She can get permission from the other crew for that, it'll only take a minute. I'll meet you at the lab . . . probably.''

He kissed me goodbye on the forehead, a chaste Neapolitan/Jersey City kiss, just in case I was gone longer than I planned. I went alone down the Spoke to Mark's office, thinking of the holo I had made. On it I had said: Brian, I don't know if you really want to be with me. But if you do, come at once to the museum, to the place where you left the seagull.

The fire was due to break out very soon. Brian was due to die. If this thing I was trying didn't work, I would have killed him.

''Mark is in conference,'' said Narses, the eternal Greek chorus. He looked at me slyly. ''I believe it's the two gentlemen that were with him before.''

He was *still* talking with his masters? What the Hell were they going on about?

''Narses, I have to go in *now*. It's an emergency.''

''He's not to be interrupted. Whatever it is, it will have to—''

I reached over before he could top me and hit the three-digit code that opened Mark's door. I'd seen Narses key it in a dozen times; it was his own fault, he should have been more discreet.

''Name of God, Ceece,'' said Narses, aghast, as the door split open.

I walked into a suddenly silent room. The environment tubes were full once again, but I was getting used to that. ''Forgive me,'' I said, very quickly, ''but this is an emergency. We'll be losing the timewave, or I wouldn't have interrupted you.''

Mark looked at me, deciding what line to take. But if he

ever forgave my breaking the rules, it would be today, when I had delivered his prize.

On the other hand, this would be the perfect time to slap me down, before I got out of hand.

"Carol," said Mark with sudden heartiness. "Please join us. We must thank you for the delightful gift you sent earlier." He inclined his head to the pedestal near his desk, where the seagull perched gracefully.

I almost hated it more when he was nice to me. But I could handle it, I said to myself; after all, Narses put up with Mark's intimacies well enough, and you only had to look at Mark to know that whatever they did together, it had to be pretty sick. "You're welcome," I said. "Darkwings is always happy to be of service. In fact, that's why I'm here—I have a suggestion, but we'll have to move quickly if you decide to go ahead with it." He looked expectant. I said, "I want to recruit Brian Cornwall."

"Brian Cornwall . . . refresh my memory."

"The native we used to retrieve the seagull." The D'drendt moved about in their tubes at that, as though surprised.

"Ah. But that case is closed, Carol, and very admirably on your part. I think you'll find we're grateful when the Merit points are posted."

"I would certainly . . . appreciate it if you would consider this recruitment. He's a classic case. I admit I have my eye on him for my crew."

He looked thoughtful, and I hoped I wasn't pushing it too far. Mark is a sadist, of course. If he could see that I wanted this badly, and he could, then he might give it to me. The trick was to keep him from seeing I wanted it desperately. Then he would turn me down just to see my reaction.

One of the D'drendt said, "These step-throughs are expensive. They must go into the record. This does not seem a wise use of funds."

I thought of Mark's occasional private step-throughs; this did not seem the time to mention them.

Mark said to the D'drendt, "But it would be a legitimate use of the budget. It would be quite proper if the record showed we had been working on a recruitment. It could even simplify matters."

"This recruit was going to die. We were told. He could speak of things, when he comes here."

Mark shook his head. "I'm sure Carol will keep him out of trouble. She has her eye on him for her crew, don't you, Carol?"

"Yes," I said, relieved, for if Mark was leaning my way I couldn't see the D'drendt as a real obstacle. "I don't think he'll be difficult."

"Well, then, go ahead; but as this was your idea entirely, I'm not going to assign anyone to help you. You'll have to find people on your own. We've spent enough of the budget already."

This was typical Mark "permission"; if I didn't already have Angelo and Banny waiting there would have been nothing I could do. "Thank you," I said, starting for the door. Time was weighing on me. By now Brian would be at the museum, waiting; and the wave could start drawing away at any moment.

"Just a minute, Carol; I'd like to speak to you outside." I stopped, impatient, on the other side of the door. Mark motioned to Narses, who scuttled away like a rabbit.

He leaned close and dropped his voice. "You know, Ceece, I've been watching your career. You're one of the only riders who might one day be able to give me trouble. I don't know when that day will come, but when it does, remember I did you a favor."

It made no sense, and my mind was on Brian. Mark said, "Will you remember that?"

"I'll remember."

He let me go. I ran down the corridor and out into the Spoke, heading for the lab. It was many, many days later before I realized that he had called me "Ceece."

"We're going," I said to Banny. She had the rest of the crew there, dragged out of bed, coaxed, persuaded, ready to work. Banny grinned a wide grin and threw open the lab doors. "Emergency lab use!" she announced, running through the lab, scattering the other crew like so many pigeons. "Clear off! Emergency! Check with Narses if you don't believe me."

They left, muttering.

Angelo wheeled in a long pile covered in white and parked it in the pit by my chair.

The crew took their places. Banny was at the console, checking Brian's movements on the recorder. She turned a worried face to me. "Ceece, I can't find him."

"What?"

"He's not at the focus. He's not down by the seagull's case, either."

"He's in the museum somewhere. Keep looking." Surely he was in the museum. A true knight, having gotten a message from his lady, would not turn over and go back to sleep.

"I've got him!" She was triumphant. "He's in his little office . . . I can barely make him out, there's something wrong with the focus."

"He's out of range."

"More than that, I can barely see a thing. Ceece—it's smoke. The fire's started."

I joined her at the console and we moved the screen to the first floor. Orange flames, smoke, and the lack of focus made a pretty pattern. "It's not supposed to start yet."

"It's not supposed to be really big yet, but maybe it took a while to get going."

I looked at the screen. "It looks like it's going pretty well to me."

"Maybe they based our schedule on fire department reports. Maybe we've been working on an estimate."

"Never mind—what difference does it make? We could lose concurrence any time, whatever happens. The deadline is still *now*."

We brought the screen back to Brian. "He's not moving," said Banny.

His office was on the second floor, near the stairs. The focus was on the third floor. We couldn't pull him through from where he was, not on this wave, and not with the concurrence about to drop at any moment.

Angelo came over to the screen. "Smoke inhalation," he said. "Your friend's unconscious."

I started down to the pit. "Step-through," I called out. "Take your pills." Reality hit me then—how was I going to get Brian's body up the stairs by myself? They say that adrenaline takes over in emergencies and gives you the strength of ten; I didn't want to count on it, though. "Any volunteers?" I added. "I could use some help." Angelo had disappeared while I was speaking; I didn't have time to figure out where. Banny waved her hand.

"Thanks, Ban. Henry, take Banny's place at the console. Three becomes two, four becomes three, down the line. Yu Kang, you'll have to do Cei's work and your own, I'm afraid."

"Not a problem, Ceece."

"Okay, no time to lose. Start it up." They shuffled their places and Banny took her pills. She joined me in the pit. Then Angelo suddenly showed up beside us, waving some gray plastic things in his hand.

"Gas masks," he said, breathing heavily. "We'll need them."

"We? Ang, this is not an excursion. If they lose concurrence while we're out there, we'll become anomalies. History can't be changed, and our bodies were never found in the fire. We'll just disappear."

"We'll argue about history later, Ceece. You and Banny can't drag that body by yourselves—not in five minutes, anyway, and who knows how long you'll have?"

I shook my head and found myself yelling, "Three to go! Somebody have that body on the cart ready!"

I saw Angelo grab Banny's pills. "Give me some of those," he said—

—And we were pulled in.

Lord, the whole place was smokey. Angelo stood next to me, beside the Indian artifact cases, looking pale. Being pushed through a timewall by a strong-willed crew is not the most pleasant of sensations. Banny walked ahead of us to the stairwell, where the smoke was rising. "Ang?" I said.

"I'm coming."

We took the stairs down to the second floor. The fire was still confined to the first floor, where it would do most of its damage; I was not worried about it at all. I as only worried about our waves drawing apart.

We entered the museum's offices and found Brian lying by the door. In the smoke I couldn't see if he was breathing. Angelo grasped him by the shoulders and he choked, a reassuring sound. "What—who—" he opened red eyes, and I knew what he saw: smoke and three alarming masks. He tried to thrash in panic. I pulled my mask up for a moment so he could see my face. "It's all right," I said. "We've come to get you."

"You're just a dream," he said.

"Not any more." Angelo lifted him roughly—there wasn't time to be gentle—and he lapsed into unconsciousness again. Banny and I took the other end. We inched him up the stairs, feet first with Banny and me leading. He weighed a ton.

We set him down by the focus. For all we knew, concurrence could be gone already . . . but it wasn't. A body materialized beside us, looking remarkably like Brian. Angelo grunted and we all heaved again, carrying it to the stairs. We dragged this one down, no need to be careful. As we banged away to the first floor, though, I found myself feeling guilty over our treatment of the corpse and apologized in my mind to the rider it had belonged to. I had nothing against him for dealing in the black market; we all did what we could, in the world we never made. We left him for the fire. Probably all the searchers would find were teeth and bones, but we had to be careful.

Then back up the stairs again. Brian still lay by the focus, not moving. Angelo said, "Pulling him through the timewall will be a shock, in his condition. I didn't realize how much until I went through myself—"

And we were jerked through, the pain and jarring-ness of it forgiven in our relief.

Angelo pulled off his mask immediately and got Brian onto the cart. He got out his medical pack and covered Brian's face with a tube. He put one hand over his heart in an interrogative sort of way. The crew gathered around the cart and Banny shooed them back, giving Angelo room.

"Angelo—" I said.

"Shut up, darling, I'm busy." He took out a gleaming needle and emptied it into Brian's neck. Then he stood there, waiting. I didn't dare say anything more. Brian's fingers moved weakly toward the tube, then stopped. Angelo placed his square Italian hand over Brian's heart again and smiled. "He'll be all right. In time."

I threw my arms around Angelo, to my total surprise. My "natural reserve" had gone out the window. "Angelo, honey!" "Paisan!" We pounded each other. Suddenly I thought of something. I pushed him back and cried, "Sono tanto felice di nederti, mio caro!" I'd picked that one up a while back, and had been saving it for a special occasion.

He looked startled, and broke into whoops of laughter. "Cara, you know why I do these things for you?"

"No, carissimo, tell me."

"Because you're crazy, like a Neapolitan!" He almost broke my ribs.

I stood in my bathroom, turning the walls to mirrors for the hundredth time. There was a pile of clothing at my feet. I kicked a Cretan gown and picked up a blue satin robe, whirling it over my head and shoulders. It did look rather madonna/goddess-like. . . . I stopped myself, ashamed. It was better that he learn the truth now. That was why I was going to the hospital, wasn't it? To disillusion him?

I had already considered and rejected my usual at-home dress (shorts and nothing else); there was no need to shock him. At last I put on my old workclothes, the outfit I liked to wear when I was doing hardware work in the lab. The holo goddess had worn her hair up, so I let mine down. I peered at the faces in the walls: plain enough for anyone, I should think.

I blacked out the mirrors and left, before I could change my mind.

Angelo had given me Brian's room number when he called. (We spoke for a while, and I thanked him for all his help. He said—and I heard the smile in his voice—"I'd have gone further than that, to see our Ceece finally fall to Venus."

"A bit premature, paisan," I said to him, rather coldly considering all he'd done.

"I guess the ice doesn't thaw overnight," he said in response to my tone. I cut the connection on him.)

I found the room easily, pushed open the door as I wondered what to say.

I stopped. Dervan was in the room. He sat sideways on the bed, smoking a cigarette, looking Brian in the eye. Brian sat propped against some pillows, his hands in his lap. He didn't look totally lost yet.

"—sure she'll be along soon," Dervan was saying. "By the way, I didn't get your name. What is it?"

"Don't answer him," I said quickly.

Dervan's head snapped around. Brian closed his mouth and looked calmly at Dervan. The silence lengthened. Dervan measured us both, and I could see him deciding to put it away for a later time. Maybe it was just the hospital light, but I thought he looked rather cheap goods next to Brian.

Dervan shrugged and headed for the door. He dropped the cigarette from his perfect hands and ground it underfoot. "You can't stay with him forever, Ceece," he said sympathetically, and left.

Damn, it was my own fault, diddling around with clothes when I should have come straight here. I would have to go to Mark and convince him to ride herd on Dervan, tell him out latest recruit was in danger of being trashed . . . or maybe Banny and the crew and I could guard him in shifts. He'd be safe enough when he got out of training school; even Dervan wouldn't dare—

"Your name is Ceece."

I turned back to Brian. "That's right. It's short for C.C.— Carol Celia."

He shook his head, as though clearing it. "The doctor told me a lot about you. He said you went to a lot of trouble for me. That you saved my life. Thank you."

"You're welcome." His face was different, too, in the light of the present. There were tiny wing-shaped scars above his cheekbones, where Angelo had placed them during his unconsciousness. They were there to protect him in the days to come. Although it had no legal significance; how could it, when as a student he had no legal significance himself? But there would be two scars on his face from now on, to show that Darkwings "took an interest" in him for good or bad. There were beings who would leave him alone because of that; it was nothing to be ashamed of. In fact, it would add to his status when he graduated.

Of course, he might not see it that way right now. I felt uncomfortable about it abruptly; Angelo had suggested it, but I had said yes, since it seemed a good idea. Perhaps we would appear high-handed to him. I asked him, and he said that he was aware of the marks.

"Maybe we were wrong to put them on you. If they offend you, you can have Medical remove them."

"I'll keep them if you think it's best," he said simply. "You know more about this place than I do."

"Thank you." I added with honesty, "It would've hurt my status if you took them off."

His compliance bothered me. Why wasn't he screaming to me, calling me a liar? Then an answer came. The holo had been too perfect. Here I was, a flawed human being, and he could not associate me in his mind with the archetypal image. He didn't realize yet how he'd been tricked.

"Brian, do you know who I am?"

"Your name is Ceece," he said with patience and a trace of amusement. "You're a timerider crew-captain—the doctor told me. He said I would learn what that meant, but it wasn't important right now."

"No, I mean . . . do you understand that I'm the one you saw, back in your room, back in the museum. I mean, there isn't anyone else—"

"Yes, I know that."

He must have seen something in my face, because he chuckled. It was a gentle sound, with the quiet strength of a force of nature. When I was very small, I was read a fairy tale about three brothers who contested for a throne. The youngest brother was always curious, so one day he followed a river to see how it began. The river became a stream, and the stream a spring; and the source of the spring, he found, splashed up from a walnut, which he stole and put in his pocket.

It had seemed marvelous and miraculous to me at the time. Since then, whenever I hear Brian chuckle I think of that story.

I went out to the corridor and passed Narses coming by, laden down with a bundle of papers. His jewelry flashed as he walked. He smiled condescendingly to show there were no hard feelings from my having coded open Mark's door.

"Well, well!" he said. "And what are we so happy about?"

"What business is it of yours?" I asked him.

PRETTY BOY CROSSOVER
by Pat Cadigan

*Every few years there appears a movement to
improve or modernize or even "futurize" the
writing of science fiction. The classic example
was the New Wave, which had an effect on the
style of SF literature and has been comfortably
tamed and digested. Now there is something
called "cyberpunk," of which we have yet to
learn a clear definition. It has something to do
with computers and their programming and
possibly—considering the derogatory term
"punk"—with snubbing accepted traditions. This
short story is said to be an example of "cyberpunk." It is certainly different from anything
H.G. Wells, Jules Verne, or Hugo Gernsback
would have dreamed up.*

First you see video. Then you wear video.
Then you eat video. Then you *be* video.

The Gospel According to Visual Mark

Watch or Be Watched.

Pretty Boy Credo

"Who made you?"
"You mean recently?"

82

Mohawk on the door smiles and takes his picture. "You in. But only you, okay? Don't try to get no friends in, hear that?"

"I hear. And I ain't no fool, fool. I got no friends."

Mohawk leers, leaning forward. "Pretty Boy like you, no friends?"

"Not in this world." He pushes past the Mohawk, ignoring the kissy-kissy sounds. He would like to crack the bridge of the Mohawk's nose and shove bone splinters into his brain but he is lately making more effort to control his temper and besides, he's not sure if any of that bone splinters in the brain stuff is really true. He's a Pretty Boy, all of sixteen years old, and tonight could be his last chance.

The club is Noise. Can't sneak into the bathroom for quiet, the Noise is piped in there, too. Want to get away from Noise? Why? No reason. But this Pretty Boy has learned to think between the beats. Like walking between the raindrops to stay dry, but he can do it. This Pretty Boy thinks things all the time—*all* the time. Subversive (and, he thinks so much that he knows that word *subversive*, sixteen, Pretty, or not). He thinks things like *how many Einsteins have died of hunger and thirst under a hot African sun* and *why can't you remember being born* and *why is music common to every culture* and especially *how much was there going on that he didn't know about and how could he find out about it.*

And this is all the time, one thing after another running in his head, you can see by his eyes. It's for def not much like a Pretty Boy but it's one reason why they want him. That he *is* a Pretty Boy is another and one reason why they're halfway home getting him.

He knows all about them. Everybody knows about them and everybody wants them to pause, look twice, and cough up a card that says, Yes, we see possibilities, please come to the following address during regular business hours on the next regular business day for regular further review. Everyone wants it but this Pretty Boy, who once got five cards in a night and tore them all up. But here he is, still a Pretty Boy. He thinks enough to know this is a failing in himself, that he likes being Pretty and chased and that is how they could end up getting him after all and that's b-b-b-bad. When he thinks abut it, he thinks it with the stutter. B-b-b-bad. B-b-b-bad for him because he doesn't God help him want it, no, no, n-n-n-no. Which may make him the strangest Pretty Boy still live tonight and every night.

Still live and standing in the club where only the Prettiest Pretty Boys can get in any more. Pretty Girls are too easy, they've got to be better than Pretty and besides, Pretty Boys like to be Pretty all alone, no help thank you so much. This Pretty Boy doesn't mind Pretty Girls or any other kind of girls. Lately, though he has begun to wonder how much longer it will be for him. Two years? Possibly a little longer? By three it will be for def over and the Mohawk on the door will as soon spit in his face as leer in it.

If they don't get to him.

And if they *do* get to him, then it's never over and he can be wherever he chooses to be and wherever that is will be the center of the universe. They promise it, unlimited access in your free hours and endless hot season, endless youth. Pretty Boy Heaven, and to get there, they say, you don't even really have to die.

He looks up the dj's roost, far above the bobbing, boogieing crowd on the dance floor. They still call them djs even though they aren't discs any more, they're chips and there's more than just sound on a lot of them. The great hyper-program, he's been told, the ultimate of ultimates, a short walk from there to the fourth dimension. He suspects this stuff comes from low-steppers shilling for them, hoping they'll get auditioned if they do a good enough shuck job. Nobody knows what it's really like except the ones who are there and you can't trust them, he figures. Because maybe they *aren't*, any more. Not really.

The dj sees his Pretty upturned face, recognizes him even though it's been awhile since he's come back here. Part of it was wanting to stay away from them and part of it was that the thug on the door might not let him in. And then, of course, he *had* to come, to see if he could get in, to see if anyone still wanted him. What was the point of

Pretty if there was nobody to care and watch and pursue? Even now, he is almost sure he can feel the room rearranging itself around his presence in it and the dj confirms this is true by holding up a chip and pointing it to the left.

They are squatting on the make-believe stairs by the screen, reminding him of pigeons plotting to take over the world. He doesn't look too long, doesn't want to give them the idea he'd like to talk. But as he turns away, one, the younger man, starts to get up. The older man and the woman pull him back.

He pretends a big interest in the figures lining the nearest wall. Some are Pretty, some are female, some are undecided, some are very bizarre, or wealthy, or just charity cases. They all notice him and adjust themselves for his perusal.

Then one end of the room lights up with color and new noise. Bodies dance and stumble back from the screen where images are forming to rough music.

It's Bobby, he realizes.

A moment later, there's Bobby's face on the screen, sixteen feet high, even Prettier than he'd been when he was loose among the mortals. The sight of Bobby's Pretty-Pretty face fills him with anger and dismay and a feeling of loss so great he would strike anyone who spoke Bobby's name without his permission.

Bobby's lovely slate-gray eyes scan the room. They've told him senses are heightened after you make the change and go over but he's not so sure how that's supposed to work. Bobby looks kind of blind up there on the screen. A few people wave at Bobby—the dorks they let in so the rest can have someone to be hip in front of—but Bobby's eyes move slowly back and forth, back and forth, and then stop, looking right at him.

"Ah . . ." Bobby whispers it, long and drawn out. "Aaaaaahhhh."

He lifts his chin belligerently and stares back at Bobby.

"You don't have to die any more," Bobby says silkily. Music bounces under his words. "It's beautiful in here. The dreams can be as real as you want them to be. And if you want to be, you can be with me."

He knows the commercial is not aimed only at him but

it doesn't matter. This is *Bobby*. Bobby's voice seems to be pouring over him, caressing him, and it feels too much like a taunt. The night before Bobby went over, he tried to talk him out of it, knowing it wouldn't work. If they'd actually refused him, Bobby would have killed himself, like Franco had.

But now Bobby would live forever and ever, if you believed what they said. The music comes up louder but Bobby's eyes are still on him. He sees Bobby mouth his name.

"Can you really see me, Bobby?" he says. His voice doesn't make it over the music but if Bobby's senses are so heightened, maybe he hears it anyway. If he does, he doesn't choose to answer. The music is a bumped up remix of a song Bobby used to party-till-he-puked to. The giant Bobby-face fades away to be replaced with a whole Bobby, somewhat larger than life, dancing better than the old Bobby ever could, whirling along changing scenes of streets, rooftops and beaches. The locales are nothing special but Bobby never did have all that much imagination, never wanted to go to Mars or even to the South Pole, always just to the hottest club. Always he liked being the exotic in plain surroundings and he still likes it. He always loved to get the looks. To be watched, worshipped, pursued. Yeah. He can see this is Bobby-heaven. The whole world will be giving him the looks now.

The background on the screen goes from street to the inside of a club; *this* club, only larger, better, with an even hipper crowd, and Bobby shaking it with them. Half the real crowd is forgetting to dance now because they're watching Bobby, hoping he's put some of them into his video. Yeah, that's the dream, get yourself remixed in the extended dance version.

His own attention drifts to the fake stairs that don't lead anywhere. They're still perched on them, the only people who are watching *him* instead of Bobby. The woman, looking overaged in a purple plastic sacsuit, is fingering a card.

He looks up at Bobby again. Bobby is dancing in place and looking back at him, or so it seems. Bobby's lips move soundlessly but so precisely he can read the words:

This can be you. Never get old, never get tired, it's never last call, nothing happens unless you want it to and it could be you. You. You. Bobby's hands point to him on the beat. *You. You. You.*

Bobby. Can you really see me?

Bobby suddenly breaks into laughter and turns away, shaking it some more.

He sees the Mohawk from the door pushing his way through the crowd, the real crowd, and he gets anxious. The Mohawk goes straight for the stairs, where they make room for him, rubbing the bristly red strip of hair running down the center of his head as though they were greeting a favored pet. The Mohawk looks as satisfied as a professional glutton after a foodrace victory. He wonders what they promised the Mohawk for letting him in. Maybe some kind of limited contract. Maybe even a try-out.

Now they are all watching him together. Defiantly, he touches a tall girl dancing nearby and joins her rhythm. She smiles down at him, moving between him and them purely by chance but it endears her to him anyway. She is wearing a flap of translucent rag over secondskins, like an old-time showgirl. Over six feet tall, not beautiful with that nose, not even pretty, but they let her in so she could be tall. She probably doesn't know that; she probably doesn't know anything that goes on and never really will. For that reason, he can forgive her the hard-tech orange hair.

A Rude Boy brushes against him in the course of a dervish turn, asking acknowledgment by ignoring him. Rude Boys haven't changed in more decades than anyone's kept track of, as though it were the same little group of leathered and chained troopers buggering their way down the years. The Rude Boy isn't dancing with anyone. Rude Boys never do. But this one could be handy, in case of an emergency.

The girl is dancing hard, smiling at him. He smiles back, moving slightly to her right, watching Bobby possibly watching him. He still can't tell if Bobby really sees anything. The scene behind Bobby is still a double of the club, getting hipper and hipper if that's possible. The music keeps snapping back to its first peak passage. Then

Bobby gestures like God and he sees *himself*. He is dancing next to Bobby, Prettier than he ever could be, just the way they promise. Bobby doesn't look at the phantom but at him where he really is, lips moving again. *If you want to be, you can be with me. And so can she.*

His tall partner appears next to the phantom of himself. She is also much improved, though still not Pretty, or even pretty. The real girl turns and sees herself and there's no mistaking the delight in her face. Queen of the Hop for a minute or two. Then Bobby sends her image away so that it's just the two of them, two Pretty Boys dancing the night away, private party, stranger go find your own good time. How it used to be sometimes in real life, between just the two of them. He remembers hard.

"B-b-b-bobby!" he yells, the old stutter reappearing. Bobby's image seems to give a jump, as though he finally heard. He forgets everything, the girl, the Rude Boy, the Mohawk, them on the stairs, and plunges through the crowd toward the screen. People fall away from him as though they were re-enacting the Red Sea. He dives for the screen, for Bobby, not caring how it must look to anyone. What would they know about it, any of them. He can't remember in his whole sixteen years ever hearing one person say, *I love my friend*. Not Bobby, not even himself.

He fetches up against the screen like a slap and hangs there, face pressed to the glass. He can't see it now but on the screen Bobby would seem to be looking down at him. Bobby never stops dancing.

The Mohawk comes and peels him off. The others swarm up and take him away. The tall girl watches all this with the expression of a woman who lives upstairs from Cinderella and wears the same shoe size. She stares longingly at the screen. Bobby waves bye-bye and turns away.

"Of course, the process isn't reversible," says the older man. The steely hair has a careful blue tint; he has sense enough to stay out of hip clothes.

They have laid him out on a lounger with a tray of refreshments right by him. Probably slap his hand if he reaches for any, he thinks.

"Once you've distilled something to pure information,

it just can't be reconstituted in a less efficient form,'' the woman explains, smiling. There's no warmth to her. *A less efficient form*. If that's what she really thinks, he knows he should be plenty scared of these people. Did she say things like that to Bobby? And did it make him even *more* eager?

"There may be no more exalted a form of existence than to live as sentient information,'' she goes on. ''Though a lot more research must be done before we can offer conversion on a larger scale.''

"Yeah?'' he says. "Do they know that, Bobby and the rest?''

"Oh, there's nothing to worry about,'' says the younger man. He looks as though he's still getting over the pain of having outgrown his boogie shoes. ''The system's quite perfected. What Grethe means is we want to research more applications for this new form of existence.''

"Why not go over yourselves and do that, if it's so *exalted*.''

"There are certain things that need to be done on this side,'' the woman says bitchily. "Just because—''

"Grethe.'' The older man shakes his head. She pats her slicked-back hair as though to soothe herself and moves away.

"We have other plans for Bobby when he gets tired of being featured in clubs,'' the older man says. "Even now, we're educating him, adding more data to his basic information configuration—''

"That would mean he ain't really *Bobby* any more, then, huh?''

The man laughs. "Of course he's Bobby. Do you change into someone else every time you learn something new?''

"Can you prove I *don't?*''

The man eyes him warily. "Look. You *saw* him. Was that Bobby?''

"I saw a video of Bobby dancing on a giant screen.''

"That *is* Bobby and it will remain Bobby no matter what, whether he's poured into a video screen in a dot pattern or transmitted the length of the universe.''

"That what you got in mind for him? Send a message to nowhere and the message is him?''

"We could. But we're not going to. We're introducing him to the concept of higher dimensions. The way he is now, he could possibly break out of the three-dimensional level of existence, pioneer a whole new plane of reality."

"Yeah? And how do you think you're gonna get Bobby to do *that*?"

"We convince him it's entertaining."

He laughs. "That's a good one. Yeah. Entertainment. You get to a higher level of existence and you'll open a club there that only the hippest can get into. It figures."

The older man's face gets hard. "That's what all you Pretty Boys are crazy for, isn't it? Entertainment?"

He looks around. The room must have been a dressing room or something back in the days when bands had been live. Somewhere overhead he can hear the faint noise of the club but he can't tell if Bobby's still on. "You call this entertainment?"

"I'm tired of this little prick," the woman chimes in. "He's thrown away opportunities other people would kill for—"

He makes a rude noise. "Yeah, we'd all kill to be someone's data chip. You think I really believe Bobby's real just because I can see him on a *screen*?"

The older man turns to the younger one. "Phone up and have them pipe Bobby down here." Then he swings the lounger around so it faces a nice modern screen implanted in a shored-up cement-block wall.

"Bobby will join us shortly. Then he can tell you whether he's real or not himself. How will that be for you?"

He stares hard at the screen, ignoring the man, waiting for Bobby's image to appear. As though they really bothered to communicate regularly with Bobby this way. Feed in that kind of data and memory and Bobby'll believe it. He shifts uncomfortably, suddenly wondering how far he could get if he moved fast enough.

"My *boy*," says Bobby's sweet voice from the speaker on either side of the screen and he forces himself to keep looking as Bobby fades in, presenting himself on the same kind of lounger and looking mildly exerted, as though he's just come off the dance floor for real. "Saw you shakin' it upstairs awhile ago. You haven't been here for such a long time. What's the story?"

He opens his mouth but there's no sound. Bobby looks at him with boundless patience and indulgence. So Pretty, hair the perfect shade now and not a bit dry from the dyes and lighteners, skin flawless and shining like a healthy angel. Overnight angel, just like the old song.

"My *boy*," says Bobby. "Are you struck, like, shy or *dead*?"

He closes his mouth, takes one breath. "I don't like it, Bobby. I don't like it this way."

"Of course not, lover. You're the Watcher, not the Watchee, that's why. Get yourself picked up for a season or two and your disposition will *change*."

"You really like it, Bobby, being a blip on a chip?"

"Blip on a chip, your ass. I'm a universe now. I'm, like, *everything*. And, hey, dig—I'm on every channel." Bobby laughed. "I'm happy I'm sad!"

"S-A-D," comes in the older man. "Self-Aware Data."

"Ooo-eee," he says. "Too clever for me. Can I get out of here now?"

"What's your hurry?" Bobby pouts. "Just because I went over you don't love me anymore?"

"You always were screwed up about that, Bobby. Do you know the difference between being loved and being watched?"

"Sophisticated boy," Bobby says. "So wise, so learned. So fully packed. On this side, there is no difference. Maybe there never was. If you love me, you watch me. If you don't look, you don't care and if you don't care I don't matter. If I don't matter, I don't exist. Right?"

He shakes his head.

"No, my boy, I *am* right." Bobby laughs. "You believe I'm right, because if you *didn't*, you wouldn't come shaking your Pretty Boy ass in a place like *this*, now, would you? You *like* to be watched, get seen. You see me, I see you. Life goes on."

He looks up at the older man, needing relief from Bobby's pure Prettiness. "How does he see me?"

"Sensors in the equipment. Technical stuff, nothing you care about."

He sighs. He should be upstairs or across town, shaking it with everyone else, living Pretty for as long as he could. Maybe in another few months, this way would begin to look good to him. By then they might be off Pretty Boys and looking for some other type and there he'd be, out in the cold-cold, sliding down the other side of his peak and no one would *want* him. Shut out of something going on that he might want to know about after all. Can he face it? He glances at the younger man. All grown up and no place to glow. Yeah, but can *he* face it?

He doesn't know. Used to be there wasn't much of a choice and now that there is, it only seems to make it worse. Bobby's image looks like it's studying him for some kind of sign, Pretty eyes bright, hopeful.

The older man leans down and speaks low into his ear. "We need to get you before you're twenty-five, before the brain stops growing. A mind taken from a still-growing brain will blossom and adapt. Some of Bobby's predecessors have made marvelous adaptation to their new medium. Pure video: there's a staff that does nothing all day but watch and interpret their symbols for breakthroughs in thought. And we'll be taking Pretty Boys for as long as they're publicly sought-after. It's the most efficient way to find the best performers, go for the ones everyone wants to see or be. The top of the trend is closest to heaven. And even if you never make a breakthrough, you'll still be entertainment. Not such a bad way to live for a Pretty Boy. Never have to age, to be sick, to lose touch. You spent most of your life young, why learn how to be old? Why learn how to live without all the things you have now—"

He puts his hands over his ears. The older man is still talking and Bobby is saying something and the younger man and the woman come over to try to do something about him. Refreshments are falling off the tray. He struggles out of the lounger and makes for the door.

"Hey, my *boy*," Bobby calls after him. "Gimme a minute here, gimme what the problem is."

He doesn't answer. What can you tell someone made of pure information anyway?"

*   *   *

There's a new guy on the front door, bigger and meaner than His Mohawkness but he's only there to keep people out, not to keep anyone *in*. You want to jump ship, go to, you poor un-hip asshole. Even if you are a Pretty Boy. He reads it in the guy's face as he passes from noise into the three A.M. quiet of the street.

R & R
by Lucius Shepard

The worst thing that Latin-American nations can do is to attempt to eliminate illiteracy, to end corruption, and to bring about a more equitable distribution of the land. This type of program induces undying fury in the chief executives of the richest country in North America and sends them off on mad military and naval crusades regardless of costs or consequences. Lucius Shepard, who knows his Americas, brings authenticity to his projections of those countries in the above political contexts. This novella, taking place just a few years into the future, has the ring of reality. R & R., incidentally, is military jargon for "Rest and Recreation." You better believe it!

1

One of the new Sikorsky gunships, an element of the First Air Cavalry with the words Whispering Death painted on its side, gave Mingolla and Gilbey and Baylor a lift from the Ant Farm to San Francisco de Juticlan, a small town located inside the green zone which on the latest maps was designated Free Occupied Guatamala. To the east of this green zone lay an undesignated band of yellow that crossed the country from the Mexican border to the Caribbean.

The Ant Farm was a firebase on the eastern edge of the yellow band, and it was from there that Mingolla—an artillery specialist not yet twenty-one years old—lobbed shells into an area which the maps depicted in black and white terrain markings. And thus it was that he often thought of himself as engaged in a struggle to keep the world safe for primary colors.

Mingolla and his buddies could have taken their r&r in Rió or Caracas, but they had noticed that the men who visited these cities had a tendency to grow careless upon their return; they understood from this that the more exuberant your r&r, the more likely you were to wind up a casualty, and so they always opted for the lesser distractions of the Guatamalan towns. They were not really friends: they had little in common, and under different circumstances they might well have been enemies. But taking their r&r together had come to be a ritual of survival, and once they had reached the town of their choice, they would go their separate ways and perform further rituals. Because they had survived so much already, they believed that if they continued to perform these same rituals they would complete their tours unscathed. They had never acknowledged their belief to one another, speaking of it only obliquely—that, too, was part of the ritual—and had this belief been challenged they would have admitted its irrationalty; yet they would also have pointed out that the strange character of the war acted to enforce it.

The gunship set down at an airbase a mile west of town, a cement strip penned in on three sides by barracks and offices, with the jungle rising behind them. At the center of the strip another Sikorsky was practicing take-offs and landings—a drunken, camouflage-colored dragonfly—and two others were hovering overhead like anxious parents. As Mingolla jumped out a hot breeze fluttered his shirt. He was wearing civvies for the first time in weeks, and they felt flimsy compared to his combat gear; he glanced around, nervous, half-expecting an unseen enemy to take advantage of his exposure. Some mechanics were lounging in the shade of a chopper whose cockpit had been destroyed, leaving fanglike shards of plastic curving from the charred metal. Dusty jeeps trundled back and forth beneath the buildings; a brace of crisply starched lieutenants were making a brisk beeline toward a fork-lift stacked high with aluminum coffins. Afternoon sunlight fired dazzles on the seams and handles of the coffins, and through the heat haze the distant line of barracks shifted like waves in a troubled olive-drab sea. The incongruity of the scene—its What's-Wrong-With-This-Picture mix of the horrid and the commonplace—wrenched at Mingolla. His left hand trembled, and the light seemed to grow brighter, making him weak and vague. He leaned against the Sikorsky's rocket pod to steady himself. Far above, contrails were fraying in the deep blue range of the sky: XL-16s off to blow holes in Nicaragua. He stared after them with something akin to longing, listening for their engines, but heard only the spacy whisper of the Sikorskys.

Gilbey hopped down from the hatch that led to the computer deck behind the cockpit; he brushed imaginary dirt from his jeans and sauntered over to Mingolla and stood with hands on hips: a short muscular kid whose blond crewcut and petulant mouth gave him the look of a grumpy child. Baylor stuck his head out of the hatch and worriedly scanned the horizon. Then he, too, hopped down. He was tall and rawboned, a couple of years older than Mingolla, with lank black hair and pimply olive skin and features so sharp that they appeared to have been hatcheted into shape. He rested a hand on the side of the Sikorsky, but almost instantly, noticing that he was touching the flaming letter W in Whispering Death, he jerked the hand away as if he'd been scorched. Three days before there had been an all-out assault on the Ant Farm, and Baylor had not recovered from it. Neither had Mingolla. It was hard to tell whether or not Gilbey had been affected.

One of the Sikorsky's pilots cracked the cockpit door. "Y'all can catch a ride into 'Frisco at the PX," he said, his voice muffled by the black bubble of his visor. The sun shined a white blaze on the visor, making it seem that the helmet contained night and a single star.

"Where's the PX?" asked Gilbey.

The pilot said something too muffled to be understood.

"What?" said Gilbey.

Again the pilot's response was muffled, and Gilbey became angry. "Take that damn thing off!" he said.

"This?" The pilot pointed to his visor. "What for?"

"So I can hear what the hell you sayin'."

"You can hear now, can'tcha?"

"Okay," said Gilbey, his voice tight. "Where's the goddamn PX?"

The pilot's reply was unintelligible; his faceless mask regarded Gilbey with inscrutable intent.

Gilbey balled up his fists. "Take that son of a bitch off!"

"Can't do it, soldier," said the second pilot, leaning over so that the two black bubbles were nearly side by side. "These here doobies"—he tapped his visor—"they got micro-circuits that beams shit into our eyes. 'Fects the optic nerve. Makes it so we can see the beaners even when they undercover. Longer we wear 'em, the better we see."

Baylor laughed edgily, and Gilbey said, "Bull!" Mingolla naturally assumed that the pilots were putting Gilbey on, or else their reluctance to remove the helmets stemmed from a superstition, perhaps from a deluded belief that the visors actually did bestow special powers. But given a war in which combat drugs were issued and psychics predicted enemy movements, anything was possible, even micro-circuits that enhanced vision.

"You don't wanna see us, nohow," said the first pilot. "The beams mess up our faces. We're deformed-lookin' mothers."

" 'Course you might not notice the changes," said the second pilot. "Lotsa people don't. But if you did, it'd mess you up."

Imagining the pilots' deformities sent a sick chill mounting from Mingolla's stomach. Gilbey, however, wasn't buying it. "You think I'm stupid?" he shouted, his neck reddening.

"Naw," said the first pilot. "We can *see* you ain't stupid. We can see lotsa stuff other people can't, 'cause of the beams."

"All kindsa weird stuff," chipped in the second pilot. "Like souls."

"Ghosts."

"Even the future."

"The future's our best thing," said the first pilot. "You guys wanna know what's ahead, we'll tell you."

They nodded in unison, the blaze of sunlight sliding across both visors: two evil robots responding to the same program.

Gilbey lunged for the cockpit door. The first pilot slammed it shut, and Gilbey pounded on the plastic, screaming curses. The second pilot flipped a switch on the control console, and a moment later his amplified voice boomed out: "Make straight past that fork-lift 'til you hit the barracks. You'll run right into the PX."

It took both Mingolla and Baylor to drag Gilbey away from the Sikorsky, and he didn't stop shouting until they drew near the fork-lift with its load of coffins: a giant's treasure of enormous silver ingots. Then he grew silent and lowered his eyes. They wangled a ride with an MP corporal outside the PX, and as the jeep hummed across the cement, Mingolla glanced over at the Sikorsky that had transported them. The two pilots had spread a canvas on the ground, had stripped to shorts and were sunning themselves. But they had not removed their helmets. The weird juxtaposition of tanned bodies and shiny black heads disturbed Mingolla, reminding him of an old movie in which a guy had gone through a matter transmitter along with a fly and had ended up with the fly's head on his shoulders. Maybe, he thought, the helmets were like that, impossible to remove. Maybe the war had gotten that strange.

The MP corporal noticed him watching the pilots and let out a barking laugh. "Those guys," he said, with the flat emphatic tone of a man who knew whereof he spoke, "are fuckin' nuts!"

Six years before, San Francisco de Juticlan had been a scatter of thatched huts and concrete block structures deployed among palms and banana leaves on the east bank of the Rió Dulce, at the junction of the river and a gravel road that connected with the Pan American Highway; but it had since grown to occupy substantial sections of both

banks, increased by dozens of bars and brothels: stucco
cubes painted all the colors of the rainbow, with a fantastic
bestiary of neon signs mounted atop their tin roofs. Dragons; unicorns; fiery birds; centaurs. The MP corporal told
Mingolla that the signs were not advertisements but coded
symbols of pride; for example, from the representation of a
winged red tiger crouched amidst green lilies and blue
crosses, you could deduce that the owner was wealthy, a
member of a Catholic secret society, and ambivalent
toward government policies. Old signs were constantly being
dismantled, and larger, more ornate ones erected in their
stead as testament to improved profits, and this warfare of
light and image was appropriate to the time and place,
because San Francisco de Juticlan was less a town than a
symptom of war. Though by night the sky above it was
radiant, at ground level it was mean and squalid. Pariah
dogs foraged in piles of garbage, hardbitten whores spat
from the windows, and according to the corporal, it was
not unusual to stumble across a corpse, probably a victim
of the gangs of abandoned children who lived in the
fringes of the jungle. Narrow streets of tawny dirt cut
between the bars, carpeted with a litter of flattened cans
and feces and broken glass; refugees begged at every
corner, displaying burns and bullet wounds. Many of the
buildings had been thrown up with such haste that their
walls were tilted, their roofs canted, and this made the
shadows they cast appear exaggerated in their jaggedness,
like shadows in the work of a psychotic artist, giving
visual expression to a pervasive undercurrent of tension.
Yet as Mingolla moved along, he felt at ease, almost
happy. His mood was due in part to his hunch that it was
going to be one hell of an r&r (he had learned to trust his
hunches); but it mainly spoke to the fact that towns like
this had become for him a kind of afterlife, a reward for
having endured a harsh term of existence.

  The corporal dropped them off at a drugstore, where
Mingolla bought a box of stationery, and then they stopped
for a drink at the Club Demonio: a tiny place whose
whitewashed walls were shined to faint phosphorescence
by the glare of purple light bulbs dangling from the ceiling
like radioactive fruit. The club was packed with soldiers

and whores, most sitting at tables around a dance floor not much bigger than a king-size mattress. Two couples were swaying to a ballad that welled from a jukebox encaged in chicken wire and two-by-fours; veils of cigarette smoke drifted with underwater slowness above their heads. Some of the soldiers were mauling their whores, and one whore was trying to steal the wallet of a soldier who was on the verge of passing out; her hand worked between his legs, encouraging him to thrust his hips forward, and when he did this, with her other hand she pried at the wallet stuck in the back pocket of his tight-fitting jeans. But all the action seemed listless, half-hearted, as if the dimness and syrupy music had thickened the air and were hampering movement. Mingolla took a seat at the bar. The bartender glanced at him inquiringly, his pupils becoming cored with purple reflections, and Mingolla said. "Beer."

"Hey, check that out!" Gilbey slid onto an adjoining stool and jerked his thumb toward a whore at the end of the bar. Her skirt was hiked to mid-thigh, and her breasts, judging by their fullness and lack of sag, were likely the product of elective surgery.

"Nice," said Mingolla, disinterested. The bartender set a bottle of beer in front of him, and he had a swig; it tasted sour, watery, like a distillation of the stale air.

Baylor slumped onto the stool next to Gilbey and buried his face in his hands. Gilbey said something to him that Mingolla didn't catch, and Baylor lifted his hand. "I ain't going back," he said.

"Aw, Jesus!" said Gilbey. "Don't start that crap."

In the half-dark Baylor's eye sockets were clotted with shadows. His stare locked onto Mingolla. "They'll get us next time," he said. "We should head downriver. They got boats in Livingston that'll take you to Panama."

"Panama!" sneered Gilbey. "Nothin' there 'cept more beaners."

"We'll be okay at the Farm," offered Mingolla. "Things get too heavy, they'll pull us back."

"Too heavy?" A vein throbbed in Baylor's temple. "What the fuck you call 'too heavy?' "

"Screw this!" Gilbey heaved up from his stool. "You

deal with him, man," he said to Mingolla; he gestured at the big-breasted whore. "I'm gonna climb Mount Silicon."

"Nine o'clock," said Mingolla. "The PX. Okay?"

Gilbey said, "Yeah," and moved off. Baylor took over his stool and leaned close to Mingolla. "You know I'm right," he said in an urgent whisper. "They almost got us this time."

"Air Cav'll handle 'em," said Mingolla, affecting nonchalance. He opened the box of stationery and unclipped a pen from his shirt pocket.

"You *know* I'm right," Baylor repeated.

Mingolla tapped the pen against his lips, pretending to be distracted.

"Air Cav!" said Baylor with a despairing laugh. "Air Cav ain't gonna do squat!"

"Why don't you put on some decent tunes?" Mingolla suggested. "See if they got any Prowler on the box."

"Dammit!" Baylor grabbed his wrist. "Don't you understand, man? This shit ain't workin' no more!"

Mingolla shook him off. "Maybe you need some change," he said coldly; he dug out a handful of coins and tossed them on the counter. "There! There's some change."

"I'm telling you . . ."

"I don't wanna hear it!" snapped Mingolla.

"You don't wanna hear it?" said Baylor, incredulous. He was on the verge of losing control. His dark face slick with sweat, one eyelid fluttering. He pounded the countertop for emphasis. "Man, you better hear it! 'Cause we don't pull somethin' together soon, *real* soon, we're gonna die! You hear that, don'tcha?"

Mingolla caught him by the shirtfront. "Shut up!"

"I ain't shuttin' up!" Baylor shrilled. "You and Gilbey, man, you think you can save your ass by stickin' your head in the sand. But I'm gonna make you listen." He threw back his head, his voice rose to a shout. "We're gonna die!"

The way he shouted it—almost gleefully, like a kid yelling a dirty word to spite his parents—pissed Mingolla off. He was sick of Baylor's scenes. Without planning it, he punched him, pulling the punch at the last instant. Kept a hold of his shirt and clipped him on the jaw, just enough to rock back his head. Baylor blinked at him, stunned, his mouth open. Blood seeped from his gums. At the opposite end of the counter, the bartender was leaning beside a choirlike arrangement of liquor bottles, watching Mingolla and Baylor, and some of the soldiers were watching, too: they looked pleased, as if they had been hoping for a spot of violence to liven things up. Mingolla felt debased by their attentiveness, ashamed of his bullying. "Hey, I'm sorry, man," he said. "I . . ."

"I don't give a shit 'bout you're sorry," said Baylor, rubbing his mouth. "Don't give a shit 'bout nothin' 'cept gettin' the hell outta here."

"Leave it alone, all right?"

But Baylor wouldn't leave it alone. He continued to argue, adopting the long-suffering tone of someone carrying on bravely in the face of great injustice. Mingolla tried to ignore him by studying the label on his beer bottle: a red and black graphic portraying a Guatemalan soldier, his rifle upheld in victory. It was an attractive design, putting him in mind of the poster work he had done before being drafted; but considering the unreliability of Guatemalan troops, the heroic pose was a joke. He gouged a trench through the center of the label with his thumbnail.

At last Baylor gave it up and sat staring down at the warped veneer of the counter. Mingolla let him sit a minute; then, without shifting his gaze from the bottle, he said, "Why don't you put on some decent tunes?"

Baylor tucked his chin onto his chest, maintaining a stubborn silence.

"It's your only option, man," Mingolla went on. "What else you gonna do?"

"You're crazy," said Baylor; he flicked his eyes toward Mingolla and hissed it like a curse. "Crazy!"

"You gonna take off for Panama by yourself? Un-unh. You know the three of us got something going. We come this far together, and if you just hang tough, we'll go home together."

"I don't know," said Baylor. "I don't know anymore."

"Look at it this way," said Mingolla. "Maybe we're all three of us right. Maybe Panama *is* the answer, but the time

just isn't ripe. If that's true, me and Gilbey will see it
sooner or later."

With a heavy sigh, Baylor got to his feet. "You ain't
never gonna see it, man," he said dejectedly.

Mingolla had a swallow of beer. "Check if they got any
Prowler on the box. I could relate to some Prowler."

Baylor stood for a moment, indecisive. He started for
the jukebox, then veered toward the door. Mingolla tensed,
preparing to run after him. But Baylor stopped and walked
back over to the bar. Lines of strain were etched deep in
his forehead. "Okay," he said, a catch in his voice.
"Okay. What time tomorrow? Nine o'clock?"

"Right," said Mingolla, turning away. "The PX."

Out of the corner of his eye he saw Baylor cross the
room and bend over the jukebox to inspect the selections.
He felt relieved. This was the way all their r&rs had
begun, with Gilbey chasing a whore and Baylor feeding
the jukebox, while he wrote a letter home. On their first
r&r he had written his parents about the war and its bizarre
forms of attrition; then, realizing that the letter would
alarm his mother, he had torn it up and written another,
saying merely that he was fine. He would tear this letter up
as well, but he wondered how his father would react if he
were to read it. Most likely with anger. His father was a
firm believer in God and country, and though Mingolla
understood the futility of adhering to any moral code in
light of the insanity around him, he had found that something of his father's tenets had been ingrained in him: he
would never be able to desert as Baylor kept insisting. He
knew it wasn't that simple, that other factors, too, were
responsible for his devotion to duty; but since his father
would have been happy to accept the responsibility, Mingolla
tended to blame it on him. He tried to picture what his
parents were doing at that moment—father watching the
Mets on TV, mother puttering in the garden—and then,
holding those images in mind, he began to write.

"Dear Mom and Dad,
    In your last letter you asked if I thought we were
winning the war. Down here you'd get a lot of blank stares
in response to that question, because most people have a

perspective on the war to which the overall result isn't relevant. Like there's a guy I know who has this rap about how the war is a magical operation of immense proportions, how the movements of the planes and troops are inscribing a mystical sign on the surface of reality, and to survive you have to figure out your location within the design and move accordingly. I'm sure that sounds crazy to you, but down here everyone's crazy the same way (some shrink's actually done a study on the incidence of superstition among the occupation forces). They're looking for a magic that will ensure their survival. You may find it hard to believe that I subscribe to this sort of thing, but I do. I carve my initials on the shell casings, wear parrot feathers inside my helmet . . . and a lot more.

"To get back to your question, I'll try to do better than a blank stare, but I can't give you a simple Yes or No. The matter can't be summed up that neatly. But I can illustrate the situation by telling you a story and let you draw your own conclusions. There are hundreds of stories that would do, but the one that comes to mind now concerns the Lost Patrol . . ."

A Prowler tune blasted from the jukebox, and Mingolla broke off writing to listen: it was a furious, jittery music, fueled—it seemed—by the same aggressive paranoia that had generated the war. People shoved back chairs, overturned tables and began dancing in the vacated spaces; they were crammed together, able to do no more than shuffle in rhythm, but their tread set the light bulbs jiggling at the end of their cords, the purple glare slopping over the walls. A slim acne-scarred whore came to dance in front of Mingolla, shaking her breasts, holding out her arms to him. Her face was corpse-pale in the unsteady light, her smile a dead leer. Trickling from one eye, like some exquisite secretion of death, was a black tear of sweat and mascara. Mingolla couldn't be sure he was seeing her right. His left hand started trembling, and for a couple of seconds the entire scene lost its cohesiveness. Everything looked scattered, unrecognizable, embedded in a separate context from everything else: a welter of meaningless objects bobbing up and down on a tide of deranged music. Then somebody opened the door, admitting a wedge of sunlight, and the room settled back to normal. Scowling, the whore danced away. Mingolla breathed easier. The tremors in his hand subsided. He spotted Baylor near the door talking to a scruffy Guatemalan guy . . . probably a coke connection. Coke was Baylor's panacea, his remedy for fear and desperation. He always returned from r&r bleary-eyed and prone to nosebleeds, boasting about the great dope he'd scored. Pleased that he was following routine, Mingolla went back to his letter.

". . . Remember me telling you that the Green Berets took drugs to make them better fighters? Most everyone calls the drugs 'Sammy,' which is short for 'samurai.' They come in ampule form, and when you pop them under your nose, for the next thirty minutes or so you feel like a cross between a Medal-of-Honor winner and Superman. The trouble is that a lot of Berets overdo them and flip out. They sell them on the black market, too, and some guys use them for sport. They take the ampules and fight each other in pits . . . like human cockfights.

"Anyway, about two years ago a patrol of Berets went on patrol up in Fire Zone Emerald, not far from my base, and they didn't come back. They were listed MIA. A month or so after they'd disappeared, somebody started ripping off ampules from various dispensaries. At first the crimes were chalked up to guerrillas, but then a doctor caught sight of the robbers and said they were Americans. They were wearing rotted fatigues, acting nuts. An artist did a sketch of their leader according to the doctor's description, and it turned out to be a dead ringer for the sergeant of that missing patrol. After that they were sighted all over the place. Some of the sightings were obviously false, but others sounded like the real thing. They were said to have shot down a couple of our choppers and to have knocked over a supply column near Zacapas.

"I'd never put much stock in the story, to tell you the truth, but about four months ago this infantryman came walking out of the jungle and reported to the firebase. He claimed he'd been captured by the Lost Patrol, and when I heard his story, I believed him. He said they had told him that they weren't Americans anymore but citizens of the jungle. They lived like animals, sleeping under palm fronds, popping the ampules night and day. They were

crazy, but they'd become geniuses at survival. They knew
everything about the jungle. When the weather was going
to change, what animals were near. And they had this
weird religion based on the beams of light that would shine
down through the canopy. They'd sit under those beams,
like saints being blessed by God, and rave about the purity
of the light, the joys of killing, and the new world they
were going to build.

"So that's what occurs to me when you ask your
questions, mom and dad. The Lost Patrol. I'm not attempting to be circumspect in order to make a point about the
horrors of war. Not at all. When I think about the Lost
Patrol I'm not thinking about how sad and crazy they are.
I'm wondering what it is they see in that light, wondering
if it might be of help to me. And maybe therein lies your
answer . . ."

It was coming on sunset by the time Mingolla left the
bar to begin the second part of his ritual, to wander
innocent as a tourist through the native quarter, partaking
of whatever fell to hand, maybe having dinner with a
Guatemalan family, or buddying up with a soldier from
another outfit and going to church, or hanging out with
some young guys who'd ask him about America. He had
done each of these things on previous r&rs, and his pre-
tense of innocence always amused him. If he were to
follow his inner directives, he would burn out the horrors
of the firebase with whores and drugs; but on that first
r&r—stunned by the experience of combat and needing
solitude—a protracted walk had been his course of action,
and he was committed not only to repeating it but also to
recapturing his dazed mental set: it would not do to half-
ass the ritual. In this instance, given recent events at the
Ant Farm, he did not have to work very hard to achieve
confusion.

The Rio Dulce was a wide blue river, heaving with a
light chop. Thick jungle hedged its banks, and yellowish
reed beds grew out from both shores. At the spot where
the gravel road ended was a concrete pier, and moored to
it a barge that served as a ferry; it was already loaded with
its full complement of vehicles—two trucks—and carried

about thirty pedestrians. Mingolla boarded and stood in the
stern beside three infantrymen who were still wearing their
combat suits and helmets, holding double-barreled rifles
that were connected by flexible tubing to backpack computers; through their smoked faceplates he could see green
reflections from the read-outs on their visor displays. They
made him uneasy, reminding him of the two pilots, and he
felt better after they had removed their helmets and proved
to have normal human faces. Spanning a third of the way
across the river was a sweeping curve of white cement
supported by slender columns, like a piece fallen out of a
Dali landscape: a bridge upon which construction had been
halted. Mingolla had noticed it from the air just before
landing and hadn't thought much about it; but now the
sight took him by storm. It seemed less an unfinished
bridge than a monument to some exalted ideal, more beautiful than any finished bridge could be. And as he stood
rapt, with the ferry's oily smoke farting out around him,
he sensed there was an analogue of that beautiful curving
shape inside him, that he, too, was a road ending in
mid-air. It gave him confidence to associate himself with
such loftiness and purity, and for a moment he let himself
believe that he also might have—as the upward-angled
terminus of the bridge implied—a point of completion
lying far beyond the one anticipated by the architects of his
fate.

On the west bank past the town the gravel road was
lined with stalls: skeletal frameworks of brushwood poles
roofed with palm thatch. Children chased in and out
among them, pretending to aim and fire at each other with
stalks of sugar cane. But hardly any soldiers were in
evidence. The crowds that moved along the road were
composed mostly of Indians: young couples too shy to
hold hands; old men who looked lost and poked litter with
their canes; dumpy matrons who made outraged faces at
the high prices; shoeless farmers who kept their backs
ramrod-straight and wore grave expressions and carried
their money knotted in handkerchiefs. At one of the stalls
Mingolla bought a sandwich and a Coca Cola. He sat on a
stool and ate contentedly, relishing the hot bread and the

spicy fish cooked inside it, watching the passing parade.
Gray clouds were bulking up and moving in from the
south, from the Caribbean; now and then a flight of XL-16s
would arrow northward toward the oil fields beyond Lake
Ixtabal, where the fighting was very bad. Twilight fell.
The lights of the town began to be picked out sharply
against the empurpling air. Guitars were plucked, hoarse
voices sang, the crowds thinned. Mingolla ordered another
sandwich and Coke. He leaned back, sipped and chewed,
steeping himself in the good magic of the land, the sweetness of the moment. Beside the sandwich stall, four old
women were squatting by a cooking fire, preparing chicken
stew and corn fritters; scraps of black ash drifted up from
the flames, and as twilight deepened, it seemed these
scraps were the pieces of a jigsaw puzzle that were fitting
together overhead into the image of a starless night.

Darkness closed in, the crowds thickened again, and
Mingolla continued his walk, strolling past stalls with
necklaces of light bulbs strung along their frames, wires
leading off them to generators whose rattle drowned out
the chirring of frogs and crickets. Stalls selling plastic
rosaries, Chinese switchblades, tin lanterns; others selling
embroidered Indian shirts, flour-sack trousers, wooden
masks; others yet where old men in shabby suit coats sat
cross-legged behind pyramids of tomatoes and melons and
green peppers, each with a candle cemented in melted wax
atop them, like primitive altars. Laughter, shrieks, vendors
shouting. Mingolla breathed in perfume, charcoal smoke,
the scents of rotting fruit. He began to idle from stall to
stall, buying a few souvenirs for friends back in New
York, feeling part of the hustle, the noise, the shining
black air, and eventually he came to a stall around which
forty or fifty people had gathered, blocking all but its
thatched roof from view. A woman's amplified voice cried
out, *"LA MARIPOSA!"* Excited squeals from the crowd.
Again the woman cried out, *"EL CUCHILLO!"* The two
words she had called—the butterfly and the knife—intrigued Mingolla, and he peered over heads.

Framed by the thatch and rickety poles, a dusky-skinned
young woman was turning a handle that spun a wire cage:

it was filled with white plastic cubes, bolted to a plank counter. Her black hair was pulled back from her face, tied behind her neck, and she wore a red sundress that left her shoulders bare. She stopped cranking, reached into the cage and without looking plucked one of the cubes; she examined it, picked up a microphone and cried, *"LA LUNA!"* A bearded guy pushed forward and handed her a card. She checked the card, comparing it to some cubes that were lined up on the counter; then she gave the bearded guy a few bills in Guatemalan currency.

The composition of the game appealed to Mingolla. The dark woman; her red dress and cryptic words; the runelike shadow of the wire cage; all this seemed magical, an image out of an occult dream. Part of the crowd moved off, accompanying the winner, and Mingolla let himself be forced closer by new arrivals pressing in from behind. He secured a position at the corner of the stall, fought to maintain it against the eddying of the crowd, and on glancing up, he saw the woman smiling at him from a couple of feet away, holding out a card and a pencil stub. "Only ten cents Guatemalan," she said in American-sounding English.

The people flanking Mingolla urged him to play, grinning and clapping him on the back. But he didn't need urging. He knew he was going to win: it was the clearest premonition he had ever had, and it was signaled mostly by the woman herself. He felt a powerful attraction to her. It was as if she were a source of heat . . . not of heat alone but also of vitality, sensuality, and now that he was within range, that heat was washing over him, making him aware of a sexual tension developing between them, bringing with it the knowledge that he would win. The strength of the attraction surprised him, because his first impression had been that she was exotic-looking but not beautiful. Though slim, she was a little wide-hipped, and her breasts, mounded high and served up in separate scoops by her tight bodice, were quite small. Her face, like her coloring, had an East Indian cast, its features too large and voluptuous to suit the delicate bone structure; yet they were so expressive, so finely cut, that their disproportion came to seem a virtue. Except that it was thinner, it might have been the face of one of those handmaidens you see on Hindu religious posters, kneeling beneath Krishna's throne. Very sexy, very serene. That serenity, Mingolla decided, wasn't just a veneer. It ran deep. But at the moment he was more interested in her breasts. They looked nice pushed up like that, gleaming with a sheen of sweat. Two helpings of shaky pudding.

The woman waggled the card, and he took it: a simplified Bingo card with symbols instead of letters and numbers. "Good luck," she said, and laughed, as if in reaction to some private irony. Then she began to spin the cage.

Mingolla didn't recognize many of the words she called, but an old man cozied up to him and pointed to the appropriate square whenever he got a match. Soon several rows were almost complete. *"LA MANZANA!"* cried the woman, and the old man tugged at Mingolla's sleeve, shouting, *"Se gano!"*

As the woman checked his card, Mingolla thought about the mystery she presented. Her calmness, her unaccented English and the upper class background it implied, made her seem out of place here. Maybe she was a student, her education interrupted by the war . . . though she might be a bit too old for that. He figured her to be twenty-two or twenty-three. Graduate school, maybe. But there was an air of worldliness about her that didn't support that theory. He watched her eyes dart back and forth between the card and the plastic cubes. Large, heavy-lidded eyes. The whites stood in such sharp contrast to her dusky skin that they looked fake: milky stones with black centers.

"You see?" she said, handing him his winnings—about three dollars—and another card.

"See what?" Mingolla asked, perplexed.

But she had already begun to spin the cage again.

He won three of the next seven cards. People congratulated him, shaking their heads in amazement; the old man cozied up further, suggesting in sign language that he was the agency responsible for Mingolla's good fortune. Mingolla, however, was nervous. His ritual was founded on a principle of small miracles, and though he was certain the woman was cheating on his behalf (that, he assumed, had been the meaning of her laughter, her "You see?"), though his luck was not really luck, its excessiveness menaced that principle. He lost three cards in a row, but thereafter won two of four and grew even more nervous. He considered leaving. But what if it *were* luck? Leaving might run him afoul of a higher principle, interfere with some cosmic process and draw down misfortune. It was a ridiculous idea, but he couldn't bring himself to risk the faint chance that it might be true.

He continued to win. The people who had congratulated him became disgruntled and drifted off, and when there were only a handful of players left, the woman closed down the game. A grimy street kid materialized from the shadows and began dismantling the equipment. Unbolting the wire cage, unplugging the microphone, boxing up the plastic cubes, stuffing it all into a burlap sack. The woman moved out from behind the stall and leaned against one of the roofpoles. Half-smiling, she cocked her head, appraising Mingolla, and then—just as the silence between them began to get prickly—she said, "My name's Debora."

"David." Mingolla felt as awkward as a fourteen-year-old; he had to resist the urge to jam his hands into his pockets and look away. "Why'd you cheat?" he asked; in trying to cover his nervousness, he said it too loudly and it sounded like an accusation.

"I wanted to get your attention," she said. "I'm . . . interested in you. Didn't you notice?"

"I didn't want to take it for granted."

She laughed. "I approve! It's always best to be cautious."

He liked her laughter; it had an easiness that made him think she would celebrate the least good thing.

Three men passed by arm-in-arm, singing drunkenly. One yelled at Debora, and she responded with an angry burst of Spanish. Mingolla could guess what had been said, that she had been insulted for associating with an American. "Maybe we should go somewhere," he said. "Get off the streets."

"After he's finished." She gestured at the kid, who was now taking down the string of light bulbs. "It's funny," she said. "I have the gift myself, and I'm usually uncomfortable around anyone else who has it. But not with you."

"The gift?" Mingolla thought he knew what she was referring to, but was leery about admitting to it.

"What do you call it? ESP?"

He gave up the idea of denying it. "I never put a name on it," he said.

"It's strong in you. I'm surprised you're not with Psicorp."

He wanted to impress her, to cloak himself in a mystery equal to hers. "How do you know I'm not?"

"I could tell." She pulled a black purse from behind the counter. "After drug therapy there's a change in the gift, in the way it comes across. It doesn't feel as hot, for one thing." She glanced up from the purse. "Or don't you perceive it that way? As heat."

"I've been around people who felt hot to me," he said. "But I didn't know what it meant."

"That's what it means . . . sometimes." She stuffed some bills into the purse. "So, why aren't you with Psicorp?"

Mingolla thought back to his first interview with a Psicorp agent: a pale, balding man with the innocent look around the eyes that some blind people have. While Mingolla had talked, the agent had fondled the ring Mingolla had given him to hold, paying no mind to what was being said, and had gazed off distractedly, as if listening for echoes. "They tried hard to recruit, me," Mingolla said. "But I was scared of the drugs. I heard they had bad side-effects."

"You're lucky it was voluntary," she said. "Here they just snap you up."

The kid said something to her; he swung the burlap sack over his shoulder, and after a rapid-fire exchange of Spanish he ran off toward the river. The crowds were still thick, but more than half the stalls had shut down; those that remained open looked—with their thatched roofs and strung lights and beshawled women—like crude nativity scenes ranging the darkness. Beyond the stalls, neon signs winked on and off: a chaotic menagerie of silver eagles and crimson spiders and indigo dragons. Watching them burn and vanish, Mingolla experienced a wave of dizziness. Things were starting to look disconnected as they had at the Club Demonio.

"Don't you feel well?" she asked.

"I'm just tired."

She turned him to face her, put her hands on his shoulders. "No," she said. "It's something else."

The weight of her hands, the smell of her perfume, helped to steady him. "There was an assault on the firebase a few days ago," he said. "It's still with me a little, y'know."

She gave his shoulders a squeeze and stepped back. "Maybe I can do something." She said this with such gravity, he thought she must have something specific in mind. "How's that?" he asked.

"I'll tell you at dinner . . . that is, if you're buying." She took his arm, jollying him. "You owe me that much, don't you think, after all your good luck?"

"Why aren't *you* with Psicorp?" he asked as they walked.

She didn't answer immediately, keeping her head down, nudging a scrap of cellophane with her toe. They were moving along an uncrowded street, bordered on the left by the river—a channel of sluggish black lacquer—and on the right by the windowless rear walls of some bars. Overhead, behind a latticework of supports, a neon lion shed a baleful green nimbus. "I was in school in Miami when they started testing here," she said at last. "And after I came home, my family got on the wrong side of Department Six. You know Department Six?"

"I've heard some stuff."

"Sadists don't make efficient bureaucrats," she said. "They were more interested in torturing us than in determining our value."

Their footsteps crunched in the dirt; husky jukebox voices cried out for love from the next street over. "What happened?" Mingolla asked.

"To my family?" She shrugged. "Dead. No one ever bothered to confirm it, but it wasn't necessary. Confirmation, I mean." She went a few steps in silence. "As for me . . ." A muscle bunched at the corner of her mouth. "I did what I had to."

He was tempted to ask for specifics, but thought better of it. "I'm sorry," he said, and then kicked himself for having made such a banal comment.

They passed a bar lorded over by a grinning red-and-purple neon ape. Mingolla wondered if these glowing figures had meaning for guerrillas with binoculars in the hills: gone-dead tubes signaling times of attack or troop movements. He cocked an eye toward Debora. She didn't look despondent as she had a second before, and that accorded with his impression that her calmness was a product of self-control, that her emotions were strong but held in tight check and only let out for exercise. From out on the river came a solitary splash, some cold fleck of life surfacing briefly, then returning to its long ignorant glide through the dark . . . and his life no different really, though maybe less graceful. How strange it was to be walking beside this woman who gave off heat like a candle-flame, with earth and sky blended into a black gas, and neon totems standing guard overhead.

"Shit," said Debora under her breath.

It surprised him to hear her curse. "What is it?"

"Nothing," she said wearily. "Just 'shit.' " She pointed ahead and quickened her pace. "Here we are."

The restaurant was a working-class place that occupied the ground floor of a hotel: a two-story building of yellow concrete block with a buzzing Fanta sign hung above the entrance. Hundreds of moths swarmed about the sign, flickering whitely against the darkness, and in front of the steps stood a group of teenage boys who were throwing knives at an iguana. The iguana was tied by its hind legs to the step railing. It had amber eyes, a hide the color of boiled cabbage, and it strained at the end of its cord, digging its claws into the dirt and arching its neck like a pint-size dragon about to take flight. As Mingolla and Debora walked up, one of the boys scored a hit in the iguana's tail and it flipped high into the air, shaking loose the knife. The boys passed around a bottle of rum to celebrate.

Except for the waiter—a pudgy young guy leaning beside a door that opened onto a smoke-filled kitchen—the place was empty. Glaring overhead lights shined up the grease spots on the plastic tablecloths and made the uneven thicknesses of yellow paint appear to be dripping. The cement floor was freckled with dark stains that Mingolla discovered to be the remains of insects. However, the food turned out to be pretty good, and Mingolla shoveled down a plateful of chicken and rice before Debora had half-finished hers. She ate deliberately, chewing each bite a long time, and he had to carry the conversation. He told her about New York, his painting, how a couple of galleries had showed interest even though he was just a student. He compared his work to Rauschenberg, to Silvestre. Not as good, of course. Not yet. He had the notion that everything he told her—no matter its irrelevance to the moment—was securing the relationship, establishing subtle ties: he pictured the two of them enwebbed in a network of luminous threads that acted as conduits for their attraction. He could feel her heat more strongly than ever, and he wondered what it would be like to make love to her, to be swallowed by that perception of heat. The instant he wondered this, she glanced up and smiled, as if sharing the thought. He wanted to ratify his sense of intimacy, to tell her something he had told no one else, and so—having only one important secret—he told her about the ritual.

She laid down her fork and gave him a penetrating look. "You can't really believe that," she said.

"I know it sounds . . ."

"Ridiculous," she broke in. "That's how it sounds."

"It's the truth," he said defiantly.

She picked up her fork again, pushed around some grains of rice. "How is it for you," she said, "when you have a premonition? I mean, what happens? Do you have dreams, hear voices?"

"Sometimes I just know things," he said, taken aback by her abrupt change of subject. "And sometimes I see pictures. It's like with a TV that's not working right. Fuzziness at first, then a sharp image."

"With me, it's dreams. And hallucinations. I don't

know what else to call them." Her lips thinned; she sighed, appearing to have reached some decision. "When I first saw you, just for a second, you were wearing battle gear. There were inputs on the gauntlets, cables attached to the helmet. The faceplate was shattered, and your face . . . it was pale, bloody." She put her hand out to cover his. "What I saw was very clear, David. You can't go back."

He hadn't described artilleryman's gear to her, and no way could she have seen it. Shaken, he said, "Where am I gonna go?"

"Panama," she said. "I can help you get there."

She suddenly snapped into focus. You find her, dozens like her, in any of the r&r towns. Preaching pacifism, encouraging desertion. Do-gooders, most with guerrilla connections. And that, he realized, must be how she had known about his gear. She had probably gathered information on the different types of units in order to lend authenticity to her dire pronouncements. His opinion of her wasn't diminished; on the contrary, it went up a notch. She was risking her life by talking to him. But her mystery had been dimmed.

"I can't do that," he said.

"Why not? Don't you believe me?"

"It wouldn't make any difference if I did."

"I . . ."

"Look," he said. "This friend of mine, he's always trying to convince me to desert, and there've been times I wanted to. But it's just not in me. My feet won't move that way. Maybe you don't understand, but that's how it is."

"This childish thing you do with your two friends," she said after a pause. "That's what's holding you here, isn't it?"

"It isn't childish."

"That's exactly what it is. Like a child walking home in the dark and thinking that if he doesn't look at the shadows, nothing will jump out at him."

"You don't understand," he said.

"No, I suppose I don't." Angry, she threw her napkin down on the table and stared intently at her plate as if reading some oracle from the chicken bones.

"Let's talk about something else," said Mingolla.

"I have to go," she said coldly.

"Because I won't desert?"

"Because of what'll happen if you don't." She leaned toward him, her voice burred with emotion. "Because knowing what I do about your future, I don't want to wind up in bed with you."

Her intensity frightened him. Maybe she *had* been telling the truth. But he dismissed the possibility. "Stay," he said. "We'll talk some more about it."

"You wouldn't listen." She picked up her purse and got to her feet.

The waiter ambled over and laid the check beside Mingolla's plate; he pulled a plastic bag filled with marijuana from his apron pocket and dangled it in front of Mingolla. "Gotta get her in the mood, man," he said. Debora railed at him in Spanish. He shrugged and moved off, his slow-footed walk an advertisement for his goods.

"Meet me tomorrow then," said Mingolla. "We can talk more about it tomorrow."

"No."

"Why don't you gimme a break?" he said. "This is all coming down pretty fast, y'know. I get here this afternoon, meet you, and an hour later you're saying, 'Death is in the cards, and Panama's your only hope.' I need some time to think. Maybe by tomorrow I'll have a different attitude."

Her expression softened but she shook her head, No.

"Don't you think it's worth it?"

She lowered her eyes, fussed with the zipper of her purse a second and let out a rueful hiss. "Where do you want to meet?"

"How 'bout the pier on this side? 'Round noon."

She hesitated. "All right." She came around to his side of the table, bent down and brushed her lips across his cheek. He tried to pull her close and deepen the kiss, but she slipped away. He felt giddy, overheated. "You really gonna be there?" he asked.

She nodded but seemed troubled, and she didn't look back before vanishing down the steps.

Mingolla sat a while, thinking about the kiss, its promise. He might have sat even longer, but three drunken soldiers staggered in and began knocking over chairs, giving the waiter a hard time. Annoyed, Mingolla went to the door and stood taking in hits of the humid air. Moths were loosely constellated on the curved plastic of the Fanta sign, trying to get next to the bright heat inside it, and he had a sense of relation, of sharing their yearning for the impossible. He started down the steps but was brought up short. The teenage boys had gone; however, their captive iguana lay on the bottom step, bloody and unmoving. Bluish-gray strings spilled from a gash in its throat. It was such a clear sign of bad luck, Mingolla went back inside and checked into the hotel upstairs.

The hotel corridors stank of urine and disinfectant. A drunken Indian with his fly unzipped and a bloody mouth was pounding on one of the doors. As Mingolla passed him, the Indian bowed and made a sweeping gesture, a parody of welcome. Then he went back to his pounding. Mingolla's room was a windowless cell five feet wide and coffin-length, furnished with a sink and a cot and a chair. Cobwebs and dust clotted the glass of the transom, reducing the hallway light to a cold bluish-white glow. The walls were filmy with more cobwebs, and the sheets were so dirty that they looked to have a pattern. He lay down and closed his eyes, thinking about Debora. About ripping off that red dress and giving her a vicious screwing. How she'd cry out. That both made him ashamed and gave him a hard-on. He tried to think about making love to her tenderly. But tenderness, it seemed, was beyond him. He went flaccid. Jerking-off wasn't worth the effort, he decided. He started to unbutton his shirt, remembered the sheets and figured he'd be better off with his clothes on. In the blackness behind his lids he began to see explosive flashes, and within those flashes were images of the assault on the Ant Farm. The mist, the tunnels. He blotted them out with the image of Debora's face, but they kept coming back. Finally he opened his eyes. Two . . . no, three fuzzy-looking black stars were silhouetted against the

transom. It was only when they began to crawl that he
recognized them to be spiders. Big ones. He wasn't usually
afraid of spiders, but these particular spiders terrified him.
If he hit them with his shoe he'd break the glass and they'd
eject him from the hotel. He didn't want to kill them with
his hands. After a while he sat up, switched on the overhead and searched under the cot. There weren't any more
spiders. He lay back down, feeling shaky and short of
breath. Wishing he could talk to someone, hear a familiar
voice. "It's okay," he said to the dark air. But that didn't
help. And for a long time, until he felt secure enough to
sleep, he watched the three black stars crawling across the
transom, moving toward the center, touching each other,
moving apart, never making any real progress, never straying
from their area of bright confinement, their universe of
curdled, frozen light.

2

In the morning Mingolla crossed to the west bank and
walked toward the airbase. It was already hot, but the air
still held a trace of freshness and the sweat that beaded on
his forehead felt clean and healthy. White dust was settling
along the gravel road, testifying to the recent passage of
traffic; past the town and the cut-off that led to the uncom-
pleted bridge, high walls of vegetation crowded close to
the road, and from within them he heard monkeys and
insects and birds: sharp sounds that enlivened him, making
him conscious of the play of his muscles. About halfway
to the base he spotted six Guatemalan soldiers coming out
of the jungle, dragging a couple of bodies; they tossed
them onto the hood of their jeep, where two other bodies
were lying. Drawing near, Mingolla saw that the dead
were naked children, each with a neat hole in his back. He
had intended to walk on past, but one of the soldiers—a
gnomish, copper-skinned man in dark blue fatigues—blocked
his path and demanded to check his papers. All the soldiers gathered around to study the papers, whispering,
turning them sideways, scratching their heads. Used to
such hassles, Mingolla paid them no attention and looked
at the dead children.

They were scrawny, sun-darkened, lying face down with their ragged hair hanging in a fringe off the hood; their skins were pocked by infected mosquito bites, and the flesh around the bullet holes was ridged-up and bruised. Judging by their size, Mingolla guessed them to be about ten years old; but then he noticed that one was a girl with a teenage fullness to her buttocks, her breasts squashed against the metal. That made him indignant. They were only wild children who survived by robbing and killing, and the Guatemalan soldiers were only doing their duty: they performed a function comparable to that of the birds that hunted ticks on the hide of a rhinoceros, keeping their American beast pest-free and happy. But it wasn't right for the children to be laid out like game.

The soldier gave back Mingolla's papers. He was now all smiles, and—perhaps in the interest of solidifying Guatemalan-American relations, perhaps because he was proud of his work—he went over to the jeep and lifted the girl's head by the hair so Mingolla could see her face. *"Bandita!"* he said, arranging his features into a comical frown. The girl's face was not unlike the soldier's, with the same blade of a nose and prominent cheekbones. Fresh blood glistened on her lips, and the faded tattoo of a coiled serpent centered her forehead. Her eyes were open, and staring into them—despite their cloudiness—Mingolla felt that he had made a connection, that she was regarding him sadly from somewhere behind those eyes, continuing to die past the point of clinical death. Then an ant crawled out of her nostril, perching on the crimson curve of her lip, and the eyes merely looked vacant. The soldier let her head fall and wrapped his hand in the hair of a second corpse; but before he could lift it, Mingolla turned away and headed down the road toward the airbase.

There was a row of helicopters lined up at the edge of the landing strip, and walking between them, Mingolla saw the two pilots who had given him a ride from the Ant Farm. They were stripped to shorts and helmets, wearing baseball gloves, and they were playing catch, lofting high flies to one another. Behind them, atop their Sikorsky, a mechanic was fussing with the main rotor housing. The sight of the pilots didn't disturb Mingolla as it had the previous day; in fact, he found their weirdness somehow comforting. Just then, the ball eluded one of them and bounced Mingolla's way. He snagged it and flipped it back to the nearer of the pilots, who came loping over and stood pounding the ball into the pocket of his glove. With his black reflecting face and sweaty, muscular torso, he looked like an eager young mutant.

"How's she goin'?" he asked. "Seem like you a little tore down this mornin'."

"I feel okay," said Mingolla defensively. " 'Course" —he smiled, making light of his defensiveness—"maybe you see something I don't."

The pilot shrugged; the sprightliness of the gesture seemed to convey good humor.

Mingolla pointed to the mechanic. "You guys broke down, huh?"

"Just overhaul. We're goin' back up early tomorrow. Need a lift?"

"Naw, I'm here for a week."

An eerie current flowed through Mingolla's left hand, setting up a palsied shaking. It was bad this time, and he jammed the hand into his hip pocket. The olive-drab line of barracks appeared to twitch, to suffer a dislocation and shift farther away; the choppers and jeeps and uniformed men on the strip looked toylike: pieces in a really neat GI Joe Airbase kit. Mingolla's hand beat against the fabric of his trousers like a sick heart.

"I gotta get going," he said.

"Hang in there," said the pilot. "You be awright."

The words had a flavor of diagnostic assurance that almost convinced Mingolla of the pilot's ability to know his fate, that things such as fate could be known. "You honestly believe what you were saying yesterday, man?" he asked. " 'Bout your helmets? 'Bout knowing the future?"

The pilot bounced the ball on the cement, snatched it at the peak of its rebound and stared down at it. Mingolla could see the seams and brand name reflected in the visor, but nothing of the face behind it, no evidence either of normalcy or deformity. "I get asked that a lot," said the pilot. "People raggin' me y'know. But you ain't raggin' me, are you, man?"

"No," said Mingolla. "I'm not."

"Well," said the pilot, "it's this way. We buzz 'round up in the nothin', and we see shit down on the ground, shit nobody else sees. Then we blow that shit away. Been doin' it like that for ten months, and we're still alive. Fuckin' A, I believe it!"

Mingolla was disappointed. "Yeah, okay," he said.

"You hear what I'm sayin'?" asked the pilot. "I mean we're livin' goddamn proof."

"Uh-huh." Mingolla scratched his neck, trying to think of a diplomatic response, but thought of none. "Guess I'll see you." He started toward the PX.

"Hang in there, man!" the pilot called after him. "Take it from me! Things gonna be lookin' up for you real soon!"

The canteen in the PX was a big, barnlike room of unpainted boards; it was of such recent construction that Mingolla could still smell sawdust and resin. Thirty or forty tables; a jukebox; bare walls. Behind the bar at the rear of the room, a sour-faced corporal with a clipboard was doing a liquor inventory, and Gilbey—the only customer—was sitting by one of the east windows, stirring a cup of coffee. His brow was furrowed, and a ray of sunlight shone down around him, making it look that he was being divinely inspired to do some soul-searching.

"Where's Baylor?" asked Mingolla, sitting opposite him.

"Fuck, I dunno," said Gilbey, not taking his eyes from the coffee cup. "He'll be here."

Mingolla kept his left hand in his pocket. The tremors were diminishing, but not quickly enough to suit him; he was worried that the shaking would spread as it had after the assault. He let out a sigh, and in letting it out he could feel all his nervous flutters. The ray of sunlight seemed to be humming a wavery golden note, and that, too, worried him. Hallucinations. Then he noticed a fly buzzing against the windowpane. "How was it last night?" he asked.

Gilbey glanced up sharply. "Oh, you mean Big Tits.

She lemme check her for lumps." He forced a grin, then went back to stirring his coffee.

Mingolla was hurt that Gilbey hadn't asked about his night; he wanted to tell him about Debora. But that was typical of Gilbey's self-involvement. His narrow eyes and sulky mouth were the imprints of a mean-spiritedness that permitted few concerns aside from his own well-being. yet despite his insensitivity, his stupid rages and limited conversation, Mingolla believed that he was smarter than he appeared, that disguising one's intelligence must have been a survival tactic in Detroit, where he had grown up. It was his craftiness that gave him away: his insights into the personalities of adversary lieutenants; his slickness at avoiding unpleasant duty; his ability to manipulate his peers. He wore stupidity like a cloak, and perhaps he had worn it for so long that it could not be removed. Still, Mingolla envied him its virtues, especially the way it had numbed him to the assault.

"He's never been late before," said Mingolla after a while.

"So what he's fuckin' late!" snapped Gilbey, glowering. "He'll be here!"

Behind the bar, the corporal switched on a radio and spun the dial past Latin music, past Top Forty, then past an American voice reporting the baseball scores. "Hey!" called Gilbey. "Let's hear that, man! I wanna see what happened to the Tigers." With a shrug, the corporal complied.

". . . White Sox six, A's three," said the announcer. "That's eight in a row for the Sox . . ."

"White Sox are kickin' some ass," said the corporal, pleased.

"The White Sox!" Gilbey sneered. "What the White Sox got 'cept a buncha beaners hittin' two hunnerd and some coke-sniffin' niggers? Shit! Every spring the White Sox are flyin', man. But then 'long comes summer and the good drugs hit the street and they fuckin' die!"

"Yeah," said the corporal, "but this year . . ."

"Take that son of a bitch Caldwell," said Gilbey, ignoring him. "I seen him coupla years back when he had a trial with the Tigers. Man, that guy could hit! Now he shuffles up there like he's just feelin' the breeze.''

"They ain't takin' drugs, man," said the corporal testily. "They can't take 'em 'cause there's these tests that show if they's on somethin'."

Gilbey barreled ahead. "White Sox ain't gotta chance, man! Know what the guy on TV calls 'em sometimes? The Pale Hose! The fuckin' Pale Hose! How you gonna win with a name like that? The Tigers, now, they got the right kinda name. The Yankees, the Braves, the . . ."

"Bullshit, man!" The corporal was becoming upset; he set down his clipboard and walked to the end of the bar. "What 'bout the Dodgers? They gotta wimpy name and they're a good team. Your name don't mean shit!"

"The Reds," suggested Mingolla; he was enjoying Gilbey's rap, its stubbornness and irrationality. Yet at the same time he was concerned by its undertone of desperation: appearances to the contrary, Gilbey was not himself this morning.

"Oh, yeah!" Gilbey smacked the table with the flat of his hand. "The Reds! Lookit the Reds, man! Lookit how good they been doin' since the Cubans come into the war. You think that don't mean nothin'? You think their name ain't helpin' 'em? Even if they get in the Series, the Pale Hose don't gotta prayer against the Reds." He laughed—a hoarse grunt. "I'm a Tiger fan, man, but I gotta feelin' this ain't their year, y'know. The Reds are tearin' up the NL East, and the Yankees is comin' on, and when they get together in October, man, then we gonna find out alla 'bout everything. Alla 'bout fuckin' everything!" His voice grew tight and tremulous. "So don't gimme no trouble 'bout the candyass Pale Hose, man! They ain't shit and they never was and they ain't gonna be shit 'til they change their fuckin' name!"

Sensing danger, the corporal backed away from confrontation, and Gilbey lapsed into a moody silence. For a while there were only the sounds of chopper blades and the radio blatting out cocktail jazz. Two mechanics wandered in for an early morning beer, and not long after that three fatherly-looking sergeants with potbellies and thinning hair and quartermaster insignia on their shoulders sat at a nearby table and started up a game of rummy. The corporal brought them a pot of coffee and a bottle of whiskey, which they mixed and drank as they played. Their game had an air of custom, of something done at this time every day, and watching them, taking note of their fat, pampered ease, their old-buddy familiarity, Mingolla felt proud of his palsied hand. It was an honorable affliction, a sigh that he had participated in the heart of the war as these men had not. Yet he bore them no resentment. None whatsoever. Rather it gave him a sense of security to know that three such fatherly men were here to provide him with food and liquor and new boots. He basked in the dull, happy clutter of their talk, in the haze of cigar smoke that seemed the exhaust of their contentment. He believed that he could go to them, tell them his problems and receive folksy advice. They were here to assure him of the rightness of his purpose, to remind him of simple American values, to lend an illusion of fraternal involvement to the war, to make clear that it was merely an exercise in good fellowship and tough-mindedness, an initiation rite that these three men had long ago passed through, and after the war they would all get rings and medals and pal around together and talk about bloodshed and terror with head-shaking wonderment and nostalgia, as if bloodshed and terror were old, lost friends whose natures they had not fuly appreciated at the time . . . Mingolla realized then that a smile had stretched his facial muscles taut, and that his train of thought had been leading him into spooky mental territory. The tremors in his hand were worse than ever. He checked his watch. It was almost ten o'clock. *Ten o'clock!* In a panic, he scraped back his chair and stood.

"Let's look for him," he said to Gilbey.

Gilbey started to say something but kept it to himself. He tapped his spoon hard against the edge of the table. Then he, too, scraped back his chair and stood.

Baylor was not be found at the Club Demonio or any of the bars on the west bank. Gilbey and Mingolla described him to everyone they met, but no one remembered him. The longer the search went on, the more insecure Mingolla became. Baylor was necessary, an essential underpinning of the platform of habits and routines that suported him, that let him live beyond the range of war's weapons and the laws of chance, and should that underpinning be destroyed . . . In his mind's eye he saw the platform tipping, him and Gilbey toppling over the edge, cartwheeling down into an abyss filled with black flames. Once Gilbey said, "Panama! The son of a bitch run off to Panama." But Mingolla didn't think this was the case. He was certain that Baylor was close at hand. His certainty had such a valence of clarity that he became even more insecure, knowing that this sort of clarity often heralded a bad conclusion.

The sun climbed higher, its heat an enormous weight pressing down, its light leaching color from the stucco walls, and Mingolla's sweat began to smell rancid. Only a few soldiers were on the streets, mixed in with the usual run of kids and beggars, and the bars were empty except for a smattering of drunks still on a binge from the night before. Gilbey stumped along, grabbing people by the shirt and asking his questions. Mingolla, however, terribly conscious of his trembling hand, nervous to the point of stammering, was forced to work out a stock approach whereby he could get through these brief interviews. He would amble up, keeping his right side forward, and say, "I'm looking for a friend of mine. Maybe you seen him? Tall guy. Olive skin, black hair, thin. Name's Baylor." He came to be able to let this slide off his tongue in a casual unreeling.

Finally Gilbey had had enough. "I'm gonna hang out with Big Tits," he said. "Meet'cha at the PX tomorrow." He started to walk off, but turned and added, "You wanna get in touch 'fore tomorrow, I'll be at the Club Demonio." He had an odd expression on his face. It was as if he were trying to smile reassuringly, but—due to his lack of practice with smiles—it looked forced and foolish and not in the least reassuring.

Around eleven 'clock Mingolla wound up leaning against a pink stucco wall, watching out for Baylor in the thickening crowds. Beside him, the sun-browned fronds of a banana tree were feathering in the wind, making a crispy sound whenever a gust blew them back into the wall. The roof of the bar across the street was being repaired: patches of new tin alternating with narrow strips of rust that looked like enormous strips of bacon laid there to fry. Now and then he would let his gaze drift up to the unfinished bridge, a great sweep of magical whiteness curving into the blue, rising above the town and the jungle and the war. Not even the heat haze rippling from the tin roof could warp its smoothness. It seemed to be orchestrating the stench, the mutter of the crowds, and the jukebox music into a tranquil unity, absorbing those energies and returning them purified, enriched. He thought that if he stared at it long enough, it would speak to him, pronounce a white word that would grant his wishes.

Two flat cracks—pistol shots—sent him stumbling away from the wall, his heart racing. Inside his head the shots had spoken the two syllables of Baylor's name. All the kids and beggars had vanished. All the soldiers had stopped and turned to face the direction from which the shots had come: zombies who had heard their master's voice.

Another shot.

Some soldiers milled out of a side street, talking excitedly. ". . . fuckin' nuts!" one was saying, and his buddy said, "It was Sammy, man! You see his eyes?"

Mingolla pushed his way through them and sprinted down the side street. At the end of the block a cordon of MPs had sealed off access to the right-hand turn, and when Mingolla ran up one of them told him to stay back.

"What is it?" Mingolla asked. "Some guy playing Sammy?"

"Fuck off," the MP said mildly.

"Listen," said Mingolla. "It might be this friend of mine. Tall, skinny guy. Black hair. Maybe I can talk to him."

The MP exchanged glances with his buddies, who shrugged and acted otherwise unconcerned. "Okay," he said. He pulled Mingolla to him and pointed out a bar with turquoise walls on the next corner down. "Go on in there and talk to the captain."

Two more shots, then a third.

"Better hurry," said the MP. "Ol' Captain Haynesworth there, he don't have much faith in negotiations."

*   *   *

It was cool and dark inside the bar; two shadowy figures were flattened against the wall beside a window that opened onto the cross-street. Mingolla could make out the glint of automatic pistols in their hands. Then, through the window, he saw Baylor pop up from behind a retaining wall: a three-foot-high structure of mud bricks running between a herbal drugstore and another bar. Baylor was shirtless, his chest painted with reddish-brown smears of dried blood, and he was standing in a nonchalant pose, with his thumbs hooked in his trouser pockets. One of the men by the window fired at him. The report was deafening, causing Mingolla to flinch and close his eyes. When he looked out the window again, Baylor was nowhere in sight.

"Fucker's just tryin' to draw fire," said the man who had shot at Baylor. "Sammy's fast today."

"Yeah, but he's slowin' some," said a lazy voice from the darkness at the rear of the bar. "I do believe he's outta dope."

"Hey," said Mingolla. "Don't kill him! I know the guy. I can talk to him."

"Talk?" said the lazy voice. "You kin talk 'til yo' ass turns green, boy, and Sammy ain't gon' listen."

Mingolla peered into the shadows. A big, sloppy-looking man was leaning on the counter; brass insignia gleamed on his beret. "You the captain?" he asked. "They told me outside to talk to the captain."

"Yes, indeed," said the man. "And I'd be purely delighted to talk with you, boy. What you wanna talk 'bout?"

The other men laughed.

"Why are you trying to kill him?" asked Mingolla, hearing the pitch of desperation in his voice. "You don't have to kill him. You could use a trank gun."

"Got one comin'," said the captain. "Thing is, though, yo' buddy got hisself a coupla hostages back of that wall, and we get a chance at him 'fore the trank gun 'rives, we bound to take it."

"But . . ." Mingolla began.

"Lemme finish, boy." The captain hitched up his gunbelt, strolled over and draped an arm around Mingolla's shoul-

der, enveloping him in an aura of body odor and whiskey
breath. "See," he went on, "we had everything under
control. Sammy there . . ."

"Baylor!" said Mingolla angrily. "His name's Baylor."

The captain lifted his arm from Mingolla's shoulder and
looked at him with amusement. Even in the gloom Mingolla
could see the network of broken capillaries on his cheeks,
the bloated alcoholic features. "Right," said the captain.
"Like I's sayin', yo' good buddy Mister Baylor there
wasn't doin' no harm. Just sorta ravin' and runnin' round.
But then 'long comes a coupla our Marine brothers. Seems
like they'd been givin' our beaner friends a demonstration
of the latest combat gear, and they was headin' back from
said demonstration when they seen our little problem and
took it 'pon themselves to play hero. Wellsir, puttin' it in a
nutshell, Mister Baylor flat kicked their ass. Stomped all
over their *esprit de corps*. Then he drags 'em back of that
wall and starts messin' with one of their guns. And . . ."

Two more shots.

"Shit!" said one of the men by the window.

"And there he sits," said the captain. "Fuckin' with us.
Now either the gun's outta ammo or else he ain't figgered
out how it works. If it's the latter case, and he does figger
it out . . ." The captain shook his head dolefully, as if
picturing dire consequences. "See my predicament?"

"I could try talking to him," said Mingolla. "What
harm would it do?"

"You get yourself killed, it's your life, boy. But it's my
ass that's gonna get hauled up on charges." The captain
steered Mingolla to the door and gave him a gentle shove
toward the cordon of MPs. " 'Preciate you volunteerin',
boy."

Later Mingolla was to reflect that what he had done had
made no sense, because—whether or not Baylor had
survived—he would never have been returned to the Ant
Farm. But at the time, desperate to preserve the ritual,
none of this occurred to him. He walked around the corner
and toward the retaining wall. His mouth was dry, his
heart pounded. But the shaking in his hand had stopped,
and he had the presence of mind to walk in such a way that
he blocked the MPs' line of fire. About twenty feet from

the wall he called out, "Hey, Baylor! It's Mingolla, man!"
And as if propelled by a spring, Baylor jumped up, staring
at him. It was an awful stare. His eyes were like bulls-
eyes, white showing all around the irises; trickles of blood
ran from his nostrils, and nerves were twitching in his
cheeks with the regularity of watchworks. The dried blood
on his chest came from three long gouges; they were
partially scabbed over but were oozing a clear fluid. For a
moment he remained motionless. Then he reached down
behind the wall, picked up a double-barreled rifle from
whose stock trailed a length of flexible tubing, and brought
it to bear on Mingolla.

He squeezed the trigger.

No flame, no explosion. Not even a click. But Mingolla
felt that he'd been dipped in ice water. "Christ!" he said.
"Baylor! It's me!" Baylor squeezed the trigger again,
with the same result. An expression of intense frustration
washed over his face, then lapsed into that dead man's
stare. He looked directly up into the sun, and after a few
seconds he smiled: he might have been receiving terrific
news from on high.

Mingolla's senses had become wonderfully acute. Somewhere far away a radio was playing a country and western
tune, and with its plaintiveness, its intermittent bursts of
static, it seemed to him the whining of a nervous system
on the blink. He could hear the MPs talking in the bar,
could smell the sour acids of Baylor's madness, and he
thought he could feel the pulse of Baylor's rage, an incon-
stant flow of heat eddying around him, intensifying his
fear, rooting him to the spot. Baylor laid the gun down,
laid it down with the tenderness he might have shown
toward a sick child, and stepped over the retaining wall.
The animal fluidity of the movement made Mingolla's skin
crawl. He managed to shuffle backward a pace and held up
his hands to ward Baylor off. "C'mon, man," he said
weakly. Baylor let out a fuming noise—part hiss, part
whimper—and a runner of saliva slid between his lips. The
sun was a golden bath drenching the street, kindling glints
and shimmers from every bright surface, as if it were
bringing reality to a boil.

Somebody yelled, "Get down, boy!"

Then Baylor flew at him, and they fell together, rolling on the hard-packed dirt. Fingers dug in behind his Adam's apple. He twisted away, saw Baylor grinning down, all staring eyes and yellowed teeth. Strings of drool flapping from his chin. A Halloween face. Knees pinned Mingolla's shoulders, hands gripped his hair and bashed his head against the ground. Again, and again. A keening sound switched on inside his ears. He wrenched an arm free and tried to gouge Baylor's eyes; but Baylor bit his thumb, gnawing at the joint. Mingolla's vision dimmed, and he couldn't hear anything anymore. The back of his head felt mushy. It seemed to be rebounding very slowly from the dirt, higher and slower after each impact. Framed by blue sky, Baylor's face looked to be receding, spiraling off. And then, just as Mingolla began to fade, Baylor disappeared.

Dust was in Mingolla's mouth, his nostrils. He heard shouts, grunts. Still dazed, he propped himself onto an elbow. A little ways off, khaki arms and legs and butts were thrashing around in a cloud of dust. Like a comic strip fight. You expected asterisks and exclamation points overhead to signify profanity. Somebody grabbed his arm, hauled him upright. The MP captain, his beefy face flushed. He frowned reprovingly as he brushed dirt from Mingolla's clothes. "Real gutsy, boy," he said. "And real, real stupid. He hadn't been at the end of his run, you'd be drawin' flies 'bout now." He turned to a sergeant standing nearby. "How stupid you reckon that was, Phil?"

The sergeant said that it beat him.

"Well," the captain said, "I figger if the boy here was in combat, that'd be 'bout Bronze-Star stupid."

That, allowed the sergeant, was pretty goddamn stupid.

" 'Course here in 'Frisco''—the captain gave Mingolla a final dusting—"it don't get you diddley-shit."

The MPs were piling off Baylor, who lay on his side, bleeding from his nose and mouth. Blood thick as gravy filmed over his cheeks.

"Panama," said Mingolla dully. Maybe it *was* an option. He saw how it would be . . . a night beach, palm shadows a lacework on the white sand.

"What say?" asked the captain.

"He wanted to go to Panama," said Mingolla.

The captain gave an amused snort. "Don't we all."

One of the MPs rolled Baylor onto his stomach and handcuffed him; another manacled his feet. Then they rolled him back over. Yellow dirt had mired with the blood on his cheeks and forehead, fitting him with a blotchy mask. His eyes snapped open in the middle of that mask, widening when he felt the restraints. He started to hump up and down, trying to bounce his way to freedom. He kept on humping for almost a minute; then he went rigid and—his gone eyes fixed on the molten disc of the sun—he let out a roar. That was the only word for it. It wasn't a scream or a shout, but a devil's exultant roar, so loud and full of fury, it seemed to be generating all the blazing light and heat-dance. Listening to it had a seductive effect, and Mingolla began to get behind it, to feel it in his body like a good rock 'n' roll tune, to sympathize with its life-hating exuberance.

"Whoo-ee!" said the captain, marveling. "They gon' have to build a whole new zoo for that boy."

After giving his statement, letting a Corpsman check his head, Mingolla caught the ferry to meet Debora on the east bank. He sat in the stern, gazing out at the unfinished bridge, this time unable to derive from it any sense of hope or magic. Panama kept cropping up in his thoughts. Now that Baylor was gone, was it really an option? He knew he should try to figure things out, plan what to do, but he couldn't stop seeing Baylor's bloody, demented face. He'd seen worse, Christ yes, a whole lot worse. Guys reduced to spare parts, so little of them left that they didn't need a shiny silver coffin, just a black metal can the size of a cookie jar. Guys scorched and one-eyed and bloody, clawing blindly at the air like creatures out of a monster movie. But the idea of Baylor trapped forever in some raw, red place inside his brain, in the heart of that raw, red noise he'd made, maybe that idea was worse than anything Mingolla had seen. He didn't want to die; he rejected the prospect with the impassioned stubbornness a child displays when confronted with a hard truth. Yet he would rather die than endure madness. Compared to what Baylor had in store, death and Panama seemed to offer the same peaceful sweetness.

Someone sat down beside Mingolla: a kid who couldn't have been older than eighteen. A new kid with a new haircut, new boots, new fatigues. Even his face looked new, freshly broken from the mold. Shiny, pudgy cheeks; clear skin; bright, unused blue eyes. He was eager to talk. He asked Mingolla about his home, his family, and said, Oh, wow, it must be great living in New York, wow. But he appeared to have some other reason for initiating the conversation, something he was leading up to, and finally he spat it out.

"You know the Sammy that went animal back there?" he said. "I seen him pitted last night. Little place in the jungle west of the base. Guy name Chaco owns it. Man, it was incredible!"

Mingolla had only heard of the pits third- and fourth-hand, but what he had heard was bad, and it was hard to believe that this kid with his air of homeboy innocence could be an afficionado of something so vile. And, despite what he had just witnessed, it was even harder to believe that Baylor could have been a participant.

The kid didn't need prompting. "It was pretty early on," he said. "There'd been a coupla bouts, nothin' special, and then this guy walks in lookin' real twitchy. I knew he was Sammy by the way he's starin' at the pit, y'know, like it's somethin' he's been wishin' for. And this guy with me, friend of mine, he gives me a poke and says, 'Holy shit! That's the Black Knight, man! I seen him fight over in Reunion awhile back. Put your money on him,' he says. 'The guy's an ace!' "

Their last r&r had been in Reunion. Mingolla tried to frame a question but couldn't think of one whose answer would have any meaning.

"Well," said the kid, "I ain't been down long, but I'd even heard 'bout the Knight. So I went over and kinda hung out near him, thinkin' maybe I can get a line on how he's feelin', y'know, 'cause you don't wanna just bet the guy's rep. Pretty soon Chaco comes over and asks the Knight if he wants some action. The Knight says, 'Yeah, but I wanna fight an animal. Somethin' fierce, man. I

wanna fight somethin' fierce.' Chaco says he's got some
monkeys and shit, and the Knight says he hears Chaco's
got a jaguar. Chaco he hems and haws, says maybe so,
maybe not, but it don't matter 'cause a jaguar's too strong
for Sammy. And then the Knight tells Chaco who he is.
Lemme tell ya, Chaco's whole attitude changed. He could
see how the bettin' was gonna go for somethin' like the
Black Knight versus a jaguar. And he says, 'Yes sir,
Mister Black Knight sir! Anything you want!' And he
makes the announcement. Man, the place goes nuts. People wavin' money, screamin' odds, drinkin' fast so's they
can get ripped in time for the main event, and the Knight's
just standin' there, smilin', like he's feedin' off the confusion. Then Chaco lets the jaguar in through the tunnel and
into the pit. It ain't a full-growed jaguar, half-growed
maybe, but that's all you figure even the Knight can
handle.''

The kid paused for breath; his eyes seemed to have
grown brighter. ''Anyway, the jaguar's sneakin' 'round
and 'round, keepin' close to the pit wall, snarlin' and
spittin', and the Knight's watchin' him from up above,
checkin' his moves, y'know. And everybody starts chantin',
'Sam-mee, Sam-mee, Sam-mee,' and after the chant builds
up loud the Knight pulls three ampules outta his pocket. I
mean, shit, man! Three! I ain't never been 'round Sammy
when he's done more'n two. Three gets you clear into the
fuckin' sky! So when the Knight holds up these three
ampules, the crowd's tuned to burn, howlin' like they's
playin' Sammy themselves. But the Knight, man, he keeps
his cool. He is *so* cool! He just holds up the ampules and
lets 'em take the shine, soakin' up the noise and energy,
gettin' strong off the crowd's juice. Chaco waves everybody quiet and gives the speech, y'know, 'bout how in the
heart of every man there's a warrior-soul waitin' to be
loosed and shit. I tell ya, man, I always thought that
speech was crap before, but the Knight's makin' me buy it
a hunnerd percent. He is so goddamn cool! He takes off his
shirt and shoes, and he ties this piece of black silk 'round
his arm. Then he pops the ampules, one after another, real
quick, and breathes it all in. I can see it hittin', catchin'
fire in his eyes. Pumpin' him up. And soon as he's popped

the last one, he jumps into the pit. He don't use the tunnel, man! He jumps! Twenty-five feet down to the sand, and lands in a crouch.''

Three other soldiers were leaning in, listening, and the kid was now addressing all of them, playing to his audience. He was so excited that he could barely keep his speech coherent, and Mingolla realized with disgust that he, too, was excited by the image of Baylor crouched on the sand. Baylor, who had cried after the assault. Baylor, who had been so afraid of snipers that he had once pissed in his pants rather than walk from his gun to the latrine.

Baylor, the Black Knight.

''The jaguar's screechin' and snarlin' and slashin' at the air,'' the kid went on. ''Tryin' to put fear into the Knight. 'Cause the jaguar knows in his mind the Knight's big trouble. This ain't some jerk like Chaco, this is Sammy. The Knight moves to the center of the pit, still in a crouch.'' Here the kid pitched his voice low and dramatic. ''Nothin' happens for a coupla minutes, 'cept it's tense. Nobody's hardly breathin'. The jaguar springs a coupla times, but the Knight dances off to the side and makes him miss, and there ain't no damage either way. Whenever the jaguar springs, the crowd sighs and squeals, not just 'cause they's scared of seein' the Knight tore up, but also 'cause they can see how fast he is. Silky fast, man! Unreal. He looks 'bout as fast as the jaguar. He keeps on dancin' away, and no matter how the jaguar twists and turns, no matter if he comes at him along the sand, he can't get his claws into the Knight. And then, man . . . oh, it was so smooth! Then the jaguar springs again, and this time 'stead of dancin' away, the Knight drops onto his back, does this half roll onto his shoulders, and when the jaguar passes over him, he kicks up with both feet. Kicks up hard! And smashes his heels into the jaguar's side. The jaguar slams into the pit wall and comes down screamin', snappin' at his ribs. They was busted, man. Pokin' out the skin like tentposts.''

The kid wiped his mouth with the back of his hand and flicked his eyes toward Mingolla and the other soldiers to see if they were into the story. ''We was shoutin', man,'' he said. ''Poundin' the top of the pit wall. It was so loud,

the guy I'm with is yellin' in my ear and I can't hear
nothin'. Now maybe it's the noise, maybe it's his ribs,
whatever . . . the jaguar goes berserk. Makin' these scuttlin'
lunges at the Knight, tryin' to get close 'fore he springs so
the Knight can't pull that same trick. He's snarlin' like a
goddamn chainsaw! The Knight keeps leapin' and spinnin'
away. But then he slips, man, grabs the air for balance, and
the jaguar's on him, clawin' at his chest. For a second
they're like waltzin' together. Then the Knight pries loose
the paw that's hooked him, pushes the jaguar's head back
and smashes his fist into the jaguar's eye. The jaguar flops
onto the sand, and the Knight scoots to the other side of
the pit. He's checkin' the scratches on his chest, which is
bleedin' wicked. Meantime, the jaguar gets to his feet, and
he's fucked up worse than ever. His one eye's fulla blood,
and his hindquarters is all loosey-goosey. Like if this was
boxin', they'd call in the doctor. The jaguar figures he's
had enough of this crap, and he starts tryin' to jump outta
the pit. This one time he jumps right up to where I'm
leanin' over the edge. Comes so close I can smell his
breath, I can see myself reflected in his good eye. He's
clawin' for a grip, wantin' to haul hisself up into the
crowd. People are freakin', thinkin' he might be gonna
make it. But 'fore he gets the chance, the Knight catches
him by the tail and slings him against the wall. Just like
you'd beat a goddamn rug, that's how he's dealin' with the
jaguar. And the jaguar's a real mess, now. He's quiverin'.
Blood's pourin' outta his mouth, his fangs is all red. The
Knight starts makin' these little feints, wavin' his arms,
growlin'. He's toyin' with the jaguar. People don't believe
what they're seein', man. Sammy's kickin' a jaguar's ass
so bad he's got room to toy with it. If the place was nuts
before, now it's a fuckin' zoo. Fights in the crowd, guys
singin' the Marine Hymn. Some beaner squint's takin' off
her clothes. The jaguar tries to scuttle up close to the
Knight again, but he's too fucked up. He can't keep it
together. And the Knight he's still growlin' and feintin'.
A guy behind me is booin', claimin' the Knight's defamin'
the purity of the sport by playin' with the jaguar. But hell,
man, I can see he's just timin' the jaguar, waitin' for the
right moment, the right move.''

Staring off downriver, the kid wore a wistful expression:
he might have been thinking about his girlfriend. "We all
knew it was comin'," he said. "Everybody got real quiet.
So quiet you could hear the Knight's feet scrapin' on the
sand. You could feel it in the air, and you knew the jaguar
was savin' up for one big effort. Then the Knight slips
again, 'cept he's fakin'. I could see that, but the jaguar
couldn't. When the Knight reels sideways, the jaguar
springs. I thought the Knight was gonna drop down like he
did the first time, but he springs, too. Feetfirst. And he
catches the jaguar under the jaw. You could hear bone
splinterin', and the jaguar falls in a heap. He struggles to
get up, but no way! He's whinin', and he craps all over the
sand. The Knight walks up behind him, takes his head in
both hands and gives it a twist. Crack!"

As if identifying with the jaguar's fate, the kid closed
his eyes and sighed. "Everybody'd been quiet 'til they
heard that crack, then all hell broke loose. People chantin',
'Sam-mee, Sam-mee,' and people shovin', tryin' to get
close to the pit wall so they can watch the Knight take the
heart. He reaches into the jaguar's mouth and snaps off
one of the fangs and tosses it to somebody. Then Chaco
comes in through the tunnel and hands him the knife.
Right when he's 'bout to cut, somebody knocks me over
and by the time I'm back on my feet, he's already took the
heart and tasted it. He's just standin' there with the jaguar's blood on his mouth and his own blood runnin' down
his chest. He looks kinda confused, y'know. Like now the
fight's over and he don't know what to do. But then he
starts roarin'. He sounds the same as the jaguar did 'fore it
got hurt. Crazy fierce. Ready to get it on with the whole
goddamn world. Man, I lost it! I was right with that roar.
Maybe I was roarin' with him, maybe everybody was.
That's what it felt like, man. Like bein' in the middle of
this roar that's comin' outta every throat in the universe."
The kid engaged Mingolla with a sober look. "Lotsa
people go 'round sayin' the pits are evil, and maybe they
are. I don't know. How you s'posed to tell 'bout what's
evil and what's not down here? They say you can go to the
pits a thousand times and not see nothin' like the jaguar
and the Black Knight. I don't know 'bout that, either. But

I'm goin' back just in case I get lucky. 'Cause what I saw last night, if it was evil, man, it was so fuckin' evil it was beautiful, too.''

3

Debora was waiting at the pier, carrying a picnic basket and wearing a blue dress with a high neckline and a full skirt: a schoolgirl dress. Mingolla homed in on her. The way she had her hair, falling about her shoulders in thick, dark curls, made him think of smoke turned solid, and her face seemed the map of a beautiful country with black lakes and dusky plains, a country in which he could hide. They walked along the river past the town and came to a spot where ceiba trees with slick green leaves and whitish bark and roots like alligator tails grew close to the shore, and there they ate and talked and listened to the water gulping against the clay bank, to the birds, to the faint noises from the airbase that at this distance sounded part of nature. Sunlight dazzled the water, and whenever wind riffled the surface, it looked as if it were spreading the dazzles into a crawling crust of diamonds. Mingolla imagined that they had taken a secret path, rounded a corner on the world and reached some eternally peaceful land. The illusion of peace was so profound that he began to see hope in it. Perhaps, he thought, something was being offered here. Some new magic. Maybe there would be a sign. Signs were everywhere if you knew how to read them. He glanced around. Thick white trunks rising into greenery, dark leafy avenues leading off between them . . . nothing there, but what about those weeds growing at the edge of the bank? They cast precise fleur-de-lis shadows on the clay, shadows that didn't have much in common with the ragged configurations of the weeds themselves. Possibly a sign, though not a clear one. He lifted his gaze to the reeds growing in the shallows. Yellow reeds with jointed stalks bent akimbo, some with clumps of insect eggs like seed pearls hanging from loose fibers, and others dappled by patches of algae. That's how they looked one moment. Then Mingolla's vision rippled, as if the whole of reality had shivered, and the reeds were transformed into rudimentary shapes: yellow sticks poking up from flat blue. On the far side of the river, the jungle was a simple smear of Crayola green; a speedboat passing with a red slash unzipping the blue. It seemed that the rippling had jostled every element of the landscape a fraction out of kilter, revealing each one to be as characterless as a building block. Mingolla gave his head a shake. Nothing changed. He rubbed his brow. No effect. Terrified, he squeezed his eyes shut. He felt like the only meaningful piece in a nonsensical puzzle, vulnerable by virtue of his uniqueness. His breath came rapidly, his left hand fluttered.

"David? Don't you want to hear it?" Debora sounded peeved.

"Hear what?" He kept his eyes closed.

"About my dream. Weren't you listening?"

He peeked at her. Everything was back to normal. She was sitting with her knees tucked under her, all her features in sharp focus. "I'm sorry," he said. "I was thinking."

"You looked frightened."

"Frightened?" He put on a bewildered face. "Naw, just had a thought is all."

"It couldn't have been pleasant."

He shrugged off the comment and sat up smartly to prove his attentiveness. "So tell me 'bout the dream."

"All right," she said doubtfully. The breeze drifted fine strands of hair across her face, and she brushed them back. "You were in a room the color of blood, with red chairs and a red table. Even the paintings on the wall were done in shades of red, and . . ." She broke off, peering at him. "Do you want to hear this? You have that look again."

"Sure," he said. But he was afraid. How could she have known about the red room? She must have had a vision of it, and . . . Then he realized that she might not have been talking about the room itself. He'd told her about the assault, hadn't he? And if she had guerrilla contacts, she would know that the emergency lights were switched on during an assault. That had to be it! She was trying to frighten him into deserting again, psyching him the way preachers played upon the fears of sinners with images of fiery rivers and torture. It infuriated him. Who the hell was she to tell him what was right or wise? Whatever he did, it was going to be *his* decision.

"There were three doors in the room," she went on. "You wanted to leave the room, but you couldn't tell which of the doors was safe to use. You tried the first door, and it turned out to be a façade. The knob of the second door turned easily, but the door itself was stuck. Rather than forcing it, you went to the third door. The knob of this door was made of glass and cut your hand. After that you just walked back and forth, unsure what to do." She waited for a reaction, and when he gave none, she said, "Do you understand?"

He kept silent, biting back anger.

"I'll interpret it for you," she said.

"Don't bother."

"The red room is war, and the false door is the way of your childish . . ."

"Stop!" He grabbed her wrist, squeezing it hard.

She glared at him until he released her. "Your childish magic," she finished.

"What is it with you?" he asked. "You have some kinda quota to fill? Five deserters a month, and you get a medal?"

She tucked her skirt down to cover her knees, fiddled with a loose thread. From the way she was acting, you might have thought he had asked an intimate question and she was framing an answer that wouldn't be indelicate. Finally she said, "Is that who you believe I am to you?"

"Isn't that right? Why else would you be handing me this bullshit?"

"What's the matter with you, David?" She leaned forward, cupping his face in her hands. "Why . . ."

He pushed her hands away. "What's the matter with me? This"—his gesture included the sky, the river, the trees—"that's what's the matter. You remind me of my parents. They ask the same sorta ignorant questions." Suddenly he wanted to injure her with answers, to find an answer like acid to throw in her face and watch it eat away her tranquility. "Know what I do for my parents?" he said. "When they ask dumb-ass questions like 'What's the matter?', I tell 'em a story. A war story. You wanna hear a war story? Something happened a few days back that'll do for an answer just fine."

"You don't have to tell me anything," she said, discouraged.

"No problem," he said. "Be my pleasure."

The Ant Farm was a large sugar-loaf hill overlooking dense jungle on the eastern border of Fire Zone Emerald; jutting out from its summit were rocket and gun emplacements that at a distance resembled a crown of thorns jammed down over a green scalp. For several hundred yards around, the land had been cleared of all vegetation. The big guns had been lowered to maximum declension and in a mad moment had obliterated huge swaths of jungle, snapping off regiments of massive tree trunks a couple of feet above the ground, leaving a moat of blackened stumps and scorched red dirt seamed with fissures. Tangles of razor wire had replaced the trees and bushes, forming surreal blue-steel hedges, and buried beneath the wire were a variety of mines and detection devices. These did little good, however, because the Cubans possessed technology that would neutralize most of them. On clear nights there was little likelihood of trouble; but on misty nights trouble could be expected. Under cover of the mist Cuban and guerrilla troops would come through the wire and attempt to infiltrate the tunnels that honeycombed the interior of the hill. Occasionally one of the mines would be triggered, and you would see a ghostly fireball bloom in the swirling whiteness, tiny black figures being flung outward from its center. Lately some of these casualties had been found to be wearing red berets and scorpion-shaped brass pins, and from this it was known that the Cubans had sent in the Alacran Division, which had been instrumental in routing the American Forces in Miskitia.

There were nine levels of tunnels inside the hill, most lined with little round rooms that served as living quarters (the only exception being the bottom level, which was given over to the computer center and offices); all the rooms and tunnels were coated with a bubbled white plastic that looked like hardened seafoam and was proof against anti-personnel explosives. In Mingolla's room, where he and Baylor and Gilbey bunked, a scarlet paper lantern had been hung on the overhead light fixture, making it seem that they were inhabiting a blood cell: Baylor had insisted on the lantern, saying that the overhead was too bright and hurt his eyes. Three cots were arranged against the walls, as far apart as space allowed. The floor around Baylor's cot was littered with cigarette butts and used Kleenex; under his pillow he kept a tin box containing a stash of pills and marijuana. Whenever he lit a joint he would always offer Mingolla a hit, and Mingolla always refused, feeling that the experience of the firebase would not be enhanced by drugs. Taped to the wall above Gilbey's cot was a collage of beaver shots, and each day after duty, whether or not Mingolla and Baylor were in the room, he would lie beneath them and masturbate. His lack of shame caused Mingolla to be embarrassed by his own secretiveness in the act, and he was also embarrassed by the pimply-youth quality of the objects taped above his cot: a Yankee pennant; a photograph of his old girlfriend, and another of his senior-year high school basketball team; several sketches he had made of the surrounding jungle. Gilbey teased him constantly about this display, calling him "the boy-next-door," which struck Mingolla as odd, because back home he had been considered something of an eccentric.

It was toward this room that Mingolla was heading when the assault began. Large cargo elevators capable of carrying up to sixty men ran up and down just inside the east and west slopes of the hill; but to provide quick access between adjoining levels, and also as a safeguard in case of power failures, an auxiliary tunnel corkscrewed down through the center of the hill like a huge coil of white intestine. It was slightly more than twice as wide as the electric carts that traveled it, carrying officers and VIPs on tours. Mingolla was in the habit of using the tunnel for his exercise. Each night he would put on sweat clothes and jog up and down the entire nine levels, doing this out of a conviction that exhaustion prevented bad dreams. That night, as he passed Level Four on his final leg up, he heard a rumbling: an explosion, and not far off. Alarms sounded, the big guns atop the hill began to thunder. From directly above came shouts and the stutter of automatic fire. The tunnel lights flickered, went dark, and the emergency lights winked on.

Mingolla flattened against the wall. The dim red lighting caused the bubbled surfaces of the tunnel to appear as smooth as a chamber in a gigantic nautilus, and this resemblance intensified his sense of helplessness, making him feel like a child trapped in an evil undersea palace. He couldn't think clearly, picturing the chaos around him. Muzzle flashes, armies of ant-men seething through the tunnels, screams spraying blood, and the big guns bucking, every shellburst kindling miles of sky. He would have preferred to keep going up, to get out into the open where he might have a chance to hide in the jungle. But down was his only hope. Pushing away from the wall, he ran full-tilt, arms waving, skidding around corners, almost falling, past Level Four, Level Five. Then, halfway between Levels Five and Six, he nearly tripped over a dead man: an American lying curled up around a belly wound, a slick of blood spreading beneath him and a machete by his hand. As Mingolla stooped for the machete, he thought nothing about the man, only about how weird it was for an American to be defending himself against Cubans with such a weapon. There was no use, he decided, in going any farther. Whoever had killed the man would be somewhere below, and the safest course would be to hide out in one of the rooms on Level Five. Holding the machete before him, he moved cautiously back up the tunnel.

Levels Five through Seven were officer country, and though the tunnels were the same as the ones above—gently curving tubes eight feet high and ten feet wide—the rooms were larger and contained only two cots. The rooms Mingolla peered into were empty, and this, despite the sounds of battle, gave him a secure feeling. But as he passed beyond the tunnel curve, he heard shouts in Spanish from his rear. He peeked back around the curve. A skinny black soldier wearing a red beret and gray fatigues was inching toward the first doorway; then, rifle at the ready, he ducked inside. Two other Cubans—slim bearded men, their skins sallow-looking in the bloody light—were standing by the arched entranceway to the auxiliary tunnel; when they saw the black soldier emerge from the room, they walked off in the opposite direction, probably to check the rooms at the far end of the level.

Mingolla began to operate in a kind of luminous panic. He realized that he would have to kill the black soldier. Kill him without any fuss, take his rifle and hope that he could catch the other two off-guard when they came back for him. He slipped into the nearest room and stationed himself against the wall to the right of the door. The Cuban, he had noticed, had turned left on entering the room; he would have been vulnerable to someone positioned like Mingolla. Vulnerable for a split-second. Less than a count of one. The pulse in Mingolla's temple throbbed, and he gripped the machete tightly in his left hand. He rehearsed mentally what he would have to do. Stab; clamp a hand over the Cuban's mouth; bring his knee up to jar loose the rifle. And he would have to perform these actions simultaneously, execute them perfectly.

Perfect execution.

He almost laughed out loud, remembering his paunchy old basketball coach saying, "Perfect execution, boys. That's what beats a zone. Forget the fancy crap. Just set your screens, run your patterns and get your shots down."

Hoops ain't nothin' but life in short pants, huh, Coach?

Mingolla drew a deep breath and let it sigh out through his nostrils. He couldn't believe he was going to die. He had spent the past nine months worrying about death, but when it got right down to it, when the circumstances arose that made death likely, it was hard to take that likelihood seriously. It didn't seem reasonable that a skinny black guy should be his nemesis. His death should involve massive detonations of light, special Mingolla-killing rays, astronomical portents. Not some scrawny little shit with a rifle. He drew another breath and for the first time registered the contents of the room. Two cots; clothes strewn everywhere; taped-up polaroids and pornográphy. Officer country or not, it was your basic Ant Farm decor; under the red light it looked squalid, long-abandoned. He was amazed by how calm he felt. Oh, he was afraid all right! But fear was tucked into the dark folds of his personality like a murderer's knife hidden inside an old coat on a closet shelf. Glowing in secret, waiting its chance to shine.

Sooner or later it would skewer him, but for now it was an ally, acting to sharpen his senses. He could see every bubbled pucker on the white walls, could hear the scrape of the Cuban's boots as he darted into the room next door, could feel how the Cuban swung the rifle left-to-right, paused, turned . . .

He *could* feel the Cuban! Feel his heat, his heated shape, the exact position of his body. It was as if a thermal imager had been switched on inside his head, one that worked through walls.

The Cuban eased toward Mingolla's door, his progress tangible, like a burning match moving behind a sheet of paper. Mingolla's calm was shattered. The man's heat, his fleshy temperature, was what disturbed him. He had imagined himself killing with a cinematic swiftness and lack of mess; now he thought of hogs being butchered and piledrivers smashing the skulls of cows. And could he trust this freakish form of perception? What if he couldn't? What if he stabbed too late? Too soon? Then the hot, alive thing was almost at the door, and having no choice, Mingolla timed his attack to its movements, stabbing just as the Cuban entered.

He executed perfectly.

The blade slid home beneath the Cuban's ribs and Mingolla clamped a hand over his mouth, muffling his outcry. His knee nailed the rifle stock, sending it clattering to the floor. The Cuban thrashed wildly. He stank of rotten jungle air and cigarettes. His eyes rolled back, trying to see Mingolla. Crazy animal eyes, with liverish whites and expanded pupils. Sweat beads glittered redly on his brow. Mingolla twisted the machete, and the Cuban's eyelids fluttered down. But a second later they snapped open, and he lunged. They went staggering deeper into the room and teetered beside one of the cots. Mingolla wrangled the Cuban sideways and rammed him against the wall, pinning him there. Writhing, the Cuban nearly broke free. He seemed to be getting stronger, his squeals leaking out from Mingolla's hand. He reached behind him, clawing at Mingolla's face; he grabbed a clump of hair, yanked it. Desperate, Mingolla sawed with the machete. That tuned the Cuban's squeals higher, louder. He squirmed and clawed at the wall. Mingolla's clamped hand was slick with the Cuban's saliva, his nostrils full of the man's rank scent. He felt queasy, weak, and he wasn't sure how much longer he could hang on. The son of a bitch was never going to die, he was deriving strength from the steel in his guts, he was changing into some deathless force. But just then the Cuban stiffened. Then he relaxed, and Mingolla caught a whiff of feces.

He let the Cuban slump to the floor, but before he could turn loose of the machete, a shudder passed through the body, flowed up the hilt and vibrated his left hand. It continued to shudder inside his hand, feeling dirty, sexy, like a post-coital tremor. Something, some animal essence, some oily scrap of bad life, was slithering around in there, squirting toward his wrist. He stared at the hand, horrified. It was gloved in the Cuban's blood, trembling. He smashed it against his hip, and that seemed to stun whatever was inside it. But within seconds it had revived and was wriggling in and out of his fingers with the mad celerity of a tadpole.

"Teo!" someone called. *"Vamos!"*

Electrified by the shout, Mingolla hustled to the door. His foot nudged the Cuban's rifle. He picked it up, and the shaking of his hand lessened—he had the idea it had been soothed by a familiar texture and weight.

"Teo! Donde estas?"

Mingolla had no good choices, but he realized it would be far more dangerous to hang back than to take the initiative. He grunted *"Aqui!"* and walked out into the tunnel, making lots of noise with his heels.

"Dete prisa, hombre!"

Mingolla opened fire as he rounded the curve, The two Cubans were standing by the entrance to the auxiliary tunnel. Their rifles chattered briefly, sending a harmless spray of bullets off the walls; they whirled, flung out their arms and fell. Mingolla was too shocked by how easy it had been to feel relief. He kept watching, expecting them to do something. Moan, or twitch.

After the echoes of the shots had died, though he could hear the big guns jolting and the crackle of firefights, a heavy silence seemed to fill in through the tunnel, as if his

bullets had pierced something that had dammed silence up.
The silence made him aware of his isolation. No telling
where the battle lines were drawn . . . if, indeed, they
existed. It was conceivable that small units had infiltrated
every level, that the battle for the Ant Farm was in micro-
cosm the battle for Guatemala: a conflict having no patterns, no real borders, no orderly confrontations, but like a
plague could pop up anywhere at any time and kill you.
That being the case, his best bet would be to head for the
computer center, where friendly forces were sure to be
concentrated.

He walked to the entrance and stared at the two dead
Cubans. They had fallen blocking his way, and he was
hesitant about stepping over them, half-believing they were
playing possum, that they would reach up and grab him.
The awkward attitudes of their limbs made him think they
were holding a difficult pose, waiting for him to try. Their
blood looked purple in the red glow of the emergencies,
thicker and shinier than ordinary blood. He noted their
moles and scars and sores, the crude stitching of their
fatigues, gold fillings glinting from their open mouths. It
was funny, he could have met these guys while they were
alive and they might have made only a vague impression;
but seeing them dead, he had catalogued their physical
worth in a single glance. Maybe, he thought, death revealed your essentials as life could not. He studied the
dead men, wanting to read them. Couple of slim, wiry
guys. Nice guys, into rum and the ladies and sports. He'd
bet they were baseball players, infielders, a double-play
combo. Maybe he should have called to them, Hey, I'm a
Yankee fan. Be cool! Meet'cha after the war for a game of
flies and grounders. Fuck this killing shit. Let's play some
ball.

He laughed, and the high, cracking sound of his laughter startled him. Christ! Standing around here was just
asking for it. As if to second that opinion, the thing inside
his hand exploded into life, eeling and frisking about.
Swallowing back his fear, Mingolla stepped over the two
dead men, and this time, when nothing clutched at his
trouser legs, he felt very, very relieved.

*   *   *

Below Level Six, there was a good deal of mist in the auxiliary tunnel, and from this Mingolla understood that the Cubans had penetrated the hillside, probably with a borer mine. Chances were the hole they had made was somewhere close, and he decided that if he could find it he would use it to get the hell out of the Farm and hide in the jungle. On Level Seven the mist was extremely thick; the emergency lights stained it pale red, giving it the look of surgical cotton packing a huge artery. Scorchmarks from grenade bursts showed on the walls like primitive graphics, and quite a few bodies were visible beside the doorways. Most of them Americans, badly mutilated. Uneasy, Mingolla picked his way among them, and when a man spoke behind him, saying, "Don't move," he let out a hoarse cry and dropped his rifle and spun around, his heart pounding.

A giant of a man—he had to go six-seven, six-eight, with the arms and torso of a weightlifter—was standing in a doorway, training a forty-five at Mingolla's chest. He wore khakis with lieutenant's bars, and his babyish face, though cinched into a frown, gave an impression of gentleness and stolidity: he conjured for Mingolla the image of Ferdinand the Bull weighing a knotty problem. "I told you not to move," he said peevishly.

"It's okay," said Mingolla. "I'm on your side."

The lieutenant ran a hand through his thick shock of brown hair; he seemed to be blinking more than was normal. "I'd better check," he said. "Let's go down to the storeroom."

"What's to check?" said Mingolla, his paranoia increasing.

"Please!" said the lieutenant, a genuine wealth of entreaty in his voice. "There's been too much violence already."

The storeroom was a long, narrow L-shaped room at the end of the level; it was ranged by packing crates, and through the gauzy mist the emergency lights looked like a string of dying red suns. The lieutenant marched Mingolla to the corner of the L, and turning it, Mingolla saw that the rear wall of the room was missing. A tunnel had been blown into the hillside, opening onto blackness. Forked roots with balls of dirt attached hung from its roof, giving it the witchy appearance of a tunnel into some world of dark magic; rubble and clods of earth were piled at its lip. Mingolla could smell the jungle, and he realized that the big guns had stopped firing. Which meant that whoever had won the battle of the summit would soon be sending down mop-up squads. "We can't stay here," he told the lieutenant. "The Cubans'll be back."

"We're perfectly safe," said the lieutenant. "Take my word." He motioned with the gun, indicating that Mingolla should sit on the floor.

Mingolla did as ordered and was frozen by the sight of a corpse, a Cuban corpse, lying between two packing crates opposite him, its head propped against the wall. "Jesus!" he said, coming back up to his knees.

"He won't bite," said the lieutenant. With the lack of self-consciousness of someone squeezing into a subway seat, he settled beside the corpse; the two of them neatly filled the space between the crates, touching elbow to shoulder.

"Hey," said Mingolla, feeling giddy and scattered. "I'm not sitting here with this fucking dead guy, man!"

The lieutenant flourished his gun. "You'll get used to him."

Mingolla eased back to a sitting position, unable to look away from the corpse. Actually, compared to the bodies he had just been stepping over, it was quite presentable. The only signs of damage were blood on its mouth and bushy black beard, and a mire of blood and shredded cloth at the center of its chest. Its beret had slid down at a rakish angle to cover one eyebrow; the brass scorpion pin was scarred and tarnished. Its eyes were open, reflecting glowing red chips of the emergency lights, and this gave it a baleful semblance of life. But the reflections made it appear less real, easier to bear.

"Listen to me," said the lieutenant.

Mingolla rubbed at the blood on his shaking hand, hoping that cleaning it would have some good effect.

"Are you listening?" the lieutenant asked.

Mingolla had a peculiar perception of the lieutenant and the corpse as dummy and ventriloquist. Despite its glowing eyes, the corpse had too much reality for any trick of the light to gloss over for long. Precise crescents showed on its fingernails, and because its head was tipped to the left, blood had settled into that side, darkening its cheek and temple, leaving the rest of the face pallid. It was the lieutenant, with his neat khakis and polished shoes and nice haircut, who now looked less than real.

"Listen!" said the lieutenant vehemently. "I want you to understand that I have to do what's right for me!" The bicep of his gun arm bunched to the size of a cannonball.

"I understand," said Mingolla, thoroughly unnerved.

"Do you? Do you really?" The lieutenant seemed aggravated by Mingolla's claim to understanding. "I doubt it. I doubt you could possibly understand."

"Maybe I can't," said Mingolla. "Whatever you say, man. I'm just trying to get along, y'know."

The lieutenant sat silent, blinking. Then he smiled. "My name's Jay," he said. "And you are . . . ?"

"David." Mingolla tried to bring his concentration to bear on the gun, wondering if he could kick it away, but the sliver of life in his hand distracted him.

"Where are your quarters, David?"

"Level Three."

"I live here," said Jay. "But I'm going to move. I couldn't bear to stay in a place where . . ." He broke off and leaned forward, adopting a conspiratorial stance. "Did you know it takes a long time for someone to die, even after their heart has stopped?"

"No, I didn't." The thing in Mingolla's hand squirmed toward his wrist, and he squeezed the wrist, trying to block it.

"It's true," said Jay with vast assurance. "None of these people"—he gave the corpse a gentle nudge with his elbow, a gesture that conveyed to Mingolla a creepy sort of familiarity—"have finished dying. Life doesn't just switch off. It fades. And these people are still alive, though it's only a half-life." He grinned. "The half-life of life, you might say."

Mingolla kept the pressure on his wrist and smiled, as if in appreciation of the play on words. Pale red tendrils of mist curled between them.

"Of course you aren't attuned," said Jay. "So you wouldn't understand. But I'd be lost without Eligio."

"Who's Eligio?"

Jay nodded toward the corpse. "We're attuned, Eligio and I. That's how I know we're safe. Eligio's perceptions aren't limited to the here and now any longer. He's with his men at this very moment, and he tells me they're all dead or dying."

"Uh-huh," said Mingolla, tensing. He had managed to squeeze the thing in his hand back into his fingers, and he thought he might be able to reach the gun. But Jay disrupted his plan by shifting the gun to his other hand. His eyes seemed to be growing more reflective, acquiring a ruby glaze, and Mingolla realized this was because he had opened them wide and angled his stare toward the emergency lights.

"It makes you wonder," said Jay. "It really does."

"What?" said Mingolla, easing sideways, shortening the range for a kick.

"Half-lives," said Jay. "If the mind has a half-life, maybe our separate emotions do, too. The half-life of love, of hate. Maybe they still exist somewhere." He drew up his knees, shielding the gun. "Anyway, I can't stay here. I think I'll go back to Oakland." His tone became whispery. "Where are you from, David?"

"New York."

"Not my cup of tea," said Jay. "But I love the Bay Area. I own an antique shop there. It's beautiful in the mornings. Peaceful. The sun comes through the window, creeping across the floor, y'know, like a tide, inching up over the furniture. It's as if the original varnishes are being reborn, the whole shop shining with ancient lights."

"Sounds nice," said Mingolla, taken aback by Jay's lyricism.

"You seem like a good person." Jay straightened up a bit. "But I'm sorry. Eligio tells me your mind's too cloudy for him to read. He says I can't risk keeping you alive. I'm going to have to shoot."

Mingolla set himself to kick, but then listlessness washed over him. What the hell did it matter? Even if he knocked the gun away, Jay could probably break him in half. "Why?" he said. "Why do you have to?"

"You might inform on me." Jay's soft features sagged into a sorrowful expression. "Tell them I was hiding."

"Nobody gives a shit you were hiding," said Mingolla. "That's what I was doing. I bet there's fifty other guys doing the same damn thing."

"I don't know." Jay's brow furrowed. "I'll ask again. Maybe your mind's less cloudy now." He turned his gaze to the dead man.

Mingolla noticed that the Cuban's irises were angled upward and to the left—exactly the same angle to which Jay's eyes had drifted earlier—and reflected an identical ruby glaze.

"Sorry," said Jay, leveling the gun. "I have to." He licked his lips. "Would you please turn your head? I'd rather you weren't looking at me when it happens. That's how Eligio and I became attuned."

Looking into the aperture of the gun's muzzle was like peering over a cliff, feeling the chill allure of falling and, it was more out of contrariness than a will to survive that Mingolla popped his eyes at Jay and said, "Go ahead."

Jay blinked but he held the gun steady. "Your hand's shaking," he said after a pause.

"No shit," said Mingolla.

"How come it's shaking?"

"Because I killed someone with it," said Mingolla. "Because I'm as fucking crazy as you are."

Jay mulled this over. "I was supposed to be assigned to a gay unit," he said finally. "But all the slots were filled, and when I had to be assigned here they gave me a drug. Now I . . . I . . ." He blinked rapidly, his lips parted, and Mingolla found that he was straining toward Jay, wanting to apply Body English, to do something to push him over this agonizing hump. "I can't . . . be with men anymore," Jay finished, and once again blinked rapidly; then his words came easier. "Did they give you a drug, too? I mean I'm not trying to imply you're gay. It's just they have drugs for everything these days, and I thought that might be the problem."

Mingolla was suddenly, inutterably sad. He felt that his

emotions had been twisted into a thin black wire, that the wire was frayed and spraying black sparks of sadness. That was all that energized him, all his life. Those little black sparks.

"I always fought before," said Jay. "And I was fighting this time. But when I shot Eligio . . . I just couldn't keep going."

"I really don't give a shit," said Mingolla. "I really don't."

"Maybe I *can* trust you." Jay sighed. "I just wish you were attuned. Eligio's a good soul. You'd appreciate him."

Jay kept on talking, enumerating Eligio's virtues, and Mingolla tuned him out, not wanting to hear about the Cuban's love for his family, his posthumous concerns for them. Staring at his bloody hand, he had a magical overview of the situation. Sitting in the root cellar of this evil mountain, bathed in an eerie red glow, a scrap of a dead man's life trapped in his flesh, listening to a deranged giant who took his orders from a corpse, waiting for scorpion soldiers to pour through a tunnel that appeared to lead into a dimension of mist and blackness. It was insane to look at it that way. But there it was. You couldn't reason it away; it had a brutal glamour that surpassed reason, that made reason unnecessary.

". . . and once you're attuned," Jay was saying, "you can't ever be separated. Not even by death. So Eligio's always going to be alive inside me. Of course I can't let them find out. I mean"—he chuckled, a sound like dice rattling in a cup—"talk about giving aid and comfort to the enemy!"

Mingolla lowered his head, closed his eyes. Maybe Jay would shoot. But he doubted that. Jay only wanted company in his madness.

"You swear you won't tell them?" Jay asked.

"Yeah," said Mingolla. "I swear."

"All right," said Jay. "But remember, my future's in your hands. You have a responsibility to me."

"Don't worry."

Gunfire crackled in the distance.

"I'm glad we could talk," said Jay. "I feel much better."

Mingolla said that he felt better, too.

They sat without speaking. It wasn't the most secure way to pass the night, but Mingolla no longer put any store in the concept of security. He was too weary to be afraid. Jay seemed entranced, staring at a point above Mingolla's head, but Mingolla made no move for the gun. He was content to sit and wait and let fate take its course. His thoughts uncoiled with vegetable sluggishness.

They must have been sitting a couple of hours when Mingolla heard the whisper of helicopters and noticed that the mist had thinned, that the darkness at the end of the tunnel had gone gray. "Hey," he said to Jay. "I think we're okay now." Jay offered no reply, and Mingolla saw that his eyes were angled upward and to the left just like the Cuban's eyes, glazed over with ruby reflection. Tentatively, he reached out and touched the gun. Jay's hand flopped to the floor, but his fingers remained clenched around the butt. Mingolla recoiled, disbelieving. It couldn't be! Again he reached out, feeling for a pulse. Jay's wrist was cool, still, and his lips had a bluish cast. Mingolla had a flutter of hysteria, thinking that Jay had gotten it wrong about being attuned: instead of Eligio becoming part of his life, he had become part of Eligio's death. There was a tightness in Mingolla's chest, and he thought he was going to cry. He would have welcomed tears, and when they failed to materialize he grew both annoyed at himself and defensive. Why should he cry? The guy had meant nothing to him . . . though the fact that he could be so devoid of compassion was reason enough for tears. Still, if you were going to cry over something as commonplace as a single guy dying, you'd be crying every minute of the day, and what was the future in that? He glanced at Jay. At the Cuban. Despite the smoothness of Jay's skin, the Cuban's bushy beard, Mingolla could have sworn they were starting to resemble each other the way old married couples did. And, yep, all four eyes were fixed on exactly the same point of forever. It was either a hell of a coincidence or else Jay's craziness had been of such magnitude that he had willed himself to die in this fashion just to lend credence to his theory of half-lives. And maybe he was still alive. Half alive. Maybe he and Mingolla were now attuned, and if that were true, maybe . . . Revolted by the prospect of joining Jay and the Cuban in their deathwatch, Mingolla scrambled to his feet and ran into the tunnel. He might have kept running, but on coming out into the dawn light he was brought up short by the view from the tunnel entrance.

At his back, the green dome of the hill swelled high, its sides brocaded with shrubs and vines, an infinity of pattern as eye-catching as the intricately carved facade of a Hindu temple; atop it, one of the gun emplacements had taken a hit: splinters of charred metal curved up like peels of black rind. Before him lay the moat of red dirt with its hedge-rows of razor wire, and beyond that loomed the blackish-green snarl of the jungle. Caught on the wire were hundreds of baggy shapes wearing bloodstained fatigues; frays of smoke twisted up from the fresh craters beside them. Overhead, half-hidden by the lifting gray mist, three Sikorskys were hovering. Their pilots were invisible behind layers of mist and reflection, and the choppers themselves looked like enormous carrion flies with bulging eyes and whirling wings. Like devils. Like gods. They seemed to be whispering to one another in anticipation of the feast they were soon to share.

The scene was horrid yet it had the purity of a stanza from a ballad come to life, a ballad composed about tragic events in some border hell. You could never paint it, or if you could the canvas would have to be as large as the scene itself, and you would have to incorporate the slow boil of the mist, the whirling of the chopper blades, the drifting smoke. No detail could be omitted. It was the perfect illustration of the war, of its secret magical splendor, and Mingolla, too, was an element of the design, the figure of the artist painted in for a joke or to lend scale and perspective to its vastness, its importance. He knew that he should report to his station, but he couldn't turn away from this glimpse into the heart of the war. He sat down on the hillside, cradling his sick hand in his lap, and watched as—with the ponderous aplomb of idols floating to earth, fighting the cross-draft, the wind of their descent whipping up furies of red dust—the Sikorskys made skillful landings among the dead.

4

Halfway through the telling of his story, Mingolla had realized that he was not really trying to offend or shock Debora, but rather was unburdening himself; and he further realized that by telling it he had to an extent cut loose from the past, weakened its hold on him. For the first time he felt able to give serious consideration to the idea of desertion. He did not rush to it, embrace it, but he did acknowledge its logic and understand the terrible illogic of returning to more assaults, more death, without any magic to protect him. He made a pact with himself: he would pretend to go along as if desertion were his intent and see what signs were offered.

When he had finished, Debora asked whether or not he was over his anger. He was pleased that she hadn't tried to offer sympathy. "I'm sorry," he said: "I wasn't really angry at you . . . at least that was only part of it."

"It's all right." She pushed back the dark mass of her hair so that it fell to one side and looked down at the grass beside her knees. With her head inclined, eyes half-lidded, the graceful line of her neck and chin like a character in some exotic script, she seemed a good sign herself. "I don't know what to talk to you about," she said. "The things I feel I have to tell you make you mad, and I can't muster any small-talk."

"I don't want to be pushed," he said. "But believe me, I'm thinking about what you've told me."

"I won't push. But I still don't know what to talk about." She plucked a grass blade, chewed on the tip. He watched her lips purse, wondered how she'd taste. Mouth sweet in the way of a jar that had once held spices. She tossed the grass blade aside. "I know," she said brightly. "Would you like to see where I live?"

"I'd just as soon not go back to 'Frisco yet." Where you live, he thought; I want to touch where you live.

"It's not in town," she said. "It's a village downriver."

"Sounds good." He came to his feet, took her arm and helped her up. For an instant they were close together, her breasts grazing his shirt. Her heat coursed around him, and he thought if anyone were to see them, they would see two figures wavering as in a mirage. He had an urge to tell her he loved her. Though most of what he felt was for the salvation she might provide, part of his feelings seemed real and that puzzled him, because all she had been to him was a few hours out of the war, dinner in a cheap restaurant and a walk along the river. There was no basis for consequential emotion. Before he could say anything, do anything, she turned and picked up her basket.

"It's not far," she said, walking away. Her blue skirt swayed like a rung bell.

They followed a track of brown clay overgrown by ferns, overspread by saplings with pale translucent leaves, and soon came to a grouping of thatched huts at the mouth of a stream that flowed into the river. Naked children were wading in the stream, laughing and splashing each other. Their skins were the color of amber, and their eyes were as wet-looking and purplish-dark as plums. Palms and acacias loomed above the huts, which were constructed of sapling trunks lashed together by nylon cord; their thatch had been trimmed to resemble bowl-cut hair. Flies crawled over strips of meat hung on a clothesline stretched between two of the huts. Fish heads and chicken droppings littered the ocher ground. But Mingolla scarcely noticed these signs of poverty, seeing instead a sign of the peace that might await him in Panama. And another sign was soon forthcoming. Debora bought a bottle of rum at a tiny store, then led him to the hut nearest the mouth of the stream and introduced him to a lean, white-haired old man who was sitting on a bench outside it. Tio Moises. After three drinks Tio Moises began to tell stories.

The first story concerned the personal pilot of an ex-president of Panama. The president had made billions from smuggling cocaine into the States with the help of the CIA, whom he had assisted on numerous occasions, and was himself an addict in the last stages of mental deterioration. It had become his sole pleasure to be flown from city to city in his country, to sit on the landing strips, gaze out the window and do cocaine. At any hour of night or day, he was likely to call the pilot and order him to prepare a flight plan to Colon or Bocas del Toro or Penonome. As the president's condition worsened, the pilot realized that soon the CIA would see he was no longer useful and would kill him. And the most obvious manner of killing him would be by means of an airplane crash. The pilot did not want to die alongside him. He tried to resign, but the president would not permit it. He gave thought to mutilating himself, but being a good Catholic, he could not flout God's law. If he were to flee, his family would suffer. His life became a nightmare. Prior to each flight, he would spend hours searching the plane for evidence of sabotage, and upon each landing, he would remain in the cockpit, shaking from nervous exhaustion. The president's condition grew even worse. He had to be carried aboard the plane and have the cocaine administered by an aide, while a second aide stood by with cotton swabs to attend his nosebleeds. Knowing his life could be measured in weeks, he pilot asked his priest for guidance. "Pray," the priest advised. The pilot had been praying all along, so this was no help. Next he went to the commandant of his military college, and the commandant told him he must do his duty. This, too, was something the pilot had been doing all along. Finally he went to the chief of the San Blas Indians, who were his mother's people. The chief told him he must accept his fate, which—while not something he had been doing all along—was hardly encouraging. Nonetheless, he saw it was the only available path and he did as the chief had counseled. Rather than spending hours in a pre-flight check, he would arrive minutes before take-off and taxi away without even inspecting the fuel gauge. His recklessness came to be the talk of the capitol. Obeying the president's every whim, he flew in gales and in fogs, while drunk and drugged, and during those hours in the air, suspended between the laws of gravity and fate, he gained a new appreciation of life. Once back on the ground, he engaged in living with a fierce avidity, making passionate love to his wife, carousing with friends and staying out until dawn. Then one day as he was preparing to leave for the airport, an American man came to his house and told him he had been replaced. "If we let the president fly with so negligent a pilot, we'll be blamed for anything that happens," said the American. The pilot did not have to ask whom he had meant by "we." Six weeks later the president's plane crashed in the Darien Mountains. The pilot was overjoyed. Panama had been ridded of a villain, and his own life had not been forfeited. But a week after the crash, after the new president—another smuggler with CIA connections—had been appointed, the commandant of the air force summoned the pilot, told him that the crash would never have occurred had he been on the job, and assigned him to fly the new president's plane.

All through the afternoon Mingolla listened and drank, and drunkenness fitted a lens to his eyes that let him see how these stories applied to him. They were all fables of irresolution, cautioning him to act, and they detailed the core problems of the Central American people who—as he was now—were trapped between the poles of magic and reason, their lives governed by the politics of the ultra-real, their spirits ruled by myths and legends, with the rectangular computerized bulk of North America above and the conch-shell-shaped continental mystery of South America below. He assumed that Debora had orchestrated the types of stories Tio Moises told, but that did not detract from their potency as signs: they had the ring of truth, not of something tailored to his needs. Nor did it matter that his hand was shaking, his vision playing tricks. Those things would pass when he reached Panama.

Shadows blurred, insects droned like tambouras, and twilight washed down the sky, making the air look grainy, the chop on the river appear slower and heavier. Tio Moises' granddaughter served plates of roast corn and fish, and Mingolla stuffed himself. Afterward, when the old man signaled his weariness, Mingolla and Debora strolled off along the stream. Between two of the huts, mounted on a pole, was a warped backboard with a netless hoop, and some young men were shooting baskets. Mingolla joined them. It was hard dribbling on the bumpy dirt, but he had never played better. The residue of drunkenness fueled his game, and his jump shots followed perfect arcs down through the hoop. Even at improbable angles, his shots fell true. He lost himself in flicking out his hands to make a steal, in feinting and leaping high to snag a rebound, becoming—as dusk faded—the most adroit of ten arm-waving, jitter-stepping shadows.

The game ended and the stars came out, looking like holes punched into fire through a billow of black silk overhanging the palms. Flickering chutes of lamplight illuminated the ground in front of the huts, and as Debora and Mingolla walked among them, he heard a radio tuned to the Armed Forces Network giving a play-by-play of a baseball game. There was a crack of the bat, the crowd roared, the announcer cried, "He got it all!" Mingolla imagined the ball vanishing into the darkness above the stadium, bouncing out into parking-lot America, lodging under a tire where some kid would find it and think it a miracle, or rolling across the street to rest under a used car, shimmering there, secretly white and fuming with home run energies. The score was three-to-one, top of the second. Mingolla didn't know who was playing and didn't care. Home runs were happening for him, mystical jump shots curved along predestined tracks. He was at the center of incalculable forces.

One of the huts was unlit, with two wooden chairs out front, and as they approached, the sight of it blighted Mingolla's mood. Something about it bothered him: its air of preparedness, of being a little stage set. Just paranoia, he thought. The signs had been good so far, hadn't they? When they reached the hut, Debora sat in the chair nearest the door and looked up at him. Starlight pointed her eyes with brilliance. Behind her, through the doorway, he made out the shadowy cocoon of a strung hammock, and beneath it, a sack from which part of a wire cage protruded. "What about your game?" he asked.

"I thought it was more important to be with you," she said.

That, too, bothered him. It was all starting to bother him, and he couldn't understand why. The thing in his hand wiggled. He balled the hand into a fist and sat next to Debora. "What's going on between you and me?" he asked, nervous. "Is anything gonna happen? I keep thinking it will, but . . ." He wiped sweat from his forehead and forgot what he had been driving at.

"I'm not sure what you mean," she said.

A shadow moved across the yellow glare spilling from the hut next door. Rippling, undulating. Mingolla squeezed his eyes shut.

"If you mean . . . romantically," she said, "I'm confused about that myself. Whether you return to your base or go to Panama, we don't seem to have much of a future. And we certainly don't have much of a past."

It boosted his confidence in her, in the situation, that she didn't have an assured answer. But he felt shaky. Very shaky. He gave his head a twitch, fighting off more ripples. "What's it like in Panama?"

"I've never been there. Probably a lot like Guatemala, except without the fighting."

Maybe he should get up, walk around. Maybe that would help. Or maybe he should just sit and talk. Talking seemed to steady him. "I bet," he said, "I bet it's beautiful, y'know. Panama. Green mountains, jungle waterfalls. I bet there's lots of birds. Macaws and parrots. Millions of 'em."

"I suppose so."

"And hummingbirds. This friend of mine was down there once on a hummingbird expedition, said there was a million kinds. I thought he was sort of a creep, y'know, for being into collecting hummingbirds." He opened his eyes and had to close them again. "I guess I thought hummingbird collecting wasn't very relevant to the big issues."

"David?" Concern in her voice.

"I'm okay." The smell of her perfume was more cloying than he remembered. "You get there by boat, right? Must be a pretty big boat. I've never been on a real boat, just this rowboat my uncle had. He used to take me fishing off Coney Island, we'd tie up to a buoy and catch all these poison fish. You shoulda seen some of 'em. Like mutants. Rainbow-colored eyes, weird growths all over. Scared the hell outta me to think about eating fish."

"I had an uncle who . . ."

"I used to think about all the ones that must be down

there too deep for us to catch. Giant blowfish, genius sharks, whales with hands. I'd see 'em swallowing the boat, I'd . . .''

"Calm down, David." She kneaded the back of his neck, sending a shiver down his spine.

"I'm okay, I'm okay." He pushed her hand away; he did not need shivers along with everything else. "Lemme hear some more 'bout Panama."

"I told you, I've never been there."

"Oh, yeah. Well, how 'bout Costa Rica? You been to Costa Rica." Sweat was popping out all over his body. Maybe he should go for a swim. He'd heard there were manatees in the Rio Dulce. "Ever seen a manatee?" he asked.

"David!"

She must have leaned close, because he could feel her heat spreading all through him, and he thought maybe that would help, smothering in her heat, heavy motion, get rid of this shakiness. He'd take her into that hammock and see just how hot she got. *How* hot *she got, how* hot *she got.* The words did a train rhythm in his head. Afraid to open his eyes, he reached out blindly and pulled her to him. Bumped faces, searched for her mouth. Kissed her. She kissed back. His hand slipped up to cup a breast. Jesus, she felt good! She felt like salvation, like Panama, like what you fall into when you sleep.

But then it changed, changed slowly, so slowly that he didn't notice until it was almost complete, and her tongue was squirming in his mouth, as thick and stupid as a snail's foot, and her breast, oh shit, her breast was jiggling, trembling with the same wormy juices that were in his left hand. He pushed her off, opened his eyes. Saw crude-stitch eyelashes sewn to her cheeks. Lips parted, mouth full of bones. Blank face of meat. He got to his feet, pawing the air, wanting to rip down the film of ugliness that had settled over him.

"David?" She warped his name, gulping the syllables as if she were trying to swallow and talk at once.

Frog voice, devil voice.

He spun around, caught an eyeful of black sky and spiky trees and a pitted bone-knob moon trapped in a weave of branches. Dark warty shapes of the huts, doors into yellow flame with crooked shadow men inside. He blinked, shook his head. It wasn't going away, it was real. What was this place? Not a village in Guatemala, naw, un-uh. He heard a strangled wildman grunt come from his throat, and he backed away, backed away from everything. She walked after him, croaking his name. Wig of black straw, dabs of shining jelly for eyes. Some of the shadow men were herky-jerking out of their doors, gathering behind her, talking about him in devil language. Long-legged licorice-skinned demons with drumbeat hearts, faceless nothings from the dimension of sickness. He backed another few steps.

"I can see you," he said. "I know what you are."

'It's all right, David," she said, and smiled.

Sure! She thought he was going to buy the smile, but he wasn't fooled. He saw how it broke over her face the way something rotten melts through the bottom of a wet grocery sack after it's been in the garbage for a week. Gloating smile of the Queen Devil Bitch. She had done this to him, had teamed up with the bad life in his hand and done witchy things to his head. Made him see down to the layer of shit-magic she lived in.

"I see you," he said.

He tripped, went backward flailing, stumbling, and came out of it running toward the town.

Ferns whipped his legs, branches cut at his face. Webs of shadow fettered the trail, and the shrilling insects had the sound of a metal edge being honed. Up ahead, he spotted a big moonstruck tree standing by itself on a rise overlooking the water. A grandfather tree, a white magic tree. It summoned to him. He stopped beside it, sucking air. The moonlight cooled him off, drenched him with silver, and he understood the purpose of the tree. Fountain of whiteness in the dark wood, shining for him alone. He made a fist of his left hand. The thing inside the hand eeled frantically as if it knew what was coming. He studied the deeply grooved, mystic patterns of the bark and found the point of confluence. He steeled himself. Then he drove his fist into the trunk. Brilliant pain lanced up his arm, and he cried out. But he hit the tree again, hit it a third time. He held the hand tight against his body, muffling the pain. It was already swelling, becoming a knuckle-less cartoon hand; but nothing moved inside it. The riverbank, with its rustlings and shadows, no longer menaced him; it had been transformed into a place of ordinary lights, ordinary darks, and even the whiteness of the tree looked unmagically bright.

"David!" Debora's voice, and not far off.

Part of him wanted to wait, to see whether or not she had changed for the innocent, for the ordinary. But he couldn't trust her, couldn't trust himself, and he set out running once again.

Mingolla caught the ferry to the west bank, thinking that he would find Gilbey, that a dose of Gilbey's belligerence would ground him in reality. He sat in the bow next to a group of five other soldiers, one of whom was puking over the side, and to avoid a conversation he turned away and looked down into the black water slipping past. Moonlight edged the wavelets with silver, and among those gleams it seemed he could see reflected the broken curve of his life: a kid living for Christmas, drawing pictures, receiving praise, growing up mindless to high school, sex, and drugs, growing beyond that, beginning to draw pictures again, and then, right where you might expect the curve to assume a more meaningful shape, it was sheared off, left hanging, its process demystified and explicable. He realized how foolish the idea of the ritual had been. Like a dying man clutching a vial of holy water, he had clutched at magic when the logic of existence had proved untenable. Now the frail linkages of that magic had been dissolved, and nothing supported him: he was falling through the dark zones of the war, waiting to be snatched by one of its monsters. He lifted his head and gazed at the west bank. The shore toward which he was heading was as black as a bat's wing and inscribed with arcana of violent light. Rooftops and palms were cast in silhouette against a rainbow haze of neon; gassy arcs of blood red and lime green and indigo were visible between them: fragments of glowing beasts. The wind bore screams and wild music. The soldiers beside him laughed and cursed, and the one guy kept on puking. Mingolla rested his forehead on the wooden rail, just to feel something solid.

At the Club Demonio, Gilbey's big-breasted whore was lounging by the bar, staring into her drink. Mingolla pushed through the dancers, through heat and noise and veils of lavender smoke; when he walked up to the whore, she put on a professional smile and made a grab for his crotch. He fended her off. "Where's Gilbey?" he shouted. She gave him a befuddled look; then the light dawned. "Meengolla?" she said. He nodded. She fumbled in her purse and pulled out a folded paper. "Ees frawm Geel-bee," she said. "Forr me, five dol-larrs."

He handed her the money and took the paper. It proved to be a Christian pamphlet with a pen-and-ink sketch of a rail-thin, aggrieved-looking Jesus on the front, and beneath the sketch, a tract whose first line read, "The last days are in season." He turned it over and found a handwritten note on the back. The note was pure Gilbey. No explanation, no sentiment. Just the basics.

> I'm gone to Panama. You want to make that trip, check out a guy named Ruy Barros in Livingston. He'll fix you up. Maybe I'll see you.
>
> G.

Mingolla had believed that his confusion had peaked, but the fact of Gilbey's desertion wouldn't fit inside his head, and when he tried to make it fit he was left more confused than ever. It wasn't that he couldn't understand what had happened. He understood it perfectly; he might have predicted it. Like a crafty rat who had seen his favorite hole blocked by a trap, Gilbey had simply chewed a new hole and vanished through it. The thing that confused Mingolla was his total lack of referents. He and Gilbey and Baylor had seemed to triangulate reality, to locate each other within a coherent map of duties and places and events; and now that they were both gone, Mingolla felt utterly bewildered. Outside the club, he let the crowds push him along and gazed up at the neon animals atop the bars. Giant blue rooster, green bull,

golden turtle with fiery red eyes. Great identities regarding
him with disfavor. Bleeds of color washed from the signs,
staining the air to a garish paleness, giving everyone a
mealy complexion. Amazing, Mingolla thought, that you
could breathe such grainy discolored stuff, that it didn't
start you choking. It was all amazing, all nonsensical.
Everything he saw struck him as unique and unfathomable,
even the most commonplace of sights. He found himself
staring at people—at whores, at street kids, at an MP who
was talking to another MP, patting the fender of his jeep as
if it were his big olive-drab pet—and trying to figure out
what they were really doing, what special significance
their actions held for him, what clues they presented that
might help him unravel the snarl of his own existence. At
last, realizing that he needed peace and quiet, he set out
toward the airbase, thinking he would find an empty bunk
and sleep off his confusion; but when he came to the
cut-off that led to the unfinished bridge, he turned down it,
deciding that he wasn't ready to deal with gate sentries and
duty officers. Dense thickets buzzing with insects narrowed the cut-off to a path, and at its end stood a line of
sawhorses. He climbed over them and soon was mounting
a sharply inclined curve that appeared to lead to a point not
far below the lumpish silver moon.

Despite a litter of rubble and cardboard sheeting, the
concrete looked pure under the moon, blazing bright, like
a fragment of snowy light not quite hardened to the material; and as he ascended he thought he could feel the bridge
trembling to his footsteps with the sensitivity of a white
nerve. He seemed to be walking into darkness and stars, a
solitude the size of creation. It felt good and damn lonely,
maybe a little too much so, with the wind flapping pieces
of cardboard and the sounds of the insects left behind.

After a few minutes he glimpsed the ragged terminus
ahead. When he reached it, he sat down carefully, letting
his legs dangle. Wind keened through the exposed girders,
tugging at his ankles; his hand throbbed and was fever-hot.
Below, multicolored brilliance clung to the black margin
of the east bank like a colony of bioluminescent algae. He
wondered how high he was. Not high enough, he thought.
Faint music was fraying on the wind—the inexhaustible

delirium of San Francisco de Juticlan—and he imagined that the flickering of the stars was caused by this thin smoke of music drifting across them.

He tried to think what to do. Not much occurred to him. He pictured Gilbey in Panama. Whoring, drinking, fighting. Doing just as he had in Guatemala. That was where the idea of desertion failed Mingolla. In Panama he would be afraid; in Panama, though his hand might not shake, some other malignant twitch would develop; in Panama he would resort to magical cures for his afflictions, because he would be too imperiled by the real to derive strength from it. And eventually the war would come to Panama. Desertion would have gained him nothing. He stared out across the moon-silvered jungle, and it seemed that some essential part of him was pouring from his eyes, entering the flow of the wind and rushing away past the Ant Farm and its smoking craters, past guerrilla territory, past the seamless join of sky and horizon, being irresistibly pulled toward a point into which the world's vitality was emptying. He felt himself emptying as well, growing cold and vacant and slow. His brain became incapable of thought, capable only of recording perceptions. The wind brought green scents that made his nostrils flare. The sky's blackness folded around him, and the stars were golden pinpricks of sensation. He didn't sleep, but something in him slept.

A whisper drew him back from the edge of the world. At first he thought it had been his imagination, and he continued staring at the sky, which had lightened to the vivid blue of pre-dawn. Then he heard it again and glanced behind him. Strung out across the bridge, about twenty feet away, were a dozen or so children. Some standing, some crouched. Most were clad in rags, a few wore coverings of vines and leaves, and others were naked. Watchful; silent. Knives glinted in their hands. They were all emaciated, their hair long and matted, and Mingolla, recalling the dead children he had seen that morning, was for a moment afraid. But only for a moment. Fear flared in him like a coal puffed to life by a breeze and died an instant later, suppressed not by any rational accommodation but

by a perception of those ragged figures as an opportunity
for surrender. He wasn't eager to die, yet neither did he
want to put forth more effort in the cause of survival.
Survival, he had learned, was not the soul's ultimate priority. He kept staring at the children. The way they were
posed reminded him of a Neanderthal grouping in the
Museum of Natural History. The moon was still up, and
they cast vaguely defined shadows like smudges of graph-
ite. Finally Mingolla turned away; the horizon was showing a distinct line of green darkness.

He had expected to be stabbed or pushed, to pinwheel
down and break against the Rió Dulce, its waters gone a
steely color beneath the brightening sky. But instead a
voice spoke in his ear: "Hey, macho." Squatting beside
him was a boy of fourteen or fifteen, with a swarthy
monkeylike face framed by tangles of shoulder-length dark
hair. Wearing tattered shorts. Coiled serpent tattooed on
his brow. He tipped his head to one side, then the other.
Perplexed. He might have been trying to see the true
Mingolla through layers of false appearance. He made a
growly noise in his throat and held up a knife, twisting it
this way and that, letting Mingolla observe its keen edge,
how it channeled the moonlight along its blade. An army-
issue survival knife with a brass-knuckle grip. Mingolla
gave an amused sniff.

The boy seemed alarmed by this reaction; he lowered
the knife and shifted away. "What you doing here, man?"
he asked.

A number of answers occurred to Mingolla, most demanding too much energy to voice; he chose the simplest.
"I like it here. I like the bridge."

The boy squinted at Mingolla. "The bridge is magic,"
he said. "You know this?"

"There was a time I might have believed you," said
Mingolla.

"You got to talk slow, man." The boy frowned. "Too
fast, I can't understan'."

Mingolla repeated his comment, and the boy said, "You
believe it, gringo. Why else you here?" With a planing
motion of his arm he described an imaginary continuance
of the bridge's upward course. "That's where the bridge

travels now. Don't have not'ing to do wit' crossing the river. It's a piece of white stone. Don't mean the same t'ing a bridge means.''

Mingolla was surprised to hear his thoughts echoed by someone who so resembled a hominid.

''I come here,'' the boy went on. ''I listen to the wind, hear it sing in the iron. And I know t'ings from it. I can see the future.'' He grinned, exposing blackened teeth, and pointed south toward the Caribbean. ''Future's that way, man.''

Mingolla liked the joke; he felt an affinity for the boy, for anyone who could manage jokes from the boy's perspective, but he couldn't think of a way to express his good feeling. Finally he said, ''You speak English well.''

''Shit! What you think? 'Cause we live in the jungle, we talk like animals? Shit!'' The boy jabbed the point of his knife into the concrete. ''I talk English all my life. Gringos they too stupid to learn Spanish.''

A girl's voice sounded behind them, harsh and peremptory. The other children had closed to within ten feet, their savage faces intent upon Mingolla, and the girl was standing a bit forward of them. She had sunken cheeks and deep-set eyes; ratty cables of hair hung down over her single-scoop breasts. Her hipbones tented up a rag of a skirt, which the wind pushed back between her legs. The boy let her finish, then gave a prolonged response, punctuating his words by smashing the brass-knuckle grip of his knife against the concrete, striking sparks with every blow.

''Gracela,'' he said to Mingolla, ''she wants to kill you. But I say, some men they got one foot in the worl' of death, and if you kill them, death will take you, too. And you know what?''

''What?'' said Mingolla.

''It's true. You and death''—the boy clasped his hands—''like this.''

''Maybe,'' Mingolla said.

''No 'maybe.' The bridge tol' me. Tol' me I be t'ankful if I let you live. So you be t'ankful to the bridge. That magic you don' believe, it save your ass.'' The boy lowered out of his squat and sat cross-legged. ''Gracela, she don' care 'bout you live or die. She jus' go 'gainst me 'cause when I leave here, she going to be chief. She's, you know, impatient.''

Mingolla looked at the girl. She met his gaze coldly: a witch-child with slitted eyes, bramble hair, and ribs poking out. ''Where are you going?'' he asked the boy.

''I have a dream I will live in the south; I dream I own a warehouse full of gold and cocaine.''

The girl began to harangue him again, and he shot back a string of angry syllables.

''What did you say?'' Mingolla asked.

''I say, 'Gracela, you give me shit, I going to fuck you and t'row you in the river.' '' He winked at Mingolla. ''Gracela she a virgin, so she worry 'bout that firs' t'ing.''

The sky was graying, pink streaks fading in from the east; birds wheeled up from the jungle below, forming into flocks above the river. In the half-light Mingolla saw that the boy's chest was cross-hatched with ridged scars: knife wounds that hadn't received proper treatment. Bits of vegetation were trapped in his hair, like primitive adornments.

''Tell me, gringo,'' said the boy. ''I hear in America there is a machine wit' the soul of a man. This is true?''

''More or less,'' said Mingolla.

The boy nodded gravely, his suspicions confirmed. ''I hear also America has builded a metal worl' in the sky.''

''They're building it now.''

''In the house of your president, is there a stone that holds the mind of a dead magician?''

Mingolla gave this due consideration. ''I doubt it,'' he said. ''But it's possible.''

Wind thudded against the bridge, startling him. He felt its freshness on his face and relished the sensation. That— the fact that he could still take simple pleasure from life— startled him more than had the sudden noise.

The pink streaks in the east were deepening to crimson and fanning wider; shafts of light pierced upward to stain the bellies of some low-lying clouds to mauve. Several of the children began to mutter in unison. A chant. They were speaking in Spanish, but the way their voices jumbled the words, it sounded guttural and malevolent, a language for trolls. Listening to them, Mingolla imagined them crouched around fires in bamboo thickets. Bloody knives lifted sunwards over their fallen prey. Making love in the green nights among fleshy Rousseau-like vegetation, while pythons with ember eyes coiled in the branches above their heads.

"Truly, gringo," said the boy, apparently still contemplating Mingolla's answers. "These are evil times." He stared gloomily down at the river; the wind shifted the heavy snarls of his hair.

Watching him, Mingolla grew envious. Despite the bleakness of his existence, this little monkey king was content with his place in the world, assured of its nature. Perhaps he was deluded, but Mingolla envied his delusion, and he especially envied his dream of gold and cocaine. His own dreams had been dispersed by the war. The idea of sitting and daubing colors onto canvas no longer held any real attraction for him. Nor did the thought of returning to New York. Though survival had been his priority all these months, he had never stopped to consider what survival portended, and now he did not believe he could return. He had, he realized, become acclimated to the war, able to breathe its toxins; he would gag on the air of peace and home. The war was his new home, his newly rightful place.

Then the truth of this struck him with the force of an illumination, and he understood what he had to do.

Baylor and Gilbey had acted according to their natures, and he would have to act according to his, which imposed upon him the path of acceptance. He remembered Tio Moises' story about the pilot and laughed inwardly. In a sense his friend—the guy he had mentioned in his unsent letter—had been right about the war, about the world. It was full of designs, patterns, coincidences, and cycles that appeared to indicate the workings of some magical power. But these things were the result of a subtle natural process. The longer you lived, the wider your experience, the more complicated your life became, and eventually you were bound in the midst of so many interactions, a web of circumstance and emotion and event, that nothing was simple anymore and everything was subject to interpretation. Interpretation, however, was a waste of time. Even the most logical of interpretations was merely an attempt to herd mystery into a cage and lock the door on it. It made life no less mysterious. And it was equally pointless to seize upon patterns, to rely on them, to obey the mystical regulations they seemed to imply. Your one effective course had to be entrenchment. You had to admit to mystery, to the incomprehensibility of your situation, and protect yourself against it. Shore up your web, clear it of blind corners, set alarms. You had to plan aggressively. You had to become the monster in your own maze, as brutal and devious as the fate you sought to escape. It was the kind of militant acceptance that Tio Moises' pilot had not had the opportunity to display, that Mingolla himself—though the opportunity had been his—had failed to display. He saw that now. He had merely reacted to danger and had not challenged or used forethought against it. But he thought he would be able to do that now.

He turned to the boy, thinking he might appreciate this insight into "magic," and caught a flicker of movement out of the corner of his eye. Gracela. Coming up behind the boy, her knife held low, ready to stab. In reflex, Mingolla flung out his injured hand to block her. The knife nicked the edge of his hand, deflected upward and sliced the top of the boy's shoulder.

The pain in Mingolla's hand was excruciating, blinding him momentarily; and then as he grabbed Gracela's forearm to prevent her from stabbing again, he felt another sensation, one almost covered by the pain. He had thought the thing inside his hand was dead, but now he could feel it fluttering at the edges of the wound, leaking out in the rich trickle of blood that flowed over his wrist. It was trying to worm back inside, wriggling against the flow, but the pumping of his heart was too strong, and soon it was gone, dripping on the white stone of the bridge.

Before he could feel relief or surprise or any way absorb what had happened, Gracela tried to pull free. Mingolla got to his knees, dragged her down and dashed her knife hand against the bridge. The knife skittered away. Gracela struggled wildly, clawing at his face, and the other children edged forward. Mingolla levered his left arm under Gracela's chin, choking her; with his right hand, he picked up the knife and pressed the point into her breast. The children stopped their advance, and Gracela went limp. He could feel her trembling. Tears streaked the grime on her cheeks. She looked like a scared little girl, not a witch.

"Puta!" said the boy. He had come to his feet, holding his shoulder, and was staring daggers at Gracela.

"Is it bad?" Mingolla asked. "The shoulder?"

The boy inspected the bright blood on his fingertips. "It hurts," he said. He stepped over to stand in front of Gracela and smiled down at her; he unbuttoned the top button of his shorts.

Gracela tensed.

"What are you doing?" Mingolla suddenly felt responsible for the girl.

"I going to do what I tol' her, man." The boy undid the rest of the buttons and shimmied out of his shorts; he was already half-erect, as if the violence had aroused him.

"No," said Mingolla, realizing as he spoke that this was not at all wise.

"Take your life," said the boy sternly. "Walk away."

A long powerful gust of wind struck the bridge; it seemed to Mingolla that the vibration of the bridge, the beating of his heart, and Gracela's trembling were driven by the same shimmering pulse. He felt an almost visceral commitment to the moment, one that had nothing to do with his concern for the girl. Maybe, he thought, it was an implementation of his new convictions.

The boy lost patience. He shouted at the other children, herding them away with slashing gestures. Sullenly, they moved off down the curve of the bridge, positioning themselves along the railing, leaving an open avenue. Beyond them, beneath a lavender sky, the jungle stretched to the horizon, broken only by the rectangular hollow made by the airbase. The boy hunkered at Gracela's feet. "Tonight," he said to Mingolla, "the bridge have set us together. Tonight we sit, we talk. Now, that's over. My heart say to kill you. But 'cause you stop Gracela from cutting deep, I give you a chance. She mus' make a judgmen'. If she say she go wit' you, we"—he waved toward the other children—"will kill you. If she wan' to stay, then you mus' go. No more talk, no bullshit. You jus' go. Understan'?"

Mingolla wasn't afraid, and his lack of fear was not born of an indifference to life, but of clarity and confidence. It was time to stop reacting away from challenges, time to meet them. He came up with a plan. There was no doubt that Gracela would choose him, choose a chance at life, no matter how slim. But before she could decide, he would kill the boy. Then he would run straight at the others: without their leader, they might not hang together. It wasn't much of a plan and he didn't like the idea of hurting the boy; but he thought he might be able to pull it off. "I understand," he said.

The boy spoke to Gracela; he told Mingolla to release her. She sat up, rubbing the spot where Mingolla had pricked her with the knife. She glanced coyly at him, then at the boy; she pushed her hair back behind her neck and thrust out her breasts as if preening for two suitors. Mingolla was astonished by her behavior. Maybe, he thought, she was playing for time. He stood and pretended to be shaking out his kinks, edging closer to the boy, who remained crouched beside Gracela. In the east a red fireball had cleared the horizon; its sanguine light inspired Mingolla, fueled his resolve. He yawned and edged closer yet, firming his grip on the knife. He would yank the boy's head back by the hair, cut his throat. Nerves jumped in his chest. A pressure was building inside him, demanding that he act, that he move now. He restrained himself. Another step should do it, another step to be absolutely sure. But as he was about to take that step, Gracela reached out and tapped the boy on the shoulder.

Surprise must have showed on Mingolla's face, because the boy looked at him and grunted laughter. "You t'ink she pick you?" he said. "Shit! You don' know Gracela, man. Gringos burn her village. She lick the devil's ass 'fore she even shake hands wit' you." He grinned, stroked her hair. " 'Sides, she t'ink if she fuck me good, maybe I say, 'Oh, Gracela, I got to have some more of that!' And who knows? Maybe she right."

Gracela lay back and wriggled out of her skirt. Between her legs, she was nearly hairless. A smile touched the corners of her mouth. Mingolla stared at her, dumbfounded.

"I not going to kill you, gringo," said the boy without looking up; he was running his hand across Gracela's stomach. "I tol' you I won' kill a man so close wit' death." Again he laughed. "You look pretty funny trying to sneak up. I like watching that."

Mingolla was stunned. All the while he had been gearing himself up to kill, shunting aside anxiety and revulsion, he had merely been providing an entertainment for the boy. The heft of the knife seemed to be drawing his anger into a compact shape, and he wanted to carry out his attack, to cut down this little animal who had ridiculed him; but humiliation mixed with the anger, neutralizing it. The poisons of rage shook him; he could feel every incidence of pain and fatigue in his body. His hand was throbbing, bloated and discolored like the hand of a corpse. Weakness pervaded him. And relief.

"Go," said the boy. He lay down beside Gracela, propped on an elbow, and began to tease one of her nipples erect.

Mingolla took a few hesitant steps away. Behind him, Gracela made a mewling noise and the boy whispered something. Mingolla's anger was rekindled—they had already forgotten him!—but he kept going. As he passed the other children, one spat at him and another shied a pebble. He fixed his eyes on the white concrete slipping beneath his feet.

When he reached the mid-point of the curve, he turned back. The children had hemmed in Gracela and the boy against the terminus, blocking them from view. The sky had gone bluish-gray behind them, and the wind carried their voices. They were singing: a ragged, chirpy song that sounded celebratory. Mingolla's anger subsided, his humiliation ebbed. He had nothing to be ashamed of; though he had acted unwisely, he had done so from a posture of strength and no amount of ridicule could diminish that. Things were going to work out. Yes they were! He would make them work out.

For a while he watched the children. At this remove, their singing had an appealing savagery and he felt a trace of wistfulness at leaving them behind. He wondered what would happen after the boy had done with Gracela. He was not concerned, only curious. The way you feel when you think you may have to leave a movie before the big finish. Will our heroine survive? Will justice prevail? Will survival and justice bring happiness in their wake? Soon the end of the bridge came to be bathed in the golden rays of the sunburst; the children seemed to be blackening and dissolving in heavenly fire. That was a sufficient resolution for Mingolla. He tossed Gracela's knife into the river and went down from the bridge in whose magic he no longer believed, walking toward the war whose mystery he had accepted as his own.

5

At the airbase, Mingolla took a stand beside the Sikorsky that had brought him to San Francisco de Juticlan; he had recognized it by the painted flaming letters of the words Whispering Death. He rested his head against the letter G and recalled how Baylor had recoiled from the letters, worried that they might transmit some deadly essence. Mingolla didn't mind the contact. The painted flames seemed to be warming the inside of his head, stirring up thoughts as slow and indefinite as smoke. Comforting thoughts that embodied no images or ideas. Just a gentle buzz of mental activity, like the idling of an engine. The base was coming to life around him. Jeeps pulling away from barracks; a couple of officers inspecting the belly of a cargo plane; some guy repairing a fork-lift. Peaceful, homey. Mingolla closed his eyes, lulled into a half-sleep, letting the sun and the painted flames bracket him with heat real and imagined.

Some time later—how much later, he could not be sure—a voice said, "Fucked up your hand pretty good, didn'tcha?"

The two pilots were standing by the cockpit door. In their black flight suits and helmets they looked neither weird nor whimsical, but creatures of functional menace. Masters of the Machine. "Yeah," said Mingolla. "Fucked it up."

"How'd ya do it?" asked the pilot on the left.

"Hit a tree."

"Musta been goddamn crocked to hit a tree," said the pilot on the right. "Tree ain't goin' nowhere if you hit it."

Mingolla made a non-committal noise. "You guys going up to the Farm?"

"You bet! What's the matter, man? Had enough of them wild women?" Pilot on the right.

"Guess so. Wanna gimme a ride?"

"Sure thing," said the pilot on the left. "Whyn't you climb on in front. You can sit back of us."

"Where your buddies?" asked the pilot on the right.

"Gone," said Mingolla as he climbed into the cockpit.

One of the pilots said, "Didn't think we'd be seein' them boys again."

Mingolla strapped into the observer's seat behind the co-pilot's position. He had assumed there would be a lengthy instrument check, but as soon as the engines had been warmed, the Sikorsky lurched up and veered northward. With the exception of the weapons systems, none of the defenses had been activated. The radar, the thermal imager and terrain display, all showed blank screens. A nervous thrill ran across the muscles of Mingolla's stomach as he considered the varieties of danger to which the pilots' reliance upon their miraculous helmets had laid them open; but his nervousness was subsumed by the whispery rhythms of the rotors and his sense of the Sikorsky's power. He recalled having a similar feeling of secure potency while sitting at the controls of his gun. He had never let that feeling grow, never let it rule him, empower him. He had been a fool.

They followed the northeasterly course of the river, which coiled like a length of blue-steel razor wire between jungle hills. The pilots laughed and joked, and the ride came to have the air of a ride with a couple of good ol' boys going nowhere fast and full of free beer. At one point the co-pilot piped his voice through the on-board speakers and launched into a dolorous country song.

"Whenever we kiss, dear, our two lips meet,
And whenever you're not with me, we're apart.
When you sawed my dog in half, that was depressin',
But when you shot me in the chest, you broke my heart."

As the co-pilot sang, the pilot rocked the Sikorsky back and forth in a drunken accompaniment, and after the song ended, he called back to Mingolla, "You believe this here son of a bitch wrote that? He did! Picks a guitar, too! Boy's a genius!"

"It's a great song," said Mingolla, and he meant it. The song had made him happy, and that was no small thing.

They went rocking through the skies, singing the first verse over and over. But then, as they left the river behind, still maintaining a northeasterly course, the co-pilot pointed to a section of jungle ahead and shouted, "Beaners! Quadrant Four! You got 'em?"

"Got 'em!" said the pilot. The Sikorsky swerved down toward the jungle, shuddered, and flame veered from beneath them. An instant later, a huge swath of jungle erupted into a gout of marbled smoke and fire. "Whee-oo!" the co-pilot sang out, jubilant. "Whisperin' Death strikes again!" With guns blazing, they went swooping through blowing veils of dark smoke. Acres of trees were burning, and still they kept up the attack. Mingolla gritted his teeth against the noise, and when at last the firing stopped, dismayed by this insanity, he sat slumped, his head down. He suddenly doubted his ability to cope with the insanity of the Ant Farm and remembered all his reasons for fear.

The co-pilot turned back to him. "You ain't got no call to look so gloomy, man," he said. "You're a lucky son of a bitch, y'know that?"

The pilot began a bank toward the east, toward the Ant Farm. "How you figure that?" Mingolla asked.

"I gotta clear sight of you, man," said the co-pilot. "I can tell you for true you ain't gonna be at the Farm much longer. It ain't clear why or nothin'. But I 'spect you gonna be wounded. Not bad, though. Just a goin'-home wound."

As the pilot completed the bank, a ray of sun slanted into the cockpit, illuminating the co-pilot's visor, and for a split-second Mingolla could make out the vague shadow of the face beneath. It seemed lumpy and malformed. His imagination added details. Bizarre growths, cracked cheeks, an eye webbed shut. Like a face out of a movie about nuclear mutants. He was tempted to believe that he had really seen this; the co-pilot's deformities would validate his prediction of a secure future. But Mingolla rejected the temptation. He was afraid of dying, afraid of the terrors held by life at the Ant Farm, yet he wanted no more to do with magic . . . unless there was magic involved in being a good soldier. In obeying the disciplines, in the practice of fierceness.

"Could be his hand'll get him home," said the pilot. "That hand looks pretty fucked up to me. Looks like a million-dollar wound, that hand."

"Naw, I don't get it's his hand," said the co-pilot. "Somethin' else. Whatever, it's gonna do the trick."

Mingolla could see his own face floating in the black plastic of the co-pilot's visor; he looked warped and pale, so thoroughly unfamiliar that for a moment he thought the face might be a bad dream the co-pilot was having.

"What the hell's with you, man?" the co-pilot asked. "You don't believe me?"

Mingolla wanted to explain that his attitude had nothing to do with belief or disbelief, that it signaled his intent to obtain a safe future by means of securing his present; but he couldn't think how to put it into words the co-pilot would accept. The co-pilot would merely refer again to his visor as testimony to a magical reality or perhaps would point up ahead where—because the cockpit plastic had gone opaque under the impact of direct sunlight—the sun now appeared to hover in a smoky darkness: a distinct fiery sphere with a streaming corona, like one of those cabalistic emblems embossed on ancient seals. It was an evil, fearsome-looking thing, and though Mingolla was unmoved by it, he knew the pilot would see in it a powerful sign.

"You think I'm lyin'?" said the co-pilot angrily. "You think I'd be bullshittin' you 'bout somethin' like this? Man, I ain't lyin'! I'm givin' you the good goddamn word!"

They flew east into the sun, whispering death, into a world disguised as a strange bloody enchantment, over the dark green wild where war had taken root, where men in combat armor fought for no good reason against men wearing brass scorpions on their berets, where crazy, lost men wandered the mystic light of Fire Zone Emerald and mental wizards brooded upon things not yet seen. The co-pilot kept the black bubble of his visor angled back toward Mingolla, waiting for a response. But Mingolla just stared, and before too long the co-pilot turned away.

LO, HOW AN OAK E'ER BLOOMING
by Suzette Haden Elgin

The power of faith is not to be underestimated. Science is often confronted with this—with recovery from incurable diseases, with events that run counter to prediction, with such items as Charles Fort or Immanual Velikovsky drag out into the light that confound conservative scientists. Here's a story of a miracle that may or may not be scientifically explained.

The day that she caused the miracle, Willow Severty was just plain tired. The women in the audience had been thrashing her a good half hour, and she'd been patiently bearing that, working away one word at a time toward somehow making them understand. But they were angry, at her and at the world, and they would not let Willow be. And when words failed her, Willow turned in utter weariness to deeds. One deed, to be precise.

She stood there sagging under the lash of their tongues, looking more and more battered and useless every minute. And then she gave herself a sort of shake, the way a tired animal will shake off water, and she raised her two hands before her to ward the other women off.

"That's enough," she said, standing there at the front of the room before the rows of chairs, beside the speaker's lectern. "That's more than enough. I'm sorry you're so dissatisfied with me, but I can't do any better. And I tell you you're wrong, with that laundry list of yours. I tell you there've been laws written down since first men could record their wickedness and their pride—and there has always been a way to make those laws no more than chicken scratches. Laws are like wars—of their making there is no end, and they're not worth warm spit. I tell you, what we need is a *miracle*."

They would have interrupted her if she'd paused, and she knew that, so she went right on.

"A miracle!" Willow said again. "Something that money and power and law and science and war *cannot do*. I've had enough of words—they ignore words anyway—it's time now for *signs*. Signs and portents. We need a miracle to show them. . . ." And she had smiled an exhausted smile and added, "Just a very small miracle will do. It doesn't have to be the levitation of the Pentagon. It will be sufficient if—" Willow looked around her, and out over their heads toward the windows at the back of the conference room, and she saw something that would serve her purpose. "It would be sufficient for that bare oak tree, standing out there naked in the snow, to burst all at once into glorious bloom. That would be miracle enough."

And she had drawn a deep breath, and it was so.

Well. It isn't every day that a big oak flowers in the middle of deep winter, or any other time. *This* flowering was preposterous; it offended all the sensibilities. The experts came in twos and threes—the botanists and the biologists and the linear and nonlinear dynamicists and the horticulturists and even the physicists. When the careful dissection of one of the perfect yellow blooms, as big as a teacup, proved beyond any question that it was indeed a real flower, a genuine plant form growing, and not—as they had first assumed—a creation of plastic or silk or some other man-made substance, there were cautious articles in the scholarly journals about the matter. With photographs of cross sections of the blossom and its parts under the microscope, from a variety of angles and points of view. The botanists, who'd been rather out of it the past decade or so, preened themselves in the center circle of scientific attention and faced the difficult questions.

"What *is* it, exactly?"

"An anomaly," they said solemnly.

"What *are* those flowers?"

"We don't know. Sorry."

"Well, how could such a thing *be*?"

"We don't know that either. That is the nature of an anomaly."

No one among the experts could explain why, when you took one golden flower from the tree, another formed immediately to take its place. They were soon sorry they had even mentioned that, because it drew great crowds of people determined to take home an armful of the wonderful blooms for themselves, and it became necessary to set up a permanent security guard around the oak, and build a ten-foot-tall steel chain-link fence and a small guardhouse, and set a Doberman loping along the perimeter of the secured area.

The media were less cautious then the scientists. The *National Enquirer* had a headline half a page high shrieking "ROSES BLOOM ON WINTER OAK! BISHOPS DECLARE MIRACLE!" Not that the blossoms were roses, or any other flower identifiable by man, but it was close enough. It conveyed the sense of the situation.

The commercial interests were not cautious either. By the end of the first week, even as the fence was still going up in the muddy trampled snow, there were hot dog stands and coffee-and-doughnut wagons. And there were souvenir vendors selling plastic oaks with yellow plastic flowers in a wide range of sizes, with a small plaque at the base reading "Replica of the Miracle Oak" in Gothic letters.

The churches were at first not only interested but eager. Miracles are not all that common, and a miracle that would go on twenty-four hours a day, standing up sturdily to every variety of scientific investigation, could not be said to exist anywhere else in the world today. But after the first wave of theologians and evangelists had spoken with Willow Severty, the churches drew back, bruised into a confused and uneasy silence.

The facts appeared to be beyond dispute; there had been forty-three witnesses inside the room when Willow called for that oak to bloom in the snow, and another dozen

passersby outside who could not possibly be claimed to
have been subject to mob hysteria. The women in the
room agreed unanimously that when they had turned to
look where Willow was looking, the tree had been there
before their eyes in its full blazing glory of golden flowers.
And the people outside were in full agreement—one minute there'd been an oak there, bare and black like any
other February oak; and then, all of an instant, the tree had
been covered branch after branch with flowers. The people
persisted, despite the scientists, in calling the flowers roses.
There seemed to be no question but that Willow Severty
had called those roses forth.

And so the churchmen went to Willow prepared to be
reverent, prepared to find *her* reverent, and they came
away in great confusion. The woman was not a Catholic,
she was not a Baptist, she was not even a Christian! The
sudden hopes of the Jews, the Muslims, the Druids, the
Wiccans—the list was endless—were promptly dashed;
Willow Severty accepted no denomination of any known
religion.

"Do you believe in God?" they asked her, and she
smiled at them and went on knitting. When they insisted
on an answer, Willow looked up with obvious distaste
and said, "Well, would you prefer to think I did it all by
my*self* gentlemen?" And she grinned in a way that offended them mightily, and added, "Or maybe you'd prefer
to say the devil did it?"

The idea that Evil might have power sufficient to set
that golden-flowered oak in the snow and maintain it there
was simply not tolerable. They writhed under the notion,
and rejected it for the sake of their sanity. On the other
hand, the idea that this unprepossessing female, dumpy
and middle-aged and badly dressed, had managed to call
forth a miracle without assistance from any organized
system of religious doctrine was also intolerable. Of course
she had not done it herself; that was silly. But Whom had
Willow Severty called upon?

They demanded to know if she could do it again, and
she did laugh at them then.

"Gentlemen," she said, "can you do it *once*?"

And when they admitted that they could not, she told

them she would wait. "You do it once," she said, "and then we'll see if I can do it twice."

They called her impudent, and blasphemous, and she laid it out for them. "You can't do it," she said. "Not for any amount of money. Not with the most powerful weapon in your arsenals. Not with the most advanced of your technologies. Not with all your mighty faiths combined. Perhaps it's time you reconsidered the value of all those things, gentlemen."

And the oak went right on blooming.

Seedlings came up around its base and were taken away in armored cars to be planted in greenhouse laboratories—where they died at once. Planted outside, set in carefully guarded circles of earth, they died equally promptly. Subjected to grafting, subjected to layering, subjected to cloning, subjected to techniques so advanced that they were military secrets—they died. Every attempt to produce or reproduce them failed. When the time came for acorns, the oak had them in abundance, side by side with the steadfast flowers, but dissection and analysis showed the acorns to be only the ordinary acorns of ordinary oaks; and seedlings forced from those acorns were ordinary seedlings. It might be a century before those seedlings burst into flower, if indeed that was what they were destined someday to do.

It wasn't enough to say, "Oh, it's just a new species of oak, which flowers when it grows to a certain age." Because it was much worse than that; it violated every natural law. There were plants known to grow with nearly miraculous speed, other and entirely acceptable plants. But there is no plant that bears flowers that never were buds and that never fade or fall; there are no *changeless* plants. True, if you took a bloom away from the oak, it faded and died like any flower fades and dies; but so long as the flowers were left on the tree, they were immune to all natural processes. High winds did not shake them loose; searing heat did not make them limp or brown the edges of their petals; the bitterest cold in no way altered their texture or fragrance. A laser would burn one away, as would a torch; but however many you burned (subject the entire time to furious shouts from worshipers demanding that you cease your desecration), another perfect flower

would form to replace the burned ones the moment you set
the implement of destruction aside. And it was the same
with chemicals, with electric currents, with sound waves,
with every mechanism the experts could devise. They were
afraid to try a nuclear weapon, right there in the middle of
Madison, Wisconsin, but they had no reason to think the
results of such a trial would have been any different.

Pressed for comment, Willow Severty said, "Well, loving kindness, what you all call 'grace,' is like that. The
more you use it, the more of it there is." And she went
back to her struggle to make ends meet, while the scientists applied for ever larger grants to study the oak tree.

Some of the women found it strange that the offers
made to Willow in the first few days—the book contracts,
the movie and television contracts, the proposals for Willow
Severty dolls and lunch boxes and bumper stickers and
coffee mugs—were all withdrawn before Willow could
decide whether any of them were worth signing.

Willow didn't find it strange. She had been a little
surprised that the media hoopla had been allowed to continue as long as it had, once it became obvious that the oak
was no seven-day wonder but proposed to *endure*. And as
the day approached that would mark the one-year anniversary of the miracle, Willow bought a ticket on the Greyhound bus and took her knitting and withdrew as quietly as
she could to a place where nobody would expect her to go.
Willow had good sense, and endless patience; she went to
the slums of Detroit.

What are we going to *do?*"
The question hovered like a banner in the air, over the
heads of the assembled members of Project Bad Oak. They
would have been pleased if an answer had hovered too, but
there was no answer. Everything had been tried, and everything had failed. The woman Willow Severty had brought
the oak tree upon the world, and no amount of money or
force of technology had proved adequate to duplicate or
explain away what she had done. A steady pressure on the
channels for dissemination of information had purged them
of all mention of the miracle or its worker, but that was
not going to be enough.

The tree was still *there*. It still *loomed*. Anyone who chose to go to Madison, Wisconsin, could see that for himself. The deadly chemicals injected into the tree's roots by stealth, in the dead of night, had had no effect at all. Sound waves, microwaves, electric shocks, salt—yes, salt, at the suggestion of an agent who knew what salt did to otherwise indestructible purple thistles on his farm—all had failed to bother the tree. It could be described only as *flourishing*.

And the people talked. In a variety of languages and social dialects, they talked, but they were all saying the same thing in the end: "Huh. *You* can't *do* that, can you? Damn straight, you can't!" People, the mass of people, were snickering.

Church attendance had fallen off, as had college enrollments and enlistments in the military. Registrations to vote were down by several percent, as were crimes of violence and hospitalizations. Physicians were reporting a decline in number of patients seen; retail sales were off just a tad; lawyers languished for lack of altercations. It was all small numbers, and any one of these taken by itself would not have been worth noticing. But as a general and pervasive trend, it was serious.

"Gentlemen," said the secretary of defense, "what we are seeing is the steady growth of a nationwide disrespect for all the institutions of our society. *Something must be done.*"

"But how the hell did—"

"Never mind how!" hissed the secretary of defense. "We don't *know* how, and we don't have time to worry about it. Willow Severty told that gaggle of hysterical feminists that a flowering oak tree was all they needed to make us look pathetic. And she was *right!*" We can't start what she started, we can't do what she did, and we look like impotent asses. We look like *wimps*. We have to stop it, before it gets out of hand. And because what we're dealing with here is not civilized or decent, but is primitive superstition, we cannot allow the first anniversary of Willow Severty's so-called miracle to arrive. We *cannot* allow that kind of symbol to be created in the public mind."

"Why 'so-called' miracle, Mister Secretary?" asked the priest who sat there as representative of religion.

"Oh, shut up, Father," said the rest of the men, and he did. It was hard to be strong from a position of total bewilderment. The priest was *absolutely* certain that God Almighty Himself had set that tree aflower and kept it so, but *why?* Why would He play so monstrous a joke upon His faithful, and for so *long?* And why had He not ended it in response to the thousands of contemplative religious praying round the clock these past six months for Him to do so? It was whispered that in the church that an abbess—an abbess!—had been heard to say, "Be not afraid; God is not mocked.' . . . . Oh, yeah?" The good father shuddered, and he crossed himself discreetly.

"Well, what do you propose we *do?*" Half a dozen of the officials present asked the same question as if they had rehearsed, all of them sounding fretful, as befit the powerful made to look foolish by the powerless.

"We're going to cut the godforsaken cursed oak tree *down!*" declared the secretary of defense, and the priest crossed himself again, too horrified at the "godforsaken" and the "cursed" to concern himself about discretion.

"That's *all?*" asked a much-decorated general in the silence. "Just cut it down?"

"Well . . . not quite all," admitted the secretary. "A story has been leaked to the press and will be appearing tomorrow. . . . It seems the tree has been discovered to be giving off powerful carcinogens into the air." He glanced at a three-by-five card in his hand and began reeling off the statistics. Leukemias, up 40 percent in Madison. Cancer of the breast, up 80 percent. Cancer of the uterus and cervix, up 60 percent. Cancer of—"

"We follow you, Mister Secretary," observed the general. "Who's breaking the story?"

"The *Washington Post*, CBS News, and *Reader's Digest*. And the *National Enquirer*."

"Dear heaven, they'll call it witchcraft!" objected the priest.

"So?" the secretary of defense sneered. "Let them! We will have *stopped* it, Father."

"Are you sure?"

"You betcha. Unless someone here can convince me that there's one good reason to do otherwise—and it will take some doing, gentlemen, I warn you—at precisely 0200 tomorrow morning, that tree will be cut to the ground, incinerated to the last centimeter of its smallest twig and root, and the ground where it grew will be sterilized. And after *that*, my friends, we will pave the entire area over, right out to the perimeter, and put up a Kentucky Fried Chicken place where the tree used to be. Madison, Wisconsin can use another fried-chicken place. And another parking lot."

He shuffled his three-by-five cards, raised his eyebrows, and waited. And then he said, "Well? Does this mean nobody intends to argue?"

Six months earlier, they might have argued. The scientists would have demanded more time to study the phenomenon. The representatives of the humanities might have pleaded for restraint in the face of such magnificence, for awe in the presence of such mystery. The men from business and industry might have hesitated—there is something about an apparently inexhaustible resource that might, under adequate controls and in the proper hands, repay further investigation. And so on. But now they were wiser men, even the men of the cloth, and they knew a menace when they saw one a-blooming. They offered no objections.

At two o'clock in the morning, the surrounding population already evacuated by grim law-enforcement and emergency personnel announcing a life-threatening emergency that could not be explained for lack of time, it began. A crew of men who were more uncomfortable than they would have been willing to admit cut and burned the oak, flat to the ground. A bulldozer made certain no least thread of a root was left, turning the ground over not once but three times, at the direct order of the Department of Defense, although the source of the order for public information was the EPA. A sterilizing substance was spread over the barren earth, and a concrete mixer brought in and parked at the ready on the site. When dawn broke over Madison, Wisconsin, the morning news carried reports of a terrible danger safely eliminated by Our Tax Dollars at

Work. Along with a picture of the blasted earth where the Doberman now ran superfluously inside the fence, with nothing left to guard but a bulldozer and a cement mixer.

There was outrage for a few days, but as people read the story in the *Reader's Digest,* and listened to CBS News, the word spread and the protests died quickly. From the pulpits, people were gravely reminded that the Holy Bible not only admits that witches are real but declares that they must not be allowed to live. In Detroit, Willow Severty smiled to herself when the agents turned up and began following her about. She understood that it would be contrary to the national interest for her to become a martyr during this brief period before the whole foolish episode faded from the public consciousness.

The feminists muttered, "All the same, she *did* it, and none of *them* could do it," but nobody pays any attention to feminists except other feminists. And the feminists themselves had never cared much for Willow Severty; they muttered awhile, but in the backs of their minds, they were thinking again of legislation.

So it was that not a single camera crew was present on the anniversary of the miracle of the oak tree in Madison, Wisconsin. Only the construction crew putting up the Kentucky Fried Chicken place, and one lone security guard, and the bored Doberman, were there when the ground began to heave and quake under the concrete. They clung to the framework of the fried-chicken place as best they could, and got out of the way as best they could.

It was a darned shame that Willow Severty could not have been there to see the spectacle. The great oak rose straight up into the air where the chicken-frying machines were to have been, its sturdy roots shoving the spanking new parking lot's surface aside and piling it up along the fissures. The tree was heavily laden with yellow flowers that looked very much like roses, and the crisp February air was filled with their fragrance. The snow was a nice touch, falling softly to cover up the broken concrete and lightly lace the edges of the blossoms' petals with white. It was a regular picture postcard, doing Madison proud; it was positively a symbol, there in the center of town. Peace on earth, it said. Good will to men.

DREAM IN A BOTTLE

By Jerry Meredith
and D. E. Smirl

More and more SF writers are discovering that there seems to be one thing faster than light—thought. For we have noted several interstellar tales based on some kind of mental projection or tie-in. This is not quite that sort of thing; it is a rather unique approach to the problem, written by two new writers who parlay dream fulfillment fantasies with galactic expeditioning—a neat marriage of opposites.

The sleepcase lid purred back. I sat up, pulled the plug from the back of my skull, stretched, and noted Buster's pale frightened eyes as he lowered himself into his own cocoon.

"Bad dreams?" I asked, grinning.

"I can't stand flying with the Ancient Mariner," he complained. "I always feel like I'm on the edge of losing it."

"What happened this time?" I clambered out of my cocoon and did a few knee bends to banish the cold from my joints.

"He won't stay in his bottle," Buster grumbled as he snapped in his plug in preparation for debriefing. "He keeps bleeding into the other dreams. I had a bad time keeping the other jinn clean. I thought they screened those brains before putting them in our ships."

"Good brains aren't necessary to run a ship," I said. "Just brains that run good."

"Then you'd better hope these run like your sweetest fantasy. The Sheik found a cloud straight ahead. We'll be hitting it in just three hours."

"What's its density?"

"About three and a half per cubic meter. Dessert time for the engines."

"Good," I yawned, feeling the chill finally burn from my bones. "We can use the kick."

"Keep your eye on the Mariner," Buster warned as he wiggled into his restraint harness. "That jinn just doesn't know his limits."

"But we needed someone who could trim the sails," I answered innocently.

Buster snorted, then jabbed the lid control. Through muffled plastic, just before the white cloud of cold sleep enveloped him, he growled, "Good luck. You know the Commander. Some people have to have a problem or they go crazy."

I headed for the bridge. The muscles in my legs un-kinked, and the nightmares—those formless memories that haunted even my cold sleep—faded. So the Mariner was bleeding into the other bottles. That was one jinn we didn't want loose. It was bad enough keeping track of eight separate fantasies without worrying about contamination. But then, it was my job to worry about it. During my tour of the bridge I monitored the jinn to make sure the Ancient Mariner, the Sheik of Araby, Sweet Alice, Bullwinkle, Naugahyde, Sigmund, Thoreau and Escoffier stayed happy as they dreamed us through space. They tuned the ramscoops, trimmed the sails, searched out food for the engines, and kept all the pretty lights on the life support modules blinking merrily. And people like Buster and Sonya and me tried to keep them from catching on to what had been done to them.

Because they weren't really jinn and they weren't kept in bottles. They were brains who labored as living comput-ers, working in concert with the ship to control systems far too important for any machine to handle. And their bottles were merely psychological restraints locking them into fantasies related to their part in running the ship—a kind of Boölean Psychology that let them go so far and no further.

At least, that's how it was supposed to work.

And a ship with jinn who learned the truth—that they had been ripped from dying bodies, placed in nutrient tanks and fooled into believing they were living perfectly normal lives, complete with friends, lovers, occupations, pleasures . . . well, such a ship died an ugly death. It had happened before. It could happen again. That's why we were careful.

Halfway to the bridge, I heard a rumble speed through the ship. The sails must have slammed through a rich field of hydrogen. Delighted, the engines gulped it down, belched it out the back, and gave us a touch more acceleration toward our rendezvous with Zeta Reticuli IV.

On the bridge, I plugged into my womb and checked the monitors. The Mariner was back where he belonged, for the time being. Good thing, too. I didn't want him shutting down the sails or leaving them spread out over five hundred kilometers of space. The magnetic fields might rip to shreds like the canvas for which they were metaphors—and a ship without sails . . .

The Ancient Mariner and Sweet Alice and all the others were nicknames invented by a shadowy figure back on Triton Base, a J. R. Mayhew, whom I'd never met but knew by virtue of the original—and perceptive—labels he'd given the jinn. I, too, had pet names for the separate systems. But as the voyage continued, I found myself thinking of them in J. R.'s terms rather than my own.

For example, the Ancient Mariner and his wife, a charming, tiny woman with wind-burned hair and nets of wrinkles fanning out from the corner of her eyes, sailed a twenty-foot ketch through the islands of the South Pacific. The seas were usually calm and the islands were always inhabited by primitive but friendly natives. Occasionally, the computer threw in a little storm just to enhance the illusion. Winds howled. Palm trees bent and hissed. The sea boiled over sand and reef. And the Mariner and his wife, safe in a hut provided by the island's chief, would make love and afterwards talk about how romantic their trip was, how much like paradise was the life they led.

But what was Sweet Alice to think when she came out of her forest, a world populated by dwarves, elves, sentient animals, and talking teapots, to find a seascape where fields had been, and a man walking on a beach who looked too real to be a part of her world?

No, that wouldn't do at all. I needed some way to strengthen the taboos keeping him in his fantasy. It wouldn't be easy. The Mariner, like most sailors, was naturally curious and too intelligent to believe in falling off the edge of the world.

I saw it was time to awaken my partner for the tour. "Good morning," I crooned perversely. "Bid your sweet dreams farewell and come back to the world of work. In short, haul your butt out of that case."

"Michael? Where are you?"

"Where else? On the bridge." I checked a screen. Alex had climbed out of her case and was pushing herself through a rigorous set of exercises. Small, wiry, with tiny breasts outlined against her jumpsuit, and black, curly hair that accentuated her boyish face, she reminded me of a child working too hard to pull her weight in a world of adults. She bobbed up and down on muscular dancer's legs, her face tight as she concentrated on getting every muscle in the right configuration. She always wanted everything just right. That's what made her such a pain in the ass.

"Any problems?" she asked.

"The Mariner again. I dispatched a couple of cretins to make sure there's no hardware malfunction."

"Any contamination?"

"Buster said an albatross showed up at the Queen of Hearts' banquet."

"Liar." She glared at me through the monitor, hands on hips breathing evenly. No sense of humor.

Then I told her about the cloud. *That* brought a smile to her face. "It's about time we had some good luck," she said. "I'll be right up."

The monitor blinked. "Take your time," I muttered. Alone, I stretched out my senses along the circuits of the ship. I felt what the sensors sensed, saw what few men could ever imagine. Our sails glowed a deep purple, ultraviolet batwings beating against an eternal vacuum. My eyes filled with stars, my fingers throbbed with each molecular annihilation. I could have remained there forever. The Company didn't need jinn, just men like me. Let them argue with their board members about applications of space technology. I didn't care. I wanted to see what was out there. I wanted to know what moved in the darkness. Maybe there was chronite in the atmosphere of Zeta Reticuli IV, maybe not. But to see it for myself, a dozen years down the line, that was my ambition.

Six-tenths Cee. One hundred and eighty thousand kilometers per second, or four and a half times around the world in the space between the ticks of a Grandfather clock. And in less than an hour, we were going to crash through a gas cloud at that velocity. Probably, it would hurt. We were trading our margin of safety for time, for a hundred kilotons of raw hydrogen snared by our sails, funneled into magnetic confinement, then fused into a second spear of thrust. We would gain a three percent increase in acceleration, and a corresponding reduction in time-until-turnover. It would hasten deceleration for the stately pass through the Zeta Reticuli system, give us time for a leisurely look at Reticuli IV and to launch the jinn called Snow White, sleeping now, into orbit over that tantalizing blue-white planet, while her seven drones went down to the surface and beamed data which she would pass on to us as we accelerated away. If we lived. If the collision with the cloud off our bow didn't smash us into stardust.

"Come down from the mountain, Michael. You can't have the stars all to yourself."

"Huh?"

"I like tasting the stars as much as you do, but why hasn't the Mariner reconfigured our sails?"

Alex, settling into her womb, was staring at me. "I asked you. . . ."

"I know what you asked. Reconfiguration isn't scheduled for another two and a half minutes."

"That's cutting it too close."

"Don't tell me about it. Argue with the manual." I sent the lines of text to her monitor, then turned back to study the words flashing across mine. The steady cadence of flickering letters seemed hypnotic, and I had to shake my head to clear my thinking.

"Where've you been?" Alexandria asked once she'd scanned the entry. "For a while, your face was as slack as your gut."

"I was thinking," I snapped. "And any time you want to go a couple of rounds with this slack gut. . . ."

"You were philosophizing again. And as to going a couple rounds, any time you think you're good enough for one. . . ." She stopped, looked away. Our bickering had taken a sudden nasty turn in a direction neither of us wanted to pursue. "I'm sorry, Michael. I didn't mean anything by it."

"The Mariner's trimming the sails now," I said. Then I watched as the sails retreated toward the ship. Their color faded, shifting from the normal deep purple through a dusky pink to mottled orange, then regained intensity to settle into a cloudy russet—a smaller, angry funnel poised to slash its narrow way through the cloud in our path.

FIVE MINUTES TO CONTACT.

The words crawled across my monitor, then were replaced by a microsecond countdown displayed in the lower right-hand corner of the screen. I tried to imagine what contact would be like, but gave up. My imagination runs too easily to scenes of Armageddon.

"Thruster termination in ninety seconds, Michael. Check your restraints."

As I fumbled with the stickystrips, I asked, "Why do we do this, Alex?"

"So we won't float around the bridge, Michael." Her hands were stabbing at her controls. Running Naugahyde was her job in this situation.

"Very funny, Alex. And you know that wasn't what I meant. I was asking why we snap at each other. Every time we have a watch together we try to rip each other to pieces."

"Don't do this to me," she gritted. "Not now. Do you

have any idea how difficult it is to turn the main thruster off?''

"Of course I do. I modify Sweet Alice's fantasy, or the Mariner's, or Bullwinkle's when I have to." *And I could handle Naugahyde's too, if the computer would just let me,* I told myself.

"I know what you're thinking, Michael, but you don't ever change the core of anyone's fantasy. For years, Naugahyde has been driving down the highway in his sports car, picking up pretty female hitchhikers. That fantasy is the core of his autonomic operation of the main thruster, and when it shuts down, he's going to experience that as an interruption of his journey. It's going to take all my concentration to keep him from trying to start his car before we're through that cloud. So will you please leave me alone?''

"I'm sorry I bothered you," I answered. She was right, of course, so I turned my attention outside once more and ignored the heat in my face. Some day, I'd be over her. Some day. I stared at the stars, blue-shifted ahead, hard points of diamond brilliance converging in our path. Their apparent dislocation only hinted at the starbow that waited for the crew who could coax another twenty-five percent from the all-too-primitive hydrogen rams we flew. And somewhere, millions of kilometers ahead, a star waited to be born from a cloud of gas. But we'd mine that cloud first.

It came so quickly, I'm not sure I ever really saw it. One moment, stars and emptiness. The next, a shimmering translucence pierced by the angry protuberance our sails had become. Then blindness, agony, a scream so profound I shall be haunted by its sound forever. They say there is only silence in the vacuum of space, but at the leading edges of our sails, at those points where they slammed into the heart of that cloud, the molecules of hydrogen accumulated into an incandescent plasma that shrieked and howled and moaned into the darkness like a chorus of mistuned violins.

On impact, the ship draped me with restraint webbing, an indestructible gossamer of molecule-chain. Startled by its sudden touch, blinded by the flash of collision, deaf-

ened by the echoes still pounding through the hull, I
fought the clinging web for a brief eternity. Then, training
took over and I relaxed. The engine rumbled, roared,
crescendoed—a perfect restart, thanks to Alexandria's brilliant touch.

The web dissolved. I fell back into my womb, exhausted. One by one, the bridge consoles flickered back to
life. Waiting for my vision to clear, I called, "Alex?
Alexandria? Are you okay?"

In a peculiar, quavering voice, she answered, "I'm not
sure, Michael."

Muscles complaining, nerves still shaken, I turned to
look her way. A figure dripped water between us. Tall,
craggily masculine, with a deep tan and white hair, he
wore sun-bleached pants and a soggy cotton shirt that
clung to broad shoulders and thick biceps. Silver hair
billowed from the opening of the shirt. Astonishment widened his blue eyes, and as he glanced from Alex to me, he
seemed breathless.

"What's happened?" he blurted. "Where's my Marcia?"

Alexandria's mouth had dropped open, and I suppose
mine had, too. The Ancient Mariner was loose on the
bridge; and if we did anything to make him suspect that
the seas he sailed were not of Earth, then looking foolish
would be the least of our worries.

I steadied my voice. "This is a dream," I said. "A
nightmare. In a moment you'll wake up and everything
will be fine."

"What kind of place is this?" He turned his gaze from
us to the monitors. The lights dripped red, green, blue
over his features. I think that's when I really began to get
scared. He was so solid—so real! I'd heard of bizarre
superimpositions creeping into experiments, ghost-like images occurring for a few seconds in labs. But not in real
life. Not on a ramship dependent on sane jinn to keep its
heart and organs running.

I'd never been in this kind of situation. No one had.
Then Alex, her voice edging toward hysteria, asked, "What
are we going to do, Michael?"

"Find out what happened."

I took a deep breath and dove into the Mariner's fantasy. Nothing. Just darkness. Then, a dance of stars above, rising, falling. Water, water everywhere. Wavelets slapped against a capsized hull. Debris bobbed in lazy swells. The collision with the cloud had blown a hole in his bottle. Frantically, I searched for the Mariner or his wife . . . and found nothing. He had broken free from the dream completely.

So where was he? He couldn't have an existence separate from his fantasy. Jinn weren't supposed to get out, no matter how hard you rubbed the bottle.

Unless I was dreaming, and he had slipped into my dream.

DON'T THINK ABOUT IT! I screamed to myself. *DON'T GET LOST DOWN THE RABBIT HOLE!*

The Sheik of Araby didn't give me any time to worry about rabbit holes. His sensors found something new and he told us about it. Warning bells, lights, and buzzers went off all at once. Alex scanned the information first. "Sweet Mother," she breathed. "There was another cloud hiding behind the first one. Not as thick, but thick enough. We'll be colliding in eight minutes."

The Mariner took a step forward, bunched his hands into fists. "This is some kind of a ship, isn't it? You rammed my boat. You murdered my wife."

"It's a dream," I insisted. "Nothing more." Somehow, I had to get the Mariner back in his bottle so he could trim the sails. "Alex—"

"Don't bother me now. I have to get us ready for the second cloud. Naugahyde isn't going to believe it—engine trouble twice in one day." Her finger brushed connodes. "Six minutes."

The ship shuddered, plowing through a fringe of the cloud ahead. Like a moan from high in the throat, the engines hummed and whined and threw us forward, ever closer to Cee.

"Not bad," Alexandria said grimly. "It could be a lot worse. It's thin, maybe two million kilometers through. Just a wisp of smoke. It's probably a shred off the main cloud."

* * *

Mesmerized by the data surging across my monitor, I almost forgot the Mariner. Then he moved. At the edge of my vision something shifted; a flash of color changed shape. When I snapped my head around, he was standing next to Alexandria, muscles bunched tight in his neck, rage purpling his face.

"Tell me what happened to my wife!" he demanded. Then he reached down and tore the filament from the back of Alexandria's head.

Alex disapppeared.

The Mariner froze. The filament fell from his hand. Blood decorated its socket. "Where is she?" he asked.

"Gone to Hell," I answered. "And she's taking us with her."

I felt cold. A quick glance at the monitors revealed some of the life support systems were already deteriating. There was no telling what damage had been done to the cerebral centers. But that wasn't the worst of it—I was no longer in control of the ship. Alex, my link with control, was gone, dead or catatonic, her fantasy shattered by the rage of the Mariner.

FOUR MINUTES flashed on the monitor. Thank you.

"She's dead," said the Mariner. He coughed, wiped the back of his hand across his mouth, then rubbed at his temples. "The seas were high. She was not a strong swimmer."

He mourned his fantasy wife. I mourned the woman I loved. Who is to say who felt the sharpest pang? My woman's name rolled from my memory with an easy rhythm. Alexandria Lightfoot N'komo, whose ancestors had maneuvered dugouts down the Niger, crept through Appalachian forests, fired on Confederates from Cemetery Ridge, marched in Selma, mined asteroids, walked the high steel as they built the cities of Titan. Alexandria, who might have wanted the stars more than I did. Against all rules we had fallen in love and considered ourselves fortunate that, together, we would see wonders beyond belief.

Until her accident.

Her flitter stalled as she attempted an unpowered landing on a strip near LookLookie on Titan. A sudden thermal crumpled one wing and all she could do was hang on.

Unavoidable, the board of inquiry ruled. Structural failure due to catastrophic stress.

They pulled her out, more dead than alive. No way to repair the damage, another board ruled. They invoked the clause written into our contracts, removed her brain, and set her up in a bottle. She was part of my ship when we launched for Zeta Reticuli IV. I was there to reinforce her fantasy.

She had what she always wanted. All I had was dross.

The command console yanked me out of my regrets. I had an incoming message. I just couldn't think of anyone who would be calling me.

"What do you want?" I growled.

"Michael?" a weak voice answered. "Is that you?"

"Alex? Where are you? Are you all right?"

"I don't know. I'm in a telephone booth. I think it's in Bullwinkle's bottle. I'm frightened. Michael, how can I be here?"

"Systems malfunction. Don't worry. You're right here on the bridge. The Mariner must have caused a line surge that blew you right into the most available dream." It was gobbledygook, but she was frightened, and there was a chance she'd believe it.

"Michael, I don't like this place."

"Look around. Tell me what you see. Try to help me wee where you are."

She hesitated a moment, then began. "I'm in a large city. Tall buildings. Paved streets filled with cars. And crowds. Everywhere I look, people pushing, shoving, hurrying. I understand some of what they say, but I can't read anything. I think the signs are written in English."

"Is there a large, red lighted sign high up on one of the nearby buildings?"

"I can't see one like that."

"Please, Alex," I urged. "You have to help me."

I suffered for long seconds before she spoke again. "Yes, I see the sign. Almost straight overhead."

"Good! Hold tight. I'll be there in a minute."

THREE MINUTES TO CONTACT. Damn it to hell! Not enough time . . . Alex was trapped in Bullwinkle's bottle, which meant she was standing on a street-corner in Manhattan some time during the latter half of the twentieth century—a Manhattan, however, formed from a Peter Max poster, in which war, murder and television blended with caped crusaders, the Fab Four, and a flying squirrel who doubled as an existential prophet. I spent as little time as possible in that dream. Unlike the other jinn who endured with pleasure a structured, almost ritualized fantasy, Bullwinkle reveled in a world in which everything was constantly in flux; forming, reforming, painting fantastic shapes on a bizarre canvas. Alex couldn't stay there long and remain sane. No one could, except Bullwinkle.

As I collected my thoughts, the Mariner moved so close I smelled the salt spray trapped in his clothes. "Are you real?" he asked, choking back a sob.

With that, I knew how to get him back in his bottle—if I had enough time. "I'm not real," I explained. "None of this is." Then I jabbed my finger at one of the monitors. "That's what's real."

In the screen, it was dawn. A rising sun gleamed off the sluggishly heaving swells with a slick light. Off to one side, a capsized hull drifted, losing its struggle with the elements to stay afloat. Beside me, the Mariner sucked in his breath.

"There it is," I said. "A raft."

"There was no raft."

"Of course there was." I made a raft, and a swell lifted it, tilting it for a split second. There was no one inside.

"She's gone," he said. "She didn't make it to the raft."

"Wait. Watch."

The light spread across the water like oil. The raft rose, fell. A hand broke the surface. Fingers scrabbled at the gunwales, clutched at the yielding rubber. A face popped out of the water and gasped.

"Marcia," the Mariner said. "My Marcia."

The woman struggled to pull herself into the raft, but she was near the end of her endurance. Her grasp on the gunwale loosened and she fell back into the sea.

"*You're* in the raft," I said. "If you don't wake from this nightmare and take her hand, your wife is going to drown. *You* have to save her. No one else can."

I turned my head from the monitor to check his reaction. He wasn't there. Back on the screen I saw him scramble out of the bottom of the raft and hoist his Marcia in. It was going to work, but I had no time to gloat. There was a sail to trim, and as yet, none on the raft.

I made oars for him, telescoping metal tubes that formed a crude mast when fit together and clamped upright in a socket on the floor of the raft. A small canvas bag contained a lightweight sail and rigging. I watched the Mariner assemble his sail, but before he could raise it, a squall moved in. He tied everything securely and waited for conditions to improve. His wife, clutched in his arms, looked into his uncertain face and smiled. I disengaged from their bottle.

Next problem. "Alex?" I shouted. No answer. A readout marched across the monitor, telling me I was running out of time. I stretched out my senses. From my previous excursions in Bullwinkle's Manhattan, I knew exactly where to find Alex. That is, if she hadn't moved, or if Bullwinkle hadn't redesigned the city. I uncapped the bottle and jumped in. Light boiled up, and sound, and smell. Crowds surged forward. Vehicles raced by, filling the air with the stench of burned petroleum. And within this sea of harsh noise and bright color, Alex, tiny and vulnerable, cowered in a telephone booth while an irate fat man in a cowboy outfit beat on the glass doors and screamed at her to leave.

"Alex!" I screamed over the din.

Her chin popped up. "Michael? Where are you?"

"Right here." The wall of the booth shimmered. A hazy glow spread over the glass, and when it faded, only a doorway remained. I reached for her. "Come on! We've run out of time!"

A shudder rippled through her body. For an instant her knees buckled and I started through the doorway to take her out. But she backed away, a piercing, cryptic look in her eyes. "I'm one of them, aren't I, Michael?"

"Don't be silly. Come on, Alex. You have to shut off the main engines."

She shook her head. "No, Michael. The Mariner pulled my plug, and now I'm not on the bridge. I'm here. That means one of us, maybe both of us, lives in a bottle. Tell me the truth, Michael. *Am I one of them?*''

She was right. She was always right. I couldn't lie to her. She knew my voice, my expressions. In the time we'd spent together, she'd unravelled all my secrets. And only my pain—knowing her truth—kept us bickering.

''Yes,'' I said. ''You're a jinn. But, listen! You have to come back. If you don't work on Naugahyde's fantasy, Buster and Sonya and all the others are going to die. *I'm* going to die.'' I beckoned, I begged through the doorway. ''Please. Come back.''

The line outside the booth was growing nasty. Someone in the back said, ''Watch me pull a rabbit out of my hat . . . ooops! Wrong hat!''

Tears wet her face. With a ragged sob, Alex took my hand, and I dragged her through.

Somewhere in the Nevada desert between Tonopah and Goldfield, the driver of a propane truck pulled out onto the highway without checking his rear-view mirror. Coming up from behind at 115 mph, a college student in a Porsche slammed into the back of the rig. The crash triggered an explosion that blew the truck a hundred feet into the air and vaporized the Porsche and a Greyhound bus that had the misfortune to be coming from the other direction at just the wrong time. The highway was completely blocked, so that when Naugahyde drove up a moment later, he had to pull to the side and wait for the wreckage to be cleared.

Two hitchhikers, a man and a woman he had picked up in Tonopah, clung together in the seat beside him. ''I think we'll be here for a while,'' Naugahyde said. He gestured at the inferno raging in the twisted metal and glass. ''And there, but for the grace of a long pit-stop, burn we.''

The woman swallowed hard. ''Perhaps you should turn off the engine,'' she suggested.

The man nodded in affirmation. ''Yeah. Don't waste your gas.''

''Humph.'' Naugahyde turned the key. The engine stopped. ''Dyin' ain't something I like bein' near,'' he said, not looking at the couple but at the gray mountains in the distance. ''But I don't mind hearin' about it on my radio.'' His tweed driver's cap had somehow turned into a straw ten-gallon hat. But the important thing was he'd killed his ignition.

The ship rammed the cloud, shuddered, tore through.

"It's all right, Michael," Alex said as she stepped into her sleepcase. "Of all the dreams I might have had, they picked the one I most wanted to see come true. That's why this is so easy to accept. I'm getting what I want—I'm going to the stars. Whether as human or part machine doesn't really matter. Not to me.''

She lay down in the sleepcase. The socket clicked into the back of her head. "Poor Michael," she said. "Poor, poor Michael. Can you be sure you're not one of us? Can you really be sure?''

The lid closed. Fog poured over her face. I stared at my monitor and cried. The ship didn't need me now. Not really. The Sheik of Araby, gazing at his thousand-member harem, would let me know when I was needed again. I hoped it would be a long time.

I eased the plug from the base of my skull, climbed down the shaft and found the lid of my sleepcase still open. I palmed a control pad. In the case next to mine, a face appeared behind plastic. The lid opened, mist escaped. With a sigh, dark-eyed Sonya sat up and shivered. "Already?" she asked. "Anything interesting happen?''

"Not a thing," I answered.

I climbed into my cocoon and fitted the plug to my head. "Sigmund?''

"Yes?''

"I'm frightened, Sigmund. I don't know what's real anymore.''

"Don't worry, Michael," he whispered as the cold mist poured over me. "We'll take care of you.''

INTO GOLD
By Tanith Lee

It is said that yesterday's magic is today's science, and today's magic is tomorrow's science in similar fashion. Tanith Lee takes us back to the days after the fall of the Roman Empire to spin a tale of marvels and wonders— which may have an explanation in today's physics—or perhaps tomorrow's. Isaac Asimov's Science Fiction Magazine *featured* Into Gold *on its cover—so if you want to dispute that this is science fiction, take it up with the world's most popular science writer.*

I

Up behind Danuvius, the forests are black, and so stiff with black pork, black bears, and black-gray wolves, a man alone will feel himself jostled. Here and there you come on a native village, pointed houses of thatch with carved wooden posts, and smoke thick enough to cut with your knife. All day the birds call, and at night the owls come out. There are other things of earth and darkness, too. One ceases to be surprised at what may be found in the forests, or what may stray from them on occasion.

One morning, a corn-king emerged, and pleased us all no end. There had been some trouble, and some of the stores had gone up in flames. The ovens were standing empty

and cold. It can take a year to get goods overland from the
River, and our northern harvest was months off.

The old fort, that had been the palace then for twelve
years, was built on high ground. It looked out across a
mile of country strategically cleared of trees, to the forest
cloud and a dream of distant mountains. Draco had called
me up to the roof-walk, where we stood watching these
mountains glow and fade, and come and go. It promised to
be a fine day, and I had been planning a good long hunt;
to exercise the men and give the breadless bellies solace.
There is also a pine-nut meal they grind in the villages,
accessible to barter. The loaves were not to everyone's
taste, but we might have to come round to them. Since the
armies pulled away, we had learned to improvise. I could
scarcely remember the first days. The old men told you,
everything, anyway, had been going down to chaos even
then. Draco's father, holding on to a commander's power,
assumed a prince's title which his orphaned warriors were
glad enough to concede him. Discipline is its own ritual,
and drug. As lands and seas away from the center of the
world caved in, soldier-fashion, they turned builders. They
made the road to the fort, and soon began on the town,
shoring it, for eternity, with strong walls. Next, they
opened up the country, and got trade rights seen to that
had gone by default for decades. There was plenty of
skirmishing as well to keep their swords bright. When the
Commander died of a wound got fighting the Blue-Hair
Tribe, a terror in those days, not seen for years since,
Draco became the Prince in the Palace. He was eighteen
then, and I five days older. We had known each other
nearly all our lives, learned books and horses, drilled,
hunted together. Though he was born elsewhere, he barely
took that in, coming to this life when he could only just
walk. For myself, I am lucky, perhaps, I never saw the
Mother of Cities, and so never hanker after her, or lament
her downfall.

That day on the roof-walk, certainly, nothing was further from my mind. Then Draco said, "*There* is something."

His clear-water eyes saw detail quicker and more finely
than mine. When I looked, to me still it was only a blur

and fuss on the forest's edge, and the odd sparkling glint of things catching the early sun.

"Now, Skorous, do you suppose . . . ?" said Draco.

"Someone has heard of our misfortune, and considerably changed his route," I replied.

We had got news a week before of a grain-caravan, but too far west to be of use. Conversely, it seemed, the caravan had received news of our fire. "Up goes the price of bread," said Draco.

By now I was sorting it out, the long rigmarole of mules and baggage-wagons, horses and men. He traveled in some style. Truly, a corn-king, profiting always because he was worth his weight in gold amid the wilds of civilization. In Empire days, he would have weighed rather less.

We went down, and were in the square behind the east gate when the sentries brought him through. He left his people out on the parade before the gate, but one wagon had come up to the gateway, presumably his own, a huge conveyance, a regular traveling house, with six oxen in the shafts. Their straps were spangled with what I took for brass. On the side-leathers were pictures of grind-stones and grain done in purple and yellow. He himself rode a tall horse, also spangled. He had a slim, snaky look, an Eastern look, with black brows and fawn skin. His fingers and ears were remarkable for their gold. And suddenly I began to wonder about the spangles. He bowed to Draco, the War-Leader and Prince. Then, to be quite safe, to me.

"Greetings, Miller," I said.

He smiled at this coy honorific.

"Health and greetings, Captain. I think I am welcome?"

"My prince," I indicated Draco, "is always hospitable to wayfarers."

"Particularly to those with wares, in time of dearth."

"Which dearth is that?"

He put one golden finger to one golden ear-lobe.

"The trees whisper. This town of the Iron Shields has no bread."

Draco said mildly, "You should never listen to gossip."

I said, "If you've come out of your way, that would be a pity."

The Corn-King regarded me, not liking my arrogance—though I never saw the Mother of Cities, I have the blood—any more than I liked his slink and glitter.

As this went on, I gambling and he summing up the bluff, the tail of my eye caught another glimmering movement, from where his house wagon waited at the gate. I sensed some woman must be peering round the flap, the way the Eastern females do. The free girls of the town are prouder, even the wolf-girls of the brothel, and aristocrats use a veil only as a sunshade. Draco's own sisters, though decorous and well brought-up, can read and write, each can handle a light chariot, and will stand and look a man straight in the face. But I took very little notice of the fleeting apparition, except to decide it too had gold about it. I kept my sight on my quarry, and presently he smiled again and drooped his eyelids, so I knew he would not risk calling me, and we had won. "Perhaps," he said, "there might be a little consideration of the detour I, so foolishly, erroneously, made."

"We are always glad of fresh supplies. The fort is not insensible to its isolation. Rest assured."

"Too generous," he said. His eyes flared. But politely he added, "I have heard of your town. There is great culture here. You have a library, with scrolls from Hellas, and Semitic Byblos—I can read many tongues, and would like to ask permission of your lord to visit among his books."

I glanced at Draco, amused by the fellow's cheek, though all the East thinks itself a scholar. But Draco was staring at the wagon. Something worth a look, then, which I had missed.

"And we have excellent baths," I said to the Corn-King, letting him know in turn that the Empire's lost children think all the scholarly East to be also unwashed.

By midday, the whole caravan had come in through the walls and arranged itself in the market-place, near the temple of Mars. The temple priests, some of whom had been serving with the Draconis Regiment when it arrived, old, old men, did not take to this influx. In spring and

summer, traders were in and out the town like flies, and
native men came to work in the forges and the tannery or
with the horses, and built their muddy thatch huts behind
the unfinished law-house—which huts winter rain always
washed away again when their inhabitants were gone. To
such events of passage the priests were accustomed. But
this new show displeased them. The chief Salius came up
to the fort, attended by his slaves, and argued a while with
Draco. Heathens, said the priest, with strange rituals, and
dirtiness, would offend the patron god of the town. Draco
seemed preoccupied.

I had put off the hunting party, and now stayed to talk
the Salius into a better humor. It would be a brief nui-
sance, and surely, they had been directed to us by the god
himself, who did not want his war-like sons to go hungry?
I assured the priest that, if the foreigners wanted to worship their own gods, they would have to be circumspect.
Tolerance of every religious rag, as we knew, was unwise.
They did not, I thought, worship Iusa. There would be no
abominations. I then vowed a boar to Mars, if I could get
one, and the dodderer tottered, pale and grim, away.

Meanwhile, the grain was being seen to. The heathen
god-offenders had sacks and jars of it, and ready flour
besides. It seemed a heavy chancy load with which to
journey, goods that might spoil if at all delayed, or if the
weather went against them. And all that jangling of gold
beside. They fairly bled gold. I had been right in my
second thought on the bridle-decorations, there were even
nuggets and bells hung on the wagons, and gold flowers;
and the oxen had gilded horns. For the men, they were
ringed and buckled and roped and tied with it. It was a
marvel.

When I stepped over to the camp near sunset, I was on
the look-out for anything amiss. But they had picketed
their animals couthly enough, and the dazzle-fringed, clink-
bellied wagons stood quietly shadowing and gleaming in
the westered light. Columns of spicy smoke rose, but only
from their cooking. Boys dealt with that, and boys had
drawn water from the well; neither I nor my men had seen
any women.

Presently I was conducted to the Corn-King's wagon. He received me before it, where woven rugs, and cushions stitched with golden discs, were strewn on the ground. A tent of dark purple had been erected close by. With its gilt-tasseled sides all down, it was shut as a box. A disc or two more winked yellow from the folds. Beyond, the plastered colonnades, the stone Mars Temple, stood equally closed and eyeless, refusing to see.

The Miller and I exchanged courtesies. He asked me to sit, so I sat. I was curious.

"It is pleasant," he said, "to be within safe walls."

"Yes, you must be often in some danger," I answered.

He smiled, secretively now. "You mean our wealth? It is better to display than to hide. The thief kills, in his hurry, the man who conceals his gold. I have never been robbed. They think, Ah, this one shows all his riches. He must have some powerful demon to protect him."

"And is that so?"

"Of course," he said.

I glanced at the temple, and then back at him, meaningly. He said, "Your men drove a hard bargain for the grain and the flour. And I have been docile. I respect your gods, Captain. I respect all gods. That, too, is a protection."

Some drink came. I tasted it cautiously, for Easterners often eschew wine and concoct other disgusting muck. In the forests they ferment thorn berries, or the milk of their beasts, neither of which methods makes such a poor beverage, when you grow used to it. But of the Semites one hears all kinds of things. Still, the drink had a sweet hot sizzle that made me want more, so I swallowed some, then waited to see what else it would do to me.

"And your lord will allow me to enter his library?" said the Corn-King, after a host's proper pause.

"That may be possible," I said. I tried the drink again. "How do you manage without women?" I added, "You'll have seen the House of the Mother, with the she-wolf painted over the door? The girls there are fastidious and clever. If your men will spare the price, naturally."

The Corn-King looked at me, with his liquid man-snake's eyes, aware of all I said which had not been spoken.

"It is true," he said at last, "that we have no women
with us."

"Excepting your own wagon."

"My daughter," he said.

I had known Draco, as I have said, almost all my life.
He was for me what no other had ever been; I had followed his star gladly and without question, into scrapes,
and battles, through very fire and steel. Very rarely would
he impose on me some task I hated, loathed. When he did
so it was done without design or malice, as a man sneezes.
The bad times were generally to do with women. I had
fought back to back with him, but I did not care to be his
pander. Even so, I would not refuse. He had stood in the
window that noon, looking at the black forest, and said in
a dry low voice, carelessly apologetic, irrefutable, "He
has a girl in that wagon. Get her for me." "Well, she may
be his—" I started off. He cut me short. "Whatever she
is. He sells things. He is accustomed to selling." "And if
he won't?" I said. Then he looked at me, with his high-
colored, translucent dyes. "Make him," he said, and next
laughed, as if it were nothing at all, this choice mission. I
had come out thinking glumly, she has witched him, put
the Eye on him. But I had known him lust like this before.
Nothing would do then but he must have. Women had
never been that way for me. They were available, when
one needed them. I like to this hour to see them here and
there, *our* women, straight-limbed, graceful, clean. In the
perilous seasons I would have died defending his sisters,
as I would have died to defend him. That was that. It was
a fact, the burning of our grain had come about through an
old grievance, an idiot who kept score of something Draco
had done half a year ago, about a native girl got on a raid.

I put down the golden cup, because the drink was going
to my head. They had two ways, Easterners, with daugh-
ters. One was best left unspoken. The other kept them
locked and bolted virgin. Mercurius bless the dice. Then,
before I could say anything, the Miller put my mind at
rest.

"My daughter," he said, "is very accomplished. She is
also very beautiful, but I speak now of the beauty of
learning and art."

"Indeed. Indeed."

The sun was slipping over behind the walls. The far mountains were steeped in dyes. This glamour shone behind the Corn-King's head, gold in the sky for him, too. And he said, "Amongst other matters, she has studied the lore of Khemia—Old Aegyptus, you will understand."

"Ah, yes?"

"Now I will confide in you," he said. His tongue flickered on his lips. Was it forked? The damnable drink had fuddled me after all, that, and a shameful relief. "The practice of the Al-Khemia contains every science and sorcery. She can read the stars, she can heal the hurts of man. But best of all, my dear Captain, my daughter has learned the third great secret of the Tri-Magae."

"Oh, yes, indeed?"

"She can," he said, "change all manner of materials into gold."

II

"Sometimes, Skorous," Draco said, "you are a fool."

"Sometimes I am not alone in that."

Draco shrugged. He had never feared honest speaking. He never asked more of a title than his own name. But those two items were, in themselves, significant. He was what he was, a law above the law. The heart-legend of the City was down, and he a prince in a forest that ran all ways for ever.

"What do you think then she will do to me? Turn me into metal, too?"

We spoke in Greek, which tended to be the palace mode for private chat. It was fading out of use in the town.

"I don't believe in that kind of sorcery," I said.

"Well, he has offered to have her show us. Come along."

"It will be a trick."

"All the nicer. Perhaps he will find someone for you, too."

"I shall attend you," I said, "because I trust none of them. And fifteen of my men around the wagon."

"I must remember not to groan," he said, "or they'll be splitting the leather and tumbling in on us with swords."

"Draco," I said, "I'm asking myself why he boasted that she had the skill?"

"All that gold: They didn't steal it or cheat for it. A witch *made* it for them."

"I have heard of the Al-Khemian arts."

"Oh yes," he said. "The devotees make gold, they predict the future, they raise the dead. She might be useful. Perhaps I should marry her. Wait till you see her," he said. "I suppose it was all pre-arranged. He will want paying again."

When we reached the camp, it was midnight. Our torches and their opened the dark, and the flame outside the Mars Temple burned faint. There were stars in the sky, no moon.

We had gone to them at their request, since the magery was intrinsic, required utensils, and was not to be moved to the fort without much effort. We arrived like a bridal procession. The show was not after all to be in the wagon, but the tent. The other Easterners had buried themselves from view. I gave the men their orders and stood them conspicuously about. Then a slave lifted the tent's purple drapery a chink and squinted up at us. Draco beckoned me after him, no one demurred. We both went into the pavilion.

To do that was to enter the East head-on. Expensive gums were burning with a dark hot perfume that put me in mind of the wine I had had earlier. The incense-burners were gold, tripods on leopards' feet, with swags of golden ivy. The floor was carpeted soft, like the pelt of some beast, and beast-skins were hung about—things I had now seen before, some of them, maned and spotted, striped and scaled, and some with heads and jewelry eyes and the teeth and claws gilded. Despite all the clutter of things, of polished mirrors and casks and chests, cushions and dead animals, and scent, there was a feeling of great space within that tent. The ceiling of it stretched taut and high, and three golden wheels depended, with oil-lights in little golden boats. The wheels turned idly now this way, now that, in a wind that came from nowhere and went to nowhere, a demon wind out of a desert. Across the space, wide as night, was an opaque dividing curtain, and on the curtain, a long parchment. It was figured with another mass of images, as if nothing in the place should be spare. A tree went up, with two birds at the roots, a white bird with a raven-black head, a soot-black bird with the head of an ape. A snake twined the tree too, round and round, and ended looking out of the lower branches where yellow fruit hung. The snake had the face of a maiden, and flowing hair. Above sat three figures, judges of the dead from Aegyptus, I would have thought, if I had thought about them, with a balance, and wands. The sun and the moon stood over the tree.

I put my hand to the hilt of my sword, and waited. Draco had seated himself on the cushions. A golden jug was to hand, and a cup. He reached forward, poured the liquor and made to take it, before—reluctantly—I snatched the vessel. "Let me, first. Are you mad?"

He reclined, not interested as I tasted for him, then let him have the cup again.

Then the curtain parted down the middle and the parchment with it, directly through the serpent-tree. I had expected the Miller, but instead what entered was a black dog with a collar of gold. It had a wolf's shape, but more slender, and with a pointed muzzle and high carven pointed ears. Its eyes were also black. It stood calmly, like a steward, regarding us, then stepped aside and lay down, its head still raised to watch. And next the woman Draco wanted came in.

To me, she looked nothing in particular. She was pleasantly made, slim, but rounded, her bare arms and feet the color of amber. Over her head, to her breast, covering her hair and face like a dusky smoke, was a veil, but it was transparent enough you saw through it to black locks and black aloe eyes, and a full tawny mouth. There was only a touch of gold on her, a rolled torque of soft metal at her throat, and one ring on her right hand. I was puzzled as to what had made her glimmer at the edge of my sight before, but perhaps she had dressed differently then, to make herself plain.

She bowed Eastern-wise to Draco, then to me. Then, in the purest Greek I ever heard, she addressed us.

"Lords, while I am at work, I must ask that you will please be still, or else you will disturb the currents of the act and so impair it. Be seated," she said to me, as if I had only stood till then from courtesy. Her eyes were very black, black as the eyes of the jackal-dog, blacker than the night. Then she blinked, and her eyes flashed. The lids were painted wath gold. And I found I had sat down.

What followed I instantly took for an hallucination, induced by the incense, and by other means less perceptible. That is not to say I did not think she was a witch. There was something of power to her I never met before. It pounded from her, like heat, or an aroma. It did not make her beautiful for me, but it held me quiet, though I swear never once did I lose my grip either on my senses or my sword.

First, and quite swiftly, I had the impression the whole tent blew upward, and we were in the open in fact, under a sky of a million stars that blazed and crackled like diamonds. Even so, the golden wheels stayed put, up in the sky now, and they spun, faster and faster, until each was a solid golden O of fire, three spinning suns in the heaven of midnight.

(I remember I thought flatly, We have been spelled. So what now? But in its own way, my stoicism was also suspect. My thoughts in any case flagged after that.)

There was a smell of lions, or of a land that had them. Do not ask me how I know. I never smelled or saw them, or such a spot. And there before us all stood a slanting wall of brick, at once much larger than I saw it, and smaller than it was. It seemed even so to lean into the sky. The woman raised her arms. She was apparent now as if rinsed all over by gilt, and one of the great stars seemed to sear on her forehead.

Forms began to come and go, on the lion-wind. If I knew then what they were, I forgot it later. Perhaps they were animals, like the skins in the tent, though some had wings.

She spoke to them. She did not use Greek any more. It was the language of Khem, presumably, or we were intended to believe so. A liquid tongue, an Eastern tongue, no doubt.

Then there were other visions. The ribbed stems of flowers, broader than ten men around, wide petals pressed to the ether. A rainbow of mist that arched over, and touched the earth with its feet and its brow. And other mirages, many of which resembled effigies I had seen of the gods, but they walked.

The night began to close upon us slowly, narrowing and coming down. The stars till raged overhead and the gold wheels whirled, but some sense of enclosure had returned. As for the sloped angle of brick it had huddled down into a sort of oven, and into this the woman was placing, with extreme care—of all things—long scepters of corn, all brown and dry and withered, blighted to straw by some harvest like a curse.

I heard her whisper then. I could not hear what.

Behind her, dim as shadows, I saw other women, who sat weaving, or who toiled at the grind-stone, and one who shook a rattle upon which rings of gold sang out. Then the vision of these women was eclipsed. Something stood there, between the night and the Eastern witch. Tall as the roof, or tall as the sky, bird-headed maybe, with two of the stars for eyes. When I looked at this, this ultimate apparition, my blood froze and I could have howled out loud. It was not common fear, but terror, such as the worst reality has never brought me, though sometimes subtle nightmares do.

Then there was a lightning, down the night. When it passed, we were enclosed in the tent, the huge night of the tent, and the brick oven burned before us, with a thin harsh fume coming from the aperture in its top.

"Sweet is truth," said the witch, in a wild and passionate voice, all music, like the notes of the gold rings on the rattle. "O Lord of the Word. The Word is, and the Word makes all things to be."

Then the oven cracked into two pieces, it simply fell away from itself, and there on a bank of red charcoal, which died to clinker even as I gazed at it, lay a sheaf of golden corn. Golden corn, smiths' work. It was pure and sound and rang like a bell when presently I went to it and struck it and flung it away.

The tent had positively resettled all around us. It was there. I felt queasy and stupid, but I was in my body and had my bearings again, the sword-hilt firm to my palm, though it was oddly hot to the touch, and my forehead burned, sweatless, as if I too had been seethed in a fire. I had picked up the goldwork without asking her anything. She did not prevent me, nor when I slung it off.

When I looked up from that, she was kneeling by the curtain, where the black dog had been and was no more. Her eyes were downcast under her veil. I noted the torque was gone from her neck and the ring from her finger. Had she somehow managed her trick that way, melting gold on to the stalks of mummified corn— No, lunacy. Why nag at it? It was *all* a deception.

But Draco lay looking at her now, burned up by another fever. It was her personal gold he wanted.

"Out, Skorous," he said to me. "Out now." Slurred and sure.

So I said to her, through my blunted lips and woollen tongue, "Listen carefully, girl. The witchery ends now. You know what he wants, and how to see to that, I suppose. Scratch him with your littlest nail, and you die."

Then, without getting to her feet, she looked up at me, only the second time. She spoke in Greek, as at the start. In the morning, when I was better able to think, I reckoned I had imagined what she said. It had seemed to be: "He is safe, for I desire him. It is my choice. If it were not my choice and my desire, where might you hide yourselves, and live?"

We kept watch round the tent, in the Easterners' camp, in the market-place, until the ashes of the dawn. There was not a sound from anywhere, save the regular quiet passaging of sentries on the walls, and the cool black forest wind that turned grey near sunrise.

At sunup, the usual activity of any town began. The camp stirred and let its boys out quickly to the well to avoid the town's women. Some of the caravaners even chose to stroll across to the public lavatories, though they had avoided the bathhouse.

An embarrassment came over me, that we should be standing there, in the foreigners' hive, to guard our prince through his night of lust. I looked sharply, to see how the men were taking it, but they had held together well. Presently Draco emerged. He appeared flushed and tumbled, very nearly shy, like some girl just out of a love-bed.

We went back to the fort in fair order, where he took me aside, thanked me, and sent me away again.

Bathed and shaved, and my fast broken, I began to feel more sanguine. It was over and done with. I would go down to the temple of Father Jupiter and give him something—why, I was not exactly sure. Then get my boar for Mars. The fresh-baked bread I had just eaten was tasty, and maybe worth all the worry.

Later, I heard the Miller had taken himself to our library and been let in. I gave orders he was to be searched on leaving. Draco's grandfather had started the collection of manuscripts, there were even scrolls said to have been rescued from Alexandrea. One could not be too wary.

In the evening, Draco called me up to his writing-room.

"Tomorrow," he said, "the Easterners will be leaving us."

"That's good news," I said.

"I thought it would please you. Zafra, however, is to remain. I'm talking her into my household."

"Zafra," I said.

"Well, they call her that. For the yellow-gold. Perhaps not her name. That might have been *Nefra*—Beautiful . . ."

"Well," I said, "if you want."

"Well," he said, "I never knew you before to be jealous of one of my women."

I said nothing, though the blood knocked about in my head. I had noted before, he had a woman's tongue himself when he was put out. He was a spoiled brat as a child, I have to admit, but a mother's early death, and the life of a forest fortress, pared most of it from him.

"The Corn-King is not her father," he said now. "She told me. But he's stood by her as that for some years. I shall send him something, in recompense."

He waited for my comment that I was amazed nothing had been asked for. He waited to see how I would jump. I wondered if he had paced about here, planning how he would put it to me. Not that he was required to. Now he said: "We gain, Skorous, a healer and diviner. Not just my pleasure at night."

"Your pleasure at night is your own affair. There are plenty of girls about, I would have thought, to keep you content. As for anything else she can or cannot do, all three temples, particularly the Women's Temple, will be up in arms. The Salius yesterday was only a sample. Do you think they are going to let some yellow-skinned harlot divine for you? Do you think that men who get hurt in a fight will want her near them?"

"You would not, plainly."

"No, I would not. As for the witchcraft, we were drugged and made monkeys of. An evening's fun is one thing."

"Yes, Skorous," he said. "Thanks for your opinion. Don't sulk too long. I shall miss your company."

An hour later, he sent, so I was informed, two of the scrolls from the library to the Corn-King in his wagon. They were two of the best, Greek, one transcribed by the hand, it was said, of a very great king. They went in a silver box, with jewel inlay. Gold would have been tactless, under the circumstances.

Next day she was in the palace. She had rooms on the women's side. It had been the apartment of Draco's elder sister, before her marriage. He treated this one as nothing less than a relative from the first. When he was at leisure, on those occasions when the wives and women of his officers dined with them, there was she with him. When he hunted, she went with him, too, not to have any sport, but as a companion, in a litter between two horses that made each hunt into a farce from its onset. She was in his bed each night, for he did not go to her, her place was solely hers: The couch his father had shared only with his mother. And when he wanted advice, it was she who gave it to him. He called on his soldiers and his priests afterwards. Though he always did so call, nobody lost face. He was wise and canny, she must have told him how to be at long last. And the charm he had always had. He even consulted me, and made much of me before everyone, because, very sensibly he realized, unless he meant to replace me, it would be foolish to let the men see I no longer counted a feather's weight with him. Besides, I might get notions of rebellion. I had my own following, my own men who would die for me if they thought me wronged. Probably that angered me more than the rest, that he might have the idea I would forego my duty and loyalty, forget my honor, and try to pull him down. I could no more do that than put out one of my own eyes.

Since we lost our homeland, since we lost, more importantly, the spine of the Empire, there had been a disparity, a separation of men. Now I saw it, in those bitter golden moments after she came among us. He had been born in the Mother of Cities, but she had slipped from his skin like water. He was a new being, a creature of the world, that might be anything, of any country. But, never having seen the roots of me, they yet had me fast. I was of the old order. I would stand until the fire had me, rather than tarnish my name, and my heart.

Gradually, the fort and town began to fill with gold. It was very nearly a silly thing. But we grew lovely and we shone. The temples did not hate her, as I had predicted. No, for she brought them glittering vessels, and laved the gods' feet with rare offerings, and the sweet spice also of her gift burned before Mars, and the Father, and the Mother, so every holy place smelled like Aegyptus, or Judea, or the brothels of Babylon for all I knew.

She came to walk in the streets with just one of the slaves at her heels, bold, the way our ladies did, and though she never left off her veil, she dressed in the stola and the palla, all clasped and cinched with the tiniest amounts of gold, while gold flooded everywhere else, and everyone looked forward to the summer heartily, for the trading. The harvest would be wondrous too. Already there were signs of astounding fruition. And in the forest, not a hint of any restless tribe, or any ill wish.

They called her by the name *Zafra*. They did not once call her "Easterner." One day, I saw three pregnant women

at the gate, waiting for Zafra to come out and touch them.
She was lucky. Even the soldiers had taken no offense.
The old Salius had asked her for a balm for his rheuma-
tism. It seemed the balm had worked.

Only I, then, hated her. I tried to let it go. I tried to
remember she was only a woman, and, if a sorceress, did
us good. I tried to see her as voluptuous and enticing, or as
homely and harmless. But all I saw was some shuttered-up,
close, fermenting thing, like mummy-dusts reviving in a
tomb, or the lion-scent, and the tall shadow that had stood
between her and the night, bird-headed, the Lord of the
Word that made all things, or unmade them. What was
she, under her disguise? Draco could not see it. Like the
black dog she had kept, which walked by her on a leash,
well-mannered and gentle, and which would probably tear
out the throat of anyone who came at her with mischief on
his mind—Under her honeyed wrappings, was it a doll of
straw or gold, or a viper?

Eventually, Draco married her. That was no surprise.
He did it in the proper style, with sacrifices to the Father,
and all the forms, and a feast that filled the town. I saw
her in colors then, that once, the saffron dress, the
Flammeus, the fire-veil of the bride, and her face bare,
and painted up like a lady's, pale, with rosy cheeks and
lips. But it was still herself, still the Eastern Witch.

And dully that day, as in the tent that night, I thought,
So what now?

III

In the late summer, I picked up some talk, among the
servants in the palace. I was by the well-court, in the
peach arbor, where I had paused to look at the peaches.
They did not always come, but this year we had had one
crop already, and now the second was blooming. As I
stood there in the shade, sampling the fruit, a pair of the
kitchen men met below by the well, and stayed to gossip
in their argot. At first I paid no heed, then it came to me
what they were saying, and I listened with all my ears.

When one went off, leaving the other, old Ursus, to fill

his dipper, I came down the stair and greeted him. He started, and looked at me furtively.

"Yes, I heard you," I said. "But tell me, now."

I had always put a mask on, concerning the witch, with everyone but Draco, and afterwards with him too. I let it be seen I thought her nothing much, but if she was his choice, I would serve her. I was careful never to speak slightingly of her to any—since it would reflect on his honor—even to men I trusted, even in wine. Since he had married her, she had got my duty, too, unless it came to vie with my duty to him.

But Ursus had the servant's way, the slave's way, of holding back bad news for fear it should turn on him. I had to repeat a phrase or two of his own before he would come clean.

It seemed that some of the women had become aware that Zafra, a sorceress of great power, could summon to her, having its name, a mighty demon. Now she did not sleep every night with Draco, but in her own apartments, sometimes things had been glimpsed, or heard—

"Well, Ursus," I said, "you did right to tell me. But it's a lot of silly women's talk. Come, you're not going to give it credit?"

"The flames burn flat on the lamps, and change color," he mumbled. "And the curtain rattled, but no one there. And Eunike says she felt some form brush by her in the corridor—"

"That is enough," I said. "Women will always fancy something is happening, to give themselves importance. You well know that. Then there's hysteria and they can believe and say anything. We are aware she has arts, and the science of Aegyptus. But demons are another matter."

I further admonished him and sent him off. I stood by the well, pondering. Rattled curtains, secretive forms—it crossed my thoughts she might have taken a lover, but it did not seem in keeping with her shrewdness. I do not really believe in such beasts as demons, except what the brain can bring forth. Then again, her brain might be capable of many things.

It turned out I attended Draco that evening, something to do with one of the villages that traded with us, some-

thing he still trusted me to understand. I asked myself if I
should tell him about the gossip. Frankly, when I had
found out—the way you always can—that he lay with her
less frequently, I had had a sort of hope, but there was a
qualm, too, and when the trade matter was dealt with, he
stayed me over the wine, and he said: "You may be
wondering about it, Skorous. If so, yes. I'm to be given a
child."

I knew better now than to scowl. I drank a toast, and
suggested he might be happy to have got a boy on her.

"She says it will be a son."

"Then of course, it will be a son."

And, I thought, it may have her dark-yellow looks. It
may be a magus too. And it will be your heir, Draco. My
future Prince, and the master of the town. I wanted to hurl
the wine cup through the wall, but I held my hand and my
tongue, and after he had gone on a while trying to coax me
to thrill at the joy of life, I excused myself and went away.

It was bound to come. It was another crack in the
stones. It was the way of destiny, and of change. I wanted
not to feel I must fight against it, or desire to send her
poison, to kill her or abort her, or tear it, her womb's fruit,
when born, in pieces.

For a long while I sat on my sleeping-couch and allowed
my fury to sink down, to grow heavy and leaden, re-
signed, defeated.

When I was sure of that defeat, I lay flat and slept.

In sleep, I followed a demon along the corridor in the
women's quarters, and saw it melt through her door. It
was tall, long-legged, with the head of a bird, or perhaps
of a dog. A wind blew, lion-tanged. I was under a tree
hung thick with peaches, and a snake looked down from it
with a girl's face framed by a flaming bridal-veil. Then
there was a spinning fiery wheel, and golden corn flew off
clashing from it. And next I saw a glowing oven, and on
the red charcoal lay a child of gold, burning and gleaming
and asleep.

When I woke with a jump it was the middle of the
night, and someone had arrived, and the slave was telling
me so.

At first I took it for a joke. Then, became serious.

Zafra, Draco's wife, an hour past midnight, had sent for me to attend her in her rooms. Naturally I suspected everything. She knew me for her adversary: She would lead me in, then say I had set on her to rape or somehow else abuse her. On the other hand, I must obey and go to her, not only for duty, now, but from sheer aggravation and raw curiosity. Though I had always told myself I misheard her words as I left her with him the first time, I had never forgotten them. Since then, beyond an infrequent politeness, we had not spoken.

I dressed as formally as I could, got two of my men, and went across to the women's side. The sentries along the route were my fellows too, but I made sure they learned I had been specifically summoned. Rather to my astonishment, they knew it already.

My men went with me right to her chamber door, with orders to keep alert there. Perhaps they would grin, asking each other if I was nervous. I was.

When I got into the room, I thought it was empty. Her women had been sent away. One brazier burned, near the entry, but I was used by now to the perfume of those aromatics. It was a night of full moon, and the blank light lay in a whole pane across the mosaic, coloring it faintly, but in the wrong, nocturnal, colors. The bed, narrow, low, and chaste, stood on one wall, and her tiring table near it. Through the window under the moon, rested the tops of the forest, so black it made the indigo sky pale.

Then a red-golden light blushed out and I saw her, lighting the lamps on their stand from a taper. I could almost swear she had not been there a second before, but she could stay motionless a long while, and with her dark robe and hair, and all her other darkness, she was a natural thing for shadows.

"Captain," she said. (She never used my name, she must know I did not want it; a sorceress, she was well aware of the power of naming.) "There is no plot against you."

"That's good to know," I said, keeping my distance, glad of my sword, and of every visible insignia of who and what I was.

"You have been very honorable in the matter of me,"

she said. "You have done nothing against me, either openly or in secret, though you hated me from the beginning. I know what this has cost you. Do not spurn my gratitude solely because it is mine."

"Domina," I said (neither would I use her name, though the rest did in the manner of the town), "you're his. He has made you his wife. And—" I stopped.

"And the vessel of his child. Ah, do you think he did that alone?" She saw me stare with thoughts of demons, and she said, "He and I, Captain. He, and I."

"Then I serve you," I said. I added, and though I did not want to give her the satisfaction I could not keep back a tone of irony, "you have nothing to be anxious at where I am concerned."

We were speaking in Greek, hers clear as water in that voice of hers which I had to own was very beautiful.

"I remain," she said, "anxious."

"Then I can't help you, Domina." There was a silence. She stood looking at me, through the veil I had only once seen dispensed with in exchange for a veil of paint. I wondered where the dog had gone, that had her match in eyes. I said, "But I would warn you. If you practice your business in here, there's begun to be some funny talk."

"They see a demon, do they?" she said.

All at once the hair rose up on my neck and scalp.

As if she read my mind, she said:

"I have not pronounced any name. Do not be afraid."

"The slaves are becoming afraid."

"No," she said. "They have always talked of me but they have never been afraid of me. None of them. Draco does not fear me, do you think? And the priests do not. Or the women and girls. Or the children, or the old men. Or the slaves. Or your soldiers. None of them fear me or what I am or what I do, the gold with which I fill the temples, or the golden harvests, or the healing I perform. None of them fear it. But you, Captain, you do fear, and you read your fear again and again in every glance, in every word they utter. But it is yours, not theirs."

I looked away from her, up to the ceiling from which the patterns had faded years before.

"Perhaps," I said, "I am not blind."

Then she sighed. As I listened to it, I thought of her, just for an instant, as a forlorn girl alone with strangers in a foreign land.

"I'm sorry," I said.

"It is true," she said, "you see more than most. But not your own error."

"Then that is how it is." My temper had risen and I must rein it.

"You will not," she said quietly, "be a friend to me."

"I cannot, and will not, be a friend to you. Neither am I your enemy, while you keep faith with him."

"But one scratch of my littlest nail," she said. Her musical voice was nearly playful.

"Only one," I said.

"Then I regret waking you, Captain," she said. "Health and slumber for your night."

As I was going back along the corridor, I confronted the black jackal-dog. It padded slowly towards me and I shivered, but one of the men stooped to rub its ears. It suffered him, and passed on, shadow to shadow, night to ebony night.

Summer went to winter, and soon enough the snows came. The trading and the harvests had shored us high against the cruelest weather, we could sit in our towers and be fat, and watch the wolves howl through the white forests. They came to the very gates that year. There were some odd stories, that wolf-packs had been fed of our bounty, things left for them, to tide them over. Our own she-wolves were supposed to have started it, the whore-house girls. But when I mentioned the tale to one of them, she flared out laughing.

I recall that snow with an exaggerated brilliance, the way you sometimes do with time that precedes an illness, or a deciding battle. Albino mornings with the edge of a broken vase, the smoke rising from hearths and temples, or steaming with the blood along the snow from the sacrifices of Year's Turn. The Wolf Feast with the races, and later the ivies and vines cut for the Mad Feast, and the old dark wine got out, the torches, and a girl I had in a shed full of hay and pigs; and the spate of weddings that come after, very sensibly. The last snow twilights were thick as soup with blueness. Then spring, and the forest surging up from its slough, the first proper hunting, with the smell of sap and crushed freshness spraying out as if one waded in a river.

Draco's child was born one spring sunset, coming forth in the bloody golden light, crying its first cry to the evening star. It was a boy, as she had said.

I had kept even my thoughts off from her after that interview in her chamber. My feelings had been confused and displeasing. It seemed to me she had in some way tried to outwit me, throw me down. Then I had felt truly angry, and later, oddly shamed. I avoided, where I could, all places where I might have to see her. Then she was seen less, being big with the child.

After the successful birth all the usual things were done. In my turn, I beheld the boy. He was straight and flaw-lessly formed, with black hair, but a fair skin; he had Draco's eyes from the very start. So little of the mother. Had she contrived it, by some other witch's art, knowing that when at length we had to cleave to him, it would be Draco's line we wished to see? No scratch of a nail, there, none.

Nor had there been any more chat of demons. Or they made sure I never intercepted it.

I said to myself, She is a matron now, she will wear to our ways. She has borne him a strong boy.

But it was no use at all.

She was herself, and the baby was half of her.

They have a name now for her demon, her genius in the shadowlands of witchcraft. A scrambled name that does no harm. They call it, in the town's argot: *Rhamthibiscan*.

We claim so many of the Greek traditions; they know of Rhadamanthys from the Greek. A judge of the dead, he is connectable to Thot of Aegyptus, the Thrice-Mighty Thrice-Mage of the Al-Khemian Art. And because Thot the Ibis-Headed and Anpu the Jackal became mingled in it, along with Hermercurius, Prince of Thieves and Whores—who is too the guide of lost souls—an ibis and a dog were added to the brief itinerary. Rhadamanthys-Ibis-Canis. The full name, even, has no power. It is a muddle, and a lie, and the invocation says: *Sweet is Truth.* Was it, though, ever sensible to claim to know what truth might be?

IV

"They know of her, and have sent begging for her. She's a healer and they're sick. It's not unreasonable. She isn't afraid. I have seen her close an open wound by passing her hands above it. Yes, Skorous, perhaps she only made me see it, and the priests to see it, and the wounded man. But he recovered, as you remember. So I trust her to be able to cure these people and make them love us even better. She herself is immune to illness. Yes, Skorous, she only thinks she is. However, thinking so has apparently worked wonders. She was never once out of sorts with the child. The midwives were amazed—or not amazed, maybe—that she seemed to have no pain during the birth. Though they told me she wept when the child was put into her arms. Well, so did I." Draco frowned. He said, "So we'll let her do it, don't you agree, let her go to them and heal them. We may yet be able to open this country, make something of it, one day. Anything that is useful in winning them."

"She will be taking the child with her?"

"Of course. He's not weaned yet, and she won't let another woman nurse him."

"Through the forests. It's three days ride away, this village. And then we hardly know the details of the sickness. If your son—"

"He will be with his mother. She has never done a foolish thing."

"You let this bitch govern you. Very well. But don't risk the life of your heir, since your heir is what you have made him, this half-breed brat—"

I choked off the surge in horror. I had betrayed myself. It seemed to me instantly that I had been made to do it. *She* had made me. All the stored rage and impotent distrust, all the bitter frustrated *guile*—gone for nothing in a couple of sentences.

But Draco only shrugged, and smiled. He had learned to

contain himself these past months. Her invaluable aid, no doubt, her rotten honey.

He said, "She has requested that, though I send a troop with her to guard her in our friendly woods, you, Skorous, do not go with them."

"I see."

"The reason which she gave was that, although there is no danger in the region at present, your love and spotless commitment to my well-being preclude you should be taken from my side." He put the smile away and said, "But possibly, too, she wishes to avoid your close company for so long, knowing as she must do you can barely keep your fingers from her throat. Did you know, Skorous," he said, and now it was the old Draco, I seemed somehow to have hauled him back, "that the first several months, I had her food always tasted. I thought you would try to see to her. I was so very astounded you never did. Or did you have some other, more clever plan, that failed?"

I swallowed the bile that had come into my mouth. I said, "You forget, Sir, if I quit you I have no other battalion to go to. The Mother of Cities is dead. If I leave your warriors, I am nothing. I am one of the scores who blow about the world like dying leaves, soldiers' sons of the lost Empire. If there were an option, I would go at once. There is none. You've spat in my face, and I can only wipe off the spit."

His eyes fell from me, and suddenly he cursed.

"I was wrong, Skorous. You would never have—"

"No, Sir. Never. Never in ten million years. But I regret you think I might. And I regret she thinks so. Once she was your wife, she could expect no less from me than I give one of your sisters."

"That bitch," he said, repeating for me my error, woman-like, "her half-breed brat—damn you, Skorous. He's my son."

"I could cut out my tongue that I said it. It's more than a year of holding it back before all others, I believe. Like vomit, Sir. I could not keep it down any longer."

"Stop saying *Sir* to me. You call her *Domina*. That's sufficient."

His eyes were wet. I wanted to slap him, the way you do a

vicious stupid girl who claws at your face. But he was my prince, and the traitor was myself.

Presently, thankfully, he let me get out.

What I had said was true, if there had been any other life to go to that was thinkable—but there was not, anymore. So, she would travel into the forest to heal, and I, faithful and unshakable, I would stay to guard him. And then she would come back. Year in and out, mist and rain, snow and sun. And bear him other brats to whom, in due course, I would swear my honor over. I had better practice harder, not to call her anything but *Lady*.

Somewhere in the night I came to myself and I knew. I saw it accurately, what went on, what was to be, and what I, so cunningly excluded, must do. Madness, they say, can show itself like that. Neither hot nor cold, with a steady hand, and every faculty honed bright.

The village with the sickness had sent its deputation to Draco yesterday. They had grand and blasphemous names for *her*, out there. She had said she must go, and at first light today would set out. Since the native villagers revered her, she might have made an arrangement with them, some itinerant acting as messenger. Or even, if the circumstance were actual, she could have been biding for such a chance. Or she herself had sent the malady to ensure it.

Her gods were the gods of her mystery. But the Semitic races have a custom ancient as their oldest altars, of giving a child to the god.

Perhaps Draco even knew—no, unthinkable. How then could she explain it? An accident, a straying, bears, wolves, the sickness after all . . . And she could give him other sons. She was like the magic oven of the Khemian Art. Put in, take out. So easy.

I got up when it was still pitch black and announced to my body-slave and the man at the door I was off hunting, alone. There was already a rumor of an abrasion between the Prince and his Captain. Draco himself would not think unduly of it, Skorous raging through the wood, slicing pigs. I could be gone the day before he considered.

I knew the tracks pretty well, having hunted them since I was ten. I had taken boar spears for the look, but no dogs. The horse I needed, but she was forest-trained and did as I instructed.

I lay off the thoroughfare, like an old fox, and let the witch's outing come down, and pass me. Five men were all the guard she had allowed, a cart with traveling stuff, and her medicines in a chest. There was one of her women, the thickest in with her, I thought, Eunike, riding on a mule. And Zafra herself, in the litter between the horses.

When they were properly off, I followed. There was no problem in the world. We moved silently and they made a noise. Their horses and mine were known to each other, and where they snuffed a familiar scent, thought nothing of it. As the journey progressed, and I met here and there with some native in the trees, he hailed me cheerily, supposing me an outrider, a rearguard. At night I bivouacked above them; at sunrise their first rustlings and throat-clearings roused me. When they were gone we watered at their streams, and once I had a burned sausage forgotten in the ashes of their cookfire.

The third day, they came to the village. From high on the mantled slope, I saw the greetings and the going in, through the haze of foul smoke. The village did have a look of ailing, something in its shades and colors, and the way the people moved about. I wrapped a cloth over my nose and mouth before I sat down to wait.

Later, in the dusk, they began to have a brisker look. The witch was making magic, evidently, and all would be well. The smoke condensed and turned yellow from their fires as the night closed in. When full night had come, the village glowed stilly, enigmatically, cupped in the forest's darkness. My mental wanderings moved towards the insignificance, the smallness, of any lamp among the great shadows of the earth. A candle against the night, a fire in winter, a life flickering in eternity, now here, now gone forever.

But I slept before I had argued it out.

Inside another day, the village was entirely renewed. Even the rusty straw thatch glinted like gold. She had worked her miracles. Now would come her own time.

A couple of the men had kept up sentry-go from the first

evening out, and last night, patrolling the outskirts of the huts, they had even idled a minute under the tree where I was roosting. I had hidden my mare half a mile off, in a deserted bothy I had found, but tonight I kept her near, for speed. And this night, too, when one of the men came up the slope, making his rounds, I softly called his name.

He went to stone. I told him smartly who I was, but when I came from cover, his sword was drawn and eyes on stalks.

"I'm no forest demon," I said. Then I asked myself if he was alarmed for other reasons, a notion of the scheme Draco had accused me of. Then again, here and now, we might have come to such a pass. I needed a witness. I looked at the soldier, who saluted me slowly. "Has she cured them all?" I inquired. I added for his benefit, "Zafra."

"Yes," he said. "It was—worth seeing."

"I am sure of that. And how does the child fare?"

I saw him begin to conclude maybe Draco had sent me after all. "Bonny," he said.

"But she is leaving the village, with the child—" I had never thought she would risk her purpose among the huts, as she would not in the town, for all her hold on them. "Is that tonight?"

"Well, there's the old woman, she won't leave her own place, it seems."

"So Zafra told you?"

"Yes. And said she would go. It's close. She refused the litter and only took Carus with her. No harm. These savages are friendly enough—"

He ended, seeing my face.

I said, "She's gone already?"

"Yes, Skorous. About an hour—"

Another way from the village? But I had watched, I had skinned my eyes—pointlessly. Witchcraft could manage anything.

"And the child with her," I insisted.

"Oh, she never will part from the child, Eunike says—"

"Damn Eunike." He winced at me, more than ever uncertain. "Listen," I said, and informed him of my suspicions. I did not say the child was half East, half spice and glisten and sins too strange to speak. I said *Draco's son*. And I did not mention sacrifice. I said there was some chance Zafra might wish to mutilate the boy for her gods. It was well known, many of the Eastern religions had such rites. The soldier was shocked, and disbelieving. His own mother—? I said, to her kind, it was not a deed of dishonor. She could not see it as we did. All the while we debated, my heart clutched and struggled in my side, I sweated. Finally he agreed we should go to look. Carus was there, and would dissuade her if she wanted to perform such a disgusting act. I asked where the old woman's hut was supposed to be, and my vision filmed a moment with relief when he located it for me as that very bothy where I had tethered my horse the previous night. I said, as I turned to run that way. "There's no old woman there. The place is a ruin."

We had both won at the winter racing, he and I. It did not take us long to achieve the spot. A god, I thought, must have guided me to it before, so I knew how the land fell. The trees were densely packed as wild grass, the hut wedged between, and an apron of bared weedy ground about the door where once the household fowls had pecked. The moon would enter there, too, but hardly anywhere else. You could come up on it, cloaked in forest and night. Besides, she had lit her stage for me. As we pushed among the last phalanx of trunks, I saw there was a fire burning, a sullen throb of red, before the ruin's gaping door.

Carus stood against a tree. His eyes were wide and beheld nothing. The other man punched him and hissed at him, but Carus was far off. He breathed and his heart drummed, but that was all.

"She's witched him," I said. Thank Arean Mars and Father Jupiter she had. It proved my case outright. I could see my witness thought this too. We went on stealthily, and stopped well clear of the tree-break, staring down.

Then I forgot my companion. I forgot the manner in which luck at last had thrown my dice for me. What I saw took all my mind.

It was like the oven of the hallucination in the tent, the thing she had made, yet open, the shape of a cauldron.

Rough mud brick, smoothed and curved, and somehow altered. Inside, the fire burned. It had a wonderful color, the fire, rubies, gold. To look at it did not seem to hurt the eyes, or dull them. The woman stood the other side of it, and her child in her grasp. Both appeared illumined into fire themselves, and the darkness of garments, of hair, the black gape of the doorway, of the forest and the night, these had grown warm as velvet. It is a sight often seen, a girl at a brazier or a hearth, her baby held by, as she stirs a pot, or throws on the kindling some further twig or cone. But in her golden arm the golden child stretched out his hands to the flames. And from her moving palm fell some invisible essence I could not see but only feel.

She was not alone. Others had gathered at her fireside. I was not sure of them, but I saw them, if only by their great height which seemed to rival the trees. A warrior there, his metal faceplate and the metal ribs of his breast just glimmering, and there a young woman, garlands, draperies and long curls, and a king who was bearded, with a brow of thunder and eyes of light, and near him another, a musician with wings starting from his forehead—they came and went as the fire danced and bowed. The child laughed, turning his head to see them, the deities of his father's side.

Then Zafra spoke the Name. It was so soft, no sound at all. And yet the roots of the forest moved at it. My entrails churned. I was on my knees. It seemed as though the wind came walking through the forest, to fold his robe beside the ring of golden red. I cannot recall the Name. It was not any of those I have written down, nor anything I might imagine. But it was the true one, and he came in answer to it. And from a mile away, from the heaven of planets, out of the pit of the earth, his hands descended and rose. He touched the child and the child was quiet. The child slept.

She drew Draco's son from his wrapping as a shining sword is drawn from the scabbard. She raised him up through the dark, and then she lowered him, and set him down in the holocaust of the oven, into the bath of flame, and the fires spilled up and covered him.

No longer on my knees, I was running. I plunged

through black waves of heat, the amber pungence of incense, and the burning breath of lions. I yelled as I ran. I screamed the names of all the gods, and knew them powerless in my mouth, because I said them wrongly, knew them not, and so they would not answer. And then I ran against the magic, the Power, and broke through it. It was like smashing air. Experienced—inexperienceable.

Sword in hand, in the core of molten gold, I threw myself on, wading, smothered, and came to the cauldron of brick, the oven, and dropped the sword and thrust in my hands and pulled him out—

He would be burned, he would be dead, a blackened little corpse, such as the Semite Karthaginians once made of their children, incinerating them in line upon line of ovens by the shores of the Inner Sea—

But I held in my grip only a child of jewel-work, of poreless perfect gold, and I sensed his gleam run into my hands, through my wrists, down my arms like scalding water to my heart.

Someone said to me, then, with such gentle sadness. "Ah Skorous. Ah, Skorous."

I lay somewhere, not seeing. I said, "Crude sorcery, to turn the child, too, into gold."

"No," she said. "Gold is only the clue. For those things which are alive, laved by the flame, it is life. It is immortal and imperishable life. And you have torn the spell, which is all you think it to be. You have robbed him of it."

And then I opened my eyes, and I saw her. There were no others, no Other, they had gone with the tearing. But she— She was no longer veiled. She was very tall, so beautiful I could not bear to look at her, and yet, could not take my eyes away. And she was golden. She was golden not in the form of metal, but as a dawn sky, as fire, and the sun itself. Even her black eyes—were of gold, and her midnight hair. And the tears she wept were stars.

I did not understand, but I whispered, "Forgive me. Tell me how to make it right."

"It is not to be," she said. Her voice was a harp, playing through the forest. "It is never to be. He is yours now, no longer mine. Take him. Be kind to him. He will know his loss all his days, all his mortal days. And never know it.''

And then she relinquished her light, as a coal dies. She vanished.

I was lying on the ground before the ruined hut, holding the child close to me, trying to comfort him as he cried, and my tears fell with his. The place was empty and hollow as if its very heart had bled away.

The soldier had run down to me, and was babbling. She had tried to immolate the baby, he had seen it, Carus had woken and seen it also. And, too, my valor in saving the boy from horrible death.

As one can set oneself to remember most things, so one can study to forget. Our sleeping dreams we dismiss on waking. Or, soon after.

They call her now, the Greek Woman. Or the Semite Witch. There has begun, in recent years, to be a story she was some man's wife, and in the end went back to him. It is generally thought she practiced against the child and the soldiers of her guard killed her.

Draco, when I returned half-dead for the fever I had caught from the contagion of the ruinous hut—where the village crone had died, it turned out, a week before—hesitated for my recovery, and then asked very little. A dazzle seemed to have lifted from his sight. He was afraid at what he might have said and done under the influence of sorceries and drugs. "Is it a fact, what the men say? She put the child into a fire?" "Yes," I said. He had looked at me, gnawing his lips. He knew of Eastern rites, he had heard out the two men. And, long, long ago, he had relied only on me. He appeared never to grieve, only to be angry. He even sent men in search for her: A bitch who would burn her own child—let her be caught and suffer the fate instead.

It occurs to me now that, contrary to what they tell us, one does not age imperceptibly, finding one evening, with cold dismay, the strength has gone from one's arm, the luster from one's heart. No, it comes at an hour, and is seen, like the laying down of a sword.

When I woke from the fever, and saw his look, all imploring on me, the look of a man who has gravely wronged you, not meaning to, who says: But I was blind— that was the hour, the evening, the moment when life's sword of youth was removed from my hand, and with no protest I let it go.

Thereafter the months moved away from us, the seasons, and next the years.

Draco continued to look about him, as if seeking the evil Eye that might still hang there, in the atmosphere. Sometimes he was partly uneasy, saying he too had seen her dog, the black jackal. But it had vanished at the time she did, though for decades the woman Eunike claimed to meet it in the corridor of the women's quarters.

He clung to me, then, and ever since he has stayed my friend; I do not say, my suppliant. It is in any event the crusty friendship now of the middle years, where once it was the flaming blazoned friendship of childhood, the envious love of young men.

We share a secret, he and I, that neither has ever confided to the other. He remains uncomfortable with the boy. Now the princedom is larger, its borders fought out wider, and fortressed in, he sends him often away to the fostering of soldiers. It is I, without any rights, none, who love her child.

He is all Draco, to look at, but for the hair and brows. We have a dark-haired strain ourselves. Yet there is a sheen to him. They remark on it. What can it be? A brand of the gods— (They make no reference, since she has fallen from their favor, to his mother.) A light from within, a gloss, of gold. Leaving off his given name, they will call him for that effulgence more often, Ardorius. Already I have caught the murmur that he can draw iron through stone, yes, yes, they have seen him do it, though I have not. (From Draco they conceal such murmurings, as once from me.) He, too, has a look of something hidden, some deep and silent pain, as if he knows, as youth never does, that men die, and love, that too.

To me, he is always courteous, and fair. I can ask nothing else. I am, to him, an adjunct of his life. I should perhaps be glad that it should stay so.

In the deep nights, when summer heat or winter snow fill up the forest, I recollect a dream, and think how I robbed him, the child of gold. I wonder how much, how much it will matter, in the end.

THE LIONS ARE ASLEEP THIS NIGHT
By Howard Waldrop

Howard Waldrop has a reputation for coming up with some of the oddest ideas in science fiction. His novelette about the last of the dodo birds is still a classic. Here he relates a tale that is harder to define. Is this taking place on an alternate Earth where things have been slightly different? Or is this in a future where the tables of social structure have been given a half-turn? Authenticity is not lacking in either case.

The white man was drunk again. Robert Oinenke crossed the narrow, graveled street and stepped up on the board-walk at the other side. Out of the corner of his eye he saw the white man raving. The man sat, feet out, back against a wall, shaking his head, punctuating his monologue with cursing words.

Some said he had been a mercenary in one of the border wars up the coast, one of those conflicts in which two countries had become one; or one country, three. Robert could not remember which. Mr. Lemuel, his history teacher, had mentioned it only in passing.

Since showing up in Onitsha town the white man had worn the same khaki pants. They were of a military cut, now torn and stained. The shirt he wore today was a dashiki, perhaps variegated bright blue and red when made,

240

now faded to purple. He wore a cap with a foreign insignia. Some said he had been a general; others, a sergeant. His loud harangues terrified schoolchildren. Robert's classmates looked on the man as a forest demon. Sometimes the constables came and took him away; sometimes they only asked him to be quiet, and he would subside.

Mostly he could be seen propped against a building, talking to himself. Occasionally somebody would give him money. Then he would make his way to the nearest store or market stall that sold palm wine.

He had been in Robert's neighborhood for a few months. Before that he had stayed near the marketplace.

Robert did not look at him. Thinking of the marketplace, he hurried his steps. The first school bell rang.

"You will not be dawdling at the market," his mother had said as he readied himself for school. "Miss Mbene spoke to me of your tardiness yesterday."

She took the first of many piles of laundry from her wash baskets and placed them near the ironing board. There was a roaring fire in the hearth, and her irons were lined up in the racks over it. The house was already hot as an oven and would soon be as damp as the monsoon season.

His mother was still young and pretty but worn. She had supported them since Robert's father had been killed in an accident while damming a tributary of the Niger. He and forty other men had been swept away when a cofferdam burst. Only two of the bodies had ever been found. There was a small monthly check from the company her husband had worked for, and the government check for single mothers.

Her neighbor Mrs. Yortebe washed, and she ironed. They took washing from the well-to-do government workers and business people in the better section.

"I shan't be late," said Robert, torn with emotions. He knew he wouldn't spend a long time there this morning and be late for school, but he did know that he would take the wide route that led through the marketplace.

He put his schoolbooks and supplies in his satchel. His mother turned to pick up somebody's shirt from the pile. She stopped, looking at Robert.

"What are you going to do with *two* copybooks?" she asked.

Robert froze. His mind tried out ten lies. His mother started toward him.

"I'm nearly out of pages," he said. She stopped. "If we do much work today. I shall have to borrow.

"I buy you ten copybooks at the start of each school year and then again at the start of the second semester. Money does not grow on the breadfruit trees, you know?"

"Yes, Mother," he said. He hoped she would not look in the copybooks, see that one was not yet half-filled with schoolwork and that the other was still clean and empty. His mother referred to all extravagance as "a heart-tearing waste of time and money."

"You have told me not to borrow from others. I thought I was using foresight."

"Well," said his mother, "see you don't go to the marketplace. It will only make you envious of all the things you can't have. And do not be late to school one more time this term, or I shall have you ever ironing."

"Yes, Mother," he said. Running to her, he rubbed his nose against her cheek. "Good-bye."

"Good day. And don't go near that marketplace!"

"Yes, Mother."

The market! Bright, pavilioned stalls covering a square Congo mile of ground filled with gaudy objects, goods, animals and people. The Onitsha market was a crossroads of the trade routes, near the river and the railway station. Here a thousand vendors sold their wares on weekdays, many times that on weekends and holidays.

Robert passed the great piles of melons, guinea fowl in cages, tables of toys and gewgaws, all bright and shiny in the morning light.

People talked in five languages, haggling with each other, calling back and forth, joking. Here men from Senegal stood in their bright red hats and robes. Robert saw a tall Wazir, silent and regal, indicating the prices he would pay with quick movements of his long fingers, while the merchant he stood before added two more each time. A few people with raised tattoos on their faces, backcountry people, wandered wide-eyed from table to table, talking quietly among themselves.

Scales clattered, food got weighed, chickens and ducks rattled, a donkey brayed near the big corral where larger livestock was sold. A goat wagon delivered yams to a merchant, who began yelling because they were still too hard. The teamster shrugged his shoulders and pointed to his bill of lading. The merchant threw down his apron and headed toward Onitsha's downtown, cursing the harvest, the wagoners, and the food cooperatives.

Robert passed by the food stalls, though the smell of ripe mangoes made his mouth water. He had been skipping lunch for three weeks, saving his Friday pennies. At the schoolhouse far away the ten-minute bell rang. He would have to hurry.

He came to the larger stalls at the far edge of the market where the booksellers were. He could see the bright paper jackets and dark type titles and some of the cover pictures on them from fifty yards away. He went toward the stall of Mr. Fred's Printers and High-Class Bookstore, which was his favorite. The clerk, who knew him by now, nodded to Robert as he came into the stall area. He was a nice young man in his twenties dressed in a three-piece suit. He looked at the clock.

"Aren't you going to be late for school this fine morning?"

Robert didn't want to take the time to talk but said, "I know the books I want. It will only be a moment."

The clerk nodded.

Robert ran past the long shelves with their familiar titles: *Drunkards Believe the Bar is Heaven; Ruth, the Sweet Honey That Poured Away; Johnny, the Most-Worried Husband; The Lady That Forced Me to Be Romantic; The Return of Mabel, in a Drama on How I Was About Marrying My Sister*, the last with a picture of Miss Julie Engebe, the famous drama actress, on the cover, which Robert knew was just a way to get people to buy the book.

Most of them were paper covered, slim, about fifty pages thick. Some had bright, stenciled lettering on them, others drawings; a few had *photographios*. Robert turned at the end of the shelf and read the titles of others quickly:

The Adventures of Constable Joe; Eddy, the Coal-City Boy; Pocket Encyclopedia of Etiquette and Good Sense; Why Boys Never Trust Money-Monger Girls; How to Live Bachelor's Life and a Girl's Life Without too Many Mistakes; Ibo Folktales You Should Know.

He found what he was looking for: *Clio's Whips* by Oskar Oshwenke. It was as thin as the others, and the typefaces on the red, green, and black cover were in three different type styles. There was even a different *i* in the word *whips*.

Robert took it from the rack (it had been well thumbed, but Robert knew it was the only copy in the store). He went down two more shelves, to where they kept the dramas, and picked out *The Play of the Swearing Stick* by Otuba Malewe and *The Raging Turk, or Bajazet II* by Thomas Goffe, an English European who had lived three hundred years ago.

Robert returned to the counter, out of breath from his dash through the stall. "These three," he said, spreading them out before him.

The clerk wrote figures on two receipt papers. "That will be twenty-four new cents, young sir." he said.

Robert looked at him without comprehension. "But yesterday they would have been twenty-two cents!" he said.

The clerk looked back down at the books. Then Robert noticed the price on the Goffe play, six cents, had been crossed out and eight cents written over that in big, red pencil.

"Mr. Fred himself came through yesterday and looked over the stock," said the clerk. "Some prices he raised, others he liberally reduced. There are now many more two-cent books in the bin out front," he said apologetically.

"But . . . I only have twenty-two new cents." Robert's eyes began to burn.

The clerk looked at the three books. "I'll tell you what, young sir. I shall let you have these three books for twenty-two cents. When you get two cents more, you are to bring them *directly* to me. If the other clerk or Mr. Fred is here, you are to make no mention of this matter. Do you see?"

"Yes, yes. Thank you!" He handed all his money

across. He knew it was borrowing, which his mother did not want him to do, but he wanted these books so badly.

He stuffed the pamphlets and receipts into his satchel. As he ran from the bookstall he saw the nice young clerk reach into his vest pocket, fetch out two pennies, and put them into the cashbox. Robert ran as fast as he could toward school. He would have to hurry or he would be late.

Mr. Yotofeka, the principal, looked at the tardy slip.

"Robert," he said, looking directly into the boy's eyes, "I am very disappointed in you. You are a bright pupil. Can you give me one good reason why you have been late to school three times in two weeks?"

"No, sir," said Robert. He adjusted his glasses, which were taped at one of the earpieces.

"No reason at all?"

"It took longer than I thought to get to school."

"You are thirteen years old, Robert Oinenke!" His voice rose. "You live less than a Congo mile from this schoolhouse, which you have been attending for seven years. You should know by now how long it takes you to get from your home to the school!"

Robert winced. "Yessir."

"Hand me your book satchel, Robert."

'But I . . .''

"Let me see."

"Yessir." He handed the bag to the principal, who was standing over him. The man opened it, took out the schoolbooks and copybooks, then the pamphlets. He looked down at the receipt, then at Robert's records file, which was open like the big book of the Christian Saint Peter in heaven.

"Have you not been eating to buy this trash?"

"No, sir."

"No, yes? Or yes, no?"

"Yes, I haven't."

"Robert, two of these are pure trash. I am glad to see you have bought at least one good play. But your other choices are just, just . . . You might as well have poured your coppers down a civet hole as buy these." He held up

Clio's Whips. "Does your mother know you read these things? And this play! *The Swearing Stick* is about the kind of primitive superstitions we left behind before independence. You want people to believe in this kind of thing again? You wish blood rituals, tribal differences to come back? The man who wrote this was barely literate, little more than just come in from the bush country."

"But . . ."

"But me no buts. Use the library of this schoolhouse, Robert, or the fine public one. Find books that will uplift you, appeal to your higher nature. Books written by learned people, who have gone to university." Robert knew that Mr. Yotofeka was proud of his education and that he and others like him looked down on the bookstalls and their books. He probably only read books published by the universities or real books published in Lagos or Cairo.

Mr. Yotofeka became stern and businesslike. "For being tardy you will do three days' detention after school. You will help Mr. Labuba with his cleaning."

Mr. Labuba was the custodian. He was large and slow and smelled of old clothes and yohimbé snuff. Robert did not like him.

The principal wrote a note on a form and handed it to Robert. "You will take this note home to your hardworking mother and have her sign it. You will return it to me before *second* bell tomorrow. If you are late again, Robert Oinenke, it will not be a *swearing* stick I will be dealing with you about."

"Yes, sir," said Robert.

When he got home that afternoon Robert went straight to his small alcove at the back of the house where his bed and worktable were. His table had his pencils, ink pen, eraser, ruler, compass, protractor, and glue. He took his copybooks from his satchel, then placed the three books he'd brought in the middle of his schoolbook shelf above the scarred table. He sat down to read the plays. His mother was still out doing the shopping as she always was when he got out of school.

Mr. Yotofeka was partly right about *The Play of the*

Swearing Stick. It was not a great play. It was about a man
in the old days accused of a crime. Unbeknownst to him,
the real perpetrator of the crime had replaced the man's
swearing stick with one that looked and felt just like it.
(Robert knew this was implausible.) But the false swearing
stick carried out justice anyway. It rose up from its place
on the witness cushion beside the innocent man when he
was questioned at the chief's court. It went out the window
and chased the criminal and beat him to death. (In the
stage directions the stick is lifted from the pillow by a
technician with wires above the stage and disappears out
the window, and the criminal is seen running back and
forth yelling and holding his head, bloodier each time he
goes by.)

Robert really liked plays. He watched the crowds every
afternoon going toward the playhouse in answer to the
drums and horns sounded when a drama was to be staged.
He had seen the children's plays, of course—*Big Magic,
The Trusting Chief, Daughter of the Yoruba.* He had also
seen the plays written for European children—*Cinderella,
Rumpelstiltskin, Nose of Fire.* Everyone his age had—the
Niger Culture Center performed the plays for the lower
grades each year.

But when he could get tickets through the schools or
his teachers, he had gone to see real plays both African
and European. He had gone to folk plays for adults,
expecially *Why the Snake Is Slick,* and he had seen Ourelay
the Congo playwright's *King of All He Surveyed* and *Scream
of Africa.* He had seen tragedies and comedies from most
of the African nations, even a play from Nippon, which he
had liked to look at but in which not much happened.
(Robert had liked the women actresses best, until he found
out they weren't women; then he didn't know what to
think.) But it was the older plays he liked best, those form
England of the early 1600s.

The first one he'd seen was *Westward for Smelts!* by
Christopher Kingstone, then *The Pleasant Historie of
Darastus* and *Fawnia* by Rob Greene. There had been a
whole week of old English European plays at the Culture
Hall, at night, lit by incandescent lights. His school had

gotten free tickets for anyone who wanted them. Robert was the only student his age who went to all the performances, though he saw several older students there each night.

There had been *Caesar and Pompey* by George Chapman, *Mother Bombey* by John Lyly, *The Bugbears* by John Jeffere, *The Tragicall History of Romeus and Juliet* by Arthur Broke, *Love's Labour Won* by W. Shaksper, *The Tragedy of Dido, Queen of Carthage* by Marlow and Nash, and on the final night, and best of all, *The Sparagus Garden* by Richard Brome.

That such a small country could produce so many good playwrights in such a short span of time intrigued Robert, especially when you consider that they were fighting both the Turks and the Italians during the period. Robert began to read about the country and its history in books from the school library. Then he learned that the Onitsha market sold many plays from that era (as there were no royalty payments to people dead two hundred fifty years). He had gone there, buying at first from the penny bin, then the two-cent tables.

Robert opened his small worktable drawer. Beneath his sixth-form certificate were the pamphlets from Mr. Fred's. There were twenty-six of them; twenty of them plays, twelve of those from the England of three hundred years before.

He closed the drawer. He looked at the cover of Thomas Goffe's play he had bought that morning—*The Raging Turk, or Bajazet II*. Then he opened the second copybook his mother had seen that morning. On the first page he penciled, in his finest hand:

MOTOFUKO'S REVENGE:
A Play in Three Acts
By Robert Oinenke

After an hour his hand was tired from writing. He had gotten to the place where King Motofuko was to consult with his astrologer about the attacks by Chief Renebe on neighboring tribes. He put the copybook down and began to read the Goffe play. It was good, but he found that after writing dialogue he was growing tired of reading it. He put the play away.

He didn't really want to read *Clio's Whips* yet: he wanted to save it for the weekend. But he could wait no longer. Making sure the front door was closed, though it was still hot outside, he opened the red, green, and black covers and read the title page:

CLIO'S WHIPS: The Abuses of Historie
by the White Races
By Oskar Oshwenke

"So the Spanish cry was Land Ho! and they sailed in the three famous ships, the *Nina*, the *Pinta*, and the *Elisabetta* to the cove on the island. Colon took the lead boat, and he and his men stepped out onto the sandy beach. All the air was full of parrots, and it was very wonderful there! But they searched and sailed around for five days and saw nothing but big bunches of animals, birds, fish, and turtles.

"Thinking they were in India, they sailed on looking for habitations, but on no island where they stopped were there any people at all! From one of the islands they saw far off the long lines of a much bigger island or a mainland, but tired from their search, and provendered from hunting and fishing, they returned to Europe and told of the wonders they had found, of the New Lands. Soon everyone wanted to go there."

This was exciting stuff to Robert. He reread the passage again and flipped the pages as he had for a week in Mr. Fred's. He came to his favorite illustration (which was what made him buy this book rather than another play). It was the picture of a hairy elephant, with its trunk raised and with that magical stuff, snow, all around it. Below was a passage Robert had almost memorized:

"The first man then set foot at the Big River (now the New Thames) of the Northern New Land. Though he sailed for the Portingals, he came from England (which had just given the world its third pope), and his name was Cromwell. He said the air above the Big River was a darkened profusion of pigeons, a million and a million times a hundred hundred, and they covered the skies for hours as they flew.

"He said there were strange humped cattle there (much like the European wisents) that fed on grass, on both sides of the river. They stood so thickly that you could have walked a hundred Congo miles on their backs without touching the ground.

"And here and there among them stood great hairy mammuts, which we now know once lived in much of Europe, so much like our elephant, which you see in the game parks today, but covered with a red-brown hair, with much bigger tusks, and much more fierce-looking.

"He said none of the animals were afraid of him, and he walked among them, petting some, handing them tender tufts of grass. They had never seen a man or heard a human voice, and had not been hunted since the very beginning of time. He saw that a whole continent of skins and hides lay before European man for the taking, and a million feathers for hats and decorations. He knew he was the first man ever to see this place, and that it was close to Paradise. He returned to Lisboa after many travails, but being a good Catholic, and an Englishman, he wasn't believed. So he went back to England and told his stories there."

Now Robert went back to work on his play after carefully sharpening his pencil with a knife and setting his eraser close at hand. He began with where King Motofuko calls in his astrologer about Chief Renebe:

MOTOFUKO: Like to those stars which blaze forth overhead, brighter even than the seven ordered planets? And having waxed so lustily, do burn out in a week?
ASTROLOGER: Just so! Them that awe to see their burning forget the shortness of their fire. The moon, though ne'er so hot, stays and outlasts all else.
MOTOFUKO: Think you then this Chief Renebe be but a five months' wonder?
ASTROLOGER: The gods themselves do weep to see his progress! Starts he toward your lands a blazing beacon, yet will his followers bury his ashes and cinders in some poor

hole 'fore he reaches the Mighty Niger. Such light makes gods jealous.

Robert heard his mother talking with a neighbor outside. He closed his copybook, put *Clio's Whips* away, and ran to help her carry in the shopping.

During recess the next morning he stayed inside, not joining the others in the playground. He opened his copybook and took up the scene where Chief Renebe, who has conquered all King Motofuko's lands and had all his wives and (he thinks) all the king's children put to death, questions his general about it on the way to King Motofuko's capital.

RENEBE: And certaine, you, all his children dead, all his warriors sold to the Moorish dogs?
GENERAL: As sure as the sun doth rise and set, Your Highness. I myself his children's feet did hold, swing them like buckets round my conk their limbs crack their necks and heads destroy. As for his chiefs, they are now sent to grub ore and yams in the New Lands, no trouble to you forevermore. Of his cattle we made great feast, his sheep drove we all to the four winds.

This would be important to the playgoer. King Motofuko had escaped, but he had also taken his four-year-old son. Motofene, and tied him under the bellwether just before the soldiers attacked in the big battle of Yotele. When the soldiers drove off the sheep, they sent his son to safety, where the shepherds would send him far away, where he could grow up and plot revenge.

The story of King Motofuko was an old one any Onitsha theatergoer would know. Robert was taking liberties with it—the story of the sheep was from one of his favorite parts of the *Odyssey*, where the Greeks were in the cave of Polyphemus. (The real Motofene had been sent away to live as hostage-son to the chief of the neighboring state long before the attack by Chief Renebe.) And Robert was going to change some other things, too. The trouble with real life, Robert thought, was that it was usually dull and

full of people like Mr. Yotofeka and Mr. Labuba. Not like
the story of King Motofuko should be at all.

Robert had his copy of *Clio's Whips* inside his Egyptian
grammar book. He read:

"Soon all the countries of Europe that could sent expeditions to the New Lands. There were riches in its islands
and vast spaces, but the White Man had to bring others to
dig them out and cut down the mighty trees for ships. That
is when the White Europeans really began to buy slaves
from Arab merchants, and to send them across to the
Warm Sea to skin animals, build houses, and to serve
them in all ways.

"Africa was raided over. Whole tribes were sold to
slavery and degradation; worse, wars were fought between
black and black to make slaves to sell to the Europeans.
Mother Africa was raped again and again, but she was also
traveled over and mapped: Big areas marked "unexplored"
on the White Man's charts shrank and shrank so that by
1700 there were very few such places left."

Miss Mbene came in from the play yard, cocked an eye
at Robert, then went to the slateboard and wrote mathe-
matical problems on it. With a groan, Robert closed the
Egyptian grammar book and took out his sums and ciphers.

Mr. Labuba spat a stream of yohimbébark snuff into the
weeds at the edge of the playground. His eyes were red
and the pupils more open than they should have been in
the bright afternoon sun.

"We be pulling at grasses," he said to Robert. He
handed him a big pair of gloves, which came up to Robert's elbows. "Pull steady. These plants be cutting all the
way through the gloves if you jerk."

In a few moments Robert was sweating. A smell of desk
polish and eraser rubbings came off Mr. Labuba's shirt as
he knelt beside him. They soon had cleared all along the
back fence.

Robert got into the rhythm of the work, taking pleasure
when the cutter weeds came out of the ground with a
tearing pop and a burst of dirt from the tenacious, octopuslike

roots. Then they would cut away the runners with trowels. Soon they had made quite a pile near the teeter-totters.

Robert was still writing his play in his head: he had stopped in the second act when Motofuko, in disguise, had come to the forgiveness-audience with the new King Renebe. Unbeknownst to him, Renebe, fearing revenge all out of keeping with custom, had persuaded his stupid brother Guba to sit on the throne for the one day when anyone could come to the new king and be absolved of crimes.

"Is he giving you any trouble?" asked the intrusive voice of Mr. Yotofeka. He had come up and was standing behind Robert.

Mr. Labuba swallowed hard, the yohimbé lump going down chokingly.

"No complaints, Mr. Yotofeka," he said, looking up.

"Very good, Robert, you can go home when the tower bell rings at three o'clock."

"Yes, sir."

Mr. Yotofeka went back inside.

Mr. Labuba looked at Robert and winked.

MOTOFUKO: Many, many wrongs in my time. I pray you, king, forgive me. I let my wives, faithful all, be torn from me, watched my children die, while I stood by, believing them proof from death. My village dead, all friends slaves. Reason twisted like hemp.

GUBA: From what mad place came you where such happens?

MOTOFUKO: (*Aside*) Name a country where this is not the standard of normalcy. (*To Guba*) Aye, all these I have done. Blinded, I went to worse. Pray you, forgive my sin.

GUBA: What could that be?

MOTOFUKO: (*Uncovering himself*): Murdering a king. (*Stabs him*)

GUBA: Mother of gods! Avenge my death. You kill the wrong man. Yonder—(*Dies*)

(*Guards advance, weapons out.*)

MOTOFUKO: Wrong man, when all men are wrong? Come, dogs, crows, buzzards, tigers. I welcome barks, beaks, claws, and teeth. Make the earth one howl. Damned, damned world where men fight like jackals over the carrion of states! Bare my bones then; they call for rest.

(Exeunt, fighting. Terrible screams off. Blood flows in from the wings in a river.)

SOLDIER *(Aghast)*: Horror to report. They flay the ragged skin from him whole!

"But the hide and fishing stations were hard to run with just slave labor. Not enough criminals could be brought from the White Man's countries to fill all the needs.

"Gold was more and more precious, in the hands of fewer and fewer people in Europe. There was some, true, in the Southern New Land, but it was high in the great mountain ranges and very hard to dig out. The slaves were worked underground till they went blind. There were revolts under those cruel conditions.

"One of the first new nations was set up by slaves who threw off their chains. They called their land Freedom, which was the thing they had most longed for since being dragged from Mother Africa. All the armies of the White Man's trading stations could not overthrow them. The people of Freedom slowly dug gold out of the mountains and became rich and set out to free others, in the Southern New Land and in Africa itself. . . .

"Rebellion followed rebellion. Mother Africa rose up. There were too few white men, and the slave armies they sent soon rebelled too and joined their brothers and sisters against the White Man.

"First to go were the impoverished French and Spanish dominions, then the richer Italian ones, and those of the British. Last of all were the colonies of the great German banking families. Then the wrath of Mother Africa turned on those Arabs and Egyptians who had helped the White Man in his enslavement of the black.

"Now they are all gone as powers from our continent and only carry on the kinds of commerce with us which put all the advanatages to Africa."

ASHINGO: The ghost! The ghost of that dead king!
RENEBE: What! What madness this? Guards, your places! What mean you, man?
ASHINGO: He came, I swear, his skin all strings, his brain a red cawleyflower, his eyes empty holes!

RENEBE: What portent this? The old astrologer, quick. To find what means to turn out this being like a goat from our crops. (*Alarums without. Enter astrologer.*)

ASTROLOGER: Your men just now waked me from a mighty dream. Your majesty was in some high place, looking over the courtyard at all his friends and family. You were dressed in regal armor all of brass and iron. Bonfires of victory burned all around, and not a word of dissent was heard anywhere in the land. All was peace and calm.

RENEBE: Is this then a portent of continued long reign?

ASTROLOGER: I do not know, sire. It was *my* dream.

His mother was standing behind him, looking over his shoulder.

Robert jerked, trying to close the copybook. His glasses flew off.

"What is that?" She reached forward and pulled the workbook from his hands.

"It is extra work for school," he said. He picked up his glasses.

"No, it is not." She looked over his last page. "It is wasting your paper. Do you think we have money to burn away?"

"No, Mother. Please . . ." He reached for the copybook.

"First you are tardy. Then you stay detention after school. You waste your school notebooks. Now you have *lied* to me."

"I'm sorry, I . . ."

"What is this?"

"It is a play, a historical play."

"What are you going to do with a play?"

Robert lowered his eyes. "I want to take it to Mr. Fred's Printers and have it published. I want it acted in the Niger Culture Hall. I want it to be sold all over Niger."

His mother walked over to the fireplace, where her irons were cooling on their racks away from the hearth.

"What are you going to *do*!!?" he yelled.

His mother flinched in surprise. She looked down at the notebook, then back at Robert. Her eyes narrowed.

"I was going to get my spectacles."

Robert began to cry.

She came back to him and put her arms around him. She smelled of the marketplace, of steam and cinnamon. He buried his head against her side.

"I will make you proud of me, Mother. I am sorry I used the copybook, but I *had* to write this play."

She pulled away from him. "I ought to beat you within the inch of your life, for ruining a copybook. You are going to have to help me for the rest of the week. You are not to work on this until you have finished every bit of your schoolwork. You should know Mr. Fred nor nobody is going to publish anything written by a schoolboy."

She handed him the notebook. "Put that away. Then go out on the porch and bring in those piles of mending. I am going to sweat a copybook out of your brow before I am through."

Robert clutched the book to him as if it were his soul.

RENEBE: O rack, ruin, and pain! Falling stars and the wind do shake the foundations of night itself! Where my soldiers, my strength? What use taxes, tribute if they buy not strong men to die for me?

(*Off*): Gone. All fled.

RENEBE: Hold! Who is there? (*Draws*)

MOTOFENE(*Entering*): He whose name will freeze your blood's roots.

RENEBE: The son of that dead king!

MOTOFENE: Aye, dead to you and all the world else, but alive to me and as constant as that star about which the groaning axle-tree of the earth does spin.

(*Alarums and excursions off.*)

Now hear you the screams of your flesh and blood and friendship, such screams as those I have heard awake and fitfully asleep these fourteen years. Now hear them for all time.

RENEBE: Guards! To me!

MOTOFENE: To you? See those stars which shower to earth out your fine window? At each a wife, child, friend does die. You watched my father cut way to bone and blood and gore and called not for the death stroke! For you I have had my Vulcans make you a fine suit. All iron and brass, as befits a king! It you will wear, to look out over

the palace yard of your dead, citizens and friends. You will have a good high view, for it is situate on cords of finest weed. (*Enter Motofene's soldiers.*) Seize him gently. (*Disarm*) And now, my former king, outside. Though full of hot stars, the night is cold. Fear not the touch of the brass. Anon you are garmented, my men will warm the suit for you.
(*Exeunt and curtain.*)

Robert passed the moaning white man amd made his way down the street, beyond the market. He was going to Mr. Fred's Printers in downtown Onitsha. He followed broad New Market Street, being careful to stay out of the way of the noisy streetcars that steamed on their rails toward the center of town.

He wore his best clothes, though it was Saturday morning. In his hands he carried his play, recopied in ink in yet another notebook. He had learned from the clerk at the market bookstall that the one sure way to find Mr. Fred was at his office on Saturday forenoon, when the Onitsha *Weekly Volcano* was being put to bed.

Robert saw two *wayway* birds sitting on the single telegraph wire leading to the relay station downtown. In the old superstitions one *wayway* was a bad omen, two were good, three a surprise.

"Mr. Fred is busy," said the woman in the *Weekly Volcano* office. Her desk was surrounded by copies of all the pamphlets printed by Mr. Fred's bookstore, past headlines from the *Volcano*, and a big picture of Mr. Fred, looking severe in his morning coat, under the giant clock, on whose face was engraved the motto in Egyptian: TIME IS BUSINESS.

The calendar on her desk, with the picture of a Niger author for each month, was open to October 1894. A listing of that author's books published by Mr. Fred was appended at the bottom of each page.

"I should like to see Mr. Fred about my play," said Robert.

"Your play?"

"Yes. A rousing historical play. It is called *Motofuko's Revenge.*"

"Is your play in proper form?"

"Following the best rules of dramaturgy," said Robert.

"Let me see it a moment."

Robert hesitated.

"Is it papertypered?" she asked.

A cold chill ran down Robert's spine.

"All manuscripts must be papertypered, two spaces between lines, with wide margins," she said.

There was a lump in Robert's throat. "But it is in my very finest book-hand," he said.

"I'm sure it is. Mr. Fred reads everything himself, is a very busy man, and insists on papertypered manuscripts."

The last three weeks came crashing down on Robert like a mud-wattle wall.

"Perhaps if I spoke to Mr. Fred . . ."

"It will do you no good if your manuscript isn't papertypered."

"Please. I . . ."

"Very well. You shall have to wait until after one. Mr. Fred has to put the *Volcano* in final form and cannot be disturbed."

It was ten-thirty.

"I'll wait," said Robert.

At noon the lady left, and a young man in a vest sat down in her chair.

Other people came, were waited on by the man or sent into another office to the left. From the other side of the shop door, behind the desk, came the sound of clanking, carts rolling, thumps, and bells. Robert imagined great machines, huge sweating men wrestling with cogs and gears, books stacked to the ceiling.

It got quieter as the morning turned to afternoon. Robert stood, stretched, and walked around the reception area again, reading the newspapers on the walls with their stories five, ten, fifteen years old, some printed before he was born.

Usually they were stories of rebellions, wars, floods, and fears. Robert did not see one about the burst dam that had killed his father, a yellowed clipping of which was in the Coptic Bible at home.

There was a poster on one wall advertising the fishing resort on Lake Sahara South, with pictures of trout and catfish caught by anglers.

At two o'clock the man behind the desk got up and pulled down the windowshade at the office. "You shall have to wait outside for your father," he said. "We're closing for the day."

"Wait for my father?"

"Aren't you Moletule's boy?"

"No. I have come to see Mr. Fred about my play. The lady . . ."

"She told me nothing. I thought you were the printer's devil's boy. You say you want to see Mr. Fred about a play?"

"Yes, I . . ."

"Is it papertypered?" asked the man.

Robert began to cry.

"Mr. Fred will see you now," said the young man, coming back in the office and taking his handkerchief back.

"I'm sorry," said Robert.

"Mr. Fred only knows you are here about a play," he said. He opened the door to the shop. There were no mighty machines there, only a few small ones in a dark, two-story area, several worktables, boxes of type and lead. Everything was dusty and smelled of metal and thick ink.

A short man in his shirtsleeves leaned against a workbench reading a long, thin strip of paper while a boy Robert's age waited. Mr. Fred scribbled something on the paper, and the boy took it back into the other room, where several men bent quietly over boxes and tables filled with type.

"Yes," said Mr. Fred, looking up.

"I have come here about my play."

"Your play?"

"I have written a play, about King Motofuko. I wish you to publish it."

Mr. Fred laughed. "Well, we shall have to see about that. Is it papertypered?"

Robert wanted to cry again.

"No, I am sorry to say, it is not. I didn't know . . ."

"We do not take manuscripts for publication unless . . ."

"It is in my very best book-hand, sir. Had I known, I would have tried to get it papertypered."

"Is your name and address on the manuscript?"

"Only my name. I . . ."

Mr. Fred took a pencil out from behind his ear. "What is your house number?"

Robert told him his address, and he wrote it down in the copybook.

"Well, Mr.—Robert Oinenke. I shall read this, but not before Thursday after next. You are to come back to the shop at ten A.M. on Saturday the nineteenth for the manuscript and our decision on it."

"But . . ."

"What?"

"I really like the books you publish, Mr. Fred, sir. I especially liked *Clio's Whips* by Mr. Oskar Oshwenke."

"Always happy to meet a satisfied customer. We published that book five years ago. Tastes have changed. The public seems tired of history books now."

"That is why I am hoping you will like my play," said Robert.

"I will see you in two weeks," said Mr. Fred. He tossed the copybook into a pile of manuscripts on the workbench.

"Because of the legacy of the White Man, we have many problems in Africa today. He destroyed much of what he could not take with him. Many areas are without telegraphy; many smaller towns have only primitive direct current power. More needs to be done with health and sanitation, but we are not as badly off as the most primitive of the White Europeans in their war-ravaged countries or in their few scattered enclaves in the plantations and timber forests of the New Lands.

It is up to you, the youth of Africa of today, to take our message of prosperity and goodwill to these people, who have now been as abused by history as we Africans once were by them. I wish you good luck.

Oskar Oshwenke,
Onitsha, Niger, 1889"

Robert put off going to the market stall of Mr. Fred's bookstore as long as he could. It was publication day.

He saw the the nice young clerk was there. (He had paid him back out of the ten Niger dollar advance Mr. Fred had had his mother sign for two weeks before. His mother still could not believe it.)

"Ho, there, Mr. Author!" said the clerk. "I have your three free copies for you. Mr. Fred wishes you every success."

The clerk was arranging his book and John-John Motulla's *Game Warden Bob and the Mad Ivory Hunter* on the counter with the big starburst saying: JUST PUBLISHED!

His book would be on sale throughout the city. He looked at the covers of the copies in his hands:

The TRAGICALL DEATH OF KING
MOTOFUKO
and HOW THEY WERE SORRY
a drama by Robert Oinenke
abetted by
MR. FRED OLUNGENE
"The Mighty Man of the Press"
for sale at Mr. Fred's High-Class Bookstore
#300 Market, and the *Weekly Volcano*
Office, 12 New Market Road
ONITSHA, NIGER
price 10¢ N.

On his way home he came around the corner where a group of boys was taunting the white man. The man was drunk and had just vomited on the foundation post of a store. They were laughing at him.

"Kill you all. Kill you all. No shame," he mumbled, trying to stand.

The words of *Clio's Whips* came to Robert's ears. He walked between the older boys and handed the white man three Niger cents. The white man looked up at him with sick, gray eyes.

"Thank you, young sir," he said, closing his hand tightly.

Robert hurried home to show his mother and the neighbors his books.

AGAINST BABYLON
By Robert Silverberg

*Los Angeles is a familiar place to most of the
world due to Hollywood and the endless stream
of movies shown on the world's theaters and
television screens that take place on its avenues and environs. This story tells of another
side of LA—that it is the subject of forest fires,
being as it is located in what is basically a dry
desert—and that it is a center on Earth most
likely to invite visitors from outer space.*

Carmichael flew in from New Mexico that morning, and
the first thing they told him when he put his little plane
down at Burbank was that fires were burning out of control
all around the Los Angeles basin. He was needed bad,
they told him. It was late October, the height of the
brushfire season in Southern California, and a hot, hard,
dry wind was blowing out of the desert, and the last time it
had rained was the fifth of April. He phoned the district
supervisor right away, and the district supervisor told
him, "Get your ass out here on the line double fast,
Mike."

"Where do you want me?"

"The worst one's just above Chatsworth. We've got
planes loaded and ready to go out of Van Nuys Airport."

"I need time to pee and to phone my wife. I'll be in
Van Nuys in fifteen, okay?"

He was so tired that he could feel it in his teeth. It was nine in the morning, and he'd been flying since half past four, and it had been rough all the way, getting pushed around by that same fierce wind out of the heart of the continent that was now threatening to fan the flames in L.A. At this moment all he wanted was home and shower and Cindy and bed. But Carmichael didn't regard fire-fighting work as optional. This time of year, the whole crazy city could go in one big fire storm. There were times he almost wished that it would. He hated this smoggy, tawdry Babylon of a city, its endless tangle of freeways, the strange-looking houses, the filthy air, the thick, chok-ing, glossy foliage everywhere, the drugs, the booze, the divorces, the laziness, the sleaziness, the porno shops and the naked encounter parlors and the massage joints, the weird people wearing their weird clothes and driving their weird cars and cutting their hair in weird ways. There was a cheapness, a trashiness, about everything here, he thought. Even the mansions and the fancy restaurants were that way: hollow, like slick movie sets. He sometimes felt that the trashiness bothered him more than the out-and-out evil. If you kept sight of your own values you could do battle with evil, but trashiness slipped up around you and infiltrated your soul without your even knowing it. He hoped that his sojourn in Los Angeles was not doing that to him. He came from the Valley, and what he meant by the Valley was the great San Joaquin, out behind Bakers-field, and not the little, cluttered San Fernando Valley they had here. But L.A. was Cindy's city, and Cindy loved L.A. and he loved Cindy, and for Cindy's sake he had lived here seven years, up in Laurel Canyon amidst the lush, green shrubbery, and for seven Octobers in a row he had gone out to dump chemical retardants on the annual brushfires, to save the Angelenos from their own idiotic carelessness. You had to accept your responsibilities, Carmichael believed.

The phone rang seven times at the home number before he hung up. Then he tried the little studio where Cindy made her jewelry, but she didn't answer there either, and it was too early to call her at the gallery. That bothered him, not being able to say hello to her right away after his three-day absence and no likely chance for it now for another eight or ten hours. But there was nothing he could do about that.

As soon as he was aloft again he could see the fire not far to the northwest, a greasy black column against the pale sky. And when he stepped from his plane a few minutes later at Van Nuys he felt the blast of sudden heat. The temperature had been in the mid-eighties at Burbank, damned well hot enough for nine in the morning, but here it was over a hundred. He heard the distant roar of flames, the popping and crackling of burning underbrush, the peculiar whistling sound of dry grass catching fire.

The airport looked like a combat center. Planes were coming and going with lunatic frenzy, and they were lunatic planes, too, antiques of every sort, forty and fifty years old and even older, converted B-17 Flying Fortresses and DC-3's and a Douglas Invader and, to Carmichael's astonishment, a Ford Trimotor from the 1930s that had been hauled, maybe, out of some movie studio's collection. Some were equipped with tanks that held fire-retardant chemicals, some were water pumpers, some were mappers with infrared and electronic scanning equipment glistening on their snouts. Harried-looking men and women ran back and forth, shouting into CB handsets, supervising the loading process. Carmichael found his way to Operations HQ, which was full of haggard people staring into computer screens. He knew most of them from other years.

One of the dispatchers said, "We've got a DC-3 waiting for you. You'll dump retardants along this arc, from Ybarra Canyon eastward to Horse Flats. The fire's in the Santa Susana foothills, and so far the wind's from the east, but if it shifts to northerly it's going to take out everything from Chatsworth to Granada Hills and right on down to Ventura Boulevard. And that's only *this* fire."

"How many are there?"

The dispatcher tapped his keyboard. The map of the San Fernando Valley that had been showing disappeared and was replaced by one of the entire Los Angeles basin. Carmichael stared. Three great scarlet streaks indicated fire zones: this one along the Santa Susanas, another nearly as big way off to the east in the grasslands north of the 210

Freeway around Glendora or San Dimas, and a third down in eastern Orange County, back of Anaheim Hills. "Ours is the big one so far," the dispatcher said. "But these other two are only about forty miles apart, and if they should join up somehow—"

"Yeah," Carmichael said. A single wall of fire running along the whole eastern rim of the basin, maybe—with Santa Ana winds blowing, carrying sparks westward across Pasadena, across downtown L.A., across Hollywood, Beverly Hills, all the way to the coast, to Venice, Santa Monica, Malibu. He shivered. Laurel Canyon would go. Everything would go. Worse than Sodom and Gomorrah, worse than the fall of Nineveh. Nothing but ashes for hundreds of miles. "Everybody scared silly of Russian nukes, and a carload of dumb kids tossing cigarettes can do the job just as easily," he said.

"But this wasn't cigarettes, Mike," the dispatcher said.

"No? What then, arson?"

"You haven't heard."

"I've been in New Mexico for the last three days."

"You're the only one in the world who hasn't heard, then."

"For Christ's sake, heard what?"

"About the E.T.s," said the dispatcher wearily. "They started the fires. Three spaceships landing at six this morning in three different corners of the L.A. basin. The heat of their engines ignited the dry grass."

Carmichael did not smile. "You've got one weird sense of humor, man."

The dispatcher said, "I'm not joking."

"Spaceships? From another world?"

"With critters fifteen feet high onboard," the dispatcher at the next computer said. "They're walking around on the freeways right this minute. Fifteen feet high, Mike."

"Men from Mars?"

"Nobody knows where the hell they came from."

"Jesus Christ, God," Carmichael said.

Wild updrafts from the blaze buffeted the plane as he took it aloft and gave him a few bad moments. But he moved easily and automatically to gain control, pulling the moves out of the underground territories of his nervous system. It was essential, he believed, to have the moves in your fingers, your shoulders, your thighs, rather than in the conscious realms of your brain. Consciousness could get you a long way, but ultimately you had to work out of the underground territories or you were dead.

He felt the plane responding and managed a grin. DC-3s were tough old birds. He loved flying them, though the youngest of them had been manufactured before he was born. He loved flying anything. Flying wasn't what Carmichael did for a living—he didn't actually do anything for a living, not anymore—but flying was what he did. There were months when he spent more time in the air than on the ground, or so it seemed to him, because the hours he spent on the ground often slid by unnoticed, while time in the air was intensified, magnified.

He swung south over Encino and Tarzana before heading up across Canoga Park and Chatsworth into the fire zone. A fine haze of ash masked the sun. Looking down, he could see the tiny houses, the tiny swimming pools, the tiny people scurrying about, desperately trying to hose down their roofs before the flames arrived. So many houses, so many people, filling every inch of space between the sea and the desert, and now it was all in jeopardy. The southbound lanes of Topanga Canyon Boulevard were as jammed with cars, here in midmorning, as the Hollywood Freeway at rush hour. Where were they all going? Away from the fire, yes. Toward the coast, it seemed. Maybe some television preacher had told them there was an ark sitting out there in the Pacific, waiting to carry them to safety while God rained brimstone down on Los Angeles. Maybe there really was. In Los Angeles anything was possible. Invaders from space walking around on the freeways even. Jesus. Jesus. Carmichael hardly knew how to begin thinking about that.

He wondered where Cindy was, what *she* was thinking about it. Most likely she found it very funny. Cindy had a wonderful ability to be amused by things. There was a line of poetry she liked to quote, from that Roman, Virgil: A storm is rising, the ship has sprung a leak, there's a whirlpool to one side and sea monsters on the other, and the captain turns to his men and says, "One day perhaps we'll look back and laugh even at all this." That was Cindy's way, Carmichael thought. The Santa Anas are blowing and three big brushfires are burning and invaders from space have arrived at the same time, and one day perhaps we'll look back and laugh even at all this. His heart overflowed with love for her, and longing. He had never known anything about poetry before he had met her. He closed his eyes a moment and brought her onto the screen of his mind. Thick cascades of jet-black hair; quick, dazzling smile; long, slender, tanned body all aglitter with those amazing rings and necklaces and pendants she designed and fashioned. And her eyes. No one else he knew had eyes like hers, bright with strange mischief, with that altogether original way of seeing that was the thing he most loved about her. *Damn* this fire, just when he'd been away three days! *Damn* the stupid men from Mars!

Where the neat rows and circles of suburban streets ended there was a great open stretch of grassy land parched by the long summer to the color of a lions hide, and beyond that were the mountains, and between the grassland and the mountains lay the fire, an enormous, lateral red crest topped by a plume of foul, black smoke. It seemed to already cover hundreds of acres, maybe thousands. A hundred acres of burning brush. Carmichael had heard once, creates as much heat energy as the atomic bomb they dropped on Hiroshima.

Through the crackle of radio static came the voice of the line boss, directing operations from a helicopter hovering at about four o'clock. "DC-3, who are you?"

"Carmichael."

"We're trying to contain it on three sides, Carmichael. You work on the east, Limekiln Canyon, down the flank of Porter Ranch Park. Got it?"

"Got it," Carmichael said.

He flew low, less than a thousand feet. That gave him a good view of the action: sawyers in hard hats and orange shirts chopping burning trees to make them fall toward the fire, bulldozer crews clearing brush ahead of the blaze, shovelers carving firebreaks, helicopters pumping water into isolated tongues of flame. He climbed five hundred feet to avoid a single-engine observer plane, then went up to five hundred more to avoid the smoke and air turbulence of the fire itself. From that altitude he had a clear picture of it, running like a bloody gash from west to east, wider at its western end. Just east of the fire's far tip he saw a circular zone of grassland perhaps a hundred acres in diameter that had already burned out, and precisely at the center of that zone stood something that looked like an aluminum silo, the size of a ten-story building, surrounded at a considerable distance by a cordon of military vehicles. He felt a wave of dizziness rock through his mind. That thing, he realized, had to be the E.T. spaceship.

It had come out of the west in the night, Carmichael thought, floating like a tremendous meteor over Oxnard and Camarillo, sliding toward the western end of the San Fernando Valley, kissing the grass with its exhaust, and leaving a trail of flame behind it. And then it had gently set itself down over there and extinguished its own brushfire in a neat little circle about itself, not caring at all about the blaze it had kindled farther back, and God knows what kind of creatures had come forth from it to inspect Los Angeles. It figured that when the UFO's finally did make a landing out in the open, it would be in L.A. Probably they had chosen it because they had seen it so often on television—didn't all the stories say that UFO people always monitored our TV transmissions? So they saw L.A. on every other show, and they probably figured it was the capital of the world, the perfect place for the first landing. But why, Carmichael wondered, had the bastards needed to pick the height of the fire season to put their ships down here?

He thought of Cindy again how fascinated she was by all this UFO and E.T. stuff those books she read, the ideas she had the way she had looked toward the stars one night when they were camping in Kings Canyon and talked of the beings that must live up there. "I'd love to see them," she said. "I'd love to get to know them and find out what their heads are like." Los Angeles was full of nut cases who wanted to ride in flying saucers, or claimed they already had, but it didn't sound nutty to Carmichael when Cindy talked that way. She had the Angeleno love of the exotic and the bizarre, yes, but he knew that her soul had never been touched by the crazy corruption here, that she was untainted by the prevailing craving for the weird and irrational that made him loathe the place so much. If she turned her imagination toward the stars, it was out of wonder, not out of madness: It was simply part of her nature, that curiosity, that hunger for what lay outside her experience, to embrace the unknowable. He had had no more belief in E.T.s than he did in the tooth fairy, but for her sake he had told her that he hoped she'd get her wish. And now the UFO people were really here. He could imagine her, eyes shining, standing at the edge of that cordon staring at the spaceship. Pity he couldn't be with her now, feeling all that excitement surging through her, the joy, the wonder, the magic.

But he had work to do. Swinging the DC-3 back around toward the west, he swooped down as close as he dared to the edge of the fire and hit the release button on his dump lines. Behind him a great crimson cloud spread out: a slurry of ammonium sulfate and water, thick as paint, with a red dye mixed into it so they could tell which areas had been sprayed. The retardant clung in globs to anything and would keep it damp for hours.

Emptying his four five-hundred-gallon tanks quickly, he headed back to Van Nuys to reload. His eyes were throbbing with fatigue, and the stink of the wet charred earth below was filtering through every plate of the old plane. It was not quite noon. He had been up all night. At the airport they had coffee ready, sandwiches, tacos, burritos. While he was waiting for the ground crew to fill his tanks he went inside to call Cindy again, and again there was no answer at home, none at the studio. He phoned the gallery, and the kid who worked there said she hadn't been in touch all morning.

"If you hear from her," Carmichael said, "tell her I'm flying fire control out of Van Nuys on the Chatsworth fire, and I'll be home as soon as things calm down a little. Tell her I miss her, too. And tell her that if I run into an E.T. I'll give it a big hug for her. You got that? Tell her just that."

Across the way in the main hall he saw a crowd gathered around someone carrying a portable television set.

Carmichael shouldered his way in just as the announcer was saying, "There has been no sign yet of the occupants of the San Gabriel or Orange County spaceships. But this was the horrifying sight that astounded residents of the Porter Ranch area beheld this morning between nine and ten o'clock." The screen showed two upright tubular figures that looked like squid walking on the tips of their tentacles, moving cautiously through the parking lot of a shopping center, peering this way and that out of enormous yellow, plattershaped eyes. At least a thousand onlookers were watching them at a wary distance, appearing both repelled and at the same time irresistibly drawn. Now and then the creatures paused to touch their foreheads together in some sort of communion. They moved very daintily, but Carmichael saw that they were taller than the lampposts—twelve feet high, maybe fifteen. Their skins were purplish and leathery looking, with rows of luminescent orange spots glowing along the sides. The camera zoomed in for a closeup, then jiggled and swerved wildly just as an enormously long elastic tongue sprang from the chest of one of the alien beings and whipped out into the crowd. For an instant the only thing visible on the screen was a view of the sky; then Carmichael saw a shot of a stunned-looking girl of about fourteen, caught around the waist by that long tongue, being hoisted into the air and popped like a collected specimen into a narrow green sack. "Teams of the giant creatures roamed the town for nearly an hour," the announcer intoned. "It has definitely been confirmed that between twenty and thirty human hostages were captured before they returned to their spacecraft. Meanwhile, fire-fighting activities desperately continue under Santa Ana conditions in the vicinity of all three landing sites, and—"

Carmichael shook his head. Los Angeles, he thought. The kind of people that live here, they walk right up and let the E.T.s gobble them like flies.

Maybe they think it's just a movie and everything will be okay by the last reel. And then he remembered that Cindy was the kind of people who would walk right up to one of these E.T.s. Cindy was the kind of people who lived in Los Angeles, he told himself, except that Cindy was *different*. Somehow.

He went outside. The DC-3 was loaded and ready.

In the forty-five minutes since he had left the fire line, the blaze seemed to have spread noticeably toward the south. This time the line boss had him lay down the retardant from the De Soto Avenue freeway interchange to the northeast corner of Porter Ranch. When he returned to the airport, intending to call Cindy again, a man in military uniform stopped him as he crossed the field and said, "You Mike Carmichael, Laurel Canyon?"

"That's right."

"I've got some troublesome news for you. Let's go inside."

"Suppose you tell me here, okay?"

The officer looked at him strangely. "It's about your wife," he said. "Cynthia Carmichael? That's your wife's name?"

"Come on," Carmichael said.

"She's one of the hostages, sir."

His breath went from him as though he had been kicked.

"Where did it happen?" he demanded. "How did they get her?"

The officer gave him a strange, strained smile. "It was the shopping-center lot, Porter Ranch. Maybe you saw some of it on TV."

Carmichael nodded. That girl jerked off her feet by that immense elastic tongue, swept through the air, popped into that green pouch. And Cindy—?

"You saw the part where the creatures were moving around? And then suddenly they were grabbing people, and everyone was running from them? That was when they got her. She was up front when they began grabbing, and maybe she had a chance to get away, but she waited just a little too long. She started to run, I understand, but then she stopped—she looked back at them—she may have called something out to them—and then—well, and then—"

"Then they scooped her up?"

"I have to tell you that they did."

"I see," Carmichael said stonily.

"One thing all the witnesses agreed, she didn't panic,

she didn't scream. She was very brave when those monsters grabbed her. How in God's name you can be brave when something that size is holding you in midair is something I don't understand, but I have to assure you that those who saw it—''

"It makes sense to me," Carmichael said.

He turned away. He shut his eyes for a moment and took deep, heavy pulls of the hot, smoky air.

Of course she had gone right out to the landing site. Of course. If there was anyone in Los Angeles who would have wanted to get to them and see them with her own eyes and perhaps try to talk to them and establish some sort of rapport with them, it was Cindy. She wouldn't have been afraid of them. She had never seemed to be afraid of anything. It wasn't hard for Carmichael to imagine her in that panicky mob in the parking lot, cool and radiant, staring at the giant aliens, smiling at them right up to the moment they seized her. In a way he felt very proud of her. But it terrified him to think that she was in their grasp.

"She's on the ship?" he asked. "The one that we have right up back here?"

"Yes."

"Have there been any messages from the hostages? Or from the aliens?"

"I can't divulge that information."

"*Is* there any information?"

"I'm sorry, I'm not at liberty to—"

"I refuse to believe," Carmichael said, "that that ship is just sitting there, that nothing at all is being done to make contact with—"

"A command center has been established, Mr. Carmichael, and certain efforts are under way. That much I can tell you. I can tell you that Washington is involved. But beyond that, at the present point in time—"

A kid who looked like an Eagle Scout came running up. "Your plane's all loaded and ready to go, Mike!"

"Yeah," Carmichael said. The fire, the fucking fire! He had almost managed to forget about it. *Almost*. He hesitated a moment, torn between conflicting responsibilities.

Then he said to the officer, "Look, I've got to get back out on the fire line. Can you stay here a little while?"

"Well—"

"Maybe half an hour. I have to do a retardant dump. Then I want you to take me over to that spaceship and get me through the cordon, so I can talk to those critters myself. If she's on that ship, I mean to get her off it."

"I don't see how it would be possible—"

"Well, try to see," Carmichael said. "I'll meet you right here in half an hour."

When he was aloft he noticed right away that the fire was spreading. The wind was even rougher and wilder than before, and now it was blowing hard from the northeast, pushing the flames down toward the edge of Chatsworth. Already some glowing cinders had blown across the city limits, and Carmichael saw houses afire to his left, maybe half a dozen of them. There would be more, he knew. In fire fighting you come to develop an odd sense of which way the struggle is going, whether you're gaining on the blaze or it's gaining on you, and that sense told him now that the vast effort that was under way was failing, that the fire was still on the upcurve, that whole neighborhoods were going to be ashes by nightfall.

He held on tight as the DC-3 entered the fire zone. The fire was sucking air like crazy now, and the turbulence was astounding: It felt as if a giant's hand had grabbed the ship by the nose. The line boss' helicopter was tossing around like a balloon on a string.

Carmichael called in for orders and was sent over to the southwest side, close by the outermost street of houses. Fire fighters with shovels were beating on wisps of flame rising out of people's gardens down there. The skirts of dead leaves that dangled down the trunks of a row of towering palm trees were blazing. The neighborhood dogs had formed a crazed pack, running desperately back and forth.

Swooping down to treetop level, Carmichael let go with a red gush of chemicals, swathing everything that looked combustible with the stuff. The shovelers looked up and waved at him, and he dipped his wings to them and headed off to the north, around the western edge of the blaze—it

was edging farther to the west too, he saw, leaping up into
the high canyons out by the Ventura County line—and
then he flew eastward along the Santa Susana foothills
until he could see the spaceship once more, standing isolated in its circle of blackened earth. The cordon of vehicles seemed to be even larger, what looked like a whole
armored division deployed in concentric rings beginning
half a mile or so from the ship.

He stared intently at the alien vessel as though he might
be able to see through its shining walls to Cindy within.

He imagined her sitting at a table, or whatever the aliens
used instead of tables, sitting at a table with seven or eight
of the huge beings, calmly explaining Earth to them and
then asking them to explain their world to her. He was
altogether certain that she was safe, that no harm would
come to her, that they were not torturing her or dissecting
her or sending electric currents through her simply to see
how she reacted. Things like that would never happen to
Cindy, he knew.

They only thing he feared was that they would depart
for their home star without releasing her. The terror that
that thought generated in him was as powerful as any kind
of fear he had ever felt.

As Carmichael approached the aliens' landing site he
saw the guns of some of the tanks below swiveling around
to point at him, and he picked up a radio voice telling him
brusquely, "You're off limits, DC-3. Get back to the fire
zone. This is prohibited air space."

"Sorry," he said. "No entry intended."

But as he started to make his turn he dropped down even
lower so that he could have a good look at the spaceship.
If it had portholes and Cindy was looking out one of those
portholes, he wanted her to know that he was nearby. That
he was watching, that he was waiting for her to come
back. But the ship's hull was blind-faced, entirely blank.

Cindy? Cindy?

She was always looking for the strange, the mysterious,
the unfamiliar, he thought. The people she brought to the
house: a Navaho once, a bewildered Turkish tourist, a kid
from New York. The music she played, the way she
chanted along with it. The incense, the lights, the medita-

tion. "I'm searching," she liked to say. Trying always to find a route that would take her into something that was wholly outside herself. Trying to become something more than she was. That was how they had fallen in love in the first place, an unlikely couple, she with her beads and sandals, he with his steady no-nonsense view of the world: She had come up to him that day long ago when he was in the record shop in Studio City, and God only knew what he was doing in that part of the world in the first place, and she had asked him something and they had started to talk, and they had talked and talked, talked all night, she wanting to know everything there was to know about him, and when dawn came up they were still together, and they had rarely been parted since. He never had really been able to understand what it was that she had wanted him for—the Valley redneck, the aging flyboy—although he felt certain that she wanted him for something real, that he filled some need for her, as she did for him, which could for lack of a more specific term be called love. She had always been searching for that too. Who wasn't? And he knew that she loved him truly and well, though he couldn't quite see why. "Love is understanding," she liked to say. "Understanding is loving." Was she trying to tell the spaceship people about love right this minute? *Cindy, Cindy, Cindy.*

Back in Van Nuys a few minutes later, he found that everyone at the airport seemed to know by this time that his wife was one of the hostages. The officer whom Carmichael had asked to wait for him was gone. He was not very surprised by that. He thought for a moment of trying to go over to the ship by himself, to get through the cordon and do something about getting Cindy free, but he realized that that was a dumb idea: The military was in charge and they wouldn't let him or anybody else get within a mile of that ship, and he'd only get snarled up in stuff with the television interviewers looking for poignant crap about the families of those who had been captured.

Then the head dispatcher came down to meet him on the field, looking almost about ready to burst with compassion, and in funereal tones told Carmichael that it would be all right if he called it quits for the day and went home

to await whatever might happen. But Carmichael shook
him off. "I won't get her back by sitting in the living
room," he said. "And this fire isn't going to go out by
itself, either."

It took twenty minutes for the ground crew to pump the
retardant slurry into the DC-3's tanks. Carmichael stood to
one side, drinking Cokes and watching the planes come
and go. People stared at him, and those who knew him
waved from a distance, and three or four pilots came over
and silently squeezed his arm or rested a hand consolingly
on his shoulder. The northern sky was black with soot,
shading to gray to east and west. The air was sauna-hot
and frighteningly dry: You could set fire to it, Carmichael
thought, with a snap of your fingers. Somebody running
by said that a new fire had broken out in Pasadena, near
the Jet Propulsion Lab, and there was another in Griffith
Park. The wind was starting to carry firebrands, then.
Dodger Stadium was burning, someone said. So is Santa
Anita Racetrack, said someone else. The whole damned
place is going to go, Carmichael thought. And my wife is
sitting inside a spaceship from another planet.

When his plane was ready he took it up and laid down a
new line of retardant practically in the faces of the fire
fighters working on the outskirts of Chatsworth. They
were too busy to wave. In order to get back to the airport
he had to make a big loop behind the fire, over the Santa
Susanas and down the flank of the Golden State Freeway,
and this time he saw the fires burning to the east, two huge
conflagrations marking the places where the exhaust streams
of the other two spaceships had grazed the dry grass and a
bunch of smaller blazes strung out on a line from Burbank
or Glendale deep into Orange County. His hands were
shaking as he touched down at Van Nuys. He had gone
without sleep now for thirty-two hours, and he could feel
himself starting to pass into that blank, white fatigue that
lies somewhere beyond ordinary fatigue.

The head dispatcher was waiting for him again as he left
his plane. "All right," Carmichael said at once. "I give
in. I'll knock off for five or six hours and grab some sleep,
and then you can call me back to—"

"No. That isn't it."

"That isn't what?"

"What I came out here to tell you, Mike. They've released some of the hostages."

"Cindy?"

"I think so. There's an Air Force car here to take you to Sylmar. That's where they've got the command center set up. They said to find you as soon as you came off your last dump mission and send you over there so you can talk with your wife."

"So she's free," Carmichael said. "Oh, Jesus, she's free!"

"You go on along, Mike. We'll look after the fire without you for a while, okay?"

The Air Force car looked like a general's limo, long and low and sleek, with a square-jawed driver in front and a couple of very tough-looking young officers to sit with him in back. They said hardly anything, and they looked as weary as Carmichael felt. "How's my wife?" he asked, and one of them said, "We understand that she hasn't been harmed." The way he said it was stiff and strange. Carmichael shrugged. The kid has seen too many old movies, he told himself.

The whole city seemed to be on fire now. Within the air-conditioned limo there was only the faintest whiff of smoke, but the sky to the east was terrifying, with streaks of red bursting like meteors through the blackness. Carmichael asked the Air Force men about that, but all he got was a clipped, "It looks pretty bad, we understand." Somewhere along the San Diego Freeway between Mission Hills and Sylmar, Carmichael fell asleep, and the next thing he knew they were waking him gently and leading him into a vast, bleak, hangarlike building near the reservoir. The place was a maze of cables and screens, with military personnel operating what looked like a thousand computers and ten thousand telephones. He let himself be shuffled along, moving mechanically and barely able to focus his eyes, to an inner office where a gray-haired colonel greeted him in his best this-is-the-tense-part-of-the-movie style and said, "This may be the most difficult job you've ever had to handle, Mr. Carmichael."

Carmichael scowled. Everybody was Hollywood in this damned town, he thought.

"They told me the hostages were being freed," he said. "Where's my wife?"

The colonel pointed to a television screen. "We're going to let you talk to her right now."

"Are you saying I don't get to see her?"

"Not immediately."

"Why not? Is she all right?"

"As far as we know, yes."

"You mean she hasn't been released? They told me the hostages were being freed."

"All but three have been let go," said the colonel. "Two people, according to the aliens, were injured as they were captured and are undergoing medical treatment aboard the ship. They'll be released shortly. The third is your wife, Mr. Carmichael. She is unwilling to leave the ship."

It was like hitting an air pocket.

"*Unwilling—?*"

"She claims to have volunteered to make the journey to the home world of the aliens. She says she's going to serve as our ambassador, our special emissary. Mr. Carmichael, does your wife have any history of mental imbalance?"

Glaring, Carmichael said, "She's very sane. Believe me."

"You are aware that she showed no display of fear when the aliens seized her in the shopping-center incident this morning?"

"I know, yes. That doesn't mean she's crazy. She's unusual. She has unusual ideas. But she's not crazy. Neither am I, incidentally." He put his hands to his face for a moment and pressed his fingertips lightly against his eyes. "All right," he said. "Let me talk to her."

"Do you think you can persuade her to leave that ship?"

"I'm sure as hell going to try."

"You are not yourself sympathetic to what she's doing, are you?" the colonel asked.

Carmichael looked up. "Yes, I am sympathetic. She's an intelligent woman doing something that she thinks is important and doing it of her own free will. Why the hell shouldn't I be sympathetic? But I'm going to try to talk her out of it, you bet. I love her. I want her. Somebody else can be the goddamned ambassador to Betelgeuse. Let me talk to her, will you?''

The colonel gestured, and the big television screen came to life. For a moment mysterious colored patterns flashed across it in a disturbing, random way; then Carmichael caught glimpses of shadowy catwalks, intricate metal strutworks crossing and recrossing at peculiar angles; and then for an instant one of the aliens appeared on the screen. Yellow platter-eyes looked complacently back at him. Carmichael felt altogether wide awake now.

The alien's face vanished and Cindy came into view. The moment he saw her, Carmichael knew that he had lost her.

Her face was glowing. There was a calm joy in her eyes verging on ecstasy. He had seen her look something like that on many occasions, but this was different: This was beyond anything she had attained before. She had seen the beatific vision, this time.

"Cindy?"

"Hello, Mike."

"Can you tell me what's been happening in there, Cindy?''

"It's incredible. The contact, the communication.''

Sure, he thought if anyone could make contact with the space people it would be Cindy. She had a certain kind of magic about her: the gift of being able to open any door.

She said, "They speak mind to mind, you know, no barriers at all. They've come in peace, to get to know us, to join in harmony with us, to welcome us into the confederation of worlds.''

He moistened his lips. "What have they done to you, Cindy? Have they brainwashed you or something?''

"No! No, nothing like that! They haven't done a thing to me, Mike! We've just talked.''

"Talked!''

"They've showed me how to touch my mind to theirs. That isn't brainwashing. I'm still me. I, me, Cindy. I'm okay. Do I look as though I'm being harmed? They aren't dangerous. Believe me.''

"They've set fire to half the city with their exhaust trails, you know."

"That grieves them. It was an accident. They didn't understand how dry the hills were. If they had some way of extinguishing the flames, they would, but the fires are too big even for them. They ask us to forgive them. They want everyone to know how sorry they are." She paused a moment. Then she said, very gently, "Mike, will you come onboard? I want you to experience them as I'm experiencing them."

"I can't do that, Cindy."

"Of course you can! Anyone can! You just open your mind, they touch you, and—"

"I know. I don't want to. Come out of there and come home, Cindy. Please. Please. It's been three days—four, now—I want to hug you, I want to hold you—"

"You can hold me as tight as you like. They'll let you onboard. We can go to their world together. You know that I'm going to go with them to their world, don't you?"

"You aren't. Not really."

She nodded gravely. She seemed terribly serious. "They'll be leaving in a few weeks, as soon as they've had a chance to exchange gifts with Earth. I've seen images of their planet—like movies, only they do it with their minds— Mike, you can't imagine how beautiful it is! How eager they are to have me come!"

Sweat rolled out of his hair into his eyes, making him blink, but he did not dare wipe it away for fear she would think he was crying.

"I don't want to go to their planet, Cindy. And I don't want you to go either."

She was silent for a time.

Then she smiled delicately and said, "I know, Mike."

He clenched his fists and let go and clenched them again. "I *can't* go there."

"No. You can't. I understand that. Los Angeles is alien enough for you, I think. You need to be in your Valley, in your own real world, not running off to some far star. I won't try to coax you."

"But you're going to go anyway?" he asked, and it was not really a question.

"You already know what I'm going to do."

"Yes."

"I'm sorry. But not really."

"Do you love me?" he said, and regretted saying it at once.

She smiled sadly. "You know I do. And you know I don't want to leave you. But once they touched my mind with theirs, once I saw what kind of beings they are—do you know what I mean? I don't have to explain, do I? You always know what I mean."

"Cindy—"

"Oh, Mike, I do love you so much."

"And I love you, babe. And I wish you'd come out of that goddamned ship."

"You won't ask that. Because you love me, right? Just as I won't ask you again to come onboard with me, because I really love you. Do you understand that, Mike?"

He wanted to reach into the screen and grab her.

"I understand, yes," he made himself say.

"I love you, Mike."

"I love you, Cindy."

"They tell me the round-trip takes forty-eight of our years, but it will only seem like a few weeks to me. Oh, Mike! Good-bye, Mike! God bless, Mike!" She blew kisses to him. He saw his favorite rings on her fingers, the three little strange star sapphire ones that she had made when she first began to design jewelry. He searched his mind for some new way to reason with her, some line of argument that would work, and could find none. He felt a vast emptiness beginning to expand within him, as though he were being made hollow by some whirling blade. Her face was shining. She seemed like a stranger to him suddenly. She seemed like a Los Angeles person, one of *those*, lost in fantasies and dreams, and it was as though he had never known her, or as though he had pretended she was something other than she was. No. No, that isn't right. She's not one of *those*, she's Cindy. Following her own star, as always. Suddenly he was unable to look at the screen any longer, and he turned away, biting his lip, making a shoving gesture with his left hand. The Air Force men in the room wore the awkward expressions of people who had inadvertently eavesdropped on someone's most intimate moments and were trying to pretend they had heard nothing.

"She isn't crazy, Colonel," Carmichael said vehemently. "I don't want anyone believing she's some kind of nut."

"Of course not, Mr. Carmichael."

"But she's not going to leave that spaceship. You heard her. She's staying aboard, going back with them to wherever the hell they came from. I can't do anything about that. You see that, don't you? Nothing I could do, short of going aboard that ship and dragging her off physically, would get her out of there. And I wouldn't ever do that."

"Naturally not. In any case, you understand that it would be impossible for us to permit you to go onboard, even for the sake of attempting to remove her."

"That's all right," Carmichael said. "I wouldn't dream of it. To remove her or even just to join her for the trip. I don't want to go to that place. Let her go: That's what she was meant to do in this world. Not me. Not me, Colonel. That's simply not my thing." He took a deep breath. He thought he might be trembling. "Colonel, do you mind if I got the hell out of here? Maybe I would feel better if I went back out there and dumped some more gunk on that fire. I think that might help. That's what I think, Colonel. All right? Would you send me back to Van Nuys, Colonel?"

He went up one last time in the DC-3. They wanted him to dump the retardants along the western face of the fire, but instead he went to the east, where the spaceship was, and flew in a wide circle around it. A radio voice warned him to move out of the area, and he said that he would.

As he circled a hatch opened in the spaceship's side and one of the aliens appeared, looking gigantic even from Carmichael's altitude. The huge, purplish thing stepped from the ship, extended its tentacles, seemed to be sniffing the smoky air.

Carmichael thought vaguely of flying down low and dropping his whole load of retardants on the creature, drowning it in gunk, getting even with the aliens for having taken Cindy from him. He shook his head. That's crazy, he told himself. Cindy would feel sick if she knew he had ever considered any such thing. But that's what I'm like, he thought. Just an ordinary, ugly, vengeful Earthman. And that's why I'm not going to go to that other planet, and that's why she is.

He swung around past the spaceship and headed straight across Granada Hills and Northridge into Van Nuys Airport. When he was on the ground he sat at the controls of his plane a long while, not moving at all. Finally one of the dispatchers came out and called up to him, "Mike, are you okay?"

"Yeah. I'm fine."

"How come you came back without dropping your load?"

Carmichael peered at his gauges. "Did I do that? I guess I did that, didn't I?"

"You're not okay, are you?"

"I forgot to dump, I guess. No, I didn't forget. I just didn't feel like doing it."

"Mike, come on out of that plane."

"I didn't feel like doing it," Carmichael said again. "Why the hell bother? This crazy city—there's nothing left in it that I would want to save anyway." His control deserted him at last, and rage swept through him like fire racing up the slopes of a dry canyon. He understood what she was doing, and he respected it, but he didn't have to like it. He didn't like it at all. He had lost Cindy, and he felt somehow that he had lost his war with Los Angeles as well. "Fuck it," he said. "Let it burn. This crazy city. I always hated it. It deserves what it gets. The only reason I stayed here was for her. She was all the mattered. But she's going away now. Let the fucking place burn."

The dispatcher gaped at him in amazement. "Mike—"

Carmichael moved his head slowly from side to side as though trying to shake a monstrous headache from it. Then he frowned. "No, that's wrong," he said. "You've got to do the job anyway, right? No matter how you feel. You have to put the fires out. You have to save what you can. Listen, Tim, I'm going to fly one last load today, you hear? And then I'll go home and get some sleep. Okay? Okay?" He had the plane in motion, going down the short runway. Dimly he realized that he had not requested clearance. A little Cessna spotter plane moved desperately out of his way, and then he was aloft. The sky was black and red. The fire was completely uncontained now, and maybe uncontainable. But you had to keep trying, he thought. You had to save what you could. He gunned and went forward, flying calmly into the inferno in the foothills, until the wild thermals caught his wings from below and lifted him and tossed him like a toy skimming over the top and sent him hurtling toward the waiting hills to the north.

Thus saith the Lord; Behold, I will raise up against Babylon, and against them that dwell in the midst of them that rise up against me, a destroying wind;

And will send unto Babylon fanners, that shall fan her, and shall empty her land: For in the day of trouble they shall be against her round about.

Jeremiah 51:1-2

STRANGERS ON PARADISE

By Damon Knight

What is the most predatory animal on Earth?
Wolves? Sharks? Rats? Tigers? None of these.
The most vicious and predatory species on this
planet is homo sapiens—*man, kindly, star-*
gazing, charitable humanity. The history of
mankind is a saga of the destruction of envi-
ronment, of other forms of life, of the warping
of the world itself, of implacable warfare within
its own species. So what shall we say when we
encounter at last an ideal peaceful society on a
paradisical new planet? Surprise, surprise!

Paradise was the name of the planet. Once it had been called something else, but nobody knew what.

From this distance, it was a warm blue cloud-speckled globe turning in darkness. Selby viewed it in a holotube, not directly, because there was no porthole in the isolation room, but he thought he knew how the first settlers had felt a century ago, seeing it for the first time after their long voyage. He felt much the same way himself; he had been in medical isolation on the entryport satellite for three months, waiting to get to the place he had dreamed of with hopeless longing all his life: a place without disease, without violence, a world that had never known the sin of Cain.

Selby (Howard W., Ph.D.) was a slender, balding man

286

in his forties, an Irishman, a reformed drunkard, an unsuccessful poet, a professor of English literature at the University of Toronto. One of his particular interests was the work of Eleanor Petryk, the expatriate lyric poet who had lived on Paradise for thirty years, the last ten of them silent. After Petryk's death in 2156, he had applied for a grant from the International Endowment to write a definitive critical biography of Petryk, and in two years of negotiation he had succeeded in gaining entry to Paradise. It was, he knew, going to be the peak experience of his life.

The Paradisans had pumped out his blood and replaced it with something that, they assured him, was just as efficient at carrying oxygen but was not an appetizing medium for microbes. They had taken samples of his body fluids and snippets of his flesh from here and there. He had been scanned by a dozen machines, and they had given him injections for twenty diseases and parasites they said he was carrying. Their faces, in the holotubes, had smiled pityingly when he told them he had had a clean bill of health when he was checked out in Houston.

It was like being in a hospital, except that only machines touched him, and he saw human faces only in the holotube. He had spent the time reading and watching canned information films of happy, healthy people working and playing in the golden sunlight. Their faces were smooth, their eyes bright. The burden of the films was always the same: how happy the Paradisans were, how fulfilling their lives, how proud of the world they were building.

The books were a little more informative. The planet had two large continents, one inhabited, the other desert (although from space it looked much like the other), plus a few rocky, uninhabitable island chains. The axial tilt was seven degrees. The seasons were mild. The planet was geologically inactive; there were no volcanoes, and earthquakes were unknown. The low, rounded hills offered no impediment to the global circulation of air. The soil was rich. And there was no disease.

This morning, after his hospital breakfast of orange juice, oatmeal, and toast, they had told him he would be released at noon. And that was like a hospital, too; it was almost two o'clock now, and he was still here.

"Mr. Selby."

He turned, saw the woman's smiling face in the holotube. "Yes?"

"We are ready for you now. Will you walk into the anteroom?"

"With the greatest of pleasure."

The door swung open. Selby entered; the door closed behind him. The clothes he had been wearing when he arrived were on a rack; they were newly cleaned and, doubtless, disinfected. Watched by an eye on the wall, he took off his pajamas and dressed. He felt like an invalid after a long illness; the shoes and belt were unfamiliar objects.

The outer door opened. Beyond stood the nurse in her green cap and bright smile; behind her was a man in a yellow jumpsuit.

"Mr. Selby, I'm John Ledbitter. I'll be taking you groundside as soon as you're thumbed out."

There were three forms to thumbprint, with multiple copies. "Thank you, Mr. Selby," said the nurse. "It's been a pleasure to have you with us. We hope you will enjoy your stay on Paradise."

"Thank you."

"Please." That was what they said instead of "You're welcome"; it was short for "Please don't mention it," but it was hard to get used to.

"This way." He followed Ledbitter down a long corridor in which they met no one. They got into an elevator. "Hang on, please." Selby put his arms through the straps. The elevator fell away; when it stopped, they were floating, weightless.

Ledbitter took his arm to help him out of the elevator. Alarm bells were ringing somewhere. "This way." They pulled themselves along a cord to the jump box, a cubicle as big as Selby's hospital room. "Please lie down here."

They lay side by side on narrow cots. Ledbitter put up the padded rails. "Legs and arms apart, please, head straight. Make sure you are comfortable. Are you ready?"

"Yes."

Ledbitter opened the control box by his side, watching the instruments in the ceiling. "On my three," he said. "One . . . two . . ."

Selby felt a sudden increase in weight as the satellite decelerated to match the speed of the planetary surface. After a long time the control lights blinked; the cot sprang up against him. They were on Paradise.

The jump boxes, more properly Henderson-Rosenberg devices, had made interplanetary and interstellar travel almost instantaneous—not quite, because vectors at sending and receiving stations had to be matched, but near enough. The hitch was that you couldn't get anywhere by jump box unless someone had been there before and brought a receiving station. That meant that interstellar exploration had to proceed by conventional means: the Taylor Drive at first, then impulse engines; round trips, even to nearby stars, took twenty years or more. Paradise, colonized in 2056 by a Gencite sect from the United States, had been the first Earthlike planet to be discovered; it was still the only one, and it was off-limits to Earthlings except on special occasions. There was not much the governments of Earth could do about that.

A uniformed woman, who said she had been assigned as his guide, took him in tow. Her name was Helga Sonnstein. She was magnificently built, clear-skinned and rosy, like all the other Paradisans he had seen so far.

They walked to the hotel on clean streets, under monorails that swooped gracefully overhead. The passersby were beautifully dressed; some of them glanced curiously at Selby. The air was so pure and fresh that simply breathing was a pleasure. The sky over the white buildings was a robin's-egg blue. The disorientation Selby felt was somehow less than he had expected.

In his room, he looked up Karen McMorrow's code. Her face in the holotube was pleasant, but she did not smile. "Welcome to Paradise, Mr. Selby. Are you enjoying your visit?"

"Very much, so far."

"Can you tell me when you would like to come to the Cottage?"

"Whenever it's convenient for you, Miss McMorrow."

"Unfortunately, there is family business I must take care of. In two or three days?"

"That will be perfectly fine. I have a few other people to interview, and I'd like to see something of the city while I'm here."

"Until later, then. I'm sorry for this delay."

"Please," said Selby.

That afternoon Miss Sonnstein took him around the city. And it was all true. The Paradisans were happy, healthy, energetic, and cheerful. He had never seen so many un-lined faces, so many clear eyes and bright smiles. Even the patients in the hospital looked healthy. They were accident victims for the most part—broken legs, cuts. He was just beginning to understand what it was like to live on a world where there was no infectious disease and never had been.

He liked the Paradisans—they were immensely friendly, warm, outgoing people. It was impossible not to like them. And at the same time he envied and resented them. He understood why, but he couldn't stop.

On his second day he talked to Petryk's editor at the state publishing house, an amiable man named Truro, who took him to lunch and gave him a handsomely bound copy of Petryk's *Collected Poems*.

During lunch—lake trout, apparently as much a delicacy here as it was in North America—Truro drew him out about his academic background, his publications, his plans for the future. "We would certainly like to publish your book about Eleanor," he said. "In fact, if it were possible, we would be even happier to publish it here first."

Selby explained his arrangements with Macmillan Schuster. Truro said, "But there's no contract yet?"

Selby, intrigued by the direction the conversation was taking, admitted that there was none.

"Well, let's see how things turn out," said Truro. Back in the office, he showed Selby photos of Petryk taken after the famous one, the only one that had appeared on Earth. She was a thin-faced woman, fragile-looking. Her hair was a little grayer, the face more lined—sadder, perhaps.

"Is there any unpublished work?" Selby asked.

"None that she wanted to preserve. She was very selective, and of course her poems sold quite well here—not as much as on Earth, but she made a comfortable living."

"What about the silence—the last ten years?"

"It was her choice. She no longer wanted to write poems. She turned to sculpture instead—wood carvings, mostly. You'll see when you go out to the Cottage."

Afterward Truro arranged for him to see Potter Hargrove, Petryk's divorced husband. Hargrove was in his seventies, white-haired and red-faced. He was the official in charge of what they called the New Lands Program: satellite cities were being built by teams of young volunteers—the ground cleared and sterilized, terrestrial plantings made. Hargrove had a great deal to say about this.

With some difficulty, Selby turned the conversation to Eleanor Petryk. "How did she happen to get permission to live on Paradise, Mr. Hargrove? I've always been curious."

"It's been our policy to admit occasional immigrants, when we think they have something we lack. *Very* occasional. We don't publicize it. I'm sure you understand."

"Yes, of course." Selby collected his thoughts. "What was she like, those last ten years?"

"I don't know. We were divorced five years before that. I remarried. Afterward, Eleanor became rather isolated."

When Selby stood up to leave, Hargrove said, "Have you an hour or so? I'd like to show you something."

They got into a comfortable four-seat runabout and drove north, through the commercial district, then suburban streets. Hargrove parked the runabout, and they walked down a dirt road past a cluster of farm buildings. The sky was an innocent blue; the sun was warm. An insect buzzed past Selby's ear; he turned and saw that it was a honeybee. Ahead was a field of corn.

The waves of green rolled away from them to the horizon, rippling in the wind. Every stalk, every leaf, was perfect.

"No weeds," said Selby.

Hargrove smiled with satisfaction. "That's the beautiful

part," he said. "No weeds, because any Earth plant poisons the soil for them. Not only that, but no pests, rusts, blights. The native organisms are incompatible. We can't eat them, and they can't eat us."

"It seems very antiseptic," Selby said.

"Well, that may seem strange to you, but the word comes from the Greek *sepsis*, which means 'putrid.' I don't think we have to apologize for being against putrefaction. We came here without bringing any Earth diseases or parasites with us, and that means there is *nothing* that can attack us. It will take hundreds of thousands of years for the local organisms to adapt to us, if they ever do."

"And then?"

Hargrove shrugged. "Maybe we'll find another planet."

"What if there aren't any other suitable planets within reach? Wasn't it just luck that you found this one?"

"Not luck. It was God's will, Mr. Selby."

Hargrove had given him the names of four old friends of Petryk's who were still alive. After some parleying on the holo, Selby arranged to meet them together in the home of Mark Andrevon, a novelist well known on Paradise in the seventies. (The present year, by Paradisan reckoning, was A.L. 102.) The others were Theodore Bonwait, a painter; Alice Orr, a poet and ceramicist; and Ruth-Joan Wellman, another poet.

At the beginning of the evening, Andrevon was pugnacious about what he termed his neglect in the English-Speaking Union; he told Selby in considerable detail about his literary honors and the editions of his works. This was familiar talk to Selby; he gathered that Andrevon was now little read even here. He managed to soothe the disgruntled author and turn the conversation to Petryk's early years on Paradise.

"Poets don't actually like each other much, I'm sure you know that, Mr. Selby," said Ruth-Joan Wellman. "We got along fairly well, though—we were all young and unheard of then, and we used to get together and cook spaghetti, that sort of thing. Then Ellie got married, and . . ."

"Mr. Hargrove didn't care for her friends?"

"Something like that," said Theodore Bonwait. "Well, there were more demands on her time, too. It was a rather strong attachment at first. We saw them occasionally, at parties and openings, that sort of thing."

"What was she like then, can you tell me? What was your impression?"

They thought about it. Talented, they agreed, a little vague about practical matters ("which was why it seemed so lucky for her to marry Potter," said Alice Orr, "but it didn't work out"), very charming sometimes, but a sharp-tongued critic. Selby took notes. He got them to tell him where they had all lived, where they had met, in what years. Three of them admitted that they had some of Petryk's letters, and promised to send him copies.

After another day or so, Truro called him and asked him to come to the office. Selby felt that something was in the wind.

"Mr. Selby," Truro said, "you know visitors like yourself are so rare that we feel we have to take as much advantage of them as we can. This is a young world, we haven't paid as much attention as we might to literary and artistic matters. I wonder if you have ever thought of staying with us?"

Selby's heart gave a jolt. "Do you mean permanently?" he said. "I didn't think there was any chance—"

"Well, I've been talking to Potter Hargrove, and he thinks something might be arranged. This is all in confidence, of course, and I don't want you to make up your mind hurriedly. Think it over."

"I really don't know what to say. I'm surprised—I mean, I was sure I had offended Mr. Hargrove."

"Oh, no, he was favorably impressed. He likes your spice."

"I'm sorry?"

"Don't you have that expression? Your, how shall I say it, ability to stand up for yourself. He's the older generation, you know—son of a pioneer. They respect someone who speaks his mind."

Selby, out on the street, felt an incredulous joy. Of all the billions on Earth, how many would ever be offered such a prize?

Later, with Helga Sonnstein, he visited an elementary school. "Did you ever have a cold?" a serious eight-year-old girl asked him.

"Yes, many times."

"What was it like?"

"Well, your nose runs, you cough and sneeze a lot, and your head feels stuffy. Sometimes you have a little fever, and your bones ache."

"That's *awful*," she said, and her small face expressed something between commiseration and disbelief.

Well, it *was* awful, and a cold was the least of it—"no worse than a bad cold," people used to say about syphilis. Thank God she had not asked about that.

He felt healthy himself, and in fact he was healthy—even before the Paradisan treatments, he had always considered himself healthy. But his medical history, he knew, would have looked like a catalog of horrors to these people—influenza, mumps, cerebrospinal meningitis once, various rashes, dysentery several times (something you had to expect if you traveled). You took it for granted—all those swellings and oozings—it was part of the game. What would it be like to go back to that now?

Miss Sonnstein took him to the university, introduced him to several people, and left him there for the afternoon. Selby talked to the head of the English department, a vaguely hearty man named Quincy; nothing was said to suggest that he might be offered a job if he decided to remain, but Selby's instinct told him that he was being inspected with that end in view.

Afterward he visited the natural history museum and talked to a professor named Morrison who was a specialist in native life-forms.

The plants and animals of Paradise were unlike anything on Earth. The "trees" were scaly, bulbous-bottomed things, some with lacy fronds waving sixty feet overhead, others with cup-shaped leaves that tilted individually to follow the sun. There were no large predators, Morrison assured him; it would be perfectly safe to go into the boonies, providing he did not run out of food. There were slender, active animals with bucket-shaped noses climbing in the forests or burrowing in the ground, and there were things that were not exactly insects; one species had a fixed wing like a maple seedpod—it spiraled down from the treetops, eating other airborne creatures on the way, and then climbed up again.

Of the dominant species, the aborigines, Morrison's department had only bones, not even reconstructions. They had been upright, about five feet tall, large-skulled, possibly mammalian. The eyeholes of their skulls were canted. The bones of their feet were peculiar, bent like the footbones of horses or cattle. "I wonder what they looked like," Selby said.

Morrison smiled. He was a little man with a brushy black mustache. "Not very attractive, I'm afraid. We do have their stone carvings, and some wall pictures and inscriptions." He showed Selby an album of photographs. The carvings, of what looked like weathered granite, showed angular creatures with blunt muzzles. The paintings were the same, but the expression of the eyes was startlingly human. Around some of the paintings were columns of written characters that looked like clusters of tiny hoofprints.

"You can't translate these?"

"Not without a Rosetta stone. That's the pity of it—if only we'd got here just a little earlier."

"How long ago did they die off?"

"Probably not more than a few centuries. We find their skeletons buried in the trunks of trees. Very well preserved. About what happened there are various theories. The likeliest thing is plague, but some people think there was a climatic change."

Then Selby saw the genetics laboratory. They were working on some alterations in the immune system, they said, which they hoped in thirty years would make it possible to abandon the allergy treatments that all children now got from the cradle up. "Here's something else that's quite interesting," said the head of the department, a blonde woman named Reynolds. She showed him white rabbits in a row of cages. Sunlight came through the open door; beyond was a loading dock, where a man with a Y-lift was hoisting up a bale of feed.

"These are Lyman Whites, a standard strain," said Miss Reynolds. "Do you notice anything unusual about them?"

"They look very healthy," said Selby.

"Nothing else?"

"No."

She smiled. "These rabbits were bred from genetic material spliced with bits of DNA from native organisms. The object was to see if we could enable them to digest native proteins. That has been only partly successful, but something completely unexpected happened. We seem to have interrupted a series of cues that turns on the aging process. The rabbits do not age past maturity. This pair, and those in the next cage, are twenty-one years old."

"Immortal rabbits?"

"No, we can't say that. All we can say is that they have lived twenty-one years. That is three times their normal span. Let's see what happens in another fifty or a hundred years."

As they left the room, Selby asked, "Are you thinking of applying this discovery to human beings?"

"It has been discussed. We don't know enough yet. We have tried to replicate the effect in rhesus monkeys, but so far without success."

"If you should find that this procedure is possible in human beings, do you think it would be wise?"

She stopped and faced him. "Yes, why not? If you are miserable and ill, I can understand why you would not want to live a long time. But if you are happy and productive, why not? Why should people have to grow old and die?"

She seemed to want his approval. Selby said, "But, if nobody ever died, you'd have to stop having children. The world wouldn't be big enough."

She smiled again. "This is a very big world, Mr. Selby."

Selby had seen in Claire Reynolds' eyes a certain guarded interest; he had seen it before in Paradisan women, including Helga Sonnstein. He did not know how to account for it. He was shorter than the average Paradisan male, not as robust; he had had to be purged of a dozen or two loathsome diseases before he could set foot on Paradise. Perhaps that was it: perhaps he was interesting to women because he was unlike all the other men they knew.

He called the next day and asked Miss Reynolds to dinner. Her face in the tube looked surprised, then pleased. "Yes, that would be very nice," she said.

An hour later he had a call from Karen McMorrow; she was free now to welcome him to the Cottage, and would be glad to see him that afternoon. Selby recognized the workings of that law of the universe that tends to bring about a desired result at the least convenient time; he called the laboratory, left a message of regret, and boarded the intercity tube for the town where Eleanor Petryk had lived and died.

The tube, a transparent cylinder suspended from pylons, ran up and over the rolling hills. The crystal windows were open; sweet flower scents drifted in, and behind them darker smells, unfamiliar and disturbing. Selby felt a thrill of excitement when he realized that he was looking at the countryside with new eyes, not as a tourist but as someone who might make this strange land his home.

They passed mile after mile of growing crops—corn, soybeans, then acres of beans, squash, peas; then fallow fields and grazing land in which the traceries of buried ruins could be seen.

After a while the cultivated fields began to thin out, and Selby saw the boonies for the first time. The tall fronded plants looked like anachronisms from the Carboniferous. The forests stopped at the borders of the fields as if they had been cut with a knife.

Provo was now a town of about a hundred thousand; when Eleanor Petryk had first lived there, it had been only a crossroads at the edge of the boonies. Selby got off the tube in late afternoon. A woman in blue stepped forward. "Mr. Selby."

"Yes."

"I'm Karen McMorrow. Was your trip pleasant?"

"Very pleasant."

She was a little older than she had looked on the holotube, in her late fifties, perhaps. "Come with me, please." No monorails here; she had a little impulse-powered runabout. They swung off the main street onto a blacktop road that ran between rows of tall maples.

"You were Miss Petryk's companion during her later years?"

"Secretary. Amanuensis." She smiled briefly.

"Did she have many friends in Provo?"

"No. None. She was a very private person. Here we are." She stopped the runabout; they were in a narrow lane with hollyhocks on either side.

The house was a low white-painted wooden building half-hidden by evergreens. Miss McMorrow opened the door and ushered him in. There was a cool, stale odor, the smell of a house unlived in.

The sitting room was dominated by a massive coffee table apparently carved from the cross section of a tree. In the middle of it, in a hollow space, was a stone bowl, and in the bowl, three carved bones.

"Is this native wood?" Selby asked, stooping to run his hand over the polished grain.

"Yes. Redwood, we call it, but it is nothing like the Earth tree. It is not really a tree at all. This was the first piece she carved; there are others in the workroom, through there."

The workroom, a shed attached to the house, was cluttered with wood carvings, some taller than Selby, others small enough to be held in the palm of the hand. The larger ones were curiously tormented shapes, half human and half tree. The smaller ones were animals and children.

"We knew nothing about this," Selby said. "Only that she had gone silent. She never explained?"

"It was her choice."

They went into Petryk's study. Books were in glass-fronted cases, and there were shelves of books and record cubes. A vase with sprays of cherry blossoms was on a windowsill.

"This is where she wrote?"

"Yes. Always in longhand, here, at the table. She wrote in pencil, on yellow paper. She said poems could not be made on machines."

"And all her papers are here?"

"Yes, in these cabinets. Thirty years of work. You will want to look through them?"

"Yes. I'm very grateful."

"Let me show you first where you will eat and sleep, then you can begin. I will come out once a day to see how you are getting on."

In the cabinets were thousands of pages of manuscript—treasures, including ten drafts of the famous poem *Walking the River*. Selby went through them methodically one by one, making copious notes. He worked until he could not see the pages, and fell into bed exhausted very night.

On the third day, Miss McMorrow took him on a trip into the boonies. Dark scents were all around them. The dirt road, such as it was, ended after half a mile; then they walked. "Eleanor often came out here, camping," she said. "Sometimes for a week or more. She liked the solitude." In the gloom of the tall shapes that were not trees, the ground was covered with not-grass and not-ferns. The silence was deep. Faint trails ran off in both directions. "Are these animal runs?" Selby asked.

"No. She made them. They are growing back now. There are no large animals on Paradise."

"I haven't even seen any small ones."

Through the undergrowth he glimpsed a mound of stone on a hill. "What is that?"

"Aborigine ruins. They are all through the boonies."

She followed him as he climbed up to it. The cut stones formed a complex hundreds of yards across. Selby stooped to peer through a doorway. The aborigines had been a small people.

At one corner of the ruins was a toppled stone figure, thirty feet long. The weeds had grown over it, but he could see that the face had been broken away, as if by blows of a hammer.

"What they could have taught us," Selby said.

"What could they have taught us?"

"What it is to be human, perhaps."

"I think we have to decide that for ourselves."

Six weeks went by. Selby was conscious that he now knew more about Eleanor Petryk than anyone on Earth, and also that he did not understand her at all. In the evenings he sometimes went into the workroom and looked at the tormented carved figures. Obviously she had turned to them because she had to do something, and because she could no longer write. But why the silence?

Toward the end, at the back of the last cabinet, Selby found a curious poem.

XC

Tremble at the coming of the light,
Hear the rings rustle on the trees.
Every creature runs away in fright;
Years will pass before the end of
    night;
Woe to them who drift upon the
    seas.
Erebus above hears not their pleas;
Repentance he has none upon his
    height—
Earth will always take what she
    can seize.

Knights of the sky, throw down
    your shining spears.
In luxury enjoy your stolen prize.
Let those who will respond to what
    I write,
Lest all of us forget to count the
    years.
Empty are the voices, and the eyes
Dead in the coming of that night.

Selby looked at it in puzzlement. It was a sonnet of sorts, a form that had lapsed into obscurity centuries ago, and one that, to his knowledge, Petryk had never used before in her life. What was more curious was that it was an awkward poem, almost a jingle. Petryk could not possibly have been guilty of it, and yet here it was in her handwriting.

With a sudden thrill of understanding, he looked at the initial letters of the lines. The poem was an acrostic, another forgotten form. It concealed a message, and that was why the poem was awkward—deliberately so, perhaps.

He read the poem again. Its meaning was incredible but clear. They had bombed the planet—probably the other continent, the one that was said to be covered with desert. No doubt it was, now. Blast and radiation would have done for any aborigines there, and a brief nuclear winter would have taken care of the rest. And the title, "XC" —Roman numerals, another forgotten art. Ninety years.

In his anguish, there was one curious phrase that he still did not understand—"Hear the rings rustle," where the expected word was "leaves." Why rings?

Suddenly he thought he knew. He went into the other room and looked at the coffee table. In the hollow, the stone bowl with its carved bones. Around it, the rings. There was a scar where the tree had been cut into, hollowed out; but it had been a big tree even then. He counted the rings outside the scar: the first one was narrow, almost invisible, but it was there. Altogether there were ninety.

The natives had buried their dead in chambers cut from the wood of living trees. Petryk must have found this one on one of her expeditions. And she had left the evidence here, where anyone could see it.

That night Selby thought of Eleanor Petryk, lying sleepless in this house. What could one do with such knowledge? Her answer had been silence: ten years of silence, until she died. But she had left the message behind her, because she could not bear the silence. He cursed her for her frailty; had she never guessed what a burden she had laid on the man who was to read her message, the man who by sheer perverse bad fortune was himself?

In the morning he called Miss McMorrow and told her he was ready to leave. She said good-bye to him at the tube, and he rode back to the city, looking out with bitter hatred at the scars the aborigines had left in the valleys.

He made the rounds to say good-bye to the people he had met. At the genetics laboratory, a pleasant young man told him that Miss Reynolds was not in. "She may have left for the weekend, but I'm not sure. If you'll wait here a few minutes, I'll see if I can find out."

It was a fine day, and the back door was open. Outside stood an impulse-powered pickup, empty.

Selby looked at the rabbits in their cages. He was thinking of something he had run across in one of Eleanor Petryk's old books, a work on mathematics. "Fibonacci numbers were invented by the thirteenth-century Italian mathematician to furnish a model of population growth in rabbits. His assumptions were: 1) it takes rabbits one month from birth to reach maturity; 2) one month after reaching maturity, and every month thereafter, each pair of rabbits will produce another pair of rabbits; and 3) rabbits never die."

As if in a dream, Selby unlatched the cages and took out two rabbits, on a buck, the other a doe heavy with young. He put them under his arms, warm and quivering. He got into the pickup with them and drove northward, past the fields of corn, until he reached the edge of the cultivated land. He walked through the undergrowth to a clearing where tender shoots grew. He put the rabbits down. They snuffed around suspiciously. One hopped, then the other. Presently they were out of sight.

Selby felt as if his blood were fizzing; he was elated and horrified all at once. He drove the pickup to the highway and parked it just outside town. Now he was frozen and did not feel anything at all.

From the hotel he made arrangements for his departure. Miss Sonnstein accompanied him to the jump terminal. "Good-bye, Mr. Selby. I hope you have had a pleasant visit."

"It has been most enlightening, thank you."

"Please," she said.

It was raining in Houston, where Selby bought, for sentimental reasons, a bottle of Old Space Ranger. The shuttle was crowded and smelly; three people were coughing as if their lungs would burst. Black snow was falling in Toronto. Selby let himself into his apartment, feeling as if he had never been away. He got the bottle out of his luggage, filled a glass, and sat for a while looking at it. His notes and the copies of Petryk's papers were in his suitcase, monuments to a book that he now knew would never be written. The doggerel of "XC" ran through his head. Two lines of it, actually, were not so bad:

> *Empty are the voices, and the eyes*
> *Dead in the coming of that night.*